IN SEARCH OF KLINGSOR

Jorge Volpi

Translated by Kristina Cordero

SCRIBNER

NEW YORK   LONDON   TORONTO   SYDNEY   SINGAPORE

SCRIBNER
1230 Avenue of the Americas
New York, NY 10020

For information about special discounts for bulk purchases,
please contact Simon & Schuster Special Sales: 1-800-465-6798 or
business@simonandschuster.com

Designed by Kyoko Watanabe
Text set in Minion

Manufactured in the United States of America

1   3   5   7   9   10   8   6   4   2

Library of Congress Cataloging-in-Publication Data
Volpi Escalante, Jorge, 1968–
[En Busca de Klingsor. English]
In search of Klingsor / Jorge Volpi.
p. cm.
1. World War, 1939–1945—Fiction. I. Title.

PQ7298.32.O47 E5313 2002
863'64—dc21   2002017582

ISBN 0-7432-0118-3

IN SEARCH
OF KLINGSOR

FOR ADRIAN, ELOY, GERARDO, NACHO, AND
PEDRO ANGEL, MY FELLOW CONSPIRATORS

CONTENTS

BOOK TWO

BOOK THREE

Science is a game—but a game with reality, a game with sharpened knives . . . if a man cuts a picture carefully into 1,000 pieces, you solve the puzzle when you reassemble the pieces into a picture; in the success or failure, both your intelligences compete. In the presentation of a scientific problem, the other player is the good Lord. He has not only set the problem but also devised the rules of the game—but they are not completely known, half of them are left for you to discover or to determine. The experiment is the tempered blade which you wield with success against the spirits of darkness—or which defeats you shamefully. The uncertainty is how much of the rules God himself has permanently ordained, and how much appears to be caused by your mental inertia, while the solution generally becomes possible only through freedom from this limitation. This is perhaps the most exciting thing in the game. For here you strive against the imaginary boundary between yourself and the Godhead—a boundary that perhaps does not exist.

—ERWIN SCHRÖDINGER

PREFACE

On September 5, the day they came for me, I was in my house on Ludwigstraße preparing some equations that Heisenberg had sent to me a few weeks earlier. Ever since July 20, when Hitler announced over the radio that the coup attempt had failed and that his life had been providentially spared, I knew that I didn't have much time. My anguish grew as I listened to the subsequent news reports: the execution of Stauffenberg and of his close friends, the preparations for the trials in the People's Court, and the massive wave of arrests that were made in the coup's aftermath.

Well aware that I could easily be the next in line, I tried to remain calm. But when I learned that Heini—Heinrich von Lutz, my childhood friend—had been arrested, I knew for sure that my days were numbered. But what could I do? Flee Germany? Hide? Escape? We were right in the middle of the very worst months of the war. It would have been impossible. All I could do was wait, quietly, for the SS or the Gestapo to break into my house. If I was lucky.

Just as I had imagined, the thugs wasted little time. A few days later, the Gestapo arrived at my house, handcuffed me, and I was taken straight to Plötzensee.

On July 20, 1944, a select group of officials of the Wehrmacht, the Armed Forces of the Third Reich, aided by dozens of civilians, had made an attempt on Hitler's life while the Führer was presiding over a meeting at his headquarters at Rastenburg, about six hundred kilometers east of Berlin. The leader of this group was Count Claus Schenk von Stauffenberg, a young colonel who had been wounded in the line of duty in North Africa. That day, Stauffenberg placed a pair of bombs in a briefcase, which was then deposited underneath the Führer's desk. Stauffenberg waited for the bombs to go off, the signal for the coup to begin, the coup that would put an end to the Nazi regime and, possibly, the entire Second World War.

The tiniest, most infuriating logistical error foiled Stauffenberg's plan. Either one of the bombs hadn't been activated or the suitcase had simply been placed too far from where Hitler had been sitting. The Führer escaped with a few scrapes and not a single one of the high commands of the party

or the army was seriously wounded. Despite the failure of their first opera-
tive, the conspirators fully intended to move ahead with their plan, but by
the early hours of the next day the Nazis had regained control of the situation. The main orchestrators of the coup—Ludwig Beck, Friedrich
Olbricht, Werner von Haeften, Albrecht Ritter Mertz von Quirnheim, and
of course, Stauffenberg—were detained and killed that night in the general
headquarters of the army, on the Bendlerstraße in Berlin. Hundreds of others were quickly arrested following the strict orders of the Reichsführer-SS
and the new minister of the interior, Heinrich Himmler.

The news of the plot came as a shock to military insiders and civilians
alike, thanks to the startling scope of people implicated: military officers,
businessmen, diplomats, members of the army and the naval intelligence
forces, professionals and merchants. In the aftermath, Himmler had all the
conspirators and their relatives arrested, on the theory that the source of evil
travels through bloodlines. By the end of August of 1944, some six hundred
people had been arrested—some for aiding and abetting the conspirators,
others simply for being related to them.

Hitler was livid about the coup, and unleashed his vengeance upon all the
people who had turned against him during the very worst moments of the
war. Scarcely a few weeks had passed since the Allied invasion of Normandy,
and already there were people ready and willing to do away with him and
place the entire Third Reich in jeopardy. So, just as Stalin—his enemy—had
done in Moscow in 1937, Hitler decided to stage a great trial so that all the
world could see just how vicious his enemies really were. Before it began,
Roland Freisler, the chief justice of the People's Court of the Greater German
Reich, and the executioner who would carry out the punishments were summoned to his headquarters, the "Wolf's Lair." There, Hitler advised them of
the following: "I want them hanged, strung up like butchered cattle!"

The trials began on August 7, in the great hall of the People's Court in
Berlin. On that day, eight defendants accused of conspiring against Hitler's
life were brought before the court: Erwin von Witzleben, Erich Hoepner,
Helmuth Stieff, Paul von Hase, Robert Bernardis, Friedrich Karl Klausing,
Peter Yorck von Wartenburg, and Albrecht von Haden. They were not permitted to wear ties or suspenders, and their own lawyers even urged them to
declare themselves guilty. Flanked on either side by two enormous Nazi
flags, Freisler ignored their protests, one after the other. Their crimes were
so patently evil in nature that any and all declarations were inadmissible.
Without flinching, Freisler condemned each of the eight defendants to
death. He directed his gaze upon them:

"Now we can return to our life and to the battle before us. The *Volk* has purged you from its ranks and is pure now. We have nothing more to do with you. We fight. The Wehrmacht cries out: 'Heil Hitler!' We fight at the side of our Führer, following him for the glory of Germany!"

By February 3, 1945, the day I was to appear before the People's Court on Bellevuestraße, Freisler had already delivered scores of death sentences. That day five of us were to stand trial. The first among us to face the judge was Fabian von Schlabrendorff, a lawyer and reserve lieutenant who had served as a liaison between various resistance leaders. He had been captured shortly after July 20, and since then had been held at the Dachau and Flössenburg concentration camps. As was his habit, Freisler interrupted him regularly, to ridicule him and the rest of the defendants, calling us pigs and traitors and proclaiming that Germany would emerge victorious—victory in 1945!—if he were able to successfully eliminate scum like us.

But then something happened, and if I hadn't witnessed it myself, I would have thought it some kind of miracle or hallucination. Suddenly, the antiaircraft signal rang out, loud and clear, and a red light went off in the hall. After a second of total silence, we heard a loud roar followed by what seemed like an endless series of explosions that reverberated through the courthouse. Bombings had become a daily fact of life in Berlin during those months, so we tried to remain calm and waited for it to end. We would never have guessed that it was anything other than a typical air raid, but it turned out to be the most intense bombing the Allies had launched since the start of the war. Before we even realized what was happening, a powerful crash blasted through the roof of the People's Court. Plaster fell from the walls like giant blocks of talcum powder, and a torrent of smoke and soot swept through the courtroom as if it had suddenly begun to snow. The plaster fell from the walls in chunks, but that seemed to be the extent of the damage. Either we would wait for the proceedings to continue or the judge would call a recess until the next day. When the smoke cleared a bit, we saw that a heavy chunk of stone had fallen onto the judge's bench, and next to it lay the head of Judge Roland Freisler, split in half, with a river of blood spilling down his face and staining the death sentence Schlabrendorff had just received. Other than Freisler, no one was injured.

The court security guards ran to the street in search of a doctor and after a few minutes returned with a little man in a white jacket who had sought shelter from the bombs in the courthouse vestibule. As soon as he approached the body, the doctor announced that nothing could be done: Freisler had died instantly. The rest of us remained exactly where we were, dumbfounded, as the security guards glared at us with hatred in their eyes, not knowing what to do next. That was when we heard the doctor's firm voice: "I won't do it. I refuse. I'm sorry. Arrest me if you want, but I won't sign that death certificate. Call someone else." Later on we found out that the doctor, a man by the name of Rolf Schleicher, was the brother of Rüdiger Schleicher, who had worked in the Institute for Aerial Legislation before being condemned to death by Freisler a few weeks earlier.

Following Freisler's death, the trial was postponed again and again as the Allied bombings continued to destroy the city. In March 1945, I was transferred from one prison to another until an American regiment finally liberated us shortly before the Nazis surrendered in May. Unlike most of my friends and fellow conspirators, I survived.

On the afternoon of July 20, 1944, a stroke of luck saved Hitler's life. If Stauffenberg's second bomb had gone off on that afternoon, or if that briefcase had been placed just a bit closer to Hitler, or if there had been a chain reaction, or if Stauffenberg had made absolutely certain to plant himself closer to Hitler . . . On the morning of February 3, 1945, a similar kind of luck saved my own life. If I had been tried on some other day, or if that bomb hadn't dropped precisely when it did, or if that piece of rock had fallen a few centimeters to the left or to the right, or if Freisler had dodged the blow or run for cover somewhere . . . I still don't know how logical—or sane—it is to establish a connection between these two events, but I do. Why do I insist, so many years after the fact, to connect these two unrelated incidents? Why do I continue to present them as one, as if they were two manifestations of one single act of will? Why do I refuse to admit that there is nothing hidden behind them, that they are no different from any other human misfortunes? Why do I cling so obstinately to these ideas of destiny, fate, and luck?

Perhaps because other unforeseeable circumstances, no less terrible than these, have forced me to write these words. Perhaps I string together these seemingly unrelated events—Hitler's salvation and my own—because this is the first time that humanity has been such a close witness to such catastrophic destruction. And our era, unlike other historical moments, has been largely determined by such twists of fate, those little signs that remind us of the ungovernable, chaotic nature of the realm in which we live. I propose, then, to tell the story of the century. *My* century. *My* version of how fate has ruled the world, and of how we men of science try in vain to domesticate its fury. But this is also the story of several lives—the one that I have endured for over eighty years and, more important, those of people that, once again by uncontrollable acts of fate, became intertwined with my own.

Sometimes I like to think that I am the thread that connects all these stories—that my existence and memory and these very words are nothing more than the vertices of the one all-encompassing, inevitable theory that brought our lives together. Perhaps my goal seems overly ambitious, or even insane. It doesn't matter. When your everyday existence becomes marked by death, when all hope is lost and all you see is the long road to your own extinction, this is the only thing that can justify your remaining days on Earth.

PROFESSOR GUSTAV LINKS
MATHEMATICIAN, UNIVERSITY OF LEIPZIG
NOVEMBER 10, 1989

BOOK ONE

Laws of Narrative Motion

LAW I: *All narratives are written by a narrator*

At first glance, this statement may appear not only paradoxical but decidedly stupid, yet it is more profound than it may seem. For years, we have been led to believe that when we read a novel or a story written in the first person—and I say this simply to illustrate a point, since this book is not a work of fiction—nobody is there to guide us through the plot and its various riddles. The plot, instead, presents itself in an almost magical manner, as if it were life itself. Through this process, we sense that a book is a parallel world which we make the active decision to enter. Nothing could be further from the truth. If there is one thing I cannot abide it is the cowardice of those authors who attempt to hide behind their words, as if nothing of their true selves filters into their phrases and verbs. They numb us with their overdoses of supposed literary objectivity. Obviously I am not the first person to identify this deceitful game, but I do want to make clear that I fully disagree with this scandalous method that certain authors employ in an effort to cover the tracks of their crimes.

Corollary I

For the reasons mentioned above, I should clarify that I, Gustav Links—a man of flesh and blood just like you—am the author of these words. But who am I, really? You can easily see this simply by glancing at the front cover of this book. But what else do you know? Forget about me for a moment and look at the cover once again. For one thing, this volume was finished—not written but finished—in 1989. And what else do you know, aside from the little that I have already told you: that I participated in the failed plot to overthrow Hitler on July 20, 1944, that I was arrested and tried, and that a twist of *fatum* finally intervened and saved my life?

Nevertheless, I hope you don't think I would be so presumptuous as to subject you to the story of my life. This has never been my intention, and as many others before me have said, I simply hope to serve as a guide who will walk you through this story: I will be a Serenus, an old, deaf Virgil who promises, from this moment on, to accompany and guide the reader. As the result of an act of luck, of the inevitable, of history, of chance, of God—call it what you like—I was forced to participate in the events I am about to describe. But I can assure you that my only goal is to gain your trust. Because of this, there is no way I could possibly trick you into thinking that I don't exist and that I haven't participated in the transcendental events I am about to describe.

LAW II: *All narrators offer one, singular truth*

I wonder if you have ever heard of a man named Erwin Schrödinger. Aside from being the celebrated physicist who discovered wave mechanics, he was also an inspired soul and one of the protagonists of this drama, a kind of Don Juan in the body of a wizened, old professor (of course, only now do I allow myself to describe him with such familiarity; when I first met him I never would have dared). He used to wear the most endearing pair of little round eyeglasses, and was forever surrounded by beautiful women . . . but that is beside the point. I only mention these details as an afterthought, out of chronological order, and only because I must. Although the notion of subjective truth certainly occurred to the Sophists in ancient Greece and to Henry James in the nineteenth century, it was our good friend Erwin who established the scientific foundations of such a theory, and his theory is one I find particularly satisfying. I won't go into detail, but I will point out one of its more unexpected consequences: *I am what I see.* What is this statement trying to communicate? A platitude: that truth is relative. Every observer, whether contemplating an electron or an entire universe in motion, unwittingly completes what Schrödinger called a "wave packet" released by all objects under observation. When subject and object make contact, what emerges is a jumbled mixture of the two, which then leads us to the none-too-surprising conclusion that, in practice, each mind is a world unto itself.

COROLLARY II

The ramifications of the previous statement must seem as transparent as a drop of morning dew; in fact, it's the oldest excuse in the book. The truth, it claims, is *my* truth, and that is that. The quantum wave functions that I complete with my act of observation are unique and immutable—and this is supported by a litany of theories I don't particularly wish to elaborate on right now (the uncertainty principle, the theory of complementarity, the exclusion principle, among others). In essence, they state that no one has the authority to declare his truth as superior to that of someone else. I am telling you this, I repeat, as a way of laying my cards out on the table. If this comes across as unbearable, deceitful, or even manipulative, please know that it is not my intention but rather the consequence of a physical law I cannot help but obey. As such, I feel no need to apologize for this.

LAW III: *All narrators possess a motive for narrating*

The problem with axioms is that they always seem so tediously obvious that many people think they could easily be mathematicians themselves. It's inevitable. But to recapitulate: If we agree with Laws I and II, that all texts must have an author, and that said author possesses a single, exclusive truth, then the next declaration will seem even more tedious. It states that if things do not appear from nowhere, it is because someone has specifically intended for it to be that way. I realize that this axiom does not apply to the world itself—at least, it seems highly unlikely that we will soon understand why someone chose to create the world as we know it—but I am not responsible for the uncertainties that exist outside these pages. We must banish the terrible theological temptation by which literary critics and scientists declare ordinary texts to be modern-day version of the Bible. No author is God, or anything like God—believe me—and no single page comes close to being even the worst imitation of the Tablets of the Law or the Gospel. And obviously, men of flesh and blood have little in common with the men we read of in books. Our metaphorical tendencies can sometimes get us into very big trouble. Here, then, is the real mystery of all mysteries: Unlike what occurs in the natural universe, books are always written with a motive, and these motives can often be quite petty indeed.

COROLLARY III

Don't assume, however, that it will be so easy to discern my motives. Scientific research, the kind that I performed for years—the kind that you will soon undertake—is much more complicated than baking a cake from an old family recipe. I only wish it were that simple! So don't get unduly excited: I have no intention of revealing my reasons in one fell swoop. I may be aware of them myself, but even I don't know if I have fully made sense of them. With a bit of patience, perhaps you will be the ones to disentangle them. Remember what Schrödinger said: For a true act of recognition to occur, an interaction must take place between observer and observed, and now I find myself in the latter (and somewhat less comfortable) category. I hope that you enjoy studying these incidents and hypothesizing upon their possible causes—a task that I have realized so many times in the past, though under very different conditions. In the world of science, this is the key to success. I could make your work easier by saying that I shall present my version of the facts and my conclusions to the world, that I will tell my own, personal truth. But at this stage of my life—I am over eighty—I am still not fully convinced by my own reasons. If you had asked me forty or even twenty years ago, I wouldn't have wasted a second in subscribing to the above-mentioned theories. No, now it is different: I see how my old, sinister friend lies in wait for me. I see how every breath requires a superhuman effort, and I see how the most trivial of human activities for you—eating, bathing, defecating—have become nothing less than minor miracles for me. And so I don't quite know if my beliefs have remained the same, either. If you are willing to accept the challenge—how pompous; let's call it a game instead—you can be the one to decide whether I am right or wrong.

CRIMES OF WAR

When Lieutenant Francis P. Bacon, former agent of the OSS, the Office of Strategic Services, and scientific adviser to the U.S. forces stationed in Germany, arrived at the Nuremberg train station at 8 A.M. on October 15, 1946, nobody was there to greet him. Gunther Sadel, officer of the counterintelligence unit attached to Brigadier General Leroy H. Watson, chief of the North American forces, was to have picked up Bacon and taken him to the gallows where the Nazi war criminals were to be executed. But when Bacon alighted from the train, Sadel was nowhere to be found. The train station was virtually empty.

Bacon waited for a few moments but quickly lost patience and asked two military policemen guarding the train depot what was going on. Nobody knew. A sudden silence fell upon them. Aside from a few railway workers—mainly POWs—whose job was to keep the train tracks in working condition, nobody there seemed to move an inch. In the distance, Bacon spotted a couple of officers and, a bit farther on, the railway station manager, but he figured they wouldn't be much help. His only option was to walk to the Palace of Justice.

Bacon was furious. The autumn wind blasted against his face. The streets remained deserted as ever, as if people were still expecting air raids. Offended and annoyed, Bacon didn't even bother to gaze at what remained of the city. At one time, it may have been the cradle of the great Meistersänger and, until recently, the proud home of the Nazi headquarters, but the war (and eleven Allied bombing raids) had reduced it to a city in ruins. Little piles of stones now lay where churches once stood; houses and buildings were now nothing more than minor, annoying obstacles in Bacon's path—all these things well-deserved losses that were hardly worth mourning. Not far off—though it hardly even crossed his mind—was the museum that had once been Germany's most important, as well as the house where Albrecht Dürer lived until his death in 1528. Now, of course, both were reduced to ashes and rubble.

As far as Bacon saw it, Nuremberg was nothing more than one of the hateful Nazi havens where thousands of young people had flaunted their gray shirts, waved their banners emblazoned with eagles, and brandished their giant torches with pride. There, they had paid homage to Hitler and venerated the swastikas which, just like prehistoric spiders perched upon their little eggs, crawled along the red ribbons that hung down from the public buildings of Germany. Every September, Nuremberg had been host to the Nazi party's annual festival, and in 1935 the Führer chose this city as the site from which he would enact his anti-Semitic laws. Nuremberg, in addition, was also the repository of the Reichskleinodien and the Reichsheiligtümer, the ancient imperial heirlooms—and symbols of Nazi power—that he had stolen from the Hofburg in Vienna after the annexation of Austria. The celebrated Lance of Longines was among these treasures, all of which eventually became emblems of Aryan authority. As far as Bacon (and the International Military Court) was concerned, tears of sorrow and shame should be shed over the Jews who perished in Auschwitz, Dachau, and other concentration camps—not the justified punishment of one of the bastions of the Third Reich.

Bacon was on the verge of turning twenty-seven, but from the moment he arrived in Europe, in February of 1943, he had made a concerted effort to appear older, stronger, and more imposing than he was. He wanted to wipe the slate clean of all the weakness that had tortured him so in the past and which, to some degree, had forced him out of the United States. He could no longer even try to be the same respectable, reasonable, sincere man he had been before. By accepting this mission—and giving up his job as a scientist at the Institute for Advanced Study at Princeton—he could not only exercise his desire for vengeance but also prove to himself that he was now a new man. He was determined to prove that he was on the side of the winners, and so he exhibited not even the slightest morsel of compassion for the defeated.

From a distance, Bacon was barely distinguishable from the handful of American soldiers patrolling the area: dark brown hair worn in a military-style haircut, pale eyes, and an angular nose which he rather liked. He fancied himself as a man who wore his uniform with panache (actually, he was a bit stiff), and he went to great pains to display his various decorations, despite the physical discomfort they produced. Upon his shoulder he bore a bulky military backpack that contained almost all his earthly possessions: a few changes of clothing, some photographs (which he hadn't dared look at since leaving New Jersey), and some old copies of *Annalen der Physik,* one of the more important journals in his field, pilfered from some or other library he had passed through.

In reality, Bacon had not gone to Nuremberg specifically for the executions. Initially, only thirty people had been granted permission to witness the event, but then General Watson invited him a bit later on, and he accepted enthusiastically. Bacon had been referred to Watson by General William J. Donovan, founder of the OSS and, for a few weeks, special assistant to the U.S. chief prosecutor at Nuremberg, Robert H. Jackson. (Not long before, in the wake of an acrimonious misunderstanding with Jackson, a veteran justice of the U.S. Supreme Court, Donovan had been forced to resign for having interviewed Hermann Goering without Jackson's permission.) Bacon, however, was on a different, perhaps more pedestrian mission: His job was to study the recorded minutes of the copious testimonies relating to scientific research under the Third Reich, and ferret out any and all "inconsistencies," to use the term favored by his superiors—that is, contradictions in the many statements made by the defendants.

The Palace of Justice was one of the few public buildings in Nuremberg that had survived the wartime bombings, and had recently been restored by Captain Daniel Kiley, a young Harvard architect also under the command of the OSS. Upon reaching the city center Bacon had little trouble identifying the building: Once protected by an ample plaza filled with trees, the large group of buildings featured archways on the ground floor, huge picture windows, and a series of pointed towers. The prison, located toward the back of the building, consisted of four rectangular blocks set in a half-moon, its exterior protected by a high semicircular wall. The Nazi prisoners were housed together in cell block C, steps away from a small chamber that was once a gymnasium but was now a gallows.

It was 9:15 when Bacon finally reached the security guards at the entrance to the Nuremberg military prison. After reviewing his credentials, the soldiers announced that they were under orders to bar all access to the building—most specifically, the gymnasium—until the executions were over. Bacon tried to explain that he had come on General Watson's invitation, but the guards were impassive, and refused his request to summon Gunther Sadel: "General Rikard's orders" was their only response.

Scores of journalists swarmed about the scene. Aside from the International Military Tribunal's official photographer, only two reporters—chosen by lottery—were granted access to the gymnasium. All the others were forced to wait, just like Bacon, for the press conference that would announce the deaths of the war criminals. In an effort to scoop the story, several newspapers had already published early editions. The *New York Herald Tribune*, for example, had given the news a full, eight-column headline:

11 NAZI CHIEFS HANGED IN NUREMBERG PRISON:
GOERING AND HENCHMEN PAY FOR THEIR WAR CRIMES

The executions were scheduled to take place in the afternoon, so Bacon still had a few hours to locate someone who might help him get in. Before anything else, however, he would go to the Grand Hotel, where a room had been reserved in his name. But bad luck seemed to dog his every step; when he arrived at the hotel, the manager declared that there were no rooms available. After patiently explaining that he was there on a special mission, Bacon asked to speak to the supervisor in charge, and a pompous bell captain cleverly rose to the occasion, becoming the de facto hotel manager for a moment, and quickly solved the problem: The hotel had not expected Bacon until the following day, when several rooms would be vacated ("The show ends today, you know?"). Since it was only for one night, however, room number 14—"Hitler's room"—could be made available.

Bacon climbed the stairs and settled into the immense suite. The luxurious appointments of the Nazi days were long gone, but they were nevertheless the most sumptuous accommodations Bacon had been offered in recent months. Although it did seem like some kind of bad joke that the walls now surrounding him had stood guard over the dead body of Adolf Hitler. Who would have ever thought? What would Elizabeth say? Oh . . . it was useless to even think about that: For better or for worse, Elizabeth wanted nothing to do with him. Bacon flung himself onto the bed, but it produced an illicit, morbid sensation, as if he were desecrating a sacred space. The idea of urinating on all the furniture crossed his mind, but then he thought better of it: Why should the hotel's housekeeping staff have to pay for his capricious behavior? He got up and walked into the bathroom. He studied the spacious tub, the sink, the toilet, the bidet. Hitler's greasy skin had surely rubbed up against all those shiny surfaces. He could just picture Hitler, naked and defenseless, admiring his flaccid member before submerging himself in the water; Bacon could even see the Führer's defecations, sliding down the hole that he now found himself peering into. . . .

Bewildered, Bacon studied himself in the mirror. Two large circles under his eyes dominated his face; not only had he matured, but he seemed to have grown old. He ran his hands through his hair and, in an attempt to concentrate on something, located one or two gray hairs and decided they were proof of his imminent decline. He was no longer a boy wonder, a child prodigy, or any of those things that had always kept him at the margins of society. As he began to take off his uniform, he mused at how very different it was from the one he used to wear. Trapped within the privileged walls of the Institute for Advanced Study in Princeton, he had very nearly married a woman he didn't love. There, his life had been a sheltered one, protected from the outside world, just like that of an insect pinned to the inside of a glass case in a museum. His departure from Princeton had been nothing less than a spectacular scandal, but it was also a miracle, a revelation. For the first time ever he sensed that life was a tangible presence that he could feel upon his skin, far from all the desks and blackboards, and the tedium of all those conferences and colloquia. He never would have dreamed that he would derive such satisfaction as a soldier fighting for his country, but now he was certain that he had made the right choice. He would have plenty of time, at some point in the future, to return to the world of science—but then it would be as a hero, not as a fugitive.

He turned on the faucet and waited for the hot water to pour out, but nothing more than a weak stream of lukewarm droplets emerged from the tap. "The Führer wouldn't have stood for this," he laughed to himself, and proceeded to bathe with the help of a towel and a freshly opened, pungent cake of soap. When he was finished, he went back to the bed and, before he knew it, fell into a deep sleep, though the unsettling dream he had nearly asphyxiated him: There he was, in the middle of a dark, rainy forest, when suddenly Vivien appeared out of nowhere. Vivien, the young black woman from Princeton with whom he had maintained a secret relationship for so long. Ruefully, he noted that his life was strewn with puddles and potholes; in fact, it seemed to have evolved into something more like a moldy, threatening swamp. In the dream, he tried to kiss Vivien when suddenly he found himself face-to-face with his ex-fiancée Elizabeth instead. "There's lipstick on your mouth," she said to him, and proceeded to wipe it off with a handkerchief. "You shouldn't do that," she reprimanded him. "It's bad, very bad." By the time Bacon managed to extricate himself, it was too late: Vivien had already disappeared.

It was almost three in the afternoon when he awoke. He kicked himself: This was the worst possible thing he could have done. Not only had he neglected his work, but he had done so thrashing about in Hitler's bedsheets! He quickly put on his clothes, scurried down the stairs, and ran as fast as he could to the pressroom at the Palace of Justice.

A few hours later, he was informed of the news which would soon travel to the rest of the world like an infectious disease. From the crumbling streets of the ancient medieval burgh, the communiqué was sent out that the Reichsmarschall Hermann Goering—the highest-ranking Nazi prisoner sentenced by the International Military Tribunal—had been found dead in his cell a few hours before Sergeant John Woods was to carry out the hanging for which he had been sentenced. According to the rumors, Goering had ingested a capsule of cyanide, a cruel, eleventh-hour joke which allowed him the last laugh over the judges' decision. "One day there will be statues of me in every plaza and little figurines in my likeness in every home in Germany," the Reichsmarschall had once arrogantly proclaimed, so certain he was that he would be redeemed in the eyes of posterity. After his death, a stack of letters was found in his cell (number 5, cell block C), all of them written with the same small, precise lettering. The first of these letters explained the reasons for his suicide:

> To the Allied Control Council: I would have had no objection to being shot. However, I will not facilitate the execution of Germany's Reichs-marschall by hanging! For the sake of Germany, I cannot permit this. Moreover, I feel no moral obligation to submit to my enemies' punishment. For this reason, I have chosen to die like the great Hannibal.

On another sheet of paper, addressed to General Roy V. Rickard, member of the Quadripartite Commission in charge of supervising the executions, Goering confessed that he had always kept a capsule of cyanide close by. He also wrote a letter to his wife: "After serious consideration and sincere prayer to the Lord, I have decided to take my own life, lest I be executed in so terrible a fashion by my enemies. . . . My last heartbeats are for our great and eternal love." Henry Gerecke, the Protestant pastor who ministered to the German prisoners, was the last recipient in this small pile of letters. In his note to Gerecke, Goering asked for pardon and explained that the motivation for his actions had been purely political.

The next day, Gunther Sadel told Bacon all he knew about the matter. At 9:35 the previous evening, October 14, the guard had informed the necessary officials that the prisoner was resting peacefully in his cot after Dr. Ludwig Pflücker had administered him a sleeping pill. Just like every night, a soldier was stationed at the door to Goering's cell, specifically to keep close watch over him until the early dawn; after all, it was to be his last night under prison surveillance. Colonel Burton Andrus, the chief officer of the prison, had suspended all external communications with the outside world as a special precaution. The guards' only source of outside contact was a telephone line connecting them to the staff at the central offices, who continually updated them, inning by inning, with the score of the World Series, which was under way at the time.

All of a sudden, someone began calling for Pastor Gerecke's aid. It was the voice of Sergeant Gregori Timishin: Something was wrong with Goering. The chaplain ran toward the cell of the once plump Reichsmarschall, but when he arrived, he knew instantly that any resuscitation attempt would be pointless. Goering's face, which had seduced so many thousands of men and women, the same face whose glare had inspired both fear and fury among his captors, was now focused on a spot somewhere far off in the distance. Only one obstinate eye remained open. His rosy complexion had turned greenish, and his body, though twenty-five kilos lighter since his imprisonment, lay like a bale of hay, impossible to move. The cell smelled like bitter almonds. Gerecke took his pulse and said, "Good Lord, this man is dead." By the time the other members of the Joint Staffs arrived, it was already too late: Out of either cowardice or pride, Goering had foiled them.

Bacon could hardly believe it: At the very last moment, that miserable fiend had gotten away with it. And Bacon was not alone. The general feeling among the Allied forces was one of bitter disappointment, and several newspapers even dared publish the following headline: GOERING CHEATS HIS EXECUTIONERS.

"Where the hell did he get that pill?" Bacon asked Sadel.

"That's what everyone wants to know," Sadel responded. "They've already launched a full-blown investigation, though for the moment are not pointing the finger at anyone. Andrus is shattered," he added, referring to the prison director. "A lot of people think it's his fault, but you know, Goering wasn't the first prisoner to commit suicide. I don't think anyone could have prevented it."

"But Goering! The day before his execution! It's unbelievable." Bacon shook his head, incredulous. "Could it have been that German doctor?"

"Pflücker? I doubt it," said Sadel. "It would have been too difficult. The guards always searched him carefully before he entered each cell, and the pill he gave Goering was only a tranquilizer. . . . No, the Reichsmarschall must have had it hidden among his things, in the storage room, and someone must have brought it to him."

"But who would want to help that pig?" Bacon asked, cracking his knuckles.

"Well, it's not as simple as it may seem. I never had contact with him, but several people have said that Hermann was quite a character. During the trial proceedings not only Germans but Americans actually sympathized with him. He was just too cynical and biting to hate."

A strange explanation, thought Bacon, especially coming from such a young man like Sadel, who was half Jewish and at age thirteen had been forced to flee Germany to find his father in the United States. Since then, he knew nothing of his mother's whereabouts or whether she was alive or dead, for she had been forced to divorce his father and remain in Berlin. When he returned to Germany with General Watson, Sadel was given permission to search for her, and when he finally found her, she agreed to be one of the witnesses for the prosecution.

"Tex Wheelis is the prime suspect," Sadel continued. "He was the officer in charge of the storage room. They say that he and Goering had become friendly, and that he might have been the one to help him. But we want to be able to find out for certain. The men in charge want to put this issue to bed. Their opinion is that it was an accident, and they feel the case should be treated as such."

"An *accident?*" Bacon was getting more and more heated. "Hundreds of people worked for months to have him hanged and at the last minute he managed to escape. Was Hitler's suicide in Berlin another 'accident'? And what about the Final Solution? Doesn't that make you feel as if all of this has been useless? That we fought against an evil that got the best of us in the end?"

"The purpose of the trials was to uncover the truth, Lieutenant. To expose the truth about the Third Reich to the entire world, and to ensure that no one can ever justify the kind of atrocities that were committed. Who can deny the horror of the Nazi regime, the gas chambers and the millions of deaths, after seeing all those photographs?"

"But given the situation, do you think the truth will ever come out? The only truth we have is the one we are capable of believing."

The following morning, Lieutenant Bacon watched from a distance as the dead bodies of the eleven Nazi chiefs—Joachim von Ribbentrop, foreign minister of the Third Reich; Hans Frank, governor-general of Occupied Poland; Wilhelm Frick, governor of Bohemia and Moravia; Alfred Jodl, chief of operation staff of the High Command of the Wehrmacht; Ernst Kaltenbrunner, head of the Reich Main Security Office and second-in-command to Himmler; Wilhelm Keitel, chief of staff of the Wehrmacht; Alfred Rosenberg, official philosopher of the regime and minister for the Eastern Occupied Territories; Fritz Sauckel, plenipotentiary for Labor Deployment; Arthur Seyss-Inquart, Reich commissioner of the Netherlands; Julius Streicher, editor and publisher of the newspaper *Der Stürmer;* and of course, Hermann Goering, Reichsmarschall and chief of the Luftwaffe and second-in-command to Hitler—were transported in military trucks to the cemetery in Ostfriedrichhof, in Munich, where they would be cremated. He stared at the long caravan of cars and armed guards that followed the trucks. The bodies had been placed in individual sacks, each one tagged with a false name. The Germans in charge of the ovens were told that the bodies were those of American soldiers who had died during the war; it was a precaution the authorities took to ensure that nothing of the cremations would ever resurface in the form of Nazi mementos. For this reason, no one was to associate those ashes with the Nazi leaders condemned to death by the International Military Tribunal in Nuremberg.

Almost instantly the oppressive tension gripping the city seemed to lift. The work was finally finished, despite the fact that nobody was satisfied with the results—especially the Soviets, who never hid their displeasure with the course the trials had taken; at one point they even accused the American and English forces of allowing Goering to commit suicide. There were still many minor Nazi functionaries waiting for their day in court, though the eyes of the entire world were not likely to remain as permanently transfixed upon the halls of the Palace of Justice.

But as I said before, Lieutenant Francis P. Bacon had not come to Nuremberg to attend the executions. His mission was of an entirely different nature, having much more to do with his insights and talents as a man of science.

About halfway through the war, while working at the Institute for Advanced Study, Bacon decided to enlist in the army. He was sent to England to make contact with the British scientists there, and in 1945 he joined the Alsos mission, led by the Dutch physicist Samuel I. Goudsmit, who was responsible for archiving all available information relating to the German scientific program, and to the Germans' work on the atomic bomb. He was also the official who ordered the capture of the German physicists who were working on it.

Once his tour of duty was over, Bacon could have returned to the United States, but he chose to continue working as a scientific consultant to the Allied Control Council, the entity responsible for governing Occupied Germany. Finally, in early October of 1946, a few days after the International Military Tribunal in Nuremberg handed down its sentences to the Nazi defendants, Bacon was summoned by the Office of Military Intelligence to review some of the documents from the trial archives. From this research he would produce a report illustrating the points he felt most relevant to his assigned task of searching for the inconsistencies in the war criminals' testimony. Of his report, one small detail emerged which caught the attention of his military commanders.

On July 30, 1946, in the main hall of the Palace of Justice in Nuremberg, seven German organizations went on trial: the Nazi party leadership; the cabinet of the Reich; the security police, known as the SS; the secret police, known as the Gestapo; the Security Service, or SD; the Storm Troops, or SA; and the Military High Command of the Third Reich. In the weeks leading up to the trials, the tribunal announced that the trial proceedings were to be broadcast throughout Germany so that anyone who had been affected by any of the accused groups might step forward and offer his or her testimony. More than 300,000 responses flooded the Palace of Justice. From this pool, 603 members of these organizations were brought to Nuremberg to testify. In the end, the court admitted the testimony of some 90 people—mostly pertaining to the SS—who had refused to commit dishonest actions in the fulfillment of their duties.

One of these testimonies caught the attention of the U.S. Intelligence Services. During this process, a little man named Wolfram von Sievers, president of the Society for German Ancestral Heritage (and, as was later discovered, the head of an office of the Ahnenerbe, the SS office of scientific investigation). Von Sievers was an extremely nervous witness; during his long hours sitting on the witness bench, he never stopped rubbing his hands, and his cheeks were perpetually drenched in perspiration. He stumbled over his words, repeated certain phrases over and over again, and, as if that weren't enough, he was also a stutterer, which further complicated the jobs of the extensive network of simultaneous translators who, for the first time in history, performed their task in the courtrooms of Nuremberg.

While being interrogated by one of the Allied prosecutors, Von Sievers made the first in a series of controversial declarations. According to an agreement signed by the Reichsführer-SS Heinrich Himmler, the SS regularly sent skulls of "Bolshevik Jews" to Von Sievers's laboratory so that he might perform experiments on them. When Von Sievers was asked if he knew how the SS obtained those craniums, he replied that they came from the prisoners of war at the Eastern Front, who were assassinated specifically for this scientific research. The prosecutor pressed on: "And what was the objective of your 'research'?" Once again Von Sievers stumbled over his words, incoherent and stuttering. Finally, after persistent pressure from the judges, he gave in and delivered a long, wildly digressive speech on phrenology and the physical development of ancient civilizations, covering everything from the Toltecs and Atlantis to Aryan supremacy and mystical shrines like Agartha and Shambhala. More specifically, however, he explained that his own task had been to establish the biological inferiority of the Semitic people, to become intimately familiar with their physiological development over the ages, which presumably would enable him to ascertain the best way to eliminate their defects.

When he was finished speaking, Von Sievers looked like one of the skulls he claimed to have been studying, and his hands were now trembling uncontrollably. The prosecutor, however, was getting fed up; he had only interrogated Von Sievers to prove that the SS and the Nazi regime in general had indeed committed atrocities. He certainly hadn't intended this to be an exposé of the repulsive scientific investigation undertaken by Von Sievers, who, it turned out, would one day be tried and convicted for crimes against humanity.

"Where did you obtain the funding for this research, Professor Von Sievers?"

"From the SS, as I have already stated," he stammered.

"Was it common procedure for the SS to commission you to perform this type of research?"

"Yes."

"And did you say that the SS provided the financing for it?"

"Yes, directly."

"What do you mean when you say 'directly,' Professor?" The prosecutor sensed that he had finally hit upon a lead that might actually get him somewhere.

Von Sievers attempted to clear his throat.

"Well, all the scientific research undertaken in Germany first had to be cleared by the supervision and control centers of the Research Council of the Third Reich."

The prosecutor had hit the nail on the head. This was exactly what he wanted to hear. The Research Council, just like so many other dependencies of the Third Reich, fell under the supervision of Reichsmarschall Hermann Goering.

"Thank you, Professor. That will be all," the prosecutor concluded.

Von Sievers, however, added one more rather unexpected statement which, by order of the judges, was stricken from the record at the defense lawyers' request. Nevertheless, the statement did appear in the transcript Bacon received from the Office of Military Intelligence, and the lieutenant studied it closely, as it was highlighted in red ink. It said: "Before any funds could be released, each project had to be approved by Hitler's scientific adviser. I never did find out the identity of this person, but according to rumor, it was a well-known figure. A man who enjoyed a prominent position in the scientific community, and who operated under the code name Klingsor."

A few days later, on August 20, the courtroom was packed, a sure sign that Hermann Goering, the Great Actor in this theater of justice, was to make his appearance. He arrived dressed in a white jacket—in his glory days, he had been known for wearing this uniform. Ruddy-faced and volatile, Goering was the heart and soul of the trials. Acerbic and straightforward, he had that special kind of impertinence that comes from years of giving orders without ever hearing a single protest. He faced his interrogators as if he were dictating his memoirs. In his best moments, he displayed an acidic, penetrating sense of humor, and in his worst, he was like a caged monster, ready and waiting to take a bite out of anyone, even Otto Stahmer, his own defense attorney. Stahmer was responsible for directing this short scene:

"Did you ever issue an order to carry out medical experiments on human subjects?" he asked. Goering took a deep breath.

"No."

"Are you acquainted with a Dr. Rascher, who has been accused of performing scientific research on human guinea pigs at Dachau, for the Luftwaffe?"

"No."

"Did you ever issue an order authorizing anyone to carry out unspeakable experiments on prisoners?"

"No."

"As president of the Research Council of the Reich, did you ever order plans for the development of a system of mass destruction?"

"No."

Sir David Maxwell-Fyfe, the British prosecutor, rose from his seat.

"You were a great pilot," he said courteously, "with an impressive service record. How is it possible that you cannot remember those experiments, which were performed so as to verify the resistance of the uniforms used by the air force?"

"I had many tasks to attend to," Goering explained, with the same civility as his interrogator. "Tens of thousands of orders were issued in my name. Justice Jackson has accused me of having 'fingers in every pie,' but it would have been impossible for me to keep track of all the scientific experiments undertaken by the Third Reich."

Maxwell-Fyfe then presented as evidence a series of letters between Heinrich Himmler and Field Marshall Erhard Milch, Goering's right-hand man. In one of these letters, Milch thanked Himmler for his assistance in facilitating Dr. Rascher's experiments with high-altitude flights. One of these experiments involved a Jewish prisoner who was flown to twenty-nine thousand feet without oxygen. The subject died after thirteen minutes.

"Is it possible," continued Maxwell-Fyfe, "that a high-ranking official directly under your command—such as Milch—could have been aware of these experiments even though you were not?"

"The areas under my control were classified in three categories," Goering explained, almost smiling. " 'Urgent,' 'Important,' and 'Routine.' The exper iments performed by the medical inspector of the Luftwaffe fell under the third category and did not require my attention."

Never again was mention made of the scientist whose job was to approve the Third Reich's scientific projects. Never again was Klingsor's name mentioned. Goering certainly didn't bring it up, and Von Sievers himself, upon a second interrogation, denied ever having uttered the name. This one dubious mention was all Bacon had to go on.

The lieutenant slammed the dossier shut.

Hypotheses: From Quantum Physics to Espionage

HYPOTHESIS I: *On Bacon's Childhood and Early Years*

On November 10, 1919, the *New York Times* ran the following front-page headlines:

LIGHTS ALL ASKEW IN THE HEAVENS
Men of Science More or Less Agog Over Results of Eclipse Observations

EINSTEIN THEORY TRIUMPHS
*Stars Not Where They Seemed or Were Calculated to Be,
but Nobody Need Worry*

A BOOK FOR 12 WISE MEN
*No More in All the World Could Comprehend It, Said Einstein When His
Daring Publishers Accepted It*

Albert Einstein was forty years old, and this was the first time his name had ever appeared in the *New York Times*. His first article on special relativity, "On the Electrodynamics of Moving Bodies," which included the famous equation $E=mc^2$, had been published fourteen years earlier, in 1905, and four years had passed since his last revision to the general relativity theory. Nevertheless, this was the moment when the public first became aware of Einstein and his significance. Einstein would become something of an oracle, the symbol of a new age, and almost every word he uttered would hereafter be recorded and reprinted by newspapers all over the world. The Treaty of Versailles had been signed only a few months earlier, putting an end to the Great War, and the world was now a different place. People everywhere seemed to sense that humanity was at the dawn of a new era, and Einstein was its prophet, a man whose advice and wisdom should be heeded. In a letter sent to his friend Max Born (one of the first interpreters of the relativity theory), Einstein actually lamented his newfound circumstance, with the modest self-confidence that he was famous for: "Just like the fairy-tale hero who transforms everything he touches into gold, everything I touch turns into scandal for the newspapers."

From 1916 to 1917, Einstein had been developing a proof that could establish the validity of the general relativity theory. Unfortunately, there were few methods that could conclusively prove his assumptions were accurate. One of them was to gauge the curvature of light as it moved closer to a sufficiently large object, but this could only be done during a solar eclipse. Unfortunately for Einstein, Europe was mired in war at the time, and communications between German scientists and the outside world had come to an abrupt halt. As such, few physicists even knew of Einstein's project, and he was forced to wait for the war to end before he could find someone who would be able to confirm his findings.

Long before the Great War started, Einstein had struck up a correspondence with Sir Arthur Eddington, and once Einstein was able to resume contact after the war ended, the illustrious English physicist immediately jumped at the chance to test the relativity theory in an experimental setting. They quickly set the date: May 29, 1919, just a few months after the armistice was signed. On this day, they would be able to observe a spectacular solar eclipse from any point close to the equator. In early 1919, Eddington secured the necessary financing—one thousand pounds—from the Astronomer Royal, Sir Frank Dyson, which enabled him to prepare two expeditions to the equator. One, which he led, would go to the island of Príncipe, off the west coast of Africa, and the other group would set off for Sobral, in the north of Brazil. According to Eddington's calculations, both were ideal points from which to measure the shift that would occur when rays of starlight approached the sun. This, following Einstein's calculations, would be 1.745 seconds of arc—double the estimate produced by traditional physics. With Dyson's support, Eddington left for Príncipe in March.

On May 29, the day of the eclipse, Eddington arose at dawn and discovered, to his dismay, that a stubborn layer of clouds was now perched directly over the island and seemed determined to ruin his plans. After all his preparations and hard work, Nature herself seemed poised to betray her students. There was the hope, however, that the team in Sobral would be able to obtain results, but even that wasn't enough to lift the astronomer's spirits. Eddington cared not for the glory that the experiment could bring him, but the pride of being the first to prove this radical, new notion of what the world *was*. It was as if fate had played a cruel practical joke at his expense:

After a few minutes, the clouds gave way to one of the most violent thunderstorms Eddington had ever seen in his entire life. The thunder reverberated in his ears like dry claps of artillery fire. If things kept going like this, the only curvature they would measure would be that of the stooped-over palm trees fighting the hurricane winds. The telescopes, the cameras, and all the other measuring instruments remained where they were, exposed to the elements, useless and defenseless against the explosions that rained down from the heavens.

By 1:30 in the afternoon, Eddington, despondent, was about ready to surrender. That was when the miracle occurred: Suddenly the clouds began to disperse, aided by a cool breeze. With only eight minutes to go before the eclipse, Eddington quickly rallied his group, all of them inspired by the sensation that they had been granted the great privilege of observing the history of the universe compressed into a few brief seconds. The sun appeared, radiant and soaring, only to be devoured moments later by the shadows of its rival, the moon. Amid this inconceivable noontime darkness, the dumbstruck birds quickly flew back into their nests while the monkeys and lizards settled in for an early night's sleep. The momentary twilight seemed enveloped in a magical, white silence. In perfect harmony, the cameras captured the moment.

During the three days that followed, Eddington locked himself away in an improvised darkroom to develop the sixteen photograms that he had taken in order to carry out the necessary calculations. The instant Eddington spied the first images taking shape from beneath the photographic solution, like lost spectra floating in the water, he knew that success was his. After double-checking the calculations several times, Eddington emerged from his inner sanctum with the pride of a bishop prepared to crown a new king. The result was conclusive, despite the tiniest margin of error: Einstein had been triumphant! It took a few weeks for the news to travel the globe, and it wasn't until November 10, 1919, almost six months after the experiment, after new measurements were taken, that it appeared in the *New York Times*.

At 7:30 that very same morning, in a small hospital in Newark, New Jersey, not far from Princeton, a baby was born. This child, in a way the first inhabitant of a new universe, would be baptized Francis Percy Bacon, son of Charles Drexter Bacon, owner of the Albany Department Store chain, and his wife, Rachel Richards, the daughter of banker Raymond Richards, of New Canaan, Connecticut.

*   *   *

One June afternoon several years later, Bacon's mother decided to teach her son how to count. She placed him in her lap and in the same indifferent voice she used for reading him bedtime stories about angels and monsters, she revealed to him the secrets of mathematics, whispering each numeral as if it were a station of the cross or a psalm inserted into her prayers. Just outside the window, a tree struggled against the first summer thundershower, and the violent gusts of wind and rain reminded them of God's presence and mercy. That day, Frank found a solution to the tempests and discovered, moreover, that numbers are sometimes better companions than people. Unlike human beings—he was thinking of his father's sudden fits of temper and his mother's cool, distant reserve—you could always rely on numbers. They are constant, he thought, and they didn't suffer from mood swings. They didn't ever cheat or betray, and they didn't pick on little boys for being scrawny and weak.

Years went by before he realized, during an intense bout of fever, that all sorts of disorders and neuroses were hidden behind the great world of numbers. Contrary to what he had initially thought, he soon realized that numbers did not belong to such a simple, unemotional realm. As the doctor bathed Frank's feverish, delirious body in ice cubes, the young patient's secret passions were suddenly awakened for the very first time. Frank watched in awe as the numbers fought among themselves with a determination that refused to surrender—just like many of the real-life men he had read about. He studied their varied behavioral patterns: They loved one another within parentheses, they had illicit sex in multiplication, they annihilated one another in subtractions, they built palaces with their Pythagorean solids, they danced from place to place on their Euclidean planes, they dreamed of utopias with differential calculus, and condemned one another to death in the vortex of square roots. Their hell was far worse than what awaited humans: Rather than languishing somewhere below zero, in the negative numbers—a stupid, infantile simplification—numbers could fall into paradoxes, anomalies, tautologies, and the painful limbo of probability.

From that moment on, numerical inventions were Frank's best friends. To him, they were the last vestige of real, existential truth. Only those people who were unfamiliar with them—like his father and the doctors—could think they were perverse, opportunistic creatures. They were wrong—numbers didn't devour the brain or turn life into a sluggish lump of mathematical conjecture. Anyway, Frank hadn't renounced the laws of man in favor of the dictums of logic; he was just reluctant to abdicate the kingdom of geometry, for that would force him to return, dolefully, to the miserable routine of his home life.

Frank was five years old when he was first seduced by the demons of algebra. His mother had found him in the basement of their New Jersey home, numb from the November frost, mesmerized by the pipes that ran around the perimeter of the room. A thick, frothy saliva bubbled at his lips, and his body had become stiff as a bamboo shoot. After consulting with a neurologist, Frank's doctor determined that the only medicine was patience. "It's as if he were sleeping," he added, unable to explain the state his patient was in, somewhere between hypnotic and autistic. It took a day and a half before Frank fulfilled the doctor's prediction. Just as the doctor had said, Frank began to paw at his bed rail, like a butterfly trying to break out of its cocoon. His mother, who had maintained a bedside vigil throughout the episode, embraced her son, convinced that her love for him had rescued him from death's door. Minutes later, however, when he finally began to move his lips, the young boy put this wayward notion to rest. "I was just trying to solve an equation," he confessed, to everyone's surprise. Then he smiled: "And I did."

In his whole life, Frank received only one gift from his father, and the memory of this occasion would always be a special, private treasure for him. He must have been about six years old when, one Sunday afternoon, without any previous warning, the old man got up from his chair and handed his son a dusty black leather box. For years he had kept it hidden away in a closet, like a secret inheritance, the greatest lesson he could pass on to his son. To Frank's shock and delight, Charles Bacon removed a most curious collection of figurines from this box: dragons, samurai, bonzos, and pagodas, which he insisted upon calling horses, pawns, bishops, and rooks. He also took out a beautiful ebony and marble board which he then placed upon the parlor table.

Frank, at first, didn't quite understand his father's momentary euphoria, nor did he comprehend why his father was suddenly so interested in taking the time to show him the way to execute checks, count the horses' moves, and construct those bizarre, labyrinthine schemes known as castlings. At his age, how could he have possibly known that this game was the one thing that allowed the aging Charles to relive a bit of his former glory? Those harmless, board-game battles, of course, were really nothing more than a simple imitation of the battles he waged among his employees at the department store.

"Very well, then. If you think you understand the rules, how about playing a little game?"

"Yes, sir," Frank responded quickly.

Despite the fact that this was supposed to be a harmless pastime, Charles focused all his energies on the game; the square chessboard became a battlefield of honor and dignity upon which he delivered martial orders against his little six-year-old son. From the minute they began, Charles weighed every move with painstaking caution, as if he really should have been consulting territorial maps or discussing strategy with the imaginary chiefs of staff who greeted him each day in his equally imaginary military headquarters. It troubled Frank to see his father like that, and he had difficulty concentrating on the baby steps of his chess game. His father's hands, covered with liver spots and bulging veins, grabbed the chess pieces with thunderous force, as if uncorking giant wine bottles. Every time he made a move Frank feared that the little plaster geishas and mandarins would go exploding into thousands of little pieces. That afternoon, Frank's father mercilessly beat his son seven times in a row, availing himself of a rather outrageous move known as the "fool's mate." Charles's chess etiquette, of course, forbade him from winning games on the basis of cheap tricks, but if his son wanted to become a real man, he would have to be able to accept legitimate defeat with humility. He needed to learn how to survive in the battlefield of life, to emerge from the trenches and face his enemies. That's what Charles Bacon thought.

"My mistake," Charles mumbled upon losing to his son for the first time. He even lit a cigar to display his sporting attitude, and added, "Although you didn't play too badly yourself." The next day, however, he didn't wait for his son to suggest a game. When Frank returned from school—he was about eight years old by now—he found his father setting up the chessboard and carefully wiping down each chess piece as if inspecting a squadron of subordinate officers.

"Shall we begin?" he asked his son. Frank nodded. He tossed his book bag onto the floor and prepared to enter into far more than a mere battle: This was a fight to the death. After several hours of play, it was safe to say that young Frank had outfoxed his father, winning the first, third, fourth, and fifth games. The befuddled Charles managed to take the second and the sixth, and he did have the consolation of winning the final round, at which point he decided that it was rather late and that he had other, more important things to do.

That day, Frank learned the meaning of the words *Pyrrhic victory* first-hand, thanks to his father's rather typical display of self-indulgence. Not long after, Charles suffered a series of misfortunes, which would fuel his bitterness and aggravate the chronic depression that set in months later. After Frank won the game, he saw the impotent look on his father's face and couldn't help savoring this vindication. But his father's temperament would not permit this kind of humiliation. After only one more year of chess games, in which his percentage of losses grew higher than that of his son, Charles simply decided not to play against Frank anymore. A few months after that, he died of a heart attack.

Before he was six years old, Frank's name never bothered him. His mother always called him Frank or Frankie; it was her way of trying to inject a bit of the New Jersey spirit into the boy. Since the death of Frank's father, nary a mention was made of that awful "Percy" which had found its way onto his baptismal certificate. No, it only appeared on the most official of documents, and then only as *P*, like some kind of scarlet letter that he prayed no one would ask him about. But in school everything changed. His first-grade teacher was the first to notice:

"Francis Bacon?" she exclaimed loudly, almost laughing.

"Yes," he replied, not understanding quite what she meant. Little did he know that from that moment on, his hopes of remaining anonymous would be dashed forever. Suddenly he found himself transformed into an object of curiosity and ridicule for students and teachers alike, sacrificed to a ritual that would repeat itself over and over again at the beginning of each school year.

At first, it wasn't such a terrible thing to discover that his name was not so original. He was consoled, in fact, by all the Johns and Marys and Roberts he saw. His mother's second husband was called Tobias Smith, and he didn't seem at all troubled by the fact that he had to share his name with thousands of his compatriots. But the taunts were what bothered Frank the most: "Bet you think you're some kind of genius, don't you, Mr. Bacon?" they asked. He did; that was the worst thing of all. Who would ever believe that there could be another brilliant scientist named Francis Bacon? The first coincidence seemed to make the second one virtually impossible. He tried defending himself by proving to everyone how talented he was, but the arrogance with which he presented his results only elicited bouts of laughter from his teachers. It was as if they thought his intellectual abilities were nothing more than an anomaly or an eccentricity rather than true genius. In any event, they never failed to compare him with the "real" Bacon, as if he were nothing more than the unfortunate, apocryphal copy of a long-dead original.

Bacon's childhood and adolescence were lonely. Hypersensitive about the qualities that set him apart from the other children, he recoiled from all human contact apart from the unavoidable. He was hardly the easiest person to live with, either, due to the persistent migraines that plagued him, sending him into nearly catatonic states in which the slightest bit of light or noise was all but unbearable. He would spend hours on end locked away in his room, dreaming up formulas and theorems until his stepfather would knock on his door, practically dragging him downstairs to supper. By this point, his mother almost regretted ever having taught him how to count: Not only had he become intransigent and rude, but he also was increasingly intolerant of anyone less intelligent than he.

The hateful games people played at his expense gradually receded from his thoughts and he found himself more and more captivated by the English scientist who had caused all the trouble to begin with. He needed to know who that fateful ancestor was, the person whose mere name had made his life a living hell. With the same dedication of a teenager who inspects himself in the mirror day after day for the most infinitesimal signs of his metamorphosis into adulthood, Francis doggedly pursued his namesake. To avoid the displeasure of reading his name in print over and over again (since it always referred to someone else), Frank chose to immerse himself in the obsessions of his "ancestor." And in the process of learning about the original Bacon's great discoveries, Francis made one of his own, the kind of vague realization that emboldens a person to take a leap of faith across the great unknown. This discovery, rather than fulfilling the predictions of his detractors, was the thing that led Frank to discover his vocation. In spite of the apparent happenstance of their shared name, Frank was inspired by the discoveries of the first Francis Bacon, and began to believe that his destiny was somehow linked to that of the old, dead scientist. Maybe it wasn't exactly a reincarnation—he couldn't think about things like that—but he felt sure it was some sort of calling, a circumstance that was too obvious to have been an act of pure coincidence.

The life history of Baron Verulam, the first Francis Bacon, transformed the life of our Francis. The more Frank learned about the baron, the more he felt that he had to continue, in some way, the work of the original Francis Bacon. As unpleasant as he had been toward those around him, Francis Bacon had managed to achieve immortality. Young Francis felt a bond with him, for he, too, felt misunderstood by his contemporaries, and he comforted himself by thinking that one day his mother, stepfather, and schoolmates would be sorry for the shoddy treatment they subjected him to. He felt especially proud of sharing his last name with a man to whom Shakespearean plays had been attributed. Just like Sir Francis, Frank had become a learned person for a variety of reasons, including curiosity, the search for truth, plus a certain amount of natural talent for his studies. But in the end Frank easily admitted that the greatest source of inspiration had been the same one Sir Francis cited: rage. For him, a happy coexistence with the precise, concrete elements of mathematics was the only solution to confronting the chaos of the universe, whose destiny was utterly independent of his. Adapting a little saying made famous by his Elizabethan hero, Frank would have said for himself: "I have studied numbers, not men."

In school, his standoffishness toward his peers gradually dissipated as the result of a growing appreciation for the natural laws, which included, at least in theory, a certain admiration for humanity in general. Although perhaps not everything that occurred in the world could be explained by reason, science at least offered a direct track to solid knowledge. And, most important, the person in possession of that knowledge—that is, a clear understanding of the laws governing the world—also possessed a power which he could then exert over other people. Francis never fully abandoned his original mistrust of others, but rather placed it in a far corner of his memory, a place he visited less and less frequently.

One morning he woke up in a most broad-minded and accepting mood. Without understanding precisely why, Francis had decided to give up theoretical mathematics, that labyrinth of abstractions and impenetrable formulae, and decided to test the slightly more solid, concrete ground of physics. This decision hardly pleased his mother, who wanted him to become an engineer, but at least it was a step closer to a world she understood. Rather than mixing and matching numbers like a schizophrenic frantically jumbling his words, his job now was to immerse himself in the basic elements of the universe: matter, light, energy. Perhaps this would be the path to satisfying his mother's hope that he make himself useful to the world around him. Unfortunately, however, he would not be able to fulfill this maternal desire: He simply couldn't manage to concentrate on such concrete problems. Instead of becoming a disciple of the realm of electronics, for example, Frank found himself drawn to perhaps the most experimental, fragile, and impractical branch of physics: the study of atoms and the recently unveiled quantum theory. Once again, there was nothing very tangible there. The names of the objects he analyzed—electrons, matrices, observable phenomena—were labels for a motley group of creatures as bizarre in nature as numbers.

In 1940, after several years of struggling with this discipline against the wishes of his mother and stepfather, Frank received his bachelor's degree, summa cum laude, in physics from Princeton University, having written his senior thesis on positrons. He was twenty years old and his future was filled with promise: As one of the very few specialists in his field, various state universities had extended invitations to him to conduct graduate-level research in their facilities. Three offers in particular stood out: one from the California Institute of Technology, where Oppenheimer worked; one from Princeton University, his alma mater; and one from the Institute for Advanced Study, located in Princeton as well. All considered, this last offer was the most tantalizing. The institute was founded in 1930 by the Bamberger brothers (owners of the eponymous Newark-based department store), but didn't really open its doors until 1933. Unlike the graduate departments of the great American universities, the institute was unique in that it neither granted degrees nor expected its professors to carry burdensome teaching schedules. Their only job was to think, and to give occasional lectures on their chosen fields of study. It rapidly became one of the most important centers of scientific research in the entire world. Albert Einstein, who decided to remain in the United States after the Nazis won the general election in Germany, was a professor there, as were the mathematicians Kurt Gödel and John von Neumann, to mention only a handful of the more famous names.

As he walked along the ample footpaths of Princeton University on his way to visit the chairman of his department, Bacon had no idea that what he was about to do would have a decisive effect on his future. The ash trees that lined the walkways were as immobile as the columns of a temple whose roof was slowly chipping away with age. A sharp wind blurred the edges of the buildings that housed the different academic departments. The faux-medieval style of the architecture—copied directly from Cambridge and Oxford—looked even less authentic than usual in the bright sunlight. Prisoners in their uncomfortable gray suits, professors and students sought refuge inside the anachronistic buildings, escaping from the frigid air that sent their hats flying off their heads. Bacon knew the dean had summoned him to tell him something quite important, but for some reason he wasn't nervous at all. He trusted that the path of modern science would carry him to the best possible place in the world. And anyway—this was the best part of all—he had finally made a rather big life decision, thanks to a certain telephone call he had received two days earlier from the Institute for Advanced Study.

The new dean was a short, loquacious little man who quickly ushered

Bacon into his office. Seated behind a great desk that obscured a good half of his chest, the man couldn't seem to stop fidgeting with his salt-and-pepper beard, as if trying to untangle the threads of destiny. He offered an outstretched hand to Bacon and invited him to have a seat. He then removed a folder among the many piled high upon his desk and, without looking twice at Bacon, began to read from its contents.

"Francis Bacon . . . of course. How could I forget a name like that? Let's see . . . summa cum laude . . . 'Excellent student, detailed analyses, slow at decision-making but an extraordinary theorist . . . In short, one of the most talented students of his generation.' So, what do you make of all this?" he asked, in a voice which reminded Bacon of the whistle of a child's toy locomotive. "There is nothing but praise here for you, my boy! Remarkable, truly remarkable."

Bacon barely heard what the dean was saying; he was too busy eyeing the collection of German physics journals—*Annalen der Physik, Zeitschrift für Physik, Naturwissenschaften*—that lined the bookcases of the tiny office. Apart from the magazines, little glass cases and flasks were the predominant decor of this office, which seemed more like an entomologist's laboratory than a physicist's administrative office. Amid the disarray, Bacon spied a photograph of the dean standing next to Einstein. In the photo, the dean stood proudly beside the discoverer of relativity like a squirrel waiting anxiously to climb a sequoia tree.

"I'm very flattered, Professor."

"I want you to know that this is not my opinion that I am sharing with you here; I am merely reading from your academic file. I would have liked to have known you better, but I guess that wasn't meant to be, and so I can't praise you quite as well as some of my colleagues can. Nothing to be done about that. Now, if you don't mind, I'd like to get to the point. I have called you here today to tell you something that you probably know better than I do."

"I think I know what you're about to tell me, Professor."

"Following the recommendation of Professor Oswald Veblen, the Institute for Advanced Study has invited you to join their team." Bacon couldn't help cracking a smile. "Of course, we would prefer that you would remain here with us, but you have the final say in the matter. If you'd like to go off and join our neighbors, I can't tell you not to. But I have to warn you that at the institute you will only be eligible for the title 'assistant,' and not 'doctoral candidate.' You *are* aware of what that means, aren't you? Do you think, perhaps, you'd like to give it some more thought, or have you already made up your mind?"

In the beginning, the institute's offices were housed in Find Hall, in Princeton's mathematics department, while the money was raised to build a proper home for the organization. From 1939 on, its main offices were located in Fuld Hall, a giant red-brick box that actually looked more like a mental institution or a government building of some sort. The new head-quarters allowed the institute to distance itself a bit from the university, although there was still a bit of bad blood between the two institutions. When the institute was just getting started, its director, Abraham Flexner, had promised not to invite Princeton professors to join its ranks, but Oswald Veblen and the Hungarian mathematician John von Neumann, both originally at Princeton, ultimately decided to sign on at the institute.

"I'm planning to accept the institute's offer, Professor."

"That's what I thought," said the dean.

Bacon had already carefully weighed the advantages and disadvantages of the offers he had received. He knew that at the institute he would not be granted the title of doctoral student, but he also knew that there he would have access to some of the greatest physicists and mathematicians in the world. He didn't doubt his decision for a second.

"Very well," said the dean. "Then I suppose there's nothing left to say. How old are you, my boy?"

"Twenty."

"You're still so young . . . too young. Perhaps you'll still be able to set things right sometime in the future. But don't waste time; the early years are essential for physicists. It's one of those unwritten rules, unfair as they may be, but you must know it by heart: After turning thirty, a physicist is through. Through. I'm telling you this from experience."

"Thank you for your advice, sir."

His appointment with Professor Von Neumann, on Tuesday at three in the afternoon, flashed through Bacon's mind, but the dean quickly inter-rupted his reverie:

"All right, then, get out of here."

HYPOTHESIS II: *On Von Neumann and the War*

"My name is Bacon, Professor. Francis Bacon."

Frank had arrived at the institute at the agreed-upon hour. He had put on one of his best suits, rat-gray, and a tie with a pattern that looked like lit-tle giraffes.

"Oh, yes, Bacon. Born January 22, 1561, at York House. Died 1626. A lunatic, unfortunately. But, oh, yes, what a fertile mind. Did you know I could recite the entire *Novum Organum* for you, line by line, right now if I wanted? But I suppose that would be rather boring for you. Anyway, I have another appointment that I don't want to be *too* late for."

Of all the men of modern science, nobody seemed able to warm up to the cunning, turbulent nature of numbers quite as John von Neumann had. As a young scholar at Princeton, where he spent a few months as a professor of mathematics, he had acquired a reputation for being one of the most intelligent men in the entire world—and, at the same time, one of the worst professors imaginable. His name in Germany was Johannes, a transliteration of the original Hungarian Janós, and so he had little apprehension about translating it into English in order to adapt to the more casual way of his adopted country. Born in Budapest in 1903, he became Johnny von Neumann in the United States, which made him an odd mix of Scotch whisky and Czech beer. He was now only thirty-seven, but his career as a child prodigy had catapulted him early on into the pantheon of contemporary mathematics. For the past few months, he was also the youngest member of the Institute for Advanced Study. Bacon had never taken any of his courses, but the Princeton campus was rife with tales of the professor's many eccentricities, and Bacon was familiar with all of them. As he would soon hear for himself, Von Neumann had a peculiar accent that was not precisely the result of his Central European provenance—in fact, many people said he had simply invented it himself. He always wore the same uniform, a neat, coffee-colored suit that he never varied, not even during the summer or for excursions into the nearby countryside. In addition to his gift for rapid-fire mathematical calculations, he also had a photographic memory: After merely scanning a page of text or quickly reading through a novel he could recite it by heart, from start to finish without committing a single error. He had done this several times with *A Tale of Two Cities.*

Impatient by nature, Von Neumann despised his students; he abhorred their slow minds and the countless unnecessary repetitions he was often obliged to parcel out, like a country farmer feeding his chickens. Worst of all, however, were the expressions of shock and fear that registered upon his students' faces whenever they attempted to decipher one of his elegant, eloquent equations. Nobody, but nobody, was able to understand his lectures, simply because of the absurd speed at which he gave them. By the time a student had begun to copy out some labyrinthine formula Von Neumann had quickly scratched out on the blackboard, the surprisingly nimble professor had already grabbed his eraser and leapt into the next problem, as if the blackboard were a giant Broadway billboard. During Von Neumann's tenure at Princeton, only one graduate student had managed to finish his thesis under Von Neumann's direction, and after that experience, the professor knew he would never again put himself through the tedium of rereading poorly written proofs and decoding someone else's muddle of arithmetic nonsense. When Abraham Flexner invited Von Neumann to join the institute, he was quick to mention that Von Neumann would have no teaching obligations whatsoever, just like all the other professors there. The mathematician gladly accepted the offer; this way, he would be forever free from the bothersome plague of busybody coeds who couldn't even tell Mozart from Beethoven.

"I have to go now. A meeting with the inner sanctum, if you know what I mean. Tea and cookies and all those illustrious names. Well, not quite as illustrious as yours, but prominent enough that I shouldn't be late, you know?" He stopped for a second. He was stocky, even slightly chubby, with a greasy double chin hiding beneath his rounded beard. His accent was truly impossible to place. "What are we going to do with you, Bacon? I'm sorry to have kept you waiting, I didn't expect . . . Well, you tell me what to do." Bacon tried in vain to say something. The way Von Neumann carried on a conversation reminded him of the caterpillar's erratic, long winded pronouncements in *Alice in Wonderland*. "All right, all right, that's a fine idea, Bacon. Listen, tomorrow I'm throwing a little party, you know. I try to do that every so often; this place can be so *boring* sometimes. I'm always telling my wife that we should open a bar here, like the kind in Budapest, but she never listens to me. All right, I have to go now. I'll expect you then, at my house tomorrow. Five o'clock, before the other guests arrive . . . One of those receptions, you know? To keep us from dying of boredom. I suppose you've heard about them. All right, I have to go. I'm sorry. Five o'clock, then. Don't forget."

"But, Professor . . ." Bacon tried interrupting him.

"I told you already, we'll discuss your problem later on. At length, I promise. Now, if you'll be so kind . . ."

After several minutes battling with an obtuse secretary to obtain the professor's home address, Bacon finally arrived at Von Neumann's house, at 26 Westcott Road, punctual as always. A pair of waiters were busy unloading trays of sandwiches from a catering truck parked in front of the main door to the house, carrying them methodically to the kitchen, like a team of laborers preparing to feed an ant farm. Bacon would never have admitted it, but of course he had heard about Von Neumann's receptions. His guest list was like a Who's Who of the Princeton intellectual scene; even Einstein was rumored to have dropped in on occasion. During this particular time, an atmosphere of war hovered over everything—after all, in less than a year Pearl Harbor would be bombed. But here, people seemed intent upon acting as if the world were the same as ever. Or perhaps people simply wanted to enjoy the last moments of calm before the storm hit.

Bacon rang the doorbell and waited a few seconds, but nobody answered. Emboldened, he entered the house along with one of the waiters and began timidly whispering, "Professor? Professor Von Neumann?" in a voice so low that nobody would have heard, even if standing three feet away. After a few minutes, a maid finally noticed him and went upstairs to announce his arrival to Von Neumann. Then the professor appeared, half dressed, with his jacket on and a tie slung over his arm.

"Bacon!"

"Yes, Professor."

"You, you again!" He sat down in one of the living room chairs and signaled for Bacon to do the same. He began buttoning his shirt with his little fingers, fat as grapes. "Your persistence doesn't bother me at all, no, not at all, but have some manners. I'm about to throw a party, you know? Wouldn't you agree that this isn't exactly the best moment to have a discussion about physics?"

"But you asked me to come, Professor."

"Nonsense, nonsense, Bacon." Now he was struggling with his tie. "Well, now that you're here, it wouldn't be right for you to leave empty-handed, would it? Manners, my friend, that's what's wrong with the Americans. Now, that's nothing personal, I assure you, but it is beginning to bother me." Von Neumann studied him, like a pathologist performing an autopsy. "I suppose that I am to decide whether you will be accepted at the institute, is that correct? Your future, sitting here in my hands. It's a terrible responsibility, my friend, just terrible. How should I know whether you're a genius or a fool?"

"I sent you my CV, Professor."

"You're a physicist, is that right?"

"That's correct, sir."

"Have you ever heard of such foolishness?" Von Neumann muttered. "Just because I wrote that tiny little book on quantum theory, why should that mean I have to review the file of every silly fool who decides to take up physics, right? Don't look at me like that, my friend, I'm not talking about you, of course not. Well, I'm afraid that those imbeciles have sent me nothing." Von Neumann got up from his chair in search of a mushroom vol-au-vent. When he located the tray, he picked it up and took it with him; he offered one to Bacon, who declined. "Can you believe it? Nothing. And the worst of all is that I bet it's time for me to present my evaluation of you to the committee, Bacon. What can I do about it?"

"I don't know, Professor."

"I've got it!" he shouted, excited by his sudden revelation. "You are aware, are you not, that we are about to enter a war?"

Bacon didn't seem to understand Von Neumann's quick change of subject.

"Yes," he said, just to say something.

"Mark my words, Bacon, we are going to war with Adolf and the Japs."

"So many people oppose the idea of a war—"

"Are you afraid, is that what you're trying to say? That you don't want to save the world from the clutches of that monster?"

Bacon didn't understand exactly where Von Neumann was headed; it almost seemed as though he was making fun of him, and so Bacon just tried to keep his answers noncommittal.

"Tell me, Bacon, what is a war?"

"I don't know, a confrontation between two or more enemies?"

"But what else than that?" Von Neumann was getting agitated. "Why do they fight, Bacon, why?"

"Because they have contradictory interests," Bacon spat out.

"For God's sake, no; it's precisely the opposite!"

"Because they have common interests?"

"Of course! They have the same objective, the same goal, but it is only available to one of them. That is why they go to war."

Bacon was confused. Von Neumann, meanwhile, was trying to calm himself down with more mushroom sandwiches.

"Let me give you a simple example. Let's take the Nazis and the British: What is their common objective? The same pie, Bacon: the Europe pie. Ever since Hitler took control of Germany in 1933, all he's done is ask for pieces. First he wanted Austria, then Czechoslovakia, then Poland, Belgium, Holland, France, Norway. Now he wants the whole pie. At first, the British tolerated his expansion, like they did at that abominable conference in Munich, but then they realized that Germany had too much. You see?"

"I follow you, Professor. War is like a game."

"Have you read my little article on the topic, the one published in 1928?" Von Neumann inquired, narrowing his eyes.

"'On the Theory of Games of Strategy,'" replied Bacon. "I've heard about it, but I haven't read it yet."

"Right," the professor mused. "All right. Suppose, then, that the war between Churchill and Hitler is a game. I will add one other condition—something that in the real case isn't necessarily true at all, but in any event—the players that intervene in the game do so rationally."

"I think I understand," ventured Bacon. "They will do whatever it takes to obtain the result they desire: victory."

"Very good." Von Neumann finally smiled. "I'm working on a theory right now together with my friend, the economist Oskar Morgenstein. The theory states that all rational games must possess a mathematic *solution*."

"A strategy."

"You've got it, Bacon. The best strategy for any game—or war—is the one that leads to the best possible result," Von Neumann cleared his throat with a swig of whisky. "Now, to my understanding, all games fall into one of two categories: zero-sum games and everything else. A game can only be considered zero-sum if the competitors are fighting over a finite, fixed object and if one person necessarily loses what the other one wins. If I only have one pie, each slice that I obtain represents a loss for my rival."

"And in the non-zero-sum games, the advantages earned by one player don't necessarily represent a loss for the other," Bacon pronounced, satisfied.

"Right. Therefore, our war between the Nazis and the British . . ."

". . . is a zero-sum game."

"Correct. Let's use it as a working hypothesis. What is the current status of the war? Hitler controls half of Europe. England barely puts up a fight. The Russians are holding out, waiting to see what happens, chained to their nonaggression pact with the Germans. If this is what things look like, Bacon, you tell me: What will be Hitler's next move?" Von Neumann asked excitedly, his chest heaving up and down like a water pump.

It was a tough question, and Bacon knew there was a catch to it. His response shouldn't reflect his intuition, he reasoned, but rather the mathematic expectations of his interrogator.

"Hitler is going to want another piece of that pie."

"That's exactly what I was hoping to hear!" Von Neumann exclaimed. "We've said that to Roosevelt over and over again. Now: Which piece, specifically?"

There were two possibilities. Bacon didn't even flinch.

"I think Hitler's going to start with Russia."

"Why?"

"Because it's the weakest of all his potential enemies, and he can't allow Stalin to continue building his war chest for much longer."

"Perfect, Bacon. Now comes the hard part." Von Neumann was enjoying the young man's astonishment. "Let's take a look at our position on this issue, that of the United States of America. Right now we're not involved, so we can be more objective. Let's try to decide, rationally, what our course of action should be."

Bacon and Von Neumann sat talking for over half an hour. In the meantime, the maid busied herself placing the plates and tablecloths in their proper places in the dining room, next to the drawing room. After a while, Klara, the professor's wife—his second wife, actually—called out to Von Neumann from the staircase, chastising him for being late for his own party. Von Neumann waved his hand dismissively and signaled to his companion to stay where he was. Although he felt a bit silly, Bacon was enjoying the conversation; its dry humor and fast-paced exchanges reminded him of those chess games with his father so many years before. Beneath the apparent simplicity of this intellectual challenge, Bacon had the feeling that he was actually waging a most unusual battle against the professor. This was the kind of conversation he could imagine taking place between two spies from enemy countries, or two lovers unsure of one another's affections. Each move was an attempt to get ahead of the next one, and so on and so on, and both men had to perform two tasks at once: They each had to carefully guard their own strategies, and at the same time figure out the other's plan of attack. The conversation itself was a kind of game.

"My theory is the following," said Von Neumann, as he took a sheet of paper from the coffee table and began outlining a neat, precise diagram. "The game we are playing with the Germans is not zero-sum because it involves the division of an even larger pie—the world—and there is a wide range of values ascribed to the different pie pieces that each side wants to keep for itself. This means that there are two strategies at play here, and four possible outcomes. The United States can decide to enter the war or not. The Axis countries can decide to attack us or not. What, then, are the four scenarios?"

Bacon responded with confidence:

"First, we attack them; second, they attack us by surprise; third, both sides attack simultaneously; fourth, things stay the way they are."

"Now let's consider the outcomes of each case. If we declare war, we have the potential advantage of surprising them, but many American lives would no doubt be lost in the process. If, on the other hand, they attack us first, they will possess that surprise margin but then they will be forced to wage a war on two fronts (provided that we are correct in assuming that they will attack the Reds at any time). Now, if we follow the third scenario and attack simultaneously, and go through all the obligatory declarations of war, etc., etc., both sides will have forfeited the surprise element, and both will suffer similar human losses. Now, if we opt for the last scenario, in which both sides leave things as they are, the likely outcome is that Hitler will take control of Europe and we will take North America, but in the long run, a conflict between the two sides will still be inevitable."

"I like your analysis, Professor."

"Thank you, Bacon. Now I'd like you to assign values to each of the possible outcomes, for our side and for theirs."

"All right," said Bacon, and he began to write on the piece of paper:

1. *The United States and the Axis attack simultaneously:* USA, 1; Axis, 1.
2. *The United States launches a surprise attack against the Axis:* USA, 3; Axis, 0.
3. *The United States waits, and the Axis launches a surprise attack:* USA, 0; Axis, 3.
4. *The situation remains the same as it has been until now:* USA, 2; Axis, 2.

Then Bacon drew the following diagram:

	The Axis attacks	*The Axis waits*
The U.S. Attacks	1,1	3,0
The U.S. Waits	0,3	2,2

"The question is," said Von Neumann, more excited than ever, "what should we do?"

Bacon contemplated the diagram as if it were a Renaissance painting. He found its simplicity as beautiful as Von Neumann did. It was a work of art.

"The worst-case scenario would be for us to wait and then get attacked by surprise. We would get a zero, and Adolf would come out with three. The problem is that we don't know what that monster has planned. From that angle, I think the only rational solution is to attack first. If we can surprise the Nazis, then we earn a lovely three. If we simply engage in a simultaneous war, at least we'd get a one and not the zero that we'd deserve for being overly indulgent," Bacon concluded, convinced. "That's the answer. This way, at least, the outcome will depend on us."

Von Neumann seemed even more satisfied than his student. Not only had Bacon proven his grit, but he and Von Neumann agreed about what decision President Roosevelt should make regarding the war. Ever since the discovery of uranium fission in 1939, Von Neumann had been one of the staunchest advocates for the establishment of a large-scale nuclear research program in the United States. An atomic bomb, if such a thing were possible, would not only take the Germans and the Japanese by surprise, but it could also end the war once and for all. Unfortunately, however, his message of warning had not seemed to have much effect on President Roosevelt.

"I think I shall have no other choice than to tolerate your tedious presence in the corridors of Fuld Hall," Von Neumann announced, slowly rising from his chair. "But don't go thinking this is paradise, Bacon. I am going to make you work like a mule until you end up despising every last equation I give you to solve. Be at my office next Monday."

Von Neumann walked toward the staircase. The irritated voice of Klara Dan once again came bounding down from the second floor. Before retiring to his upstairs quarters, Von Neumann turned to Bacon one last time.

"If you don't have anything better to do, you can stay for the party."

In December of 1941, John von Neumann's prediction came true, and the United States of America had no other choice but to enter the war. President Roosevelt had decided to remain neutral until the last possible moment, and the Japanese executed the best possible strategy: the surprise attack. The American public was shocked and outraged. Citizens from every walk of American life were angered and horrified.

HYPOTHESIS III: *On Einstein and Love*

By the time he had settled into his life in the United States, toward the end of 1933, Einstein was already something of an international genius, his mere image capable of inspiring even those unable to comprehend the slightest bit of physics. Having achieved this mythic status, the author of relativity amused himself by responding to his admirers' innocent questions with riddles and paradoxes, brief as Buddhist parables. With his long, tangled mane of graying hair and his eyes, encircled by a frame of wrinkles, he was a hermit delivered to save the modern world, so desperately in need of his help. Journalists flocked to his home on Mercer Street seeking his opinion on every topic under the sun. A modern-day cross between Socrates and Confucius, Einstein obliged them with the serene benevolence of a teacher addressing the timid ignorance of his pupils. Stories of these press conferences quickly began to circulate from one end of the country to the other, as if every one of his answers were some kind of Zen koan, a Sufi poem, or a Talmudic aphorism. On one occasion, a reporter asked Einstein the following question:

"Is there such a thing as a formula for success in life?"

"Yes, there is."

"What is it?" asked the reporter, impatient.

"If a represents success, I would say that the formula is $a=x+y+z$, in which x is work and y is luck," explained Einstein.

"What is z, then?" questioned the reporter.

Einstein smiled, and then answered: "Keeping your mouth shut."

These stories, brief and concise, only served to enhance his prestige, but at the same time, they fueled the ire of his enemies. In those days, the world was divided into two camps: those who adored Einstein and those who, like the Nazis, would have done anything to see him dead.

In 1931, when Einstein was in Pasadena to deliver a lecture at the California Institute of Technology, Abraham Flexner first approached him to join the Institute for Advanced Study, which was soon to be inaugurated at Princeton University. Flexner would make the same proposal to Einstein once again, when the two men found themselves at Oxford University in 1932.

"Professor Einstein," he said as they walked through the gardens of Christ Church College, "it is not my intention to dare to offer you a position at our institute, but if you think about it and feel that it might meet your needs, we would be more than disposed to accommodate whatever requirements you might have." Einstein replied that he would think about it, and in early 1933 the political climate in Germany forced him to accept the offer.

By the early 1930s, members of Hitler's party were winning more and more seats in the Reichstag. In the 1932 elections, for example, more than two hundred Nazi deputies joined the ranks of the Reichstag, which was now under the control of the artful, cagey Hermann Goering. Around that time, Einstein and his second wife, Elsa, realized that sooner or later they would have to flee Germany. A third telephone call from Abraham Flexner, this time to Einstein's home in Caputh, in the outskirts of Berlin, convinced the couple to cross the Atlantic. Taking advantage of the new season of conferences and lectures in the United States, Einstein promised Flexner that he would pay a visit to the institute, which would allow him to finally make a decision regarding the offer. Upon leaving their home, Einstein looked at his wife's careworn face and in the admonishing tone he reserved for truly tragic moments, he said to her: *"Dreh' dich um. Du siehst's nie wieder."* That is, "Don't turn around. You'll never see it again." In January of 1933, Einstein was at the conference in Pasadena when Hitler was named chancellor of the Reich by President Von Hindenburg. In one interview, Einstein confirmed the prediction he had recently made to his wife: "I won't be going home."

Taking care not to go anywhere near Germany, Albert and Elsa returned to Europe, where Einstein still had several academic commitments to fulfill. Goering, in the meantime, wasted no time in denouncing the communist conspiracy behind "Jewish science" during one of his incendiary speeches in the Reichstag, disavowing Albert Einstein as well as his life's work. Several Nazi assault units broke into the physicist's home in Caputh, in search of the armaments that they were certain the communists had stored there.

Einstein then paid a brief visit to the Belgian coast, and upon ensuring that Flexner was indeed prepared to agree to his conditions—an annual salary of $15,000 and a position for one of his assistants—he accepted the appointment at Princeton. On the seventeenth of October 1933, he disembarked from the steamship *Westmoreland* on Quarantine Island, New York, and from there he took a motorboat that whisked him away, incognito, to the New Jersey shore and then straight to the Peacock Inn, in the town of Princeton.

The new institute seemed to have been created exclusively for Einstein. In Flexner's own words, it was a haven that would allow scholars and scientists to work "without being carried off in the maelstrom of the immediate." Contrary to the current trend at universities all over the world, the study of physics at the Institute for Advanced Study was to be purely theoretical; no classes at all would be offered. At the institute, Einstein would have no other obligation than to think. A new koan would come to epitomize his life in the United States. The same—or maybe it was another—reporter asked the wise man:

"Professor, you have developed theories that have changed the way we see the world, a giant step forward for science. So tell us, where is your laboratory?"

"Here," replied Einstein, pointing to the fountain pen that peeked out from his jacket pocket.

*   *   *

Einstein had a method, a practice he resorted to frequently which enabled him to contemplate certain scientific issues that otherwise would have been impossible to envision. This technique was known as *Gedankenexperiment*, or "mental experiment," and despite its contradictory-sounding name, it was common practice in the days of ancient Greece. All modern science, especially physics, was based upon the use of practical experiments to prove hypotheses. A theory was considered valid if and only if reality did not betray it, if its predictions could be fulfilled rigorously and without exception. Nevertheless, since the close of the previous century, very few pure physicists were amused by the idea of locking themselves in laboratories to battle against increasingly sophisticated machinery that, in the end, only proved things they already knew. The gulf between the theorists and the experimental physicists grew wider and wider, fiercer even than the rift between mathematicians and engineers. Due to this mutual animosity, the two camps only made contact when the circumstances absolutely required it. Though they were, in fact, mutually dependent, they did all they could to avoid one another, inventing the most far-fetched excuses to get out of attending one another's seminars and conferences.

One of the most important—and controversial—of Einstein's mental experiments was the EPR Paradox of 1935, which took its name from the initials of the three scientists who worked together on the experiment: Albert Einstein, Boris Podolsky, and Nathan Rosen. Based entirely on a mental experiment (since the instruments to prove it didn't exist), the EPR Paradox was an attempt to refute, once again, the quantum physics that so irked Einstein—the same quantum physics he himself had helped bring about. As defended by the Danish physicist Niels Bohr in the so-called Copenhagen Interpretation, quantum mechanics posited, among other things, the notion that chance was no accident at all, but rather a perfectly integral feature of the laws of physics. Einstein, of course, could not accept this idea. "God does not play dice with the universe," he said to the physicist Max Born, and the EPR Paradox was a way of demonstrating certain aspects of quantum mechanics that he felt were scientifically unacceptable. Bohr and his followers, in turn, insinuated that Einstein had lost his mind.

Bacon belonged, as did Einstein, to the theoretical camp. Ever since the awakening of his youthful passion for theoretical mathematics, he had done everything possible to distance himself from concrete problems, focusing instead on formulas and equations that were increasingly more abstract, and in most cases exceedingly difficult to explain in real-world terms.

Rather than struggle with particle accelerators and spectroscopic methods, Bacon chose instead to hide himself away in the far more pleasant realm of the imagination. There, he never ran the risk of dirtying his hands with things like radioactive waste, or exposing himself to dangerous X rays. To carry out his research, all that was required of him were perseverance and ingenuity. It was an approach to physics that, in a way, was a lot like chess.

Princeton, despite being one of the country's great centers of academia, was an insipid place: too small, too American, too clean-cut, and too hypocritical. And contrary to the supposed "university tradition," or perhaps because of it, a kind of stiff formality, a sameness, an uncomfortable kind of morality seemed to infect all the relationships one might cultivate there. The university itself was known for having a history of racism and anti-Semitism. To make matters worse, people felt even less able to express any kind of natural, day-to-day happiness, what with the war raging in Europe.

In order to escape these inconveniences, Bacon convinced himself very early on that the one area in which the theoretical world was useless and perhaps even perverse was sex. Theory, when you came down to it, was just fantasy. The tragedy was that almost nobody in the town of Princeton seemed able or willing to accept this basic idea—not the dean, the ministers, the mayor, the professors' wives, the policemen, the doctors, not even the students themselves. No, they all insisted on performing endless mental experiments on the topic, and in the most unthinkable of places: in church, in lecture halls, in the eating clubs, at family gatherings, while taking their children to nursery school, as they walked their little dogs at sunset. And just like the men at the Institute for Advanced Study, the opaline community of Princeton limited itself to *thinking* about the pleasures no one dared consummate. For this very reason, Bacon detested his neighbors; they were insincere, provincial, and prudish. In this matter, Bacon could not be pacified with abstraction and fantasy: no intellect—not even that of Einstein—could come close to revealing the abundant diversity of life that was the female gender. Rational thought was fine for articulating laws and theories, for formulating hypotheses and corollaries, but it could never capture the infinite array of aromas, sensations, and pure intoxication swept together in a moment of passion. In other words: Because he was utterly incapable of relating to women of his own social class, Bacon had decided to invest his money in the world's oldest profession.

In a moment of weakness, he met Vivien. He rarely spoke with her. It wasn't that he didn't care about her life or what she had to say—there were lots of women he cared little about yet tolerated long conversations with them. He just wanted to hold on to the idea that there was something mysterious and terrible about this woman. Her eyes, framed by a little halo that shone like a moon in eclipse, *had* to be hiding some kind of ancient secret, or maybe an accident or a crime, that could explain her evasive nature. Perhaps it wasn't that at all—he never dared to ask—but he liked holding on to that illusion of living with a difficult soul; he treasured the trepidation he felt whenever he was in her presence. He envisioned Vivien, and with her he felt he could lose himself in a new, unknown land.

This was the closest he had ever come to love. Despite the passion he felt for her, however, Bacon took great pains to ensure that nobody ever caught sight of him walking through the streets of Princeton with Vivien. He always insisted on seeing her at his house, where she arrived with a ritual precision, as if offering up some kind of weekly sacrifice to the gods. Bacon, with the childish pleasure of committing a sin, of breaking an ironclad law, found himself in an emotional state the likes of which he had never known. He threw himself into proving this theory on Vivien between the sheets of his bed, with the tenacity that is the pride of the experimental physicist. Vivien, on the other hand, allowed herself to be manipulated with a serenity bordering on indolence; she had worked at a newsstand for a long time and, given all the alarming news she read daily, nothing could shock her. Vivien's lovemaking was languorous and sweaty, like dancing to the blues. Her temperament reminded Bacon of that of a quiet little guinea pig or those calm, lazy caterpillars nestled in their moth-eaten leaves, indifferent to their predators lurking above.

As soon as she was finished undressing, Bacon would place Vivien facedown on the bed on the crisp, white sheets and turn on all the lights so he could study that optical antithesis, unbothered, for several minutes. When he was done, he would rest his body on top of hers and cover her with kisses. Every step of the way his lips tested the perfection of those beautiful little spherical equations that he knew he could never resolve. When he was through, he would turn her over as if she were a rag doll, and only then did he undress. Carefully he would separate Vivien's thighs, and he would then nestle his face in the warm, welcoming space between her legs. This prelude was a kind of axiom from which several theorems emerged each time they came together, and this was where his analytic prowess was evident: this prelude, or groundwork, occasionally led him to Vivien's tiny feet and, other times, to her nipples, her eyelashes, her belly button. It was more than mere lust: Bacon was studying sex in all its different incarnations, and was observing his own pleasure as it grew and evolved. In the end, the orgasm was just the logical, necessary consequence of the calculations he had mapped out earlier.

"I think it's time for you to go," he said to her, once he had recovered.

Maybe he did truly love her, but he just couldn't stand the idea of her staying in his bed for very long, or having to kiss her when it was all over. By then, the heat they had created and the droplets of sweat that dotted her skin like translucent eyes made him sick—a repulsion as strong as the ecstasy he had just experienced. Suddenly, inevitably, he would become acutely aware of the animal quality of it all, and he couldn't help imagining them as a couple of pigs rolling around in their own filth. His theory proven, he allowed Vivien just enough time to put herself back together and then he would simply ask her to leave. With the same indifference that, in some way, he sensed in her as well, he would watch her gather up her clothes and dress in silence as if watching an inanimate object or a doll. Once he was finally alone, Bacon felt nothing but sadness, *quod erat demonstrandum,* and usually fell into a dreamless slumber.

Despite having been raised with the proper manners of a New Jersey society boy, Bacon had made little contact with girls of his own age. The girls he always felt attracted to were, inevitably, the ones who ignored him: carefully coiffed, religious and austere, unattainably beautiful. At first, Bacon tried to act as though it didn't bother him. To fend off potential rejection, he would tell himself, a priori, that they were all so stupid they probably thought a square root was some kind of orchid bulb. After many fruitless efforts at maintaining a conversation that lasted longer than five minutes, Bacon gave up on them, frustrated and depressed. He felt that he would never find someone who could understand, much less love him. This was the kind of thinking that led him, for the first time, to one of the *non sanctos* establishments that one of his loudmouth classmates had suggested he try. There he would never have to make small talk or feign interest in the weather, parties, or fancy designer dresses. According to his friend, at these places everything was reduced to a silent, discreet procedure, a release of pleasure that implied absolutely no obligations of any sort. The first time he tried it, Bacon was terrified: He tried to concentrate on mathematical formulas in an effort to hide his discomfort and to allow his body to respond the way he wanted it to. He selected a thin, timid girl—it made him feel better to think that she was even more nervous than he—who turned into an emotionless machine when she got into bed. She took her clothing off all at once, displaying a microscopic pair of nipples that seemed to protrude directly out of her chest, and which she allowed Bacon to lick briefly before she took over. When it was over, he felt no remorse, and no emptiness, either. In fact, he had rather enjoyed it. He had *really* enjoyed it. In fact, it had been even better than his fast-talking classmate had said it would be. This was the perfect thing for chasing away the demons of lust, for it allowed him to concentrate harder on more important things, like quantum physics. Whenever this bodily urge arose, all he had to do was lay out a few dollars. And like a true scientist—they all have a bit of the entomologist in them—he certainly appreciated the diversity. He was constantly surprised at the unbelievable variety he found from woman to woman. The smallest details became an inexhaustible source of arousal for him: a new beauty mark, a curve he had never seen before, a slightly misshapen belly button. They all filled him with a pleasure that, until now, he had only ever felt before when solving algebra problems. He explored those specimens with the eagle eye of the collector, and somehow this always prevented him from ever coming close to anything like tenderness.

For some reason, Vivien was not like the other girls. It had been several months since Bacon had first laid eyes on her brave, sad face. Later he would try to remember the exact date of their first encounter, to identify the precise starting point of their relationship, but for some reason he never managed to mentally retrieve the information. He couldn't even remember if it had been summer or fall, or if it had been before or after his twentieth birthday. All he could remember was the distant sound of his voice when he finally spoke to that young woman who seemed little more than a girl. That day, instead of grabbing the *New York Times* from the pile and leaving the coins on top of some women's fashion magazine, as he usually did, Bacon looked straight at Vivien and asked her for the paper himself. As she handed it to him, Bacon noted a stifled expression of pain in her eyes. The exchange may have lasted only a few seconds, but it was enough time for her somber, delicate face, like a pin stuck into a piece of cloth, to pierce his imagination and remain imbedded in his mind. This woman possessed a certain kind of beauty that he had never appreciated until just then. From that day onward, he would go to the newsstand every Sunday hoping to find her there and, perhaps, learn a bit more about her.

The way the young woman looked at him made him feel both uncomfortable and intrigued. One day he tried striking up a conversation with her, commenting on some aspect of current events—the war was always a good pretext—but she didn't take the bait. All she did was smile wanly, without even opening her lips, and then returned to whatever she had been thinking about.

"Cat got your tongue?" asked Bacon in a playful tone that he immediately regretted. "How old are you, anyway?"

"Seventeen," she responded. Her voice was low and deep.

Bacon paid for the paper and slowly walked away, as if he was waiting for her to call out to him at the last minute. She, on the other hand, didn't even seem to have noticed the anonymous face that had just asked her age. The next day, Bacon returned. His legs trembling, he somehow managed to speak in a neutral, firm tone of voice.

"Would you like to go to the movies with me?" he asked her.

For the first time, she looked up at Bacon, displaying a set of teeth that made the newsprint in front of her look yellow and old. She watched him with imploring eyes. Was this some kind of joke?

"I can't."

"Why not?"

"Because I can't."

"Are you afraid?"

"No."

This scene would be repeated over and over again during the months that followed. Bacon would stop by, pay for his *New York Times*, and tell her about the various movies playing at the nearby theaters, in the hopes of finally eliciting a yes from her. But she always just shook her head violently from side to side, as if trying to scare away a bothersome fly. Bacon refused to be discouraged, however; from his perspective, the situation was slowly evolving into a weekly routine. He was genuinely surprised, then, when one morning, she finally granted his request. At the end of the day, he met her in front of the box office of one of the local movie theaters, a highly undesirable place, it was said. The movie was (how could he forget?) *Gone With the Wind*, which had just recently opened, and was the first film Bacon had ever seen in color. Later on he would remember little of the plot, having been far more interested in sneaking covert glimpses of his companion's profile, silvery blue in the light reflecting off the movie screen. He did, however, manage to memorize both the name and the gestures of the film's starring actress, Vivien Leigh. And that was the name with which he chose to baptize his new lady friend. Later on, she told him her real name, but he stated quite plainly that he preferred calling her Vivien. By doing this, he had invented a new creature, blessed with the qualities and characteristics that he saw fit to imbue her with.

The following Sunday they repeated the scene from the previous week, even seeing *Gone With the Wind* again, as if testing the full range of laws of inertia. Again, they spoke very little. It was as if they had signed a tacit agreement to spend time together, nothing else. Their first kiss took place on the way to the movies. Just like almost everything Bacon ever did, this kiss was inspired by a curiosity that was more scientific than romantic. After a few weeks, they added a twist to their incipient tradition: the small cottage in the country that was the one thing Bacon's father had left him when he died. Even there, they never spoke more than they absolutely had to. But he would have liked to know, for example, if she felt the same pleasure he did, or if she was subjecting herself to this intimate physical activity just to make him happy. He really had no idea of the emotions that they felt for one another; to speak frankly and openly about their relationship, prohibited and precarious as it was, would have been an unnecessary provocation. And as the days stretched on, he slowly accepted that his relationship with Vivien could exist only by observing this vow of silence.

One day, Bacon was just returning home from a statistics class when he received an unexpected visitor: his mother, who now called herself Rachel Smith. After her husband's death, she had become a wealthy, haughty woman. She dressed like a New Yorker: tailored black dresses, an anachronistic gamine haircut, and a grayish animal wrapped around her neck, his dead eyes a pitiable sight. Though born into middle-class America, she had managed to find her place among the local aristocracy, thanks to her second marriage. She considered herself an equal to the women around her, and she carefully noted and copied all their habits and idiosyncrasies. For a long time Bacon didn't even notice this new attitude, until one day when she happened to unleash her venom on the city sanitation workers.

"How can you humiliate me this way?" she implored as she burst through Bacon's front door, on the verge of tears, as her turquoise-colored purse fell upon his desk. Her tone was timid, almost inaudible, despite her worldly appearance. "I had to learn from one of my friends that instead of studying, my son uses the money he inherited from his father to go out on dates with a whore. Is this true?"

"She's not a prostitute, Mother."

"Don't be coy with me, Frank."

They argued for several minutes until, worn down by his mother's histrionics, Bacon swore that he would stop seeing Vivien for good. Of course, he didn't really intend to keep the promise, at least not fully. The next time he saw Vivien, he simply told her that he would rather not see her out of doors. Vivien's eyes filled with tears when she heard this, but just as he had imagined, she said nothing. Not one single reproach or protest, just the same sadness. Nor did Vivien say anything when Bacon refused to go to the movies with her the following week. From that day on, they never went out together again. Bacon didn't even have to explain why: Vivien knew the reason all too well, and the last thing she needed was the additional humiliation of being lied to. Finally, when Bacon mentioned something about a job in a newsstand being beneath the dignity of a girl like her, Vivien began working in a cafeteria.

It didn't take Bacon long to realize that when you despise the woman you love, the love becomes a cruel, solitary vice. He trusted her, but he was also aware of the hatred that was slowly building up behind the wall of her submissiveness. Vivien, however, acted as though she had no idea of what was going on in her lover's head, behaving as if nothing at all had changed between them. She continued visiting his house, twice a week at least, with the apathy of a rabbit who allows himself to be fattened up, knowing full well that the day will soon come when he will have to take his place on his master's dining room table.

One day, at one of the little social gatherings she loved to organize, Bacon's mother introduced her son to a perky, freckled young woman from "one of the best families in Philadelphia," as Bacon's mother noted with great pride. When the girl actually seemed interested in what he had to say, young Frank decided it wouldn't be so terrible to dance with her, or tell her that he was currently unattached. Vivien didn't even cross his mind; she had evolved into something of a sexual phantom that appeared at his bedside like a figure from one of his erotic dreams. Vivien, in fact, did materialize at Bacon's apartment several times over the next few weeks, but she never found him there; he had failed to mention that he had made a number of dinner dates with the parents of his spectacular new girlfriend.

"Don't leave me," Vivien said to him the next time they were together, in a quiet, firm, determined voice.

"This was going to have to end sooner or later, Vivien. I'm sorry, really I am."

"Why?"

"There's no other way."

"I promise not to tell anyone about us."

The more Vivien talked, the more Bacon despised her—and loved her, in some odd, inexplicable way.

"There's something I haven't told you," he added, looking away. "I'm engaged." His voice trailed off. "It couldn't be any other way, you have to understand."

Of course she could understand. Bacon knew she would—he could predict her reactions by now, otherwise he wouldn't have told her, or at least not so abruptly. Perhaps Vivien would surprise him and actually get angry, and leave him for good. But Bacon suspected that she would do none of those things; he was betting that she would come back to him, and that once again they would love one another wordlessly, reverting to the same wretched habits they had maintained for so long.

"All right, Vivien. Whatever you wish."

The Institute for Advanced Study was a moldy, dismal place. It had neither laboratories nor noisy, impertinent students, and the professional tools of its occupants were reduced to the bare minimum: a few blackboards, chalk, paper. If mental experiments were what you wanted, this was the place to perform them. There, safely tucked away behind the thick walls of Fuld Hall, some of the greatest minds in the world were at work: professors Veblen, Gödel, Alexander, Von Neumann, plus a handful of celebrated thinkers who made regular pilgrimages to the institute as a stop on the university lecture circuit. This, of course, was to say nothing of the institute's most famous occupant, the patron saint of theoretical physics, Albert Einstein himself. Nevertheless, Bacon was bored.

Bacon had been working with Von Neumann for only three months, but he was already bothered that he hadn't found anything that really excited him. It wasn't that he disliked his work with the Hungarian mathematician—it was rather effortless, and after all, there was no better place to continue his education. But in his heart, he had discovered that something was pulling him away from the field of pure theory, or at least from the wordless science that was practiced at the institute. A few times, he had tried approaching the professors who gathered together for tea and cookies at three in the afternoon every day, but his attempts at striking up conversations were always frustrated by their utter lack of interest in him. Worn-out from being alone with their thoughts, they talked among themselves about such pressing scientific topics as baseball scores, the best way to acquire European wines, or the greasy quality of North American cuisine. The serious questions Bacon was trying to pose always dissolved amid a flurry of nervous titters and sudden, distracted gestures. Although he respected Bacon, Veblen limited their interactions to a condescending nod before moving away as quickly as possible. Von Neumann managed to tolerate him, as Bacon had suspected he would, but all the other scientists, the ones he scarcely knew, didn't even acknowledge his existence.

Bacon, who was accustomed to excelling at all his academic endeavors, felt himself plummeting into a state of despondence at this lack of attention, a sensation that felt a lot like the depressions he had suffered while living with his family. In these moments, he wondered if he wouldn't have been better off somewhere else, Caltech, maybe, where at least he would have been working on more pressing issues. Despite the fact that Von Neumann had published one of the most important documents of modern physics, *Mathematical Foundations of Quantum Mechanics,* in 1932, it was all too clear that he was now primarily concerned with his game theories and, even worse, the programming of mechanical calculators. Neither of these subjects compelled Bacon in the least; his mentor's ingenious formulations were occasionally entertaining, but they weren't enough to sustain Bacon's interest.

In addition to all this, Bacon's relationship with Elizabeth was growing more and more serious with each passing day, and the prospect of a formal engagement caused him nothing less than total panic. At first, he had treated their relationship as a test—after all, this was the first time a woman from his social class had ever declared her love for him. But he never imagined that it would all happen so fast. On the other hand, there was no way he could publicly formalize his relationship with Vivien: The ensuing scandal would alienate him from everyone, even in the academic world. The brilliant future that he had laid out by joining the institute suddenly seemed like a trap, and he saw no way out. But he couldn't give up on it, either; he had to hold out for at least a year before he could even think of going to Caltech.

"What's wrong with you, Bacon?" Von Neumann asked him one day, blunt and direct as always. "Is something the matter? Oh, I think I know what it is. Women, right? Men are forever in torment at the hands of women. That is the quintessential problem of the age we live in, Bacon. If we took one quarter of the time we spend resolving romantic problems and applied it instead to physics or mathematics, why, scientific progress would advance in geometric proportions. But it is one of life's great pleasures, isn't it?"

"Pleasure and pain, Professor," mumbled Bacon.

"Of course, of course! That's what makes it so very fascinating! I have to confess, I also spend hours thinking about this subject. I'm a married man, you understand. You even met my wife, Klara, at the party the other day. But I'm still young. I have a right to wonder if I will ever know another woman's body, wouldn't you agree?" Von Neumann's cheeks grew pink, livened by the topic of conversation. "Why don't we have a little drink at the end of the day, to talk more? Yes, let's do it, Bacon. In the meantime, let's get to work."

As the afternoon wore on, the sun transformed the red-brick exterior of the institute into a wall of fiery rose and violet, breaking through the somber cloud cover that normally settled in above the building. Once again, Von Neumann told Bacon to meet him at his home. Klara had gone out to play bridge with one of their neighbors, so they had the house to themselves and could talk freely. Bacon was beginning to feel more and more at home in that drawing room.

"When they first told me that alcohol was forbidden in the United States, I thought it was a joke," said Von Neumann as he removed two glasses from the bar. "You can imagine how horrified I was when I found out it was true. Truly insane, those Americans. I tell you, I only accepted the position of visiting professor at the university under the condition that I could return to Europe each summer and replenish this drought." He took out a bottle of bourbon and expertly poured the honey-colored liquid into two tall glasses. "Thank God they realized their mistake. Water? I take mine neat. All right, here you are . . . So, tell me, Bacon, what's the matter with you?"

"I don't know," Frank lied. "I guess it would be different if . . ." He tried to correct himself: "It's not that I'm unhappy at the institute, Professor, it's just that I'm afraid that it might not be the right place for me right now."

"Well, where else would you want to be?"

"That's my problem. On one hand, I can't think of any other place I'd rather be. Everyone is here. But for that reason, I get the feeling that my own work will never be very important at the institute."

The professor shook his head, as if he was sincerely distressed. "I've always said that one's mathematic capacity begins to decline after age twenty-six, so let's see, you have how many years left?"

"Four."

"Four! It's terrible, isn't it? Well, anyway, I am thirty-eight, though I think I hide it rather well." He took a few sips from his glass, then wiped his lips with a linen napkin. "Nevertheless, I get the sense that the institute isn't the only thing on your mind. You've got a problem with the girls, don't you?"

Bacon was grateful for his tutor's advice, but he wasn't altogether convinced that he wanted to discuss his private life with him. The truth was, he didn't like discussing his private life with anyone.

"So tell me, what's the matter?"

"Well, it's about two women. . . ."

"I knew it! See what a good nose I've got, Bacon? People think that mathematicians are completely out of touch with the real world, but it's just not true. Sometimes we are even better observers than regular people. We see things that others don't." He paused. "Do you love them both?"

"In a way, yes. I'm not sure. One of them is my fiancée. She's a fine girl, very sweet."

"But you don't love her."

"No."

"So then marry the other one."

"I can't do that, either. I . . . I wouldn't know how to explain it to you, Professor." Bacon took a gulp of bourbon to fortify himself. "The other girl is very different. I don't even know if I truly know her, much less love her. We barely even talk."

"That's a problem, that's for sure . . . you've got a real problem on your hands," Von Neumann mused. "Do you see how, once again, I was right? These are the issues that affect us all the time, even if we can't admit it to ourselves. But don't think that mathematics doesn't come in handy at times like this." The professor finished his drink and immediately poured himself another. Aside from his one sip, Bacon had barely touched his. "That's why I'm so taken with game theory. Or did you just think it was some eccentricity of mine, passing the time with heads and tails and poker games? No, Bacon, what makes these games truly fascinating is that they mimic the behavior of men. And they serve, above all, to clarify the nature of three very similar issues: the economy, the war, and love. I'm not kidding. These three activities effectively represent all the battles we men wage against one another. In all three, there are always at least two wills in conflict. Each one attempts to take the greatest possible advantage of the other, at the least possible risk to himself."

"Like in your war example."

"Exactly, Bacon. Now, recently I have been more worried about the economic application of this theory, but your case would be a fine exercise to test. Let's see. There are three players: you and your two girlfriends, whom we will call—in the interest of discretion—A and B. You will be C. Now you tell me what each person wants."

Bacon's hands grew clammy, as if he were preparing for confession. "The first one, the one you call A, is my fiancée. She wants us to get married. She's always hinting at it and pressuring me—it's all she thinks about. Girl B, on the other hand, only wants to be with me, but that, obviously, will be impossible if I agree to marry A."

"Understood. And you, what do you want?"

"That's the worst part of it. I don't know. I think I'd like to keep things just as they are right now. I don't want things to change."

Von Neumann got up from his chair and began to pace around the room. He clapped his hands, as if he were applauding something, and then contemplated Bacon with a paternal, ever so slightly condescending look in his eyes.

"I'm afraid that you are trying to bet on inaction, perhaps the most dangerous thing you can do in a case like this. You can try, of course, but even the laws of physics would be against you on this one. In games, one always attempts to move ahead, to advance to new objectives, and slowly destroy the adversary. That's how your two women are behaving. Both of them are trying to corner you, bit by bit, while you simply assume a defensive stance." Von Neumann returned to his chair and rested his fat hand upon Bacon's shoulder. "As your friend, I have to warn you that your strategy is doomed to fail. Sooner or later, one of them is going to wear you down. In fact, they don't even realize it but they are actually competing with one another. You're not a player in this, boy! You're only the prize!"

"So what should I do, then?"

"Oh, dear Bacon. I'm only referring to game theory, not real life. Reason is one thing—as you so astutely observed in our last discussion—but human will is an entirely different animal. All I can say is that if I were in your shoes, there would only be one thing to do."

"And are you going to tell me what that is, Professor?"

"I'm sorry, Bacon. I'm a mathematician, not a psychologist." From somewhere deep beneath Von Neumann's flushed countenance, an almost imperceptible, feline smile began to emerge across his lips.

Bacon knew that Einstein, ever since his Berlin days, loved to go on walks. Every day he would set out on the path between his house and the institute, and he particularly enjoyed chatting with a walking companion. The talks never lasted more than a few moments, but his companions treated them as if they were precious pearls of wisdom. Many illustrious physicists visited Princeton specifically to catch the professor on one of these walks, because it was during those moments that his mind was at its most relaxed and fertile.

One day Bacon decided to wait for Einstein outside of his office, cubicle 115 of Fuld Hall, hidden behind the staircase landing. He was scared, secretly embarrassed, like someone who chases after a movie star in the hopes of getting an autograph. That was the reason he was in Princeton, after all—to get to know men like Einstein, not to listen to Von Neumann's eccentric psychology, and certainly not to put up with the indifference of his older colleagues.

Just like the journalists who had dedicated themselves to popularizing—or, rather, misinterpreting—Einstein's theories, Bacon quickly learned the meaning of relativity. The seconds crawled by, agonizingly slowly; it was as if all the underground arteries connecting the universe were somehow, maddeningly, all blocked up. He had been waiting for about forty minutes now. Like a spy or a sentinel, or someone waiting for a miracle to happen, he maintained his vigil, waiting for the physicist to emerge from his office. Each time someone walked past him, Bacon waved hello timidly, and then raised his hand to his head as if to indicate that he had finally remembered the reason that had brought him there, and then walked in the opposite direction until he was certain the coast was clear. He felt like some kind of inept bodyguard, the anachronistic sentry of the Institute for Advanced Study.

Finally the door opened, and Einstein emerged, walking straight toward the exit. He wore a black suit and his hair, Bacon noticed, wasn't nearly as white or as messy as it appeared in photographs. This was the moment he had been waiting for. But at the last minute Bacon faltered, and that one moment was all it took. Einstein scurried past him down the staircase. The great physicist hadn't even noticed Bacon as he ran downstairs; he simply went on his way, indifferent to that dim shadow. By the time Bacon realized his mistake, it was too late. The professor was already out of the building. There was no way he could run and catch him by surprise; the idea was to make the encounter appear casual. If it seemed premeditated, Einstein would just get rid of him as quickly as possible. Bacon was furious at himself, but he was not about to give up so quickly. In an almost dreamlike state, Bacon began to follow Einstein—at a prudent distance, of course   digging deep into his coat pockets, leaving Fuld Hall behind.

Determined and giddy, Bacon was barely conscious of what he was doing, and of what an absurd endeavor it was. He was too focused on hiding behind the cars and ash trees that lined the streets to realize exactly what he was getting himself into. As Einstein advanced down the street, Bacon followed him. Finally, Einstein arrived at number 112 Mercer Street, where he lived with his secretary, Helen Dukas. Upon seeing Einstein disappear into his house, Bacon breathed a sigh of relief. Using his shirtsleeve, he wiped the perspiration from his forehead and headed back toward the institute.

The next day, Bacon was prepared to make up for his previous ineptitude. Today he would face Einstein for real, and if the circumstances allowed, he would confess his earlier conduct. It was said that the professor had a good sense of humor, and perhaps this would be the best way to break the ice with him. Just after noon, Bacon returned to his spot, like a soldier determined to fulfill his mission. Only moments after Bacon had reassumed his position at the stairwell, Einstein emerged from his office, once again at full speed. Bacon was unprepared for this surprise attack and, once again, the professor sped past him toward the exit, barely noticing Bacon.

His pursuit of the professor eventually evolved into yet another one of his daily routines, just like the calculations he executed for Professor Von Neumann, the phone calls he received from Elizabeth, and Vivien's evening visits. Even if he were bold enough to confess it to anyone, who would believe him? That he was pursuing Einstein, like a spectrum, a wave that kept trying to move closer to the author of relativity? Out of the question. In the meantime, Bacon worked on his technique; as time went by he felt surer and surer of himself, certain that he was becoming nearly invisible. . . . Slowly, the walk toward 112 Mercer Street became as natural as afternoon tea, or the solution of a couple of matrices; he did it out of necessity, or like a bad habit. Einstein almost always walked home alone, although every so often someone would join him—old or young, famous or unknown, each occupied the spot that was supposed to belong to Bacon, the most devoted of his disciples.

Only once did Einstein notice him. A thick fog hung in the air that lay like a greasy film covering the faces of the passersby with an unbecoming, yellowish tint. The birds' chirping rang through the air like a fire alarm signal sent out from one nest to the other. Suddenly, without any warning, Einstein turned on his heels and fixed his gaze squarely on Bacon, who was now frightened as a deer. It looked as though his sophomoric game was up. Bacon had lost.

"Do you work at the institute?" Einstein said upon recognizing him.

Perhaps this was the moment he had been waiting for, Bacon thought: the chance to initiate a friendship, albeit distant, with the man whose story he had followed more than any other, and to whom he felt connected by a profound, almost mysterious sense of awe and admiration.

"Yes, I do," Bacon replied, breathlessly awaiting the professor's next pronouncement, as if hanging on to the words of an oracle.

"It's cold," exclaimed Einstein, dazed.

That was all he said. Nothing more, no revelation, no prophecy. He didn't even ask Bacon's name. He bent his head slightly, as if to say good-bye, and continued on his way alone, absent, beneath the weak light whose structure intrigued him so. Now—finally!—Bacon could boast to the rest of the world that yes, he had received a dose of the genius's wisdom, and he would treasure those marvelous words as if God himself had bellowed them: *It's cold.* Bacon laughed to himself, still trembling, and waited for Einstein's gray silhouette to recede, like the brilliant glow of the stars which he spoke of so eloquently. The next day, Bacon resumed his pursuit of the professor, but now with the serenity of a man who had completed his mission.

HYPOTHESIS IV: *On Gödel's Theory and Marriage*

When her soul was tranquil, Elizabeth's eyes were the color of olives. But Bacon could always be sure that the tranquillity would soon give way to thunder whenever they began to acquire a slightly coppery tone. At those times, all he could do was remain quiet and wait for the angry torrent of words to come pouring out of Elizabeth's mouth, dying down to a trickle only after a few minutes. Her wrists were so slender that he could hold them between his thumb and pinky, and her neck was as strong and firm as a sunflower's stem, but when she became incensed—a fairly frequent occurrence—her diminutive proportions grew exponentially, like those of a cobra in heat. All the innocence and courtesy she so carefully exhibited during social functions would evaporate, replaced by a torrent of fiery reproaches and menacing threats, a snit of such proportions that by the time it was over, she had nearly asphyxiated herself. Only then would she begin to feel remorseful, and as she allowed sweet tears to rain down on her cheeks, Bacon, moved by such a show of emotion, would have no other choice than to caress her delicate chin and run his fingers through her tousled hair, calming her down until she could muster enough strength for her next attack.

Elizabeth was the kind of woman who always looked as if she had just stepped out of the pages of a fashion magazine: Her dresses were fitted, her jewelry took the form of tiny insects, and her hats sprouted feathers the likes of which Bacon had seen only in the movies. Her violet eye shadow and colorful rouge only enhanced her childlike complexion, reminding Bacon of a little girl trying to be like her mother by stealing and applying globs of her makeup. Bacon was always touched by this curious spectacle; in that inharmonious combination of lust and innocence, vanity and naïveté, he saw evidence of the sensitivity his fiancée hid behind her haughty appearance.

Aside from Elizabeth's undeniable beauty and artistic talents (she was a student at an art academy in New York), there was something else about her that appealed to Bacon's mother: her aristocratic lineage. Elizabeth, she explained to her son, was the only daughter of a rich banker from Philadelphia whose greatest desire was to see his daughter happy. When he saw her for the first time at a French restaurant on Fifth Avenue, Bacon knew that she would play an important role in his life—though not for any of the qualities his mother had mentioned. It was the tiny adolescent figure, the cascade of curls that tumbled out from under her hat, and the way that, in spite of her well-cultivated manners, she couldn't help twisting and untwisting her fingers in her lap. Bacon had always appreciated that rather aggressive quality found in many spoiled girls, for he sensed it was simply their way of masking their inability to solve the problems of day-to-day life. In short, he liked Elizabeth because she was the opposite of Vivien.

That afternoon, somewhere between the lobster and the chocolate cake, Elizabeth made a confession—that is, she recited the words she assumed a liberal scientist like Bacon would want to hear from a girl: She was a painter. She spoke eloquently of the importance of art and freedom, and explained that money, to her way of thinking, was simply one among many means to happiness. The significance of her declarations was largely lost on Bacon— the champagne they drank took care of that—and Elizabeth worked hard to soften her sharp, grating voice into something closer to sensual. Meanwhile, Bacon's mind was mainly focused on discerning the shape of her breasts beneath the cherry-colored blouse and the fine European lingerie that (he was certain) lay beneath it. He never once lifted his gaze to meet her eyes, but Elizabeth continued on, undeterred, with her detailed lecture on the history of art, convinced that a promising young scientist like Bacon couldn't help falling in love with a woman of such great intellect.

One day, Bacon grabbed her hand and attempted to kiss her in the middle of the street. Elizabeth, employing her family's old husband-catching technique, slapped him hard on the cheek, hard enough to call the attention of several passersby. She then told him to behave like a gentleman, and asked him to please walk her home. Once again, the tactic proved highly effective: Dazzled by this flash of temper, Bacon asked when he could see her again. After considering the idea for a few moments, Elizabeth accepted. From then on, they averaged about two dates a week, generally on Saturday mornings and Sunday afternoons, although almost an entire month went by before she would allow Bacon's lust-filled lips to settle upon her own tightly pursed pair.

In theory, Bacon despised Elizabeth's games, and he continued sleeping with Vivien about three times a week, though without the slightest trace of any sort of courtship ritual. Yet he nevertheless remained enthusiastic about the progress of his relationship with Elizabeth, precisely because she refused to let him touch her. In one of nature's absurd paradoxes, he would dream of Elizabeth's tiny body while savoring the largesse of Vivien; he yearned for Vivien's silence as he endured Elizabeth's insufferable discourses.

Bacon knew that the laws of civilized society—inspired by the laws of classical mechanics—were inflexible. Sooner or later, his double life would have to end; he could have only one of them. And it would have to be Elizabeth. His mother, his friends, his professors, his fellow graduate students—none of them would forgive him if he abandoned the delightful young lady who they always assumed would become his wife for a cafeteria worker. Resigned to a fate that seemed beyond his control, Bacon went out and bought a ring with a tiny blue diamond and gave it to Elizabeth one windy evening in March of 1942, beneath the moonlight, as prescribed by the laws of romantic love.

They hadn't settled on a wedding date, but from that day forward, Elizabeth did little more than visit bridal shops to study the endless array of available wedding dresses. Each time she saw her fiancé she would describe, with the very same patience she dedicated to her lectures on surrealism and the avant-garde, the complicated floral patterns of each model, since she found herself incapable of deciding on one single gown. The decision, Bacon quickly realized, was going to be as agonizing as determining the quadrature of a circle.

Aside from Elizabeth's new obsession with gowns, fabrics, veils, and laces, another idiosyncrasy came to light during this prewedding period: her ever-increasing jealousy. Marriage, to Elizabeth, was nothing less than complete and total surrender. Soon she began demanding more frequent visits from him. In addition to his usual Saturday and Sunday trips to New York, he now found himself traveling there several days a week, often to be with her for no more than a few hours. Unfortunately for Bacon, these trips offered no opportunity for increased intimacy. Bacon, then, was reduced to coming and going at Elizabeth's behest, like a yo-yo in the hands of a child.

As a kind of punishment for his disobedience, Elizabeth began to demand, sometimes with shrill cries and other times with gentle caresses, a detailed report of his daily activities. "Where did you go?" "Why?" "With whom?" were the three basic questions, the tenets of a belief system she practiced with the fervent devotion of the recent convert. Any sudden observation, pointless comment, or unexpected turn of conversation would instantly become the motive for an interrogation that could last hours. She acted as though any activity that didn't specifically focus on her represented a crime against their love. As far as Elizabeth was concerned, Bacon's schedule of conferences, classes, and work assignments at the institute were little more than transparent alibis aimed at hiding his infidelity.

The most surprising thing of all was that Bacon responded to Elizabeth's inventory of complaints with sweet nothings and apologies. Over and over again during those months he would ask himself exactly why he was subjecting himself to this military discipline which, in the end, was going to kill his spirit. The answer, alas, was simple: guilt. He knew that in spite of her temper tantrums, Elizabeth trusted him. And he also knew that her suspicions—though exaggerated at times—were not entirely unfounded. As he had explained to Professor Von Neumann, Bacon tried to maintain the relationship as it was by drawing Elizabeth's attention to such banal topics as his oppressive job, so as to prevent her from inferring the real reason for his occasional absences. But gradually he learned that a man with a double life is a man condemned—not simply to lying but to inventing and defending half-lies, as if his world could be divided into two separate spheres, incompatible and complementary at the same time.

In late March of 1942, Von Neumann informed Bacon that Kurt Gödel, the eminent mathematics professor, would be coming to the institute in a few days to present one of his recent papers to a private audience. Unfortunately, this was to take place on the same day that Bacon had promised Elizabeth they would travel to Philadelphia. When Bacon told her, he explained the importance of the event and assured her they would make the trip the following month. Elizabeth, however, simply told him to go straight to hell. This wasn't the first time she had threatened him—in fact, she was usually the one who would run back to him. But Bacon resolved not to give in this time. He was too determined to meet Gödel to let one of his fiancée's idle threats get in the way. In fact, he thought, this might just be the perfect excuse to take a rest from her for a few weeks, to be alone and to think about his future.

"I'm sorry, Elizabeth," he told her over the telephone, "but I have to be there." He was suddenly aware that these final few days of freedom were nothing more than a brief prelude to a lifetime of indentured servitude, so he decided to take advantage of the time.

Professor Gödel was a short, taciturn man with the body of a flagpole; his general appearance called to mind an opossum or a field mouse, certainly not a genius of contemporary logic. Yet, it was true. He had become affiliated with the institute two years earlier, eight years after writing an article that overturned the foundations of modern mathematics.

In the course of over two millennia, mathematics had evolved in a disorderly fashion, like a tree with wild branches, twisting and wrapping around one another. Thanks to the discoveries of the Babylonians, the Egyptians, the Greeks, the Arabs, and the Indians, as well as the advances made in the modern West, mathematics had become something of a monster with a thousand heads, a discipline whose true nature nobody could even begin to understand. Mathematics was the most objective and evolved scientific instrument known to mankind, used daily by millions to resolve practical problems of everyday life. But amid all that infinite diversity, nobody knew for sure if mathematics might contain, somewhere within itself, a germ in decomposition, a fungus or a virus capable of refuting its own results.

The Greeks were the first to recognize this possibility in their discovery of the paradox. As Zeno and subsequent arithmetics and geometry scholars would prove, the strict application of logic occasionally produced impossibilities or contradictions that were not so easily resolved. The notion of the paradox went as far back as classical antiquity, in the dialogues of Achilles and the Tortoise, which refuted the notion of movement, or Epimenides' paradox, which said a statement could be proven and refuted at the same time. Yet it wasn't until the late Middle Ages that these irregularities began to multiply like malignant tumors. This heresy, which escaped the Pythagoreans as well as the fathers of the Church, proved that science indeed could be proven wrong, contrary to previous belief.

To put an end to this chaos, legions of scientific thinkers attempted to systematize mathematics and the laws that governed them. One of the first people to do so was Euclid. In his *Elements*, he attempted to derive all the rules of geometry from five basic axioms. Later on, philosophers and mathematicians like René Descartes, Emmanuel Kant, George Boole, Gottlob Frege, and Giuseppe Peano tried to do the very same thing in fields as far-flung as statistics and infinitesimal calculus, although their results were hardly conclusive. In the meantime, new paradoxes were emerging as well, such those introduced by Georg Cantor in his set theory.

At the dawn of the twentieth century, the situation was more bewildering than ever. Conscious of Cantor's theories and the aberrations they produced, the English mathematicians Bertrand Russell and Alfred North Whitehead joined forces in an effort to reduce the entire scope of mathematics to a few basic principles, just as Euclid had done two thousand years earlier. Together they devised something they called the type theory, which led to the publication, in 1919, of a monumental treatise entitled *Principia Mathematica,* which was based on an earlier tract by Russell. The purpose of the *Principia Mathematica,* which they worked on from 1903 to 1910, was to erase all the uncomfortable contradictions known to contemporary mathematics.

Unfortunately, the work was so vast and complex that in the end, nobody was truly convinced that all mathematical statements could be reduced to their theories without falling into contradiction at some point or another. Just a few years earlier, in 1900, a mathematician at the University of Göttingen named David Hilbert had presented a paper at the opening session of the International Conference of Mathematicians in Paris, which explained a theory that would thereafter be known as Hilbert's Program. In this treatise he laid out a list of all the great unresolved mathematical problems, as a kind of blueprint for future mathematical research. One of these conundrums was the so-called axiom of completeness, which questioned whether the system later described in the *Principia*—or any axiomatic system, for that matter—was comprehensive, complete, and free of contradiction. Could any arithmetic proposition be derived through his postulates? Hilbert thought the answer was yes, as he said to his colleagues gathered together in Paris: "All mathematical problems are solvable, we all agree with that. After all, when we set out to solve a mathematical problem, one of the primary things that draws us in is that calling we h ar inside: Here's the problem, it needs a solution. And this can only be found through pure thinking, because in mathematics there is no such thing as *ignorabimus.*"

"Hilbert's Program became the bible of mathematicians and logicians of the world," Von Neumann explained to Bacon one day. "To solve even one of his equations would mean instant fame. Can't you just picture it? Hundreds of young minds, in every corner of the world, banging their heads to solve one of the pieces of Hilbert's great puzzle. Maybe, as a physicist, you can't grasp the magnitude of the challenge, but everyone wanted to prove himself. Everyone wanted to show that he was the best of them all. And it wasn't just a race against unknown rivals, either; it was a race against time. It was madness."

"I'm supposing you had tried to solve one of Hilbert's problems," Bacon interjected, knowing in advance what the answer would be, but giving Von Neumann a chance to unleash his vanity like a hungry tiger.

"Well, of course I tried it, Bacon, we *all* tried it. In fact, we're still trying. For months I became obsessed by the completeness axiom and the chal-

lenge it presented." Von Neumann scratched his chin reflectively and low-
ered his voice a notch, as if he were narrating a great suspense novel. "Just as
Professor Gödel did later on, though he had more success with it than I. At
first, I thought I had found the correct approach. My intuition told me that
the goal was not impossible to achieve, as I had previously thought. Have
you ever had that feeling of your skin tingling, like when someone scratches
their nails against a blackboard? It was *incredible*."

"And so what happened?"

"All of a sudden, I was stopped cold, as if a brick wall had suddenly
appeared in the middle of the road." Von Neumann rubbed his hands as if he
were about to explode. "My mind was frozen, paralyzed. I fell to pieces. The
depths of failure, you know. The only thing I could do was get into bed and
go to sleep until the next day. Then, when I woke up, I realized that something truly amazing had occurred: In my dreams, I had found a way to
advance my equations. I had *dreamed* it, Bacon, like a prophet inspired by the
voice of the Creator! I was frantic, and I plunged back into my papers. Now I
felt certain I had it." His hands seemed to curl around an imaginary trophy.
"But then, once again, as I reached the last little bit, the inspiration vanished.
Again. Just like that. And there I was again, just like the time before. Stuck."

"Oh, wow!" Bacon knew that he was supposed to utter an exclamation of
enthusiasm and beg Von Neumann to go on with the story. "So then what
happened?"

"Well, I waited until nighttime, and just as I had figured, I fell into yet
another deep sleep."

"And you found the missing link?"

"Exactly! It was a kind of miracle. My proof followed a complicated, perfect line of reasoning. I was convinced that with one of Hilbert's problems
on my CV, I would become famous."

"So why didn't it happen that way, Professor?"

"My good friend Bacon," said Von Neumann, his thick, dry lips breaking
into a smile, "it was a great stroke of luck for the world of mathematics that
I did not dream a thing that night!"

When Gödel finally solved the problem in 1931, he was still a young,
unknown mathematician. His paper, entitled "On Formally Undecidable
Propositions of *Principia Mathematica* and Related Systems, 1," was like a
bucket of cold water soaking the optimism of Hilbert's ideas. In his article,
Gödel showed that the *Principia Mathematica* allowed for the existence of
propositions that were true yet unprovable—that is, "undecidable." He then
went even further by proving that this phenomenon would hold true in any

axiomatic system, in all existing or future fields of mathematics. Against what all the experts had predicted, Gödel had proved beyond a doubt that mathematics were *incomplete*.

With shockingly simple reasoning, Gödel refuted the romantic notion that mathematics could fully interpret the world, free of the contradictions inherent in philosophical inquiry. His paper was so successful that he didn't have to write the follow-up chapter he had originally planned. His explosive mission was over. The most astonishing aspect of Gödel's achievement, however, was its simplicity. Reformulating Epimenides' ancient paradox—of course, the bedrock of all mathematical paradoxes—he had hit upon the theorem which proved his hypothesis. It said:

> To every w-consistent recursive class k of *formulae* there correspond recursive *class-signs* r such that neither v Gen r nor Neg (v Gen r) belongs to Flg(k) (where v is the *free variable* of r)

An approximate translation of this might be: "All consistent axiomatic formulations of number theory include undecidable propositions." In simpler terms, Gödel said the following: "The system of *Principia Mathematica* offers no proof for this statement of number theory." A possible expansion of the same: "This proposition of number theory has no proof within number theory," which might also be stated in the following manner: "This logical proposition is unprovable by the very laws of logic." The statement could even be extended to the realm of psychology: "It is impossible for me to prove this idea I have about myself."

To recapitulate, Gödel stated that in any system—scientific, linguistic, mental—there will always exist statements that are true but unprovable. No matter how hard one tries, no matter how perfect a system one creates, there will nevertheless exist unprovable holes and voids, paradoxical arguments that behave like termites and devour the things that seem most solid. Gödel did for mathematics exactly what Einstein's relativity theory, Bohr's quantum theory, and the discoveries of their collective disciples did when they proved that physics was no longer an *exact* science—that is, an amalgam of absolutes. Nobody was safe in a world that was suddenly dominated by uncertainty. Thanks to Gödel, truth became more slippery and elusive than it had ever been before.

Vivien's body stretched out again across Bacon's bedsheets like a sinewy brown stain. She had arrived at his apartment just after dusk. Her long, bare arms were now lost in the darkness of the night, coated with a kind of dew from the persistent rain that fell outside. Only three days had passed since Bacon's acrimonious telephone conversation with Elizabeth. As he began to kiss Vivien's earlobes, he remembered that he had considered leaving her, too. But the moment she had arrived at his house, he knew that he would be unable to resist the temptation of possessing her once again.

As if freed from a prison sentence, for the first time in a very long time Bacon was overcome by the desire to be tender with his lover. Suddenly she seemed fragile and innocent, not pained and mysterious, and he wanted to make up for his many months of betrayal. Perhaps he was simply projecting the love he wanted for himself, but instead of watching her with cold eyes, he now decided to undress her, bit by bit, as if preparing a little girl for her bath. Then he kissed her on the lips slowly and tenderly (an indulgence he normally avoided) and stroked her curly black hair. And then, finally, he made love to her with the kind of tenderness usually reserved for love affairs with virgins. The only aspect of his routine that remained unchanged was the stubborn silence he maintained while penetrating her body.

"Do you love her?"

Nestled amid the sheets, Vivien looked like a drowning woman trying to defend herself against an enormous wave crashing down upon her. Bacon was lying on her back, and as he stretched himself on top of her body, he wondered if he had become the wave she was struggling against.

"No, well, I don't know," Bacon stammered.

"Are you going to marry her?"

"Yes."

"Why, if you don't love her?"

"Don't ask me those questions. That's just the way it has to be, I suppose. There are things a person has to do: get married, have children, die. Listen, from the beginning you knew. I never led you on, Vivien."

"You don't even remember my name. How could you possibly lead me on?" Vivien moved away from Bacon and got up from the bed. She didn't seem angry, or even disappointed. She began gathering up her clothes, strewn across the floor.

Bacon looked at her as if he were staring at an ancient armoire that had suddenly sprung open, emptying bundles of photographs and lost memories onto the floor.

"Can I ask you something?" he finally said to her, haltingly, not even rising from the bed. "Just this once, Vivien, don't go. Stay with me tonight. It's raining. And I want to see your face in the morning."

*   *   *

The next day, Bacon woke up very early, doubly vexed: by the unfamiliar presence of Vivien, and by the conference that Professor Gödel was to give that morning. For a few seconds he remained still, contemplating Vivien's body as she continued sleeping peacefully. In the early morning light, she seemed lovelier than ever to him. Without making a noise, Bacon arose from the bed and got ready for the day. As he showered, he couldn't shake the strange feeling of peace that he felt upon opening his eyes and finding Vivien at his side. He told himself he had to forget about her, but her perfume clung stubbornly to his skin. Much as he tried, he could not rub out her scent with soap and water.

During the past few days, Bacon had begun to read up on Gödel's life, as if he were planning to discuss the man's biography at some later date. All the professors at the institute seemed to admire and respect him, even if they often dropped hints indicating that his personality was as difficult as his theorems. But he was one of Einstein's close friends.

Gödel had first come to the institute as a visiting professor in 1933, while still a professor at the University of Vienna. His lectures at that time (obviously) focused on the incompleteness of mathematics, and he tended to inspire intense (verging on obsessive) interest among those who came to hear him speak on the topic. Very few men of science, with the possible exception of Einstein, could boast of such an attentive audience. Oswald Veblen, who organized the event, was delighted by the enthusiastic turnout. And though Gödel used the very weakest voice to expound upon the fundamental theories of logic, the students devoured his sentences, as if deciphering them was an additional privilege that would grant them greater and deeper access to their master's incredible conclusions.

Everything had gone according to schedule until one morning, when Gödel announced to Veblen that he *had* to return to Europe immediately. He would not be able to finish his lecture series. Unable to invent an excuse, he simply said that he felt a pressing need to return home, that he was terribly sorry but he couldn't do a thing about it. After apologizing to the other professors at the institute, Gödel returned to Europe. Later on, in the fall of 1934, it was discovered that upon his return he had checked into the Westend Sanitarium, on the outskirts of Vienna, for psychiatric treatment, the victim of a profound clinical depression.

A year after this panic attack, Gödel reestablished ties with the academic community in Princeton and embarked upon another series of conferences. In 1939, shortly after Hitler had annexed Austria to the Third Reich, Gödel lost his position at the University of Vienna. To make matters worse, he was soon called into active duty by the Austrian authorities, despite his fragile state of health. In January of 1940, he and his new wife, Adèle Nimbursky, decided to leave for the United States. It was, however, the strangest sort of odyssey. Instead of traveling across the Atlantic, which they felt was too dangerous, Gödel and his wife set out for Russia, where they boarded the Trans-Siberian Railway headed for Japan. At Yokohama they set sail for San Francisco, where they arrived on March 4, 1940. A few days later, Einstein welcomed them to Princeton.

Bacon arrived at the institute and sat down in one of the last rows of the auditorium to await Gödel's arrival, feeling the same anticipation he often felt before Vivien's visits. He watched the mathematician enter and it seemed to him that the thirty-six-year-old professor looked more like a priest or a rabbi than a mathematician. His nose looked like the tiny protuberance on a turkey's beak. His little eyes, shielded by thick, dark glasses, didn't seem to radiate any particular intelligence. Nevertheless, Bacon and the others present were convinced that the skinny, bedraggled soul before them was a prodigy, a melancholy genius whose talent clearly came at the expense of his own mental health.

One of the unexpected revelations of Gödel's theorem was the confirmation of the idea that genius and insanity are inextricably linked. If all mathematical systems contain statements that are true yet unprovable, couldn't the same be true for the realm of the human mind? Just like mathematics, the mind is incapable of protecting itself in the face of chaos and confusion. It is impossible to discern one's own sanity or insanity because there exists no such external mark of reference outside one's own brain to prove the truth definitively. The insane person can judge himself only through the logic of the insane, and the genius, through the logic of genius.

On this occasion, Gödel gave a speech that was nothing more than a compulsive variation on the original theme he had sketched out during his previous lecture series at Princeton. He read his speech in an erratic, weak voice, offering little in the way of professorial showmanship, and the examples he provided were skimpy, pale sketches of his brilliant metaphors. In short, he was the polar opposite of Von Neumann, whose explications overflowed with wit and cleverness. Gödel's reflections were somber and serious, as gray and boring as his personality. At the end of the lecture, Bacon went up to him, along with some other members of the institute, and, as planned, Von Neumann made all the introductions.

"Kurt," he said, "you won't believe me when I tell you this young man's name."

Gödel made a gesture indicating he wasn't especially interested. Bacon tried extending his hand, but the professor did not even seem to notice the gesture.

"Francis Bacon. Can you believe that?" Von Neumann laughed. "Nothing less than Francis Bacon. Only this one, as opposed to the original, is a physicist."

"I don't believe in the natural sciences," Gödel responded, in a tone that wasn't trying to be condescending, but simply rational.

"But don't you find it amusing, Kurt?"

Gödel's eyes rested on Bacon's for a moment, but rather than scrutinize him, Gödel was trying to understand this strange joke his American friends were making. Finally, Von Neumann took him by the arm, as if he were a stone sphinx on loan from a foreign art museum, and the others hurriedly dispersed. Only Bacon stood where he was, in the middle of the corridor, nonplussed by the mathematician's listlessness.

When Bacon returned home that evening, Vivien was there. He was the one who had needed her so badly the night before, and now it was her turn to expose her weakness, against both her better judgment and their mutual agreement never to do such a thing. Just as she had done so many times before, Vivien was sprawled out on the bed, though this time dressed in a violet-colored blouse and black skirt, waiting for him with the serenity of a woman waiting for her executioner to arrive.

"What are you doing here?" was all he dared to ask. He let his briefcase fall to the floor with the subtlety of an anvil.

"I knew you wouldn't like it."

Bacon moved closer to Vivien, as cautious as a panther waiting to pounce on a deer. She didn't even have time to sit up. Unable to hold back, Bacon began to kiss her bare feet, her legs, and, finally, after peeling off her clothes like the skin on a piece of tropical fruit, his lips found their way to her belly and then her breasts. He was certain that this was a mistake (even worse: this was the second time he had made the *same* mistake), but he didn't care. He melted into Vivien's warm skin, and would have happily stayed there for at least another night. After a few hours, however, it was Vivien who put an end to it all.

"I have to go now," she said, still lying in his arms.

"Why?"

"It's getting late."

"So what? You can stay if you want."

Vivien knew as well as he did that it wasn't true, that they were deceiving one another, but there is nothing more false than an unwanted truth. It was better to imagine that the future was nothing more than one among many possibilities, a potential reality as nonexistent as the past. Just as adamant as Bacon had been in deciding not to see Elizabeth for the duration of Gödel's lecture series, he was determined to savor this time with Vivien, like the derelict who squeezes his last orange down to the very last drop of juice.

For several weeks, Elizabeth had been unable to sleep more than a few hours at a time. For her, the inclement nights had turned into a kind of prolonged torture in which images of her fiancé passed before her eyes like a movie reel. She envisioned him involved in all sorts of terrible activities, most of them incompatible with marriage. She began to lose her appetite, and soon realized that if she carried on like this, she would end up a skinny, desperate woman. The first few days of their separation, she wanted to teach him a lesson, and resisted the temptation to track him down. She was too sure of herself to doubt, even for a moment, that he would swallow his pride and come back to her. Once he realized how pigheaded he was being, Francis would begin to woo her in earnest, and then she would lay down the law once and for all, and spell out the conditions which would govern their future together. Her present hardships and deprivation were worth it; they were the guarantee of a glorious future that lay ahead.

They had never been apart for such a long period. And with each passing day it became more and more difficult. It was a kind of race, and the winner would simply be the one whose willpower and tenacity held out longer (later on, Bacon would liken it to the race between Achilles and the Tortoise, his fate being that of the Tortoise). Fully aware that this challenge would determine the course of the rest of her adult life, Elizabeth decided she was prepared to go the distance. Whenever a bout of anxiety would weaken her resolve and tempt her to call him, she consoled herself with the reminder that he was surely suffering the very same anguish as a result of their separation.

A nightmare was what finally broke her will. In it, she fell victim to a horrible sickness, and instead of lamenting her death, Bacon went out and celebrated it! Elizabeth woke up in tears, convinced that her dream was a sign that her strategy was failing. What if he didn't come after her? If he never really loved her in the first place? For the first time in her life she regretted her intransigence and hot temper; perhaps she had demanded too much of him. She loved him. She loved him more than before, more than she ever had. She thought of how stupid she had been. Why wait and become embittered by this separation? Why had she tested their love at all, when all she wanted was to have him by her side? Pride and vanity had no right to keep them apart! But there was still a chance to make amends for her mistake.

The morning after her nightmare, Elizabeth decided it was time to make peace with Bacon. By the time she arrived at Bacon's house, it was eleven in the morning—he would be at the institute, naturally. She could barely move as she struggled beneath the packages piled high in her arms. From a distance, her slow, teetering walk evoked that of a robot in a science fiction movie. In her arms she carried wine and cheese, fruit, balloons, and even an adorable model train. In spite of the fact that she had never before set foot in Bacon's apartment (she preferred him either to visit her at her home or to meet her at cafeterias and restaurants), from the beginning of their relationship she had insisted that he give her a key. Now she was ready to use that little device to surprise him, to delight him, and to convince him that the time had come for their reconciliation.

The lecture hall was filled to capacity. Bacon was certain, however, that only a small fraction of the audience would be able to understand the true significance of the words that fell from Kurt Gödel's lips with such surprising ease. Veblen and Von Neumann were sitting in the first row, watching as Gödel shuffled around with the grace of a hippopotamus, scrawling formulas onto the blackboard like a caveman making stick drawings of a buffalo on a cave wall. The mathematician looked frightened, and he made every effort not to look directly at his audience, losing himself in the infinity point above the back wall of the room. That day, Gödel had turned his attention, and that of his audience, to the problem known as the continuum hypothesis, sketched out by the mathematician Georg Cantor in his set theory.

"Cantor's continuum hypothesis," he said softly, as if he were the only one in the auditorium, "can be reduced to this simple question: How many points are there in a straight line on a Euclidean plane?" Gödel waited for a moment, as if to allow the question to seep into his mind before tossing it back out like a giant marble. "Obviously, this question is only possible when we extend the concept of the word *number* to infinite sets."

All of a sudden, Gödel stopped cold in his tracks, unable to comprehend why someone would interrupt his lecture. A heavy wooden door opened and then slammed shut, producing a resounding thud that destroyed the otherworldly mood that had settled over Gödel's audience. Veblen and the other professors rose from their seats, while all eyes focused on the woman who had suddenly burst into the lecture hall.

"Where are you?" she screamed, unfazed by the strangers witnessing the scene. Every last bit of Elizabeth's beauty had evaporated and what was left was a cold scowl as she scanned the rows for the face of her double-crossing fiancé. "You lied to me! Admit it!"

Seated in the back row, Bacon made out the silhouette of Elizabeth. He didn't know what to do, whether to stand up and try to calm her down, or try to hide from her wrath altogether. Elizabeth, meanwhile, remained utterly indifferent to the suddenly uncomfortable atmosphere in the auditorium. Gödel was horrified.

Veblen quickly admonished her: "For goodness' sake, miss, I don't know who you are or whom you are looking for, but this is a university lecture. I must ask you to leave immediately, so the professor may continue his presentation."

Elizabeth did not hear a word. She was too busy searching for her terrorized victim.

"Don't try to hide!" she screamed. "Did you think I wouldn't find out? That you could keep seeing that whore? How stupid do you think I am?"

"Elizabeth, please," begged Bacon. Painfully aware of his audience, he tried his best to placate his fiancée. "We'll fix all this later."

"Later? Forget about later! I'm not going anywhere until you start explaining!" And she began to advance toward him, her face stained with tears that were as hot as the anger Bacon was beginning to feel.

"Mr. Bacon," said Veblen pointedly, gesturing toward the exit. "Would you please explain to this young lady that we are in the middle of a *very* important lecture? *Do you understand?*"

By this time, Elizabeth was face-to-face with her fiancé. When he took her by the arm and tried to direct her toward the back of the lecture hall, she responded with a resonant slap across the face. The entire audience—with the exception of Gödel—breathed a prolonged *oh!* at the sound made by her hand, like that of a flyswatter slamming against a windowpane. Unable to endure any more humiliation, without even thinking, Bacon responded in kind. His blow was much less powerful but, due to an unfortunate matter of acoustics, much louder.

"This is unacceptable, Bacon!" Veblen exploded, though next to him Von Neumann let out an amused chuckle. "I will ask you again to please leave this room so we can go on."

Elizabeth, stung by the slap, was not aware of what was happening around her. She had single-handedly caused a most disastrous scene which now felt more like a hazy, chaotic nightmare. The only thing she wanted was to embrace Bacon and fall into a long, deep sleep by his side. At the front of the lecture hall, Gödel watched the scene unfold in a state of complete and utter shock.

"You let her into your house," Elizabeth sobbed as Bacon guided her toward the exit amid the stares of his colleagues. "You had that whore in your house."

The last thing Bacon was able to see before leaving the auditorium was the furious face of Professor Veblen, which wordlessly told him that his currently favorable position and his no less brilliant future at the institute were both ruined. As he supported the exhausted body of his fiancée (now his ex-fiancée, he told himself), Bacon could scarcely begin to fathom the manifold consequences of the scene. Suddenly the three stable elements of his life—Elizabeth, the institute, and, yes, even Vivien—had crashed into each other like runaway trains. What would Von Neumann think of this, the unforeseeable outcome of his romantic games? Bacon led Elizabeth to a nearby room and sat her down in a chair. He remained there for a while, not touching or hugging her. He waited for a few minutes more. When she came to, she insulted him again and then, still trembling, got up and left the institute alone.

Meanwhile, back in the auditorium Professor Gödel made the announcement that he would be unable to continue with his lecture, and then he began to cry uncontrollably until Von Neumann walked up to the lectern to console him.

HYPOTHESIS V: *On Bacon's Departure for Germany*

When Bacon returned to the institute a few days later, he went straight to Frank Aydelotte's office. Aydelotte, the institute's director and Flexner's successor, had been looking everywhere for Bacon. Bacon had no idea what fate this meeting would hold for him, though he was reasonably certain it was nothing positive. He figured it to be somewhere between a strong reprimand and unequivocal expulsion. To make matters worse, he had another of his terrible migraines. He felt as if a knife were lodged in his skull, splitting his cranium in two: One side was healthy and resilient while the other was trembling with the frenetic, uncontrollable energy of a piston charging at full blast. These headaches were always precipitated by nerves or a great shock, and they came on with lightning force, like a shooting star in the night sky. As soon as he saw the lights twinkling, followed by the ominous symptoms of vertigo and nausea, Bacon knew that the pain wasn't far off. It was useless to try and resist it. He had tried household remedies like tea (which only made him more jittery), or ice cubes on his neck (which only made him feel like a filet of sole on display at a fish market), or the useless, bizarre massages of his earlobes or pinky finger. They never provided even a moment's relief. And then the inevitable pain would come. Just as inevitable as the merciless tongue-lashing that he was about to receive from Aydelotte.

It was ten in the morning, and his body was already at the breaking point. The rays of sunlight sliced through his contracted pupils like splinters, and the faraway noises of the Princeton streets reverberated loudly in his atrophied eardrums. The vermilion walls of Fuld Hall looked like gelatin to him. Bacon breathed in, trying to pull himself together, and announced himself to the director's fat secretary. The director ushered him in immediately; without getting up from his desk, he indicated a chair, the location of Bacon's imminent torture. Behind Aydelotte, a tall man dressed in gray, burly as a football player, studied him expectantly.

"Sit down," Aydelotte said.

Bacon obeyed. He didn't want to make his discomfort too apparent, but he also didn't want to seem too inhibited. The role of the punished child was unpleasant enough; he certainly did not wish to exacerbate it with an explanation of his physical ills.

"Relax, Bacon," the director said generously. "This isn't a court-martial, nor is it a firing line."

"Before anything, I want to apologize," Bacon interrupted abruptly. "I never meant for my personal problems . . . Could I at least see Professor Gödel to apologize to him myself?"

Aydelotte gave him a reproachful look.

"Slow down, Bacon. Unfortunately, it isn't that simple. Professor Gödel had another one of his nervous episodes. He's a very sensitive man."

"Is he unwell?"

"Let's just say that this is not one of his better moments. I suppose it will pass. But for the moment, he has decided to stay inside for the week." Aydelotte coughed, on purpose, indicating the end of that part of their conversation. "I told him, Bacon, that the situation was truly an embarrassment. Can you imagine the impression it left on the other assistants? Professor Veblen has initiated a rather heated campaign against you, Bacon. Do you follow what I'm saying?"

"I would do anything at all to make up for what happened."

"*Anything at all*," repeated Aydelotte in a severe tone of voice. "It's a shame, Bacon. I have examined your file carefully and I must tell you the truth. It's quite impressive. First as an undergraduate and then here, you have performed your duties with brilliance and discretion—two qualities I admire immensely, especially in men of science."

As Bacon watched him, it seemed that Aydelotte's lips moved too much; they looked like two eels wrestling with each other.

"In any event, Professor Von Neumann has taken up your defense. He says that you are one of our most gifted colleagues. Moreover, he said he is certain that in the future, once you've gained the maturity that comes only with time, you will doubtless make great contributions to the field of physics." A slight exaggeration, Bacon thought, but Aydelotte continued, "As you can imagine, your situation here is a difficult one, though not hopeless. You have so many points in your favor that one little episode such as that of the other day is hardly fatal."

Bacon wasn't completely sure if this solemn, officious tone of voice was a figment of his imagination or if it was just Aydelotte's way of getting rid of him in the nicest way possible.

"Don't worry, Bacon, I'm not saying all this as a prelude to firing you," Aydelotte said. He stopped looking at Bacon and concentrated instead on screwing and unscrewing the cap of his fountain pen. "Of course, I do have to say what must be said, son: You no longer have a place at the institute. Your behavior the other day only confirmed this unfortunate fact." Bacon felt a shock, as if the director had just poked him in the eye. "We have been delighted to have you here with us, yet I think—and correct me if I am mistaken—that you feel you are being wasted. Your talents are not very well suited to our style of work."

Aydelotte turned briefly to look at the man in the gray suit behind him. His face impassive, the man nodded to indicate his approval. Aydelotte continued.

"I don't mean to suggest you become an experimental physicist. Rather, I am trying to say that your character is—how can I explain it? Too *curious*. We feel that if things were to continue as they are now, you would eventually leave the institute without making any of the great achievements we all feel are within your grasp. You need more action, son. More *life*."

"I . . . I don't know what to say," stuttered Bacon. "I promise, if you'd simply let me—"

"I've already told you, what happened during Gödel's lecture was unfor-

tunate but not a determining factor." Aydelotte was starting to grow irritated. "Allow me to introduce you to Mr. Bird."

The man in gray offered the faintest hint of a smile.

"Mr. Bird works for the government. A few weeks ago he contacted me,
inquiring if I might recommend someone with the qualities necessary to
carry out a special mission. The government needs a young person who also
happens to be a competent physicist. When I learned the details of the
request, I spoke with Professor Von Neumann and he couldn't think of a
better candidate than yourself."

Aydelotte's words burned in Bacon's ears, for they carried the sting of
what amounted to an invitation to resign. After the ambiguous introduction,
Bacon contemplated the man before him, a man with a firm, formidable
constitution. He was slightly burly, like a former athlete retired for several
years. Bacon guessed that he was in the military, perhaps an ex-marine.

"I want you to know, dear Bacon"—Aydelotte was clearly uneasy using
this uncharacteristically personal epithet—"that we would be very happy if
you would work with Mr. Bird, but of course it is not an order. We'd just like
you to listen to his ideas and then decide—under no pressure at all—what
would be most appropriate. I think this could be a dignified solution for
everyone involved."

As he finished his speech, Aydelotte got up and, with forced enthusiasm,
offered his hand to Bacon. Mr. Bird coughed slightly, indicating the end of
that part of the conversation, and walked toward the door.

"Why don't we go for a walk," he said to Bacon, in a voice that clearly
wasn't about to take no for an answer. Bacon followed him. Aydelotte's talk
was like an electric charge that made him forget about his headache.

"Good luck, Bacon," said the director.

Just as had occurred with his migraine, that one single sentence seemed
to be a sign telling Bacon that he would not see Aydelotte—or the institute—for a long, long time.

"Have you ever visited here before?" Bacon asked Mr. Bird to break the ice.

"Once or twice, yes."

They started their walk as good friends would, going nowhere in particular. Mr. Bird did not seem to be in a rush; he would occasionally stop to
admire the daisies and the decorative shrubs along the way, as if he were an
amateur horticulturist.

"So, you work for the government?" Bacon asked, starting to feel nause-
ated again. "Is there somewhere specific you'd like to go?"

"No."

They walked through the entire campus and when they were finished, started over again. One thing was certain: Mr. Bird had all the time in the world. But then, all of a sudden, he stopped and looked Bacon squarely in the face, as if he finally deigned to reveal the purpose of his visit.

"Is it true that Einstein discovered the fourth dimension?"

At first, Bacon wasn't sure he understood the question. He wondered if his headache was making him hear things.

"No, not exactly," he said after a few seconds. "In his theory, time is the fourth dimension. Human beings live within a four-dimensional universe, one of space-time."

"What about the formula that was published in the newspapers—does it prove the existence of the human soul?"

"No. All it says is that energy is equal to mass times the speed of light squared."

Mr. Bird scratched his head theatrically. Then, as if he had merely asked the question to set the scene for his own monologue, he launched into his theory.

"I'm not so convinced about that relativity theory. I think there are certain things that simply aren't relative. Good and evil, for example, are not relative. That line of reasoning only leads to crime, don't you think? I know too many scoundrels who use the idea of relativity to try and escape punishment. Can you imagine what would happen if we all thought everything was relative and that every single one of us could do as we pleased? There is nothing relative about being a traitor. There's nothing relative about being a murderer. To start a war that kills millions of people, as Hitler has done, why, there's nothing relative about that."

Bacon felt intimidated.

"I agree with you. But what you're talking about doesn't have anything to do with the relativity theory or with Einstein," Bacon replied. "He was only speaking in terms of physics, not human nature."

"To me it's the same thing."

"No. Einstein asserts that movement is relative only for those observers who are in motion themselves (as we are walking, for example, the women walking toward us seem to be advancing faster than they really are). He states that light is the only objective point of reference, since its velocity always remains the same, independent of where we are when we measure it. Moral issues have nothing to do with these facts, Mr. Bird."

"And do you consider this a truly important discovery?"

"Of course I do."

"I apologize for my insistence, but I have to disagree. If things were that way, wouldn't we all realize it? I don't believe there exists a fourth dimension, nor do I believe in atoms or any of those things, because I have never seen them for myself."

"You aren't the only one," Bacon replied resignedly. He was beginning to get exasperated. Discussing physics with a man who probably didn't even know the meaning of π was ridiculous. And Mr. Bird seemed too convinced of his own beliefs to be persuaded that Einstein might know more than he did.

"Is this what you wanted to talk to me about?"

"Oh, no. I'm sorry, it was just a curiosity of mine." Bird suddenly seemed chagrined by the digression. "I have met so many men like you that I've often wondered what in God's name you think about all the time. Physicists spend hours and hours just thinking. They do it while running around their offices, when they're at home, in the shower, before going to bed. I bet they even think about all those numbers while they make love to their wives."

"We're not all like that," Bacon said, hoping to lighten the mood. "But why do you know so much about physicists and their habits?"

"I have had to familiarize myself with you. It's my job."

"You still haven't told me exactly what your job is, Mr. Bird."

"I will, in due course. Why don't you start off by telling me why you have been following Professor Einstein every day."

Over and over again in his dreams, Bacon had imagined someone asking him this very question. He had even invented several possible explanations, although they all flew out of his head when confronted by Bird's question.

"Please, don't try to deny it," Mr. Bird assured him in a velvety voice, the kind you hear in the movies. "You have been following Professor Einstein, and we have been following you."

"So who are you, then?"

"You haven't answered my question, Professor." Bird's voice grew more menacing.

"You won't believe my answer," said Bacon, trying to smile.

"Why don't you let me be the judge of that."

"I swear to you I don't know why. One day I thought I would try to strike up a conversation with him as he walked home for lunch, but I didn't have the nerve, so I decided just to walk with him . . . from afar."

"Walk with him from afar. And you decided to do that every day?"

"Yes. I know it sounds crazy, but it's the truth."

"And do you think Professor Einstein never saw you doing this?"

"Well, once, but I didn't think he noticed."

"And what would you say if I told you Professor Einstein had alerted the police?"

"You're not serious." Bacon started to perspire. "It was a harmless thing, I mean, I never meant—"

"These are difficult times, Professor," said Bird, returning to his previous courtesy. "You do know that the Nazis despise Professor Einstein, and they are not the only ones. There are so many deranged people in this world. The United States is his new home and the United States must ensure the security of its citizens. Especially the security of someone like Professor Einstein, wouldn't you agree?"

"So you're a policeman?" Bacon asked, growing alarmed.

"Not exactly," Bird said, in a voice that attempted to inspire confidence. "At least not in the usual sense. Let's just say that I am in charge of making sure Professor Einstein feels at home. That no one bothers him. I'm his shadow, so to speak."

"You were watching me, then? So you must know it was just a game, right?"

"Yes, I know. Still, we were forced to take the proper precautions. It took me some time to investigate it, but, thank goodness, I didn't find anything suspicious."

"Well, now that you know I'm not a murderer, may I go?"

"I'm afraid not." Mr. Bird remained firm. "They tell me you're a very competent physicist. Commendable record. Commendable behavior—well, aside from your problems with women, although that doesn't bother me. It was for precisely that reason that we agreed with professors Aydelotte and Von Neumann when they approached us about you. We think you are just the person we need to carry out a very delicate mission that has us very concerned."

"What can I possibly do?"

"A lot, Professor. You're young, you're a competent scientist, you certainly court danger, you speak German fluently, and, as it turns out, you're now without a job and without obligations. We think you're the ideal candidate."

"Ideal for what?"

"I've already told you: for working with us. An *investigation,* if you will. You care deeply about your country, do you not?"

"Of course I do."

"Then it's time you did something for it. Don't forget, Professor, we're in the middle of a war. Priorities tend to get shifted around at a time like this."

"I suppose there's no way I can refuse you."

"You won't. You owe a good deal to this country and the moment has finally arrived for you to give back a little bit of what you've received. Doesn't that seem fair? In addition, as Professor Aydelotte mentioned, you don't belong to the institute anymore. Your staying on at the institute would only cause problems, not to mention the ones you already have before you. I think you know what I'm talking about." Bird spoke to Bacon as if he were a small child who needed to hear the reasons for doing his chores. "Obviously, I must have total confidentiality. You mustn't discuss this with anyone, and I'm afraid you'll only be permitted to say good-bye to those closest to you, and without many details as to the reasons for your departure."

"How can I tell them if I don't know anything myself?"

"Tell them you're enlisting in the army. That you've finally decided to do it. Later on, if things calm down, you can write to them and tell them the truth."

"This is awfully strange. I'll have to think about it."

"I'm sorry, Professor Bacon, but there isn't time for that. You'll have to trust us—just as your country trusts you."

Bacon knocked loudly on Von Neumann's door, as desperate as a dying man looking for a priest to issue his last rites. His headache had disappeared entirely, replaced by a feeling of unreality, possibly brought on by his fever.

"What's going on?" Von Neumann asked him as he opened the door, brusque as usual. Bacon walked into his office without waiting to be invited in.

"I've come to thank you for your recommendation," he announced. "And to say good-bye."

Von Neumann sat down in his chair and studied Bacon for a few moments. A paternal expression came over his face. As always, his initial surly attitude gave way to a mellow friendliness.

"I'm glad you took the offer, my friend. You made a good decision."

"You already knew, didn't you?"

"After the . . . incident, Aydelotte called me into his office. Veblen was demanding that you be expelled immediately from the institute. I simply told them the truth: that you're an excellent physicist but that your future doesn't lie here. Aydelotte thought it over and then told me that perhaps there was a better opportunity for you, a 'research trip,' he called it." Von

Neumann allowed himself a slight, acidic smile. "In the age we find ourselves in, my dear Bacon, we *all* have to make sacrifices. You are an intelligent man, one who can do a great deal of good for his country—but
somewhere else, not here in Princeton, in this ivory tower. I know you're
anxious and upset, but I can't say any more than this: You were chosen to
participate in an important mission because you're a physicist. You won't be
an ordinary soldier; your work is going to be terribly important."

"I would have rather made the decision under less pressure."

"But in a way you *did* make the decision, my boy. The circumstances
worked in your favor. Don't you remember our last conversation?" Von
Neumann patted Bacon's shoulder affectionately. "You yourself told me
about your romantic problems, about your dilemma with those two
women. I tried to explain to you that game theory also works when applied
to romantic strategies. Do you follow me so far?"

"Of course."

"Ever since that day, I knew that if you insisted on maintaining your life
as it was, allowing nothing to change, that eventually you would lose everything. Instead of solving your problem, you would only make it worse. And
that is exactly what happened."

"I suppose so. You told me that I was caught in the middle of a rivalry
between Vivien and Elizabeth and that the moment would inevitably arrive
in which I would be forced to choose between the two. It was either that or
the inverse: that one of them would leave me."

"I'm sorry to have to tell you that I wasn't mistaken."

"Even so, I think you fell short. You saw what happened. In the end, they
came face-to-face, and the end result is that I lost both of them."

"That's what I expected." There was a touch of compassion in Von Neumann's voice that Bacon had never heard before. "It makes sense. To fall in
love with two women—which is very different from sleeping with two
women—is the worst thing that can happen to a man. At first you think of
it as a blessing, as a sign of virility, but in fact it's more like a calamity, of bib-
lical proportions at that. The truth always comes out in the end, and by that
time you don't know how or why you ever got involved in the game to begin
with. It's hard enough to love one woman, Bacon, let alone two." Von Neumann seemed to be recalling his own turbulent romantic history. "The
competition established between two women in love with the same man is
a zero-sum game. If one woman wins, the other necessarily loses, and vice
versa. It is impossible to satisfy both. No matter how fair he tries to be, the
man in question always ends up betraying both women. In the long run this

behavior provokes suspicion and in the worst cases (like your own), a confrontation between the two rivals. I wouldn't want to be in your shoes, Bacon."

"But you told me that there might be a logical solution to this mess."

"There is!" It amused Von Neumann to play the role of the deus ex machina. "Once all three trains have collided, so to speak, the only possible strategy is to abandon the game altogether and begin another. That's it."

"Leave them both?"

"Once and for all."

"That's why you recommended me for the position?"

"Well, that was the catalyst. I hope you're not upset. In all honesty, I do believe this is your only option. It isn't running away, but rather saving what little you have left. Or would you rather stay in the little hell that seems to have swallowed you up?"

Bacon was silent. He was still reeling from the effects of the recent chain of events—Elizabeth's pain and subsequent rage; Vivien's abrupt disappearance; the scandalized murmurs in the hallways of the institute. He could barely think about what he wanted to do with the rest of his life. Maybe Aydelotte, Von Neumann, and Mr. Bird were right. Maybe the best thing was for him to forget about them before *they* could forget about *him*—or hunt him down.

"So . . . should I be thanking you?" Bacon asked, slightly incredulous.

"Not right now, but someday. It's a rare opportunity to fight for a good cause. But don't be sad—I'm afraid you and I have no choice but to remain in contact."

"What do you mean?" asked Bacon.

"Mr. Bird may be a decent naval attaché, but he isn't exactly an exemplar of wisdom."

"You know him?"

"Of course I know him! But that's not important right now. I'm going to tell you a secret, Bacon, because I trust you. I work for them as well."

"You?"

"It's one of my side projects. Perhaps not the most interesting, but one of them. In my house, I keep a small suitcase packed with clothes and, of course, a bulletproof vest. I'm only allowed to bring what's absolutely essential. When Klara's not looking, I can usually sneak a good medieval history book in there. Anyway, at any given moment they can summon me, and the flights to London can be very tedious."

"London!"

"That may be the next place we see each other, Bacon. That's where you'll be going. At the very least we can get together for a nice cup of tea."

"So I'm going to London?"

"You're quick, Bacon. Yes, you're going to Europe, under the auspices of the United States Navy. You'll know war by then. You'll know the world, and I promise you, you'll be much happier than you have been here."

Bacon sat still for a few moments, digesting Von Neumann's words. He was going to be an agent in the service of the United States in Europe. He repeated this to himself several times over until it finally sank in and he actually believed it.

"The one thing that still troubles me is Professor Gödel," Bacon suddenly said. It was the only aspect of his conversation with Aydelotte which he hadn't discussed with Von Neumann. "I think that the incident had a terrible impact on him."

"Oh, that!" Von Neumann smiled knowingly. "On the contrary, Bacon. Kurt may have been the one person in that lecture hall who actually understood what happened."

"What do you mean?"

"Do you thing Gödel was scandalized by your fiancée's behavior?" His laugh degenerated into a cackle. "Don't be naive. The reason for his breakdown had nothing to do with you. Not unlike yourself, Professor Gödel's greatest problems have to do with love."

"With *love?* Gödel?"

"I know. Who would have ever guessed? But that's what it is: The timid, sensitive Kurt Gödel is madly in love with his wife. He has done everything for her, Bacon. He pursued her endlessly, showering her with gifts until she finally agreed to marry him. Only a woman could be capable of transforming a genius like him into such a beast."

"So what happened?"

"I'll tell you, Bacon, as long as you promise to be discreet. Very few people in the United States know what I am about to say to you. It is the greatest of all the secrets you will learn during the course of the war. In Vienna, Adèle was a dancer in a nightclub of ill repute. Gödel's parents were always against the idea that their son would associate with a woman like that."

"But Gödel must have been almost thirty years old by then."

"His parents were extremely conservative, Bacon, and they exerted a strong influence upon him. It was a real tragedy. For many years Kurt didn't dare to defy his family. Don't you realize? To see you fighting with your fiancée, the professor was reminded of his own passionate affair, and that's what reduced him to tears."

"I can hardly believe it."

"Of course, it was a shock to me, too." Von Neumann was a gifted raconteur, making it seem as though he felt as strongly as Bacon did regarding Gödel's human shortcomings—which were, after all, so very similar to Bacon's. "You and Gödel have something in common. The professor's great conflict is not the problem of the continuum, or the incompleteness theorem, or the formally undecidable propositions, but rather the tumultuous and heartbreaking love he feels for his wife."

Brief Autobiographical Disquisitions: From Set Theory to Totalitarianism

---

DISQUISITION I: *Infancy and the End of an Era*

Having now provided you with the story of Lieutenant Francis P. Bacon's life, I can easily understand how a somewhat uncomfortable question remains hanging in the balance. If this Mr. Gustav Links, professor of mathematics at the University of Leipzig, is the narrator of the facts, as he insists, how is it possible that he knows the most intimate personal details of another person, that is, of Lieutenant Bacon?

This doubt is a legitimate one, and for this reason I have taken the liberty of including a brief digression. It is a reasonable doubt, because the credibility of my story depends upon its resolution. A man of science like myself is well aware that without sufficient proof, theories simply vanish into thin air. And this is my response: I cannot state that all the facts I have presented are true—for that reason I have called some of them *hypotheses*—because they were events I did not have the privilege of witnessing. What, then, can I state in my defense? Something very simple: Lieutenant Francis P. Bacon took it upon himself to tell me about his life during the many hours we spent together. At times, he would abandon his role as interrogator, and I would lighten up on my lengthy discourses, and a surprising fraternity developed between us, a bond that connected our hearts as well as our minds. In those moments of empathy, I would listen to his confessions with a patience and attentiveness that would be the envy of a great many psychoanalysts and more than a few priests. We would exchange roles, and for a few moments he would become the object of my analysis.

Naturally, one question leads to another. What were Lieutenant Bacon and I doing together? When did we first meet? What was *our* mission? How did our parallel lives intersect? To answer these questions, I have no other choice but to talk about myself.

In the great map of my imagination, I locate my birth as a tiny point in the middle of a Cartesian plane. High up on the y axis lie all the positive things that have ever happened to me, yet as I move down on the same vertical line, I find all the misfortunes, setbacks, and failures I have experienced in my life. To the far right of the x axis, I can see the things that define my character, that have become the focus of my life: my desires, my wishes, my obsessions. To the far left of the same axis, however, I see those aspects of my character that—against my will and my better judgment—have made me who I am, those seemingly unpredictable and spontaneous qualities that, for better or for worse, have led me to where I am today. What will be the end result of an exercise such as this? What shape will appear in the middle of the graph? Will I be able to draw a line through the coordinates of this journey, to derive the formula that summarizes the whole of me, in both body and soul?

As I contemplate my life from the distance afforded by time, I see myself as an abstract problem or, better yet, as a bacterium that painfully replicates itself beneath the light of a microscope. In doing this, I realize that, since the moment of my birth, my fate has been inextricably linked to the events of this century. My existence bears the scars of both the turbulent era I was born into, and the people that destiny placed in my path. For that reason, if only due to sheer circumstance, I have witnessed both the most glorious and the most infamous moments of humanity: two world wars, Auschwitz and Hiroshima, and the birth of the new science.

I digress. I am trying to concentrate, to come up with a first sentence that will somehow describe me, a shocking phrase that will spark some interest, a brilliant move that will dazzle my readers. Unfortunately, I can't think of anything. So instead, I shall begin with the obvious. My name—as I said before—is Gustav Links, and I was born on March 21, 1905, in Munich, the capital of Bavaria. I hardly need elaborate on the grandeur of my native city: All I will say is that, in addition to the tradition of madness established by King Ludwig II and his brother Otto, the region enjoyed a period of splendor marked by the contributions of men like Richard Wagner, Thomas Mann, Richard Strauss, Frank Wedekind, Werner Heisenberg, and so many others.

My father, Jürgen Links, was a professor of medieval history at the university. As shown in the genealogical tree he kept, our family's ancestry can be traced back to the seventeenth century. The Nazi authorities, in search of an incriminating Jewish ancestor, scanned the document several times over, to no avail. Our forefathers included, among others, a music conductor in the Court of Berlin, a pharmacist from Soest, and a saddler from Munich in service of King Max Joseph of Bavaria during the Napoleonic era.

My mother's name was Elsa Schwartz, though I only have a faint memory of her, for when I was three years old she died following a miscarriage. I can't say anything about her. From the few photographs my father once showed me, all I know is that she had a wide, strong forehead; light blond, almost white hair that reached just above her breasts; and a stern gaze that belied the kindness which—as I was told—was her greatest virtue. Due to this sad circumstance, I was an only child and was spared the experience of sharing my few privileges with a long list of stepsiblings, as was customary in those days, as my father never remarried.

In this respect, as in many others, my father was different from average mortals. He was born in Munich in 1871, just at the time when Bavaria became part of the German Reich under the Emperor Wilhelm I and his minister Bismarck. Almost half of my father's lifetime was spent under the ironclad regimes of these two men, and he was a staunch supporter of the empire. He may have been tough, arrogant, harsh, and rigid, but I admired him tremendously, more than almost anyone else. From a young age he was fascinated by the history of ancient Germany, something he would study his entire life. He was the wisest in an age of wise men, and could recite from memory entire passages from medieval legends of Tristan and Isolde, and the Nibelungs, and from Wolfram von Eschenbach's *Parzival*. During my childhood, however, I had almost no contact with him. In our *Bildungsbürger* milieu, that of the enlightened bourgeoisie, children were always kept separate from the adults.

When I was born, the world was an ordered environment, a serious and meticulously arranged cosmos in which flaws—war, pain, fear—were nothing more than unfortunate aberrations that were the result of inexperience. My parents and my parents' parents believed that humanity advanced in a linear fashion, from the horrors of the Stone Age to the brilliance of the future. They saw history as nothing more than a cable suspended by two lampposts or, to use a metaphor more appropriate to the twentieth century, like a railway line uniting two remote villages. In this context, the fact of being born was little more than a mere detail. From that point on, the formal education we received was what shaped us, made us into good men, and ensured our rosy future. In those days, the values we were taught were simple ones: discipline, austerity, nationalism. Such a beautiful, simple enterprise! If progress was to characterize the modern world, then individuals should conform to the larger plan. How could the system fail? If childhood education was mapped out carefully enough, if youngsters were given the tools to cultivate their physical development and spiritual growth, and if their characters were molded like a bronze plate pressed against the anvil of morality, then society could eventually rid itself of lunatics, criminals, and beggars and create a community of honorable, rich, happy, and pious men.

Luckily, my early years were not dominated by the rigorous world of science. One activity in particular had a profound, transformative effect upon my childhood: the *Wandervögel,* or "wandering birds," as we members of this youth movement were called. Just like the Boy Scouts in other countries, the *Wandervögel* played an important role in the moral development of many young Germans in those days. I met Heinrich von Lutz, my best friend for many years and one of the greatest influences in my life, in the *Wandervögel,* and I also met Werner Heisenberg there as well. Four years older than Heinrich and me, Werner was already in charge of his own group of boys when I first met him.

I still have fond memories of those years: the gaslights suspended from the lampposts in the city streets; the throngs strolling along the Marienplatz; the interminable wait to view the Glockenspiel, the lovely mechanical clock in the tower of the Neues Rathaus; the great shock of seeing a car drive by the Alte Pinakothek; the woman who carried milk to our house and to whom all the little boys shouted, *"Millimadl, Millimadl, mit'n dicken Wadl!"* (Milkmaid, Milkmaid with the fat legs!); the songs of the traveling minstrels. I suppose none of this exists anymore. Perhaps the image I recall most vividly is of the Bavarian soldiers marching to the beat of drums along the Hohenzollernstraße, and accompanied by enthusiastic military bands on their way to their base in the Oberwiesenfeld. What I didn't know was how soon that idyllic scene would turn into a nightmare.

As we all know, in July of 1914, when I was nine years old, a Serbian extremist in Sarajevo assassinated the heir to the royal and imperial throne of the neighboring Austro-Hungarian Empire, which began a war against the Slavs. Because of our alliance with Franz Joseph, Germany entered into the war a few days later. Neither of these events would have made a bit of difference to me if it hadn't been for the fact that my father was called to duty. He soon left for the front, leaving me in the care of his mother. Old Ute Links was an extraordinary woman: At age seventy, she still went on excursions in the nearby mountains and was eminently prepared to defend her home in the event that the dreaded French—or English, or Russians—decided to attack her. I stayed with her for the duration of the war.

In early 1915, my father had my grandmother send me to the Maximil-ians-Gymnasium; at one time its director was Dr. Wecklein, maternal grandfather of Werner Heisenberg. One of the most prestigious academies in all of Bavaria, it was a required stop for all young members of the bour-geoisie who wished to eventually go on to the university. Originally, the Max-Gymnasium, as we called it, was located in an enormous building on the corner of the Morawitzkystraße and the Karl Theodor-Straße, but when the war began, the Bavarian army used it as a bunker for some of its troops. When I began my studies, its three hundred or so students attended class at the Ludwig-Gymnasium, not far from the Marienplatz. A year after the end of the war, we were able to return to the school's old building.

My first years at the Max-Gymnasium were not only difficult but practi-cally useless. From the middle of 1915, several of the teachers and older stu-dents who were members of the *Wehrkraftverein,* the military group associated with the school, went to the front and many of them never returned. To keep us busy, we were obliged to take interminable classes in *Vaterlandsliebe,* lessons in patriotism that were intended to instill in us the fortitude we would need to endure difficult times. Later on, shortages of coal and food forced the school to reduce our class hours. There were peri-ods in which we only attended the Gymnasium once a week, simply to receive lists of assignments from our teachers.

The armistice of November 11, 1918, came as a great shock to the Ger-mans. Much of our army still occupied French territory and, despite set-backs, was largely intact, so it was just when we thought we were winning the war that we learned that our generals had capitulated. It was hard to believe. On the ninth day of that same month, in Berlin, Emperor Wilhelm II abdicated. The day before in Munich, Kurt Eisner, the Jewish leader of the Bavarian socialists, had proclaimed the end of the empire and the establish-ment of a *Räterepublik* (a conciliar republic, following the Soviet model). For us, it was the beginning of a turbulent era.

In the weeks that followed, Munich became a battlefield. The new regime was quick to foment antagonism between the workers and the wealthy classes. As prime minister of Bavaria, Eisner attempted to do away with the army, but all he did was lose the support of the military. Both the bour-geoisie and the aristocracy, fearful that Eisner's Bolsheviks would rob them of their privileges, funded private militias to defend them if necessary. Almost every right-wing association participated in this movement, espe-cially the secretive ultranationalist groups that had begun to proliferate throughout Bavaria. One such group, the Thule Bund, quickly assumed a pivotal role in German history: On February 21, 1919, the count of Arco-Valley, a member of Thule Bund, shot Kurt Eisner in the middle of the street.

The communists as well as the private armies waged their battles up and down Munich's main avenues. Amid the general chaos, the Social Democratic Party (SPD) took control of the new government. The first measures it took during this period, which came to be known as the "red terror," included the elimination of the monarchy and all aristocratic titles, the closure of the *Gymnasiums,* universities, and newspapers—institutions considered to be the focal points of conservatism—and the confiscation of arms. In April of 1919—to think that Francis P. Bacon still hadn't been born!—the central government in Berlin intervened in an effort to calm the strife in Bavaria. Gustav Noske, the socialist war minister, organized an army of *Freikorpen*—volunteer soldiers—and sent them to Munich under the command of General Von Oven. After several skirmishes, Von Oven occupied the city and ordered the assassination of anyone found armed with a weapon. The "white" armies used the opportunity to take revenge on their "red" enemies in a massacre that lasted several days. The forces from Berlin remained in Munich until the first of July, when they finally gained control of the situation. The Weimar republic—and with it, the rest of the ordered universe—had barely managed to keep itself afloat.

DISQUISITION II: *Youth and Irrationality*

Just like me, Heinrich was a student at the Max-Gymnasium, and belonged to the same *Wandervögel* group that I belonged to. And just like the English Boy Scouts, we were conservative and puritan, filled with an enthusiasm for life and for our peers, and our main task was to prepare ourselves to one day enter adulthood. In 1919, however, the Bavarian youth movement felt that many of these ideals had been betrayed by elders who had lost the war. These young leaders created a new movement that was a return to the original precepts of the *Wandervögel,* and they christened it the *Jungbayernbund,* or Bavarian Youth League.

On August 1, 1919, hundreds of young Germans and Austrians gathered in Prunn Castle in the Altmühl Valley to decide the future of our youth movement. After the debacle of the war, we had to reestablish the basic tenets of our organization. Heinrich and I were fourteen when we attended the meeting, accompanied by our *Gruppenführer.* Together we witnessed the incredible sight of over 250 young people joined together from every corner of the German realm. For three days, we discussed the way in which young people should handle the brutal political realities we faced. The results of this examination of conscience were published in *Der Weisse Ritter,* the official publication of the movement. There, we stated that as young Germans we categorically rejected modern civilization and its process of industrialization. We felt that these two things were directly responsible for the recent armed conflict and our subsequent defeat. For that reason, we said, young people had to fight for a society that held fast to its ancient traditions. Basing ourselves on the ideas that were circulating at the time—like Spengler's *The Decline of the West*—we were convinced that our civilization had entered into a period of decline that condemned us to a world of ever-increasing mechanization. As one of our leaders wrote in *Der Weisse Ritter,* "The youth movement is one of freedom. We have freed ourselves from the soulless mechanization and materialism of modern civilization. Our movement has triumphantly defended its right and the right of all young people to live against the limitations of tradition and authority."

At age fourteen, Heinrich and I were scarcely old enough to understand the magnitude of those words. But with time and distance, it now seems clear to me that those declarations were at the bottom of all the intellectual debates that arose in Germany from that point until our final defeat in 1945. In 1920, the general feeling that came out of the Prunn Castle meeting turned into something much more extreme. A splinter group, separate from the mainstream, soon formed to protest the youth movement's general policy of nonparticipation in political issues. Heinrich and I immediately joined. It was called the *Neudeutsche Pfadfinderschaft,* the New German Explorers. The basis of this new organization could be summarized by three driving principles: *Gemeinschaft, Führer,* and *Reich:* community, leader, and empire. Our emblem was, of course, a white horse, which symbolized the battle each of us was supposed to fight. Just like Saint George against the dragon, our mission was to vanquish the moral corruption around us and to create a new German Reich, a pure and virtuous state in which moral rectitude and truth would reign.

If I were asked to summarize my experience during that time, I would have to say that, in fact, I had two childhoods and two adolescences, different and complementary. My friendship with Heinrich was so intense, so close, that it was as if each of us also lived the life of the other. I knew every one of his gestures, appetites, and obsessions, and he knew all there was to know about me. If it hadn't been for the fact that he was stocky and solid, while I was tall and skinny as a snake, we could have passed for one another without anyone knowing. Contrary to the customs of the day—a person was to exercise reserve at all times, in the interest of preserving one's personal dignity—Heinrich and I never kept secrets from one another. It was as if a transparent light united us like brothers. Never—not before or after—have I known a friendship as noble and as pure as the one I shared with him.

I think it necessary to mention that Heini was the son of a rich man, a *very* rich businessman from Thuringia; I believe he owned a steel plant. As the German mark was devalued over and over again, he managed to amass quite a substantial fortune through crafty speculation. He and his wife, a Dutch woman of impeccable manners, traveled constantly—they only spent two days out of every month in Munich—and Heini grew up in a terribly disorganized environment, far from the iron discipline that a father like mine, being close by, inflicted upon me. Although I was never the brightest student at school, I was sufficiently frightened by the prospect of facing my father with poor grades that I was usually somewhere near the top ten. Heini, on the other hand, couldn't be bothered with things like Greek, Latin, and mathematics. He wasn't stupid—far from it, in fact. He simply preferred to devote his time to subjects that really mattered to him, like history and philosophy, ignoring other bothersome distractions.

My father grew to appreciate Heini. As I was occupied with my mathematics, which had long since become the focus of my attention, Heini became the son that just might follow in my father's footsteps. He would visit our house often, even when I wasn't there, and would spend long hours talking with my father, something inconceivable to me. Nevertheless, I wasn't jealous; just as he came to my house unannounced, I felt free to do the same at his. There, his mother—who had one of the loveliest faces I've ever laid eyes on—would tolerate my adolescent flirtation with smiles, always offering me a slice of her splendid apple tart. It was hard to believe that Heini could spend so much time arguing with such a charming woman. A tacit agreement allowed us to "exchange" parents, and it also enabled Heinrich and me to fully carry out this experiment of our shared personality.

From a very early age, Heinrich had a certain ethereal quality that would one day lead him down the path of the philosopher. He was restless and wild, but he also possessed unusual powers of observation. A glimpse of the smallest gesture or nervous tic was often all he needed to discern a person's character or temperament. I remember being amazed the first time it happened: Walking down the street, we had bumped into a tall, somber-looking woman, maybe thirty years old, and Heini whispered in my ear that she was a virgin. The same thing happened a week later when we came face-to-face with the other side of that coin, a thick-waisted Polish girl who waited on us at one of the beer gardens in the city. In a cryptic tone, Heini said, "That one doesn't ever get tired of screwing. She does it every night."

Heinrich had a well-deserved reputation as a womanizer. We lived in an environment in which any contact with women was practically a sin; the majority of my friends waited years to get married, and even when they finally did, I suspect they never fully understood their wives. Heini, on the other hand, was the complete opposite, a rarity. He had several female cousins more or less his age whom he saw on a regular basis, and one of them apparently couldn't resist the temptation of instructing him in the secrets of romantic relations. From then on, women became something of an obsession for him; he was forever talking about them, and in typical incorrigible fashion, classifying them. Sometimes the criteria were typical, like hair or eye color, and other times more creative. For example, the way he suspected they made love (dominant or submissive) or the color of their nipples (the most fascinating category to me).

As one might expect in friends as close as we were, his passion quickly became my passion as well. When we were seventeen years old, we visited our first whorehouse together, and even asked the prostitute to service us at the same time. We wanted her to touch us simultaneously, so we could observe each other's ridiculous expressions of sexual excitement. We spent hours laughing about that, imitating each other's moans of pleasure. Against all the rules we had been raised with, by the time we were eighteen we had acquired vast sexual repertoires, far beyond those of our classmates and friends.

Nevertheless, chasing skirts down Munich's dark alleys was far from our only activity. Despite his consistently bad marks, Heini was quite brilliant, always happy to participate in thoughtful philosophical discussions on the meaning of life. He was especially inspired by all the patriotic notions we had learned in the *Gymnasium* and in the youth groups, feeling that the world around us was in decline and that we Germans had to search through our history to find a way to triumph over this current adversity. These ever-present themes led Heini into a deeper, more profound rumination: Although he was still unsure of his exact path in life, he knew he wanted to become famous, to be some kind of spiritual leader to his peers. All those medieval sagas he had read had filled him with a kind of mysticism, an idealistic vision of the "German race." As we completed our studies at the Max-Gymnasium, Heini grew to become a fierce defender of irrationalism.

According to him, the stubborn causality taught in our schools was the root of all that was wrong with our civilization. Like Spengler, he felt that causality was "as rigid as death," and that the only way to combat it was with force.

It was 1924, and we had just completed, successfully, our course of studies at the Max-Gymnasium. From that moment on, our destinies would no longer be one and the same. I had been accepted to study mathematics at the University of Leipzig, while Heinrich had decided to go to Berlin to study his favorite philosopher at that time: Friedrich Nietzsche, about whose final years he would write his thesis.

DISQUISITION III: *The Arithmetics of Infinity*

Leipzig is located at the confluence of the rivers Weisse Elster and Pleisse, and the first mention of the city dates back to the beginning of the year 1000. The *Diary of the Bishop Thietmar of Merseburg*, written in that same period, recounts the tragic death of the bishop in the "urbs Lipsi." The *Alma Mater Lipsiensis*, as the university was known, was founded in 1409 and was among the greatest universities in all of Germany.

When I arrived there in September of 1924, the economy entered a period of readjustment, which allowed the Weimar republic for several years to enjoy a state of relative calm. I would have rather attended the University of Göttingen, where German mathematics was at its height, thanks to the work of David Hilbert, but I was certainly satisfied to have been accepted at Leipzig. Perhaps it wasn't as beautiful as Dresden, but it was every bit as interesting, and the city gave me the opportunity to discover myself, far removed from my father's stern gaze and—I must admit it—the severe dictums of the youth movements. I didn't have much money, but at least I would be able to choose how and where I spent it.

My chosen field—and I say this with a certain pride—was mathematical logic, specifically the theory of infinite sets developed by Georg Cantor at the end of the nineteenth century. It was a novel plan of study in those days; very few mathematicians undertook such a contemporary topic at so young an age. The minute I discovered Cantor's theories in my last year at the Max-Gymnasium, I knew I wanted to dedicate all my energy to completing his ideas. As a mathematician, he chose to confront one of the most intriguing subjects in the history of philosophy: infinity. As I began to read his work, I felt as though I had hit upon a gold mine. One of the issues raised in Hilbert's Program addressed the theory of "transfinite numbers," which

Cantor had been unable to resolve: the so-called continuum problem. When I met with Karl Huttenlocher, *Privatdozent* at the University of Leipzig, I told him I wanted to work on this delicate, complicated subject.

"You, too" was all Huttenlocher said, with a gesture of resignation.

Georg Ferdinand Ludwig Philipp Cantor was born on March 3, 1845, near the luminous, icy river Neva in St. Petersburg. He was the eldest son of a family with Jewish-German origins. His father, Georg Woldemar, had been born in Copenhagen and later converted to the Lutheran faith, while his mother, Maria Anna Bolm, was a Russian whose mother had converted from Judaism to Catholicism. When young Georg was eleven years old, the family moved to Germany, first to Wiesbaden and then to Frankfurt. After attending elementary school in St. Petersburg, he continued his schooling in various German academies before attending the Grand-Ducal Realschule of Darmstadt and, finally, the prestigious Höhere Gewerbeschule, where he remained until 1862.

From an early age, Cantor was drawn to his father's strong Lutheran faith as well as his appreciation of music, painting, and literature. But his thoughts were primarily occupied by one discipline: mathematics. To him, science was the vehicle for communication with the divine. Despite his Protestant faith, he was fascinated by the doctors of the Catholic Church and their abstruse theories about human existence and the qualities of the Creator. He was convinced that these wise souls had hit upon certain thought processes that would guide humans toward God. And in the middle of that theological discourse, Cantor had the genius to envision the pillar of his own mathematical theories: *Multitudo est id quod est ex unis quorum unum non est alterum* ("A set is an aggregate whose entities are distinct from one another"), a definition extracted from Saint Thomas Aquinas that he would remember as long as he lived.

Aware of his son's aptitude, Cantor's father thought that engineering was the proper way to channel his son's talents. Georg, however, did not share his father's opinion: His spirit couldn't be bothered with things like commerce or bridge building; it was the subtlety of pure mathematics and their theological implications that appealed to him the most. The Lutheran obsession with financial success—which his father embodied—led him to feel that he would never be capable of engaging in truly productive pursuits. Wracked by this feeling of failure, he would lock himself in his room, rarely leaving his home even for a walk down the street.

Despite these recurring bouts of melancholy, Cantor was accepted at the University of Zurich in 1862, and by age twenty-two he had graduated from the University of Berlin. His doctoral thesis on number theory, at only twenty-six pages, earned him a magna cum laude distinction, but it did little to advance the hypotheses of his later investigations. In 1869 he transferred to the University of Halle, and from then on he dedicated himself to weaving his many diverse interests—religion, mathematics, and philosophy—into one single discipline: the study of infinity. Cantor intended to create a new branch of arithmetics that would successfully decipher the relationship between divinity and numbers. As if trying to reconstruct the mind of the Eternal, he utilized the ancient Thomist idea regarding aggregates of elements to establish the bases for a new theory of sets.

Around the same time, Cantor's friend, the mathematician Richard Dedekind, published the book *Continuity and Irrational Numbers* (1872), which would have a profound effect on him. Before Dedekind's book, the concept of mathematical infinity had never been clearly defined, and scholars had to settle for flimsy assumptions or antiquated terminology dating back to the age of scholasticism. Dedekind was the first mathematician to offer a consistent—and astoundingly elegant—explanation of this idea. His theory stated that a set is infinite when one of its subsets is the same size as the original set.

In 1874, Cantor married a woman by the name of Velle Guttman. For their honeymoon, the young couple decided to visit the picturesque Swiss village of Interlaken, in the hopes of meeting Dedekind, who was vacationing there at the time. In that hilly region near Bern, Cantor had an experience as illuminating to him as his childhood lessons in medieval theology so many years earlier. He and his bride would take day trips by the banks of the river Aare and near the tranquil lakes of Thun, though his preferred activities were the long walks he took with Dedekind through the main streets of Interlaken. As they discussed their ideas of infinity, they would occasionally stop, suddenly overwhelmed by the frozen beauty of the Jungfrau that loomed like a watchful God high above their heads.

A few months later, inspired by the memory of his holiday, Cantor began to write the articles for which he would become famous. Scarcely stopping to rest, he would sit down to work and write until dusk, inspired by a voice that—he was certain—was not his own. Like the scribes of yesteryear, he would sketch his unwieldy ideas on a few pieces of paper with the same certainty and faith that he applied to his morning prayers. Armed with his new theory of sets and inspired by Dedekind's ideas, Cantor was now ready to attempt his own foray into infinity. He added and subtracted sets, treating them like abstractions independent of all reality, and then fashioned them according to traditional mathematical analysis. He shook them up and down, infusing them with a life force as if they were his own little babies. But then he arrived at a dead end. It was a kind of sickness, a disorder that threatened to push him toward madness. This anomaly, this symptom of insanity inscribed in mathematics, arose when he realized that infinity could indeed be measured.

Unlike Dedekind, Cantor believed that infinite sets could possess distinct magnitudes and have different "powers." In other words, Cantor's conclusion was that infinities came in different sizes. "As a result of this method," wrote Cantor in 1883, "it is always possible to arrive at new sets of numbers and, with them, the many different powers, ever growing, that are found in both physical and spiritual life. New numbers obtained through this method will always have the same concrete precision and the same objective reality as all other numbers." Upon realizing the meaning of his discovery, Cantor felt he had opened a Pandora's box, and he wrote as much to Dedekind: *Je le vois mais je ne le crois pas!*

If Cantor was shocked by his results, his contemporaries considered them sheer madness. His first few articles appeared in surprisingly rapid succession in the celebrated *Journal de Crèlle*, but the editors, fearful of risking their journal's academic prestige, soon began to postpone the publication of the pieces he sent in. However, the worst blow would come from an influential businessman from Berlin named Leopold Kronecker.

Born in 1823, Kronecker grew prosperous after completing his thesis on algebraic number theory in 1845. As a student, he had come into contact with some of the best mathematicians of the time—Weierstrass, Jacobi, and Steiner—and Kronecker had directed his efforts toward the universal arithmetization of mathematical theory, with the blind faith that arithmetics were necessarily finite. "God created the integers, and the rest is the work of men," he said, in a clear allusion to Cantor.

In 1883, after many years dedicated to the world of business, Kronecker accepted a professorship at the University of Berlin. There, he launched a vicious campaign that successfully thwarted Cantor's chances of receiving a post similar to his own. From then on, Kronecker devoted himself to mercilessly refuting Cantor's work on infinities. Cast aside, Cantor was forced to spend the rest of his years at the rather average University of Halle, just as his friend Dedekind was reduced to a position at a *Gymnasium* in Brunswick.

Beaten down by the bile and venom of his critics, Cantor suffered a series of nervous breakdowns that left him bedridden for weeks. Nevertheless, in

1884 he managed to finish a lengthy treatise that effectively summarized his major contributions to mathematics. Entitled the *Principles of a General Theory of Variables,* its main objective was to challenge the questions Kronecker had raised. In this book, Cantor reasserted his theory that infinite sets could have the same kind of finite enumerations that finite sets had. To prove this, he didn't bother with the theological issues that had so captivated him in his youth. Instead, he asserted that one might not be able to comprehend God by way of reason, but that it was possible to come closer to him (in the manner of the mystics) through Cantor's theory.

Kronecker refused to discuss his dispute with Cantor in public, though on one occasion he did receive Cantor in his home. It was a meeting of two opposing minds, from two different centuries and of two very distinct temperaments. In the end, both men refused to yield, and Cantor's miserable fate remained the same. In spite of it all, he continued to believe in the validity of his discoveries. He wrote: "My theory remains solid as a rock; every arrow shot against it quickly ricochets back to its assailant. How do I know this? Because I have studied it from every possible angle over the course of several years; because I have examined all the cases against infinite numbers; and most of all, because I have followed its roots, as it were, from the first infallible cause of all things created in this world."

More than Kronecker's arguments, it was one of his own discoveries that finally and definitively drove him insane. It was the continuum hypothesis. In his arithmetics of infinity, Cantor thought that there must exist an infinite set with a "greater" force than that of natural numbers, yet "lesser" than that of real numbers. Unfortunately it was something he was never able to prove. As if God had slapped him in the face, the continuum hypothesis became a kind of curse, an example of human limitations that would never find a solution.

Disillusioned, Cantor abandoned mathematics and began teaching philosophy in the rare moments of peace he enjoyed. Trembling and fatigued, he increasingly fell victim to bouts of depression, which grew longer and longer as time went by. Despite the fact that he had always placed God at the center of his work (as he once wrote to a friend), he felt that the angel of mathematics had abandoned him. In 1899, despondent at the lack of solid proof for his continuum hypothesis, he requested permission to be relieved of his teaching obligations without giving up his salary, in the hope of dedicating himself entirely to the problem's solution. In 1905 he finally gave up. In the end, he would never resolve this one final assertion, the refined torture to which his soul had been subjected.

DISQUISITION IV: *Liberty and Lust*

In the middle of October of 1926, I received a letter from Heinrich that contained surprising news: Not only was he doing extraordinarily well in his classes, but he had met the girl of his dreams and was planning to marry her. And not only was Natalia intelligent and beautiful, but she was head over heels in love with him, too. She was slightly younger than he was (if memory serves me correctly, Heinrich was almost twenty-two) and as he himself put it, "perfect" was simply the only word to describe her. He wanted me to meet her as soon as possible.

In an equally enthusiastic letter of response I said I would do whatever I could to travel to Berlin, and that it would be an honor to meet his beloved. After a few more letters, Heinrich confirmed the date we would be able to meet in Berlin, where he promised to take us out to see "one of the greatest shows in the world," a performance by the great Josephine Baker. "A little monkey in a cage," he cynically noted, adding that Natalia would bring along a girl for me. It was the best news I could have possibly received; my life at that time consisted of walking back and forth between my pension and the university, with Cantor's theories my only companion. "How are we going to get into a show like that?" I asked him. "How are we going to pay for it?" "Just be dressed and ready," he cabled me, telling me to meet him at the Berlin train station the following Saturday at noon.

I had never been in the German capital before. I had imagined it would be like Munich, but I was wrong: Berlin in those days seemed like the very center of the universe or, as the novelist Stefan Zweig wrote, the new Babel. In 1926 it was, in fact, the third largest city on the planet. That Saturday I put on my best jacket and when I arrived at the station, I was suddenly aware of how odd I must have looked amid all the other passengers. I sat down on a bench and waited anxiously, until I spotted Heinrich and two pretty girls walking toward me. At first I couldn't tell which one was to be my date, but I was too shy to ask. One was blond and freckly, with a perfectly shaped body that didn't look like it could possibly belong to an eighteen-year-old. The other girl, though, was even more dazzling: a redhead with the kind of shy smile often found in women who feel unsure of themselves. I prayed that she was my date, but she wasn't. I should have known.

"Allow me to introduce you," said Heini. "This is the love of my life, Natalia." Of course, he was right: "perfect" was the only word to describe her. "And this little gem answers to the name Marianne."

"*Enchanté,*" I said, and proceeded to kiss their hands.

Their eyes held back laughter as they looked at me.

"My friend has always been very formal," Heini said, apologizing for me. "Well, let's go, we don't have much time."

Natalia and Marianne hurried forward, to walk a few steps ahead of us, and I moved closer to Heinrich.

"Aren't they pretty?" he whispered in my ear.

"Where did you find the money for all this?" I asked him. "And your parents, how could they?"

"Forget about all of those lessons in Christian morals," Heinrich cut me off.

Heini hailed a taxi and told the driver to take us to the Café Bauer, on the Friedrichstraße, where we had a simple lunch. The atmosphere improved as the afternoon wore on, and I had the chance to get to know our female guests a bit better. As I had suspected, Marianne was two years older than us but behaved like a spoiled schoolgirl, ordering a double portion of dessert and barely acknowledging my presence for the two hours we sat there. Instead she chatted away with Natalia, making comments about the elegant bar, the other ladies' dresses, the waiter's service. Natalia simply listened to her, saying almost nothing at all. Once she dared to ask me if I studied mathematics—I felt profoundly flattered by the attention—and I tried to answer her with a short discourse on Cantor and infinity theory, but Heinrich interrupted me to make some typically impertinent comment.

"This city is filled with degenerate entertainment," he said to the girls. "Doesn't it bother you that we're taking you into a world of such decadence?"

"Of course not!" exclaimed Marianne excitedly, and for the first time that evening she turned toward me with a suggestive look in her eyes. I felt a flush seep into my cheeks.

"This city must have more cabarets than any other place in the world," Heini continued. "In the Café Nationale all the waitresses go topless," he said, and then paused, waiting for the girls to register their shock. "And at the Apollo, you can dance nude, with a woman or a man, whichever you like. But the best place is Forget-Me-Not; there you can see men dressed as women, women dressed as men. Anyway, perhaps later, if you'd like, we can go to the Kabarett der Komiker, the Katakombe, or the Megalomania."

I was surprised at Heinrich's breadth—it was as if he had taken a crash course in the depravities of Berlin. Then I thought perhaps he'd gotten this information from his father, though I could hardly imagine Heini discussing this sort of thing with him. The girls, however, found it delightful.

"Go on," said Marianne predictably.

"The best singers in the world are in Berlin. Have you heard of Renate Müller? Or Evelyn Künnecke? The best of them all is a short, ugly woman—she's like a barrel—named Claire Waldorff. And then just this year a new actress has appeared, named Marlene Dietrich, and everyone is talking about her performance in *Mouth to Mouth.*"

It was a whole new universe for me. And I quickly discovered that I liked it."

"Unfortunately," Heini continued, putting his arm around my shoulder, "those princesses wouldn't give me or Gustav a second thought. Can you guess why? I'll give you a hint: Whenever you see someone with a lavender twig on their lapel, it means they prefer the company of members of their own sex."

We all laughed and got up, euphoric. All of a sudden I felt like making love to the uninhibited Marianne, who, after her initial indifference, now had her arm slung through mine.

"All right, all right," I said to Heini. "Why don't you tell us a little about this woman we're about to see."

"Josephine Baker is the latest, the very latest thing!" Heini was starting to get droll. I could feel Marianne's body close to mine. "The one and only Max Reinhardt, director of the Deutsches Theater, was speechless after seeing her. Would you like to hear a story about her?"

"Yes! Yes!" we shouted in unison.

"They say Reinhardt went to see her backstage after her show one night, he was so taken by her beauty. Baker had just recently arrived in Paris." Heini loved being the center of attention. "You can imagine it: 'Oh, made-moiselle, what a pleasure it is to meet you!' and all that nonsense. Josephine returns the courtesy, saying, 'Sir, the pleasure is all mine,' and so on and so forth. And suddenly a black dancer is the most famous woman in all of Berlin. All the aristocrats fight to have her as a guest in their homes, as if she's some sort of traveling act. Baker, cynically, gets carried away with all this. One evening, Reinhardt introduces her to some friends of his, they introduce her to others, and this goes on until one evening, at one of those endless parties in Berlin, she meets Count Harry Kessler."

Kessler, the Red Count. I'd heard his name before. An eccentric million-aire, communist sympathizer, and friend of Heinrich's father's. It was all coming together.

"Just picture the scene: Kessler arrives at the party and what do you think he sees? You guessed it: Josephine dancing naked, completely naked, in front of all the guests. At that very moment, the count decides this woman, this *wild animal* (those were his words), would be his."

"And did he get her?" Marianne asked.

"What do you think?" Heini paused for effect. "It wasn't so easy. Like all stars, Baker had a certain attitude. She could take her clothes off in front of a thousand men and then refuse to make love to one. Of course she attended the party the count threw in her honor, but wouldn't dance. Kessler, who had already promised the other guests a truly transcendental experience, was beside himself. But like the good aristocrat he was, he managed to distract his friends with his sculpture collection. 'Just look at this Rodin,' he said to them, things like that. Suddenly they stopped before Aristide Maillol's *Woman Squatting*. For Josephine it was a revelation. Without saying a word, she removed her clothes and began to dance in front of the sculpture. The white marble and her black skin swirled into one another. The undulating union of two opposite elements! According to the people there"—of course, I knew he was referring to his father—"it was one of the most spectacular, passionate moments of the Berlin scene."

We were all mesmerized by the story. Heini had introduced us to a world that neither the girls nor I had ever dreamed of. He then took us to the club (whose name escapes me now) where the famous show was to take place, and went straight to the manager. It was all arranged. Heini got us a table not far from the stage, and a waitress soon came over with a bottle of champagne.

The show was called, appropriately, *The Chocolate Kiddies*, set to music by Duke Ellington. From the moment it began, I was fascinated: I never imagined that Josephine Baker would be so beautiful, the most beautiful woman I had ever seen. In person, she surpassed all of Heinrich's descriptions. Wrapped up in a skirt made of bananas, she danced feverishly, shaking her small breasts with their wine-colored nipples. Baker did have a somewhat savage appeal, but at the same time she was a subtle incarnation of pure movement: not a single part of her body could resist the rhythms of the drums.

"Enjoy it," Heini whispered in my ear. "You'll never find anything like it in Leipzig."

I wasn't in the mood for chatting with him; I was too excited, too focused on Josephine Baker's slick hair and lustrous skin, covered in perspiration. Beside me, the girls seemed hypnotized.

When it was over, the audience applauded wildly. One could hear shouts and see people moving around frantically, as if they had just witnessed a murder. When Baker reemerged to take her bow, the expression on her face was not a happy one. She had simply been doing her job. I, however, was dazzled. I suppose we all were, because Natalia then proposed that we try another club. After a brief discussion, we decided on Forget-Me-Not. Marianne, who was already a bit tipsy, wanted to see the women dressed up as men. On the way there, she waited for Heini and Natalia to walk ahead of us so she could kiss me on the lips and tell me she was crazy about me. Proudly, I slipped my arm around her waist.

Forget-Me-Not was something of a disappointment, though some of the tables were occupied by stocky young women with slicked-back hair, dressed in black smoking jackets and white bow ties. The other women there, those who dressed normally, clearly didn't use brassieres or corsets.

"Do you like this?" Marianne asked me.

"I guess so."

"And me?"

"Yes, very much." I took her face in my hands and kissed her, long and deep.

We didn't exchange another word for the remainder of the evening. All we did was drink, kiss, and fondle each other under the table. I did my best to maneuver her body on top of mine, to block out Heini and Natalia.

I returned to Leipzig with an odd feeling inside of me, as if my experience in Berlin had been nothing more than a dream. I returned to my old routine profoundly uninspired; everything seemed gray, predictable, planned. Without much enthusiasm I attempted to go back to my classes and my studies of the continuum hypothesis.

One day I received a letter from Berlin. It was from Marianne:

> *Dear Gustav: Heini has told me that your father won't be in Munich for the Christmas holiday, and that you don't feel it's worth it to go home, that you will be spending a sad holiday season in Leipzig. Coincidentally, I am in a similar situation: my mother has gone to America to visit her brother, and I will be alone in Berlin. If you're interested, I thought perhaps we could spend the vacation together and ring in 1927. If your plans don't change and the idea appeals to you, please let me know. Marianne.*

I considered the proposal for a few moments. I was behind in my work, I had to prepare for exams, and Huttenlocher had me working night and day. So I did the obvious: I wrote to Marianne and told her I would be delighted to see her. I even knew of a small village halfway between Berlin and Leipzig where we might meet. Perhaps from there we could go skiing. She said yes immediately.

How could I have known that so much of my future would hinge upon that seemingly insignificant decision to write or not to write a letter? Once we were alone together I discovered that Marianne was far more intelligent and clever than I had originally thought. In addition to being warm and affectionate, she possessed the extraordinary talent of knowing how to listen. Not only was she interested in my mathematical pursuits—something I found quite incredible in a woman—but she asked me to tell her more about Cantor. She was curious about him simply because he was important to me.

"He was a fascinating subject. Someone who went looking for God through the study of mathematics," I said, my eyes glued to her breasts.

We were in a little cabin, and the log fire crackled away, sounding like a tiny army of elves marching through the room.

"And did he find him?"

"I couldn't tell you," I said, kissing her. "He had many enemies who made his life hell. They thought he was mad."

"And was he, really?"

"Well, he was a man with a very fragile emotional makeup. He spent quite a bit of time in hospitals and sanitariums to treat his various anxieties."

"Poor devil! What a terrible existence!"

"It was only just before his death that the new generation of mathematicians finally began to appreciate him." I felt a bit as if we were reading from a script, but even that couldn't dampen the excitement of discussing mathematics with a naked woman. "He began to receive all sorts of medals and diplomas, but time ran out. In the end, he did become famous, but it was too late for him. Astounded by his baffling discoveries, and suffocated by the envy of his detractors, Cantor died in an insane asylum in Halle on June 6, 1918, a few months before the end of the war."

I could hardly believe what was happening; this was a paradise that I had thought was unattainable. By the end of that holiday, I realized I was madly in love with Marianne. I couldn't bear to be separated from her for very long; I craved her scent, her understanding, her tenderness. Just as I had said to her one drunken evening in Berlin, something told me that I could spend my life with her. And I was right. On October 30, 1928, Marianne Sieber became my wife. Two months earlier, on August 7, Heinrich had exchanged vows of eternal devotion with Natalia Webern. In those days, happiness seemed so simple, like a fairy tale or a solution to an algebraic equation.

DISQUISITION V: *The Search for the Absolute*

From 1928 to 1932, innumerable events transformed the Weimar republic: Kurt Weill and Bertolt Brecht unveiled their *Threepenny Opera;* the philosopher Rudolf Carnap published *The Logical Structure of the World*; and Marlene Dietrich was catapulted into stardom, just as Heini had predicted, by her performance in *The Blue Angel.* The *Graf Zeppelin* circumnavigated the globe and Alfred Döblin published *Berlin Alexanderplatz.* The Munich authorities prohibited Josephine Baker from performing in the city's theaters, and Adolf Hitler and his Nazi party received broad support in the 1930 Reichstag elections. Gödel concocted his famous theorem; Hindenburg was elected president of the republic in 1932 and finally, in that same year, 230 Nazi ministers took control of the Reichstag, thus fulfilling Hitler's dream.

This brief enumeration, of course, could never come close to describing the sudden anxiety, fear, and rage that spread through Germany. Why, then, have I chosen to discuss this era without pausing to describe it in detail, to wrestle with its contradictions, and to explain the factors which conspired to bring the Nazi regime to power? I am slightly embarrassed by my response: because those four years represent the most tranquil period of my entire life. Sometimes, when I think back, those years seem to have passed in a kind of vacuum. One by one, as I recall each day, I blush at the realization that my mind failed to register even one significant event of that era. For four years— four years!—all I find are little, everyday details, fragmented chapters of married life, a tableaux of social engagements, nights of blazing passion, and peaceful vacations in the Alps. It was a time in which the world was about to change forever—quantum physics was changing our perceptions of reality; Europe was preparing to combat fascism; art, music, and literature were reaching dizzying heights of grandeur—but my greatest concerns were kissing my wife's tender belly, completing my tasks in the mathematics department at the university, and preparing for my future *Habilitationsschrift.* Nothing worth mentioning here. Much as I tried, I couldn't solve the puzzle of the continuum, but I did discover other problems, mostly in the field of physics, which I found satisfying and which impressed my advisers.

Of course, I should mention Marianne. After the initial revelation, I learned to love her, deeply and without reservations. Why do I say it this way? In that early phase of electrifying passion, we would make love all day, every day, and could scarcely wait to be alone with one another. Inevitably, we soon fell into a routine that wasn't particularly bad—as long as we didn't confuse things by comparing it with our previous ardor. We intended to be together forever, and we knew that we couldn't go on using sex as the foundation of our shared life. If we continued that way, our fire and passion would eventually consume us, leaving us both embittered. So instead, we opted for a perverse kind of moderation: We would let our mutual desire grow slowly, for days at a time. The idea, of course, was to heighten the pleasure on those special nights when we finally did consummate our passion.

Marianne's face was angular; I would almost call it feline if it wasn't for the fact that cats tend to be associated with alertness and arrogance, qualities that Marianne most definitely lacked. On the contrary: She possessed a subtle tenderness, especially in bed. It was almost as if her excessive gaiety in front of others was a wall that hid a deep, inner shyness. And she was so aware of her introverted nature that she did everything possible to go to the opposite extreme. All the daring adventures we undertook in those days were purely her initiative. She always felt the need to exceed her own limitations, to prove herself somehow. We frequently visited Berlin, the city where we first met, sometimes with Heini and Natalia and other times alone, and there we would continue to explore that dark and tortured nocturnal underworld that we had barely penetrated. The discovery of decadent cabarets and new perversions seemed to excite Marianne even more than it excited me, if possible.

It was also the golden age of our friendship with Heini and Natalia. The four of us shared the same anxieties, dreams, dilemmas. Even our weddings occurred almost simultaneously, more evidence of that desire we had to share everything. Natalia and Marianne were just as close as Heini and I had been. Born and raised in Hamburg, as children they had sealed a pact of friendship, in which they swore never to part, no matter what. By marrying us, they had sealed that agreement and Heini and I were all too happy to accommodate their wishes, and the four of us saw each other often. Our evenings with them were unforgettable. Our feelings were so strong and ran so deep that to call us a family would hardly be an exaggeration but rather a simple way to describe the bond that held us together.

Heinrich's studies were progressing better than ever—at times I envied him—and it seemed certain that when he finished up his studies in Berlin he would be accepted into the doctoral program at Freiburg, supervised by Martin Heidegger, the rector of the university. The future couldn't have been brighter. And that was how life was when we reached 1933, that crucial year in which all our plans changed so dramatically. The city that had seen us grow up also changed, though we didn't realize it at the time.

In the previous year's elections, Hitler's party obtained close to forty percent of the popular vote. After a series of confrontations erupted in Berlin between the communists and the Nazis, Hitler saw to it that Field Marshal Paul von Hindenburg, president of the Reich, named him chancellor on January 30, 1933. Though his cabinet was composed almost entirely of the opposition—only two other Nazis, Wilhelm Frick and Hermann Goering, were ministers in his government—it was one of his most surprising triumphs, and marked the beginning of his ascent to power.

Barely a month after Von Hindenburg's appointment, an unexpected event helped accelerate the victory of the Nazis. For no apparent reason, the Reichstag was set on fire. The following day, Hitler signed an emergency decree granting him extensive powers, in an effort to control the chaos provoked by the communists: "Articles 114–118, 123–124, and 153 of the Constitution of the German Reich are to be suspended temporarily. Therefore, the limitation of personal liberties, such as the right to free expression of opinion—including the freedoms of the press, of organization, and of association—as well as the surveillance of correspondence, telegrams, and telephone communication; the forcible entry into private residences; and the confiscation and restriction of personal property are hereby extended beyond the limits that have previously been placed upon them by the law."

From amid the flames, the police extracted a tall, gawky man who had been shouting: "I object! I object!" His long face, swollen and black from soot, looked like that of a lunatic. Later on he would be identified as Marinus Van der Lubbe, a young Dutchman and communist sympathizer. From the moment of his arrest until the day of his trial he was unable to explain exactly why he had caused such a tragedy, and through it all he claimed to have been acting of his own accord. The same night of Van der Lubbe's arrest, the communist deputy Ernst Torgler was also arrested as his possible accomplice. And ten days later, they were joined in prison by the directors of the International Communist party, Gyorgy Dimitrov, Simon Popov, and Vassily Tanev. The Führer was at his height.

I was in Leipzig on September 20, 1933, when the official trial against Van der Lubbe, Torgler, Dimitrov, Popov, and Tanev began. The newspapers wrote of nothing else. The proceedings stretched out over several weeks, long sessions punctuated only by the occasional presence of Goering or Goebbels, and Dimitrov's fiery, melodramatic tirades. After a few weeks, the verdict arrived, and it shocked everyone. The four communist leaders were exonerated; only Van der Lubbe was found guilty, and he was executed shortly thereafter.

I paid little attention to the case, as I was in the middle of preparing for an endless series of tests, papers, and applications to present to the doctoral studies program at the University of Berlin. In January of 1934 I received notice of my acceptance into the mathematics department. It was marvelous: After all the recent upheaval in our lives, the four of us would finally be reunited, as two months earlier Heinrich and Natalia had returned to the capital of the Reich.

From the moment I arrived, I could see that Berlin was not the same city that had so seduced us a few years back. The recklessness and the euphoria had all but disappeared, replaced by an omnipresent sense of resignation—on the Alexanderplatz, in the box seats at the opera, at the university and the Kaiser Wilhelm Institutes, at the Academy of Sciences of Prussia, on the Kudamm. Berlin's transformation was astonishing. As per our usual nocturnal habits of hopping from cabaret to cabaret, one evening Heini, Natalia, Marianne, and I visited the Tanzfest. It was the nightclub of the moment, the popular spot among foreign diplomats and tourists. The atmosphere was as decadent—if not more so—as it had been during the Weimar period, but the effect, somehow, was the very opposite of the carefree frivolity of the old days. The naked women and cross-dressers were gone, and in their place were boys dressed up as skeletons—in retrospect a crude parody of Himmler's *Totenkopfverbände,* the death squads that would later guard the concentration camps. Together, they would sing, *"Berlin, dein Tänzer ist der Tod,"* a refrain from the most popular song at that time, the macabre foxtrot called *"Totentanz,"* the Dance of Death.

Nevertheless, to me all these changes seemed minor, unrelated to our lives. The more conservative sectors of German society had always had a predilection toward nationalism and anti-Semitism, and of course I was aware that the Nazis were encouraging these tendencies. But like everyone else, I assumed these were temporary measures simply intended to boost Hitler's prestige. Before long, those annoyances would be a thing of the past, we thought.

It wasn't until the spring of 1934 that I realized how mistaken we were, and for me it went beyond what was going on in the world beyond our set. Much worse than the Röhm murder or the Enabling Act, which granted unlimited authority to the Führer. It was even worse than the boycott against the Jewish merchants or the Civil Service Reform Law, which eliminated all non-Aryans from government posts.

Marianne and I were at Heini and Natalia's house one evening. For a few hours we had been trying to bang out an audible version of Beethoven's "Archduke" Trio. I don't know if I mentioned this before, but Heini played violin, Natalia, the piano, and I played cello. Marianne was our only audience, and it was her enthusiastic applause that allowed us to believe that we weren't nearly as dismal as we actually were. Anyway, it was one of the many nights the four of us spent together. When we finished, Natalia went into the kitchen to prepare dinner as the rest of us settled back into our seats in the living room, filled with that peaceful sensation that comes only from music. Then suddenly, without any advance warning—as if he were talking about the weather or a distant relative who was suffering from some or other illness—Heinrich announced that he had decided to join the Wehrmacht.

At first I thought I hadn't heard correctly, but the solemn, firm look on Heini's face told me I had. The blood rushed to my temples. I was horrified. I couldn't comprehend it.

"What?"

"I've decided to join the Wehrmacht," he repeated in a neutral voice.

"Are you telling me that a civilized man like you—a philosopher, yet—wants to become a soldier? Of a Nazi-controlled army? I don't believe you."

Marianne tried to calm me down, and Natalia came back into the room, to stand alongside her husband. It was clear to me now that the objective of the evening had been to tell me the news.

"My God, Heinrich, why?" I pressed.

"You can't understand, Gustav. This is the most philosophical decision I have ever made."

"You can't be serious! This is madness. Hitler is deranged, all he wants is war. Do you want to go to the front? Is that it? Do you want a bullet through your skull?" I felt trapped in some kind of terrible nightmare.

"I told you already," he said, implacable. "After much reflection on the issue, I've realized what I have to do."

I couldn't take my eyes off Natalia, but she could only look down at the floor as she held on to Heinrich's arm. It was a horrifying scene.

"This isn't possible," I continued desperately. "You can't change your mind like that from one day to the next—not you. Tell me the truth: You're doing it to hold on to your privileges, right?"

"You insult me." I recognized neither the voice nor the gesture; this was another man, not the friend with whom I had shared my entire childhood. "I am an honest man, Gustav. How many times do I have to repeat it? This is an act of intellectual integrity."

"Who put these ideas in your head, Heini? Was it that idiot Schmitt? He's one of the party's 'old fighters,' isn't he? You tell me, Natalia, please." She still couldn't look me in the eye.

"I'm his wife," she said, unwavering, as if coached on how to endure her martyrdom. "If Heinrich says it's for the best, I believe him."

I wanted to strike him. I wondered if the devil hadn't suddenly possessed him. We had never discussed the topic before, but I had always simply assumed that he felt as I did. How could he betray me—how could he betray *us*—like that? We were brothers—more than brothers. I couldn't believe it.

"I think it's best if we leave," Marianne said. "Maybe another time, when both of you have calmed down a bit, you can discuss it rationally."

"We don't have anything left to talk about!" I shouted.

Marianne and I gathered our things and prepared to leave. I was afraid I would explode from the rage I felt.

"Gustav, for the love of God," Natalia implored, calling after me.

"May God forgive you" was all I said.

THE URANIUM CIRCLE

"Klingsor."

Francis P. Bacon read the word again and again from a mimeographed page of one of the Nuremberg trial transcripts. But it refused to reveal its hidden meaning. He had to be honest with himself: He hadn't the foggiest notion of what he was looking for, nor did he have any idea of how he would go about finding it, whatever it was. In spite of his determination to tackle his assignment, and despite the experience he had gained in the Alsos mission, he had no idea where to begin. In theory, he was the American military's scientific expert, so he had no one to turn to for guidance as he entered this labyrinth. More than a scientific problem, it seemed like an enigma laid out specifically to bewilder him. How many archives would he have to search through? How many people would he have to track down and interrogate? Moreover, after all was said and done, his efforts might turn out to be pointless: In all likelihood he was dealing with an incidental issue that could easily turn out to be one of the countless projects initiated but never completed by the Nazi bureaucracy.

Bacon left his room at the Grand Hotel and walked toward the Allied Forces' Nuremberg headquarters. At General Watson's office he could send a cable to the army's information office in Washington to see if they had any information on Klingsor. It was a thankless task: Ever since the dissolution of the OSS on November 20, 1945, the U.S. intelligence operations had gone to pieces. And despite the fact that J. Edgar Hoover, the all-powerful director of the FBI, was adamantly opposed to the idea, rumor had it that President Truman was ready to approve the creation of the CIA. Nevertheless, toward the end of 1946 nothing was official, and so veteran officers of the OSS like Bacon had to report either to military intelligence, the High Command of the Armed Forces in Europe, or the State Department. Amid all this chaos, the identity of Klingsor could hardly be expected to be of much importance to anyone.

Where should he begin? Bacon asked himself this again as he walked toward the command center. He reread the transcript of Wolfram von Sievers's testimony: "Before any funds could be released, each project had to be approved by Hitler's scientific adviser. I never did find out the identity of this person, but according to rumor, it was a well-known figure. A man who enjoyed a prominent position in the scientific community, and who operated under the code name Klingsor." Should he try to obtain another statement from Von Sievers? Perhaps he would do so later on, although in his gut he knew it wouldn't lead to much. After making that initial statement, Von Sievers recanted over and over again. In fact, he claimed to have never uttered the name at all.

Bacon stopped for a few minutes to think, realizing that sometimes, the greatest ideas of all are in fact the simplest, the most obvious ones. Rather than cabling Washington, where he would be forced to deal with some unhelpful official who would never be able to address his query, he decided he would be better off contacting Samuel I. Goudsmit, his supervisor during the war and one of the best-informed men on the topic of scientific research in Nazi Germany.

Until the end of 1945, Bacon had been a member of the Alsos mission, the scientific division that fell under Goudsmit's command. During the 1920s, Goudsmit had belonged to a group of prominent young physicists focused on the burgeoning field of quantum physics, and his efforts contributed significantly to the discovery of electron spin. After obtaining his doctorate under the tutelage of Paul Ehrenfest, Goudsmit, a Dutch Jew, was offered a teaching position at the University of Michigan. Unfortunately, his parents couldn't go with him, and were forced to remain in The Hague after the war began. When the Nazis invaded Holland, Goudsmit tried everything possible to get them to America, and after an endless battle of paperwork and negotiating, he secured the necessary papers, but by then it was too late. In 1943, during one of the massive deportations of the Jewish community, his parents were arrested and sent to Auschwitz.

Desperate, Goudsmit appealed to the physicist Dirk Coster, who had helped save Lise Meitner's life in 1938, in the hope that Coster might be able to enlist Werner Heisenberg's aid. He did, and Heisenberg responded with a letter—intended, of course, for the Nazi authorities—which made specific mention of the Goudsmit family and the great hospitality they had shown German physicists who had visited Holland in the past. This assistance, sadly, didn't help much: Five days after Heisenberg sent off the letter, Goudsmit's parents died in the gas chambers at Auschwitz, the very day Goudsmit's father turned seventy. Goudsmit never forgave Heisenberg for not doing more to save them.

Thanks to the influence of John von Neumann, who had begun to travel to London on a regular basis in 1943, Bacon arrived in London to join the group of American scientists hired to study the German atomic project. At the end of 1943, Bacon was formally hired by the newly formed scientific branch of the Alsos mission, under the OSS's command. Goudsmit had been appointed director of this section, thanks to his intimate understanding of nuclear physics and European languages, as well as his lack of knowledge regarding the Manhattan Project, which would work in his favor if he were to be captured by the Nazis.

The Alsos mission disembarked at Normandy just after D Day. Its main objective was to capture the ten scientists involved in the German atomic project: Walter Gerlach, Kurt Diebner, Erich Bagge, Otto Hahn, Paul Harteck, Horst Korsching, Max von Laue, Carl Friedrich von Weizsäcker, Karl Wirtz, and, of course, Werner Heisenberg.

For several days, Goudsmit and Bacon traveled through the devastated northern regions of France and Belgium, until finally reaching Holland. Goudsmit had insisted upon going straight to The Hague, where he and Bacon visited the remains of what had once been his house. Tears of rage, impotence, and guilt rolled down the physicist's cheeks. Bacon hardly knew what to say to console him. The sight of that tall, robust, slightly cross-eyed man sobbing amid the ruins of his home, clutched by the heartbreaking memory of his parents' brutal death, was one of so many images that embodied the horror of war, and it would be etched permanently in Bacon's mind and soul. How could you not despise the enemy? How could you not feel somehow superior to the Nazis? How could you not want revenge?

After The Hague, they set off for Paris, where Alsos had its base of operations. Here its members dedicated themselves to gathering information in the laboratories of Frédéric Joliot-Curie, previously used by the Nazis during their occupation of the city. Later they went on to Strasbourg, where a German-style university had been established, and where Carl Friedrich von Weizsäcker, one of Heisenberg's close allies, had once been director of the physics institute. In February of 1945, Goudsmit, Bacon, and Colonel Pash, the mission's military commander, crossed the Rhine alongside the Allied troops. By the end of March they had reached the ancient university town of Heidelberg, where they detained the physicists Hans Bothe and Walter Genter. There, they established their southern base of operations.

Goudsmit and the other members of the Alsos mission knew that the Nazi nuclear science program had started out in Berlin, but was later transferred to a safer location as the Allied bombing intensified. A team led by Diebner had remained in Stadtilm, but the lion's share of the Nazi operation had moved to Hechingen, with Heisenberg at the helm. By subjecting Bothe and Genter to a series of exhaustive interrogations, Goudsmit and Bacon learned the role that each German physicist had played in the Nazis' nuclear program, as well as the specific places where their investigations had been carried out. They also confirmed one of the most pressing suspicions they had harbored since the beginning of the war: It was practically certain that the atomic bomb was not among Hitler's alleged secret arsenal of weapons.

General Leslie R. Groves, director of the American bomb program, a bit calmer now thanks to this latest bit of news, reassessed the priorities of the Alsos mission from his post in Washington. Given that so many German scientists were now living in areas that had fallen under the control of French and Russian forces at the end of the war, Groves decided that they had to be captured as soon as possible. Goudsmit was more excited than ever. Bacon, on the other hand, had mixed feelings about the change of assignment: He had always envisioned himself as a researcher, but the current developments had turned him into more of a spy than a scientist. Instead of hunting for the results of a particular theory, he was being asked to hunt down his fellow scientists, who, in the end, didn't stop being scientists just because they were working for the enemy.

"The entire area to the south of Stuttgart will be controlled by the French," explained Colonel Landsdale, the military attaché to the mission. "Our job, then, is to catch those physicists and confiscate the material they've used before the frogs do. If that's not possible, then we'll have to destroy everything."

In Washington the mood escalated to such a degree that there was even talk of invading southern Germany, but the advancing French army, recently reoutfitted and reorganized, was moving far too quickly. Finally it was decided that Colonel Pash would lead an assault brigade and head straight for Haigerloch, where the Germans had built an atomic battery, and then Hechingen. Goudsmit did not participate in this particular mission—it was considered far too dangerous for him—but Bacon joined Colonel Pash's team.

For the first time in his life, Bacon was about to come face-to-face with the reality of war. The agony of his day-to-day problems disappeared entirely; he wouldn't have time now to mull over his life decisions or to carefully map out the potential consequences of his actions. He was now a soldier just like any other, whose job was to carry out the orders of his superiors, and to trust his own intuition when it came time to face the enemy. Up until then, Bacon was accustomed to the notion of fighting a war of ideas, far from the front. But it was one thing to gather information in cities already controlled by the Allied forces, and quite another to make his way through the Black Forest, with the assignment of capturing Heisenberg and his team of scientists. Bacon had always believed that underneath it all he wasn't a coward, but now he truly understood the meaning of fear. It wasn't a feeling or a state of mind, but rather a growing fever that seemed to take physical control over his body—after all, the most dangerous circumstances he had ever known were the bombings that he had lived through in London.

"I don't know if this is some kind of physical law, Lieutenant," Pash said to him on one occasion, "but when a man is struck by fear, the worst thing he can do is remain still. Because it just gets worse, that's the bad part. You have to fight it the minute it hits you. At the first attack, you have to conquer it, because if you don't, it'll get the best of you—and all of us."

On Saint George's day, April 23, scarcely an hour before the French troops advanced toward the same target, the Alsos command reached Haigerloch under the able leadership of Colonel Pash. There, with almost no complications, they proceeded to arrest Karl Wirtz, Erich Bagge, Carl Friedrich von Weizsäcker, and Max von Laue, though Von Laue, it turned out, had had nothing to do with the German atomic program. After dismantling the atomic stockpile, Pash and Bacon went straight to the nearby town of Taifingen, where they captured Otto Hahn, the man who discovered atomic fission. At this point, the scientists—as well as what remained of their laboratories—were shipped off to Heidelberg.

But they still hadn't completed the most sensitive part of the entire mission. Three of the most important German scientists were still at large: Diebner and Gerlach in Munich, and Heisenberg, who had gone off to fetch his family 250 kilometers away in Urfeld soon after Pash and Bacon arrived in Hechingen. The Alsos mission would have to divide its forces. While one squadron set out for Munich on the trail of Diebner and Gerlach, the other group, led by Pash, headed for Urfeld. Bacon found himself in the latter group. The first part of the mission was successfully completed on April 30, the same day that Hitler committed suicide in Berlin.

"This is the most important assignment we have ever received," said Pash to his men.

Bacon repeated this sentence over and over again like a prayer, as the ten men (including Pash), traveling in a caravan of four vehicles, arrived at the small settlement of Kochel in Bavaria on the first of May. Urfeld was just on the other side of a small hill, the Kesselberg, but it was part of a zone that had yet to be reached by the Allied forces, so it was entirely possible that they would encounter stragglers from the German army, or a still-active Waffen-SS.

Upon reaching the Kesselberg, the men realized that the small bridge that led to Urfeld had been destroyed during the bombings, which meant the only way to reach the town was by foot, and Pash led his troops over a hill. In addition to the brisk wind that penetrated his uniform, Bacon felt a suspicious sense of calm that kept him in a constant, heightened state of awareness. Adrenaline rushed into his brain and his muscles, impeding his faculties for reasoning, which at that moment was probably something of an advantage. The bleached-white rocks seemed a fitting metaphor for his state of mind: He was exhausted but at the same time determined to continue. The group, after skirting a particularly rocky promontory, finally caught their first glimpse of the houses in Urfeld. It was tiny and harmless, a typically folkloric German village. Fatigued and ravenous, Pash's ten men quickly began their descent down the hill. Suddenly, Bacon heard a violent noise that ripped through the serene winter landscape. Bullets. Real bullets. He threw himself on the ground and prepared to fire. What was the probability that the enemy would get him? And worse, what was the probability that he would be capable of killing someone? True, the army had put him through an accelerated training course before he embarked for London, but this would be his first time firing against a human target. He trembled. It wouldn't be long before he would become an entirely different person.

In the middle of this scuffle, Bacon realized that if he wanted to come out alive, he would have to stop thinking so much. Neither science nor the calculation of probability meant anything now: Theory was garbage whose only use was to men who, sitting quietly at their desks, dedicated themselves to analyzing the actions of other people without ever facing a real battle themselves. Convinced that this was the only way to resolve the problem, Bacon fired again and again, trying to use his reflexes as his guide, until he was jolted by a prolonged silence that filled the cold Bavarian air. It had all happened far too quickly. From far off he could hear the stern voices of Colonel Pash, of one of his fellow officers, and then he finally emerged from the thick underbrush where he had sought refuge. He took a few steps forward. In the distance, he could see the bloody bodies of two German soldiers. Indifferent to such petty disputes, a splendid twilight announced the arrival of the sun's daily descent.

Pash moved closer to see if they were still breathing. Negative. Seconds later, Bacon appeared at his side. This was the first time he had come face-to-face with a cadaver since the death of his father so many years before. A wave of nausea came over him, threatening to empty his stomach, but he controlled himself, conscious of the stoic presence of his commanding officer.

"All right, Lieutenant." Pash seemed to read his thoughts. "There's no time to lose. We only have a little light left."

They stepped over the bodies as if they were a couple of dead rats on a highway. The silence had suddenly become unpleasant, unbearable.

"And the others, sir?" Bacon asked.

"They must have gotten away, but stay on your guard."

How could he know if one of his bullets had brought one of those soldiers to his death? Did it matter, really? So strong was the hatred he felt for himself right then that he had no other choice but to transfer that hatred to his victims. He struggled to recall Goudsmit's weeping face in front of his house that day in The Hague. Those Germans deserved it. Of course they did.

The ten men in Pash's troop quickly dispersed to their assigned locations in the village. Bacon reminded the colonel that Heisenberg's home had to be a few kilometers away, on the banks of the river.

"Everything in due time," Pash responded. And he began to inspect the town's public buildings in search of snipers.

In a matter of moments, two German officials, unarmed, presented themselves to Pash. Where had they come from? Bacon tried to translate their responses.

"It's a whole battalion," he explained. "Not far from here. And they want to surrender."

Pash didn't flinch.

"Tell them to come right here, tomorrow morning, Lieutenant."

"But, Colonel . . ."

"Obey my command."

Bacon quickly translated and then let the two officers go.

"What else could I do?" explained Pash. "Tell them that we're only ten men, when they might very well be a hundred? I couldn't let them think we were vulnerable, Lieutenant."

For the first time, Bacon felt admiration for that brutish, sweaty man who, from what little he could see, always seemed to get his way.

"Now let's go for that other sonofabitch," Pash announced. It hurt Bacon to hear the colonel speak that way about his childhood idol, the winner of the Nobel Prize.

All through the night, Pash's outfit worked to rebuild the bridge that connected the town to the main highway. At 6 A.M., the combat unit entered Urfeld, reinforced a few hours later by an infantry battalion stationed near Kochel. When they finally arrived at Heisenberg's property the next morning, they found the physicist sitting in a chair, staring out at the stagnant tranquillity of the lake. His face revealed no anger, no resentment; nothing more than an implacable serenity, which only made Bacon more uneasy. He was tall and thin, with facial features that seemed almost childlike. His blond hair, so classically German, only enhanced his disturbingly innocent semblance. Heisenberg possessed the quiet dignity of the hero who realizes he has met defeat. Bacon would always remember that adolescent countenance, impassive and serene, and those clear blue eyes that seemed like reflections in miniature of the lake that stretched out before him.

"Would you like to come in, gentlemen?" Heisenberg asked as Pash and Bacon approached him.

During this encounter, Heisenberg's wife, Elisabeth, remained inside the house with their six small children. Rail-thin, her face was visibly marked by fear and the shortage of food, and her children looked no better. After a minimal display of courtesy, Pash informed Heisenberg that he was under arrest, on orders of the United States Armed Forces. The physicist listened, his face registering a certain surprise—he hadn't expected to be taken into custody so soon, having assumed that the Allies would first attempt to take control of the area. But he said nothing.

The sound of gunshots rang out in the distance. Pash guessed that it was the snipers or the soldiers from the battalion that had surrendered the day before. There wasn't time to be civilized: He asked Heisenberg to quickly gather his personal belongings and gestured to Bacon to lead the prisoner to one of the armored vehicles waiting outside. Their orders were to take no risks whatsoever and to deliver Heisenberg directly to Kochel, while his family would remain at their home in Urfeld.

Bacon would never again be alone with Heisenberg after the few hours they spent together traveling in the armored car, but it was all he needed to realize who he was and what he thought about the events of the past few years. For the entire trip Bacon sat facing Heisenberg, waiting for the right moment to say something, but the right words never came. How could he explain to Heisenberg that he, too, was a physicist, that he had followed Heisenberg's career for years and years, and that he held his work in the highest esteem? Under the circumstances, it seemed that such a comment would only seem impertinent. He and his detachment had just marched through the devastated hills of Bavaria, Heisenberg's homeland, and Bacon wanted to talk of science! Ashamed, Bacon tried not to meet his gaze, not to see himself reflected in the blue of Heisenberg's eyes. They went on that way for several minutes, until finally Heisenberg ventured to talk.

"Did you have much trouble finding me?" he asked in English, in a tremulous, mellifluous voice in which Bacon couldn't help but detect a certain note of pride.

"Yes, actually, it was quite difficult," Bacon responded in German.

"Ah!" Heisenberg was surprised, though he resisted any show of emotion. "Did you study German in the army?"

The car sputtered a bit.

"No, sir. At Princeton University."

"Princeton? What was your degree?" asked Heisenberg.

Bacon hardly wanted to tell him the truth.

"Economics." It was the first thing that came to mind.

After a few minutes, Heisenberg continued talking.

"It's a lovely city, Princeton. You know, I've been there a few times. Scientific conferences, that sort of thing."

"When was the last time you were in the United States?"

"Nineteen thirty-nine, just before the war began." He stopped himself then, as if reflecting upon all that had happened since. "That was only six years ago, yet it seems like an eternity, doesn't it? Several times I was tempted to live in your country, did you know that?"

Bacon didn't mean to be rude, but he just couldn't think of anything to say. After mulling it over for a moment or two, he summoned up the courage to ask:

"Why didn't you?"

Heisenberg fell silent once again. He stroked his hair and interlaced his smooth, white, feminine fingers, forming a small oval with his hands.

"You know, one can drink beer anywhere in the world," he explained. "One can find good beer, bad beer, dark beer, beer that tastes like malt, or even pepper-flavored beer. Hundreds of different varieties. Nevertheless, one can't help but prefer the beer that's brewed in Bavaria. And even if the quality of Bavarian beer starts to decline—if it gets worse, say, than Belgian or Dutch beer—the best thing to do is stay in Bavaria and try to make it better. And if politicians do things to hurt the industry, one should fight them and do whatever it takes to make every day better. Do you see what I mean?"

"I think so," mused Bacon.

The truth was, he didn't. He could understand that a man could be a nationalist, and love his homeland, and feel so innately bound to his country that he wouldn't abandon it even in the worst of circumstances, but he could not accept someone who would voluntarily work for a government of criminals without ever raising his voice in protest. Bacon could not accept

someone who would use his science and knowledge in the service of evil—
yes, he repeated to himself: *evil*—without ever questioning the morality of
his actions. True, he did admire Heisenberg, but he also felt a deep repulsion
for the obtuse tranquillity that allowed him to remain silent in the face of a
man like Hitler. The memory of Goudsmit's parents was too powerful for
Bacon to feel any kind of sympathy for Heisenberg.

Silence filled the armored car once again. Heisenberg looked down, as if
searching for something—a lost coin, or forgiveness, perhaps. The principle
of uncertainty that he himself had discovered had taken on a new relevance:
Its creator now had no idea as to whether he had served his moral purpose,
or if he was just plain guilty.

The next day, Bacon and Heisenberg arrived at the southern base of
operations of the Alsos mission in Heidelberg. The city and its ancient university, one of the most prestigious in the world, seemed sinister and
macabre. The reflection of the Neckar irritated Bacon, as did the celebrated
castle that towered above one of the hills dominating the cityscape. Further
beyond, the forests cast a threatening, somber shadow upon the area. For
the first time it occurred to Bacon that, in reality, the physical world was a
neutral entity, its grace or lack thereof determined by the emotions felt by
its beholder.

Back at the base, Goudsmit was busy processing the recent arrivals.
Heisenberg greeted him with a cold, stiff salute, an imperturbable gesture
that made him seem proud and unrepentant. Goudsmit turned to Bacon
and thanked him for his work, and then ushered Heisenberg inside, where
he spent the next several hours interrogating him. The last time they had
seen one another had been at the University of Michigan, in Ann Arbor, on
Heisenberg's last visit before war broke out. But the thing that separated the
two men now went far deeper than time—which is only an empty construct
of the mind, anyway. The schism was far more profound than that, a moral
abyss that lay between victim and executioner, accuser and accused. On one
side there stood a man who felt betrayed by his friend, and on the other side
stood his friend who, in all likelihood, knew he had been a traitor. Bacon
was not present during the interrogation, but at the end of the day, over dinner, Goudsmit couldn't help talking about the prisoner.

"I actually invited him to come and work with us in the United States,"
he admitted in a biting tone of voice. Goudsmit had made the offer to
Heisenberg during his Ann Arbor visit. "And do you know what he said,
Lieutenant?"

"No, sir."

"With that superior, German smile, all he said to me was: 'I don't want to go. Germany needs me.'" Goudsmit covered his forehead with his hands and closed his eyes. " 'Germany needs me.' Can you believe that, Lieutenant?"

Shortly afterward, Goudsmit handed over the ten prisoners—Bagge, Diebner, Gerlach, Hahn, Harteck, Korsching, Von Laue, Von Weizsäcker, Wirtz, and Heisenberg—to the United States military authorities. The Alsos mission was over now, and the prisoners were sent on to the Dustbin internment camp, near Versailles.

Bacon had no further contact with the prisoners after that day, but through the Scottish physicist R. V. Jones, a former professor of natural philosophy at Aberdeen University and chief of staff of the Royal Air Force, he learned that the ten men had been transferred to Farm Hall, a country estate belonging to MI6, not far from Godmanchester. There at Farm Hall, where they remained until the year's end, they heard the news, via the British press and the BBC radio, that the first atomic bomb had been dropped over Hiroshima on August 6, 1945. The Americans had beaten the Germans to it. The defeat was far more than military for them. In a letter to Bacon, Goudsmit described the reaction of Walter Gerlach, the head of the German atomic program. Upon hearing the news, Gerlach locked himself in his room and wept all night long. What Bacon didn't know, however, was that R. V. Jones had hidden tiny microphones in the walls of all the dormitories and recorded all the conversations between the ten German physicists during their entire stay in Farm Hall.

In response to Bacon's request for help, Goudsmit told him about something called Operation Epsilon, and sent a portion of the corresponding transcripts to the American military office in Nuremberg. Among these documents were recorded conversations that had taken place at Farm Hall. According to Goudsmit, they might well offer some clues as to the identity of Klingsor.

With an almost imperceptible smile on his lips, Bacon turned toward the satisfying task of transcribing those incomprehensible masses of letters into the words and sentences uttered by Werner Heisenberg and his colleagues. Bacon would have loved to have read more of the transcripts from Farm Hall—who wouldn't have been fascinated by what the physicists said when they heard the news of the Allied victory?—but Goudsmit only sent him the documents that he thought most pertinent to the Klingsor investigation. From those files, Walter Gerlach emerged as a particularly key player, given his position as the last director of the physics department of the *Reichs-*

forschungsrat, the Scientific Research Council of the Third Reich. Kurt Diebner, a member of the Nazi party, also figured prominently, while Heisenberg
and Hahn did not. As Bacon quickly found out, Gerlach and Diebner's
involvement had less to do with the technical details of the work carried out
by the German scientists, and more to do with acting as liaison between the
council and the other secret programs that Hitler had established. Yet after
reading over the transcribed documents for the first time, Bacon couldn't
help feeling a bit disappointed. There wasn't one single reference to Klingsor, Hitler's purported scientific adviser. Far less enthusiastic now, Bacon
nevertheless proceeded with a thorough review of the documents:

*[August 6, 1945. A few hours after the BBC confirmed the nuclear attack on
Hiroshima.]*

HAHN: If the Americans have a uranium bomb, all of you are second-
rate scientists.

WIRTZ: Our problem wasn't technical knowledge, it was the method we
used to carry out our scientific research. German science was ruined
by politics.

GERLACH: We were only following orders. We were subjected to a much
larger plan whose implications extended far beyond what we were
doing.

WIRTZ: Plans, plans . . . But from the beginning we focused our attention
on one single objective, nothing more. . . . Why didn't we achieve it?
That's the only question that matters.

GERLACH: Ours was one among many, many projects. He never
authorized the kind of resources that would have suggested it was a
top priority.

BAGGE: But what else could have possibly been more important?

GERLACH: For him there were certainly other priorities. Crazy schemes
that were never carried out. Larks that meant the rest of us had to
make do without the resources that would have been necessary to
execute even the most minimal, small-scale experiment. . . . The
Reichsforschungsrat put all the money toward crazy, "extra-scientific"
foolishness. . . . The same thing happened in the Ahnenerbe. . . .

[August 10, 1945]

HEISENBERG: Our calculations were accurate. Including the critical mass
that we estimated to be necessary to produce the chain reaction.

DIEBNER: So what went wrong, then?

GERLACH: The decision to produce uranium industrially, in large
   quantities. In the Scientific Research Council we never thought that
   we could have a bomb ready for deployment before the end of the
   war. We kept having to go from one office to the other, from
   Himmler to Speer to Bormann to Goering, to ensure that they would
   continue to support the program. They always had other priorities.
   He never paid us much attention.
DIEBNER: Our final objective was much less ambitious: We had to
   produce a reactor and, hopefully, a self-sustaining chain reaction.
   That was all.
GERLACH: I repeat: He consistently refused to authorize the necessary
   resources, and for that reason we failed. He spent his budget in other
   areas.

The other pages were no better. Complaints, regrets, endless accusations
of one another, a general, vague sense of failure. That was all. Reading
between the lines, the only thing that caught Bacon's attention was Gerlach's
repeated complaint that much of the resources that could have been spent
on the atomic project were instead allocated to other "secret" programs. But
who determined the allocation of those resources? Who was this "he" of
whom Gerlach complained so bitterly? Bacon was growing uncomfortable.
Based on these skimpy references, could he even assume that there *was* a
Klingsor? Or was Klingsor merely a means to justify his investigation, for
which he would assume nonexistent risks and invent his work as he went
along? Wouldn't it be better to quit and simply say that Klingsor was a quantum event, nothing more than an amalgam of many men, one among many,
many executioners?

PARALLEL UNIVERSES

Nuremberg, 2 November 1946
To: Professor John von Neumann
From: Lieutenant Francis P. Bacon

Dear Professor:

I don't know quite where to begin. We have been out of touch for so long that I find myself overflowing with things I'd like to tell you. We are living in an era that has produced more history than we are capable of digesting, as Winston Churchill put it (more or less). The game of war, as you used to call it, is far more boring and merciless (please excuse the platitudes) than either of us could have imagined. In any event, I don't want to bore you with things you surely already know better than I. All I can add is that the only solution to this game seems to be, for better or for worse, not to play at all.

Now I find myself involved in another game, much less dangerous but, perhaps for that very reason, far more perplexing. Who would have thought that I would become a soldier, or rather a detective responsible for hunting down real people, instead of a physicist responsible for hunting down abstractions? To a certain degree, you were the catalyst in this transformation, and for this reason I feel emboldened to call upon you for help. Might I explain the situation without worrying that you will throw away this letter? I hope so.

My problem is that I am already involved in this aforementioned game, but to my dismay, I know neither its name nor its rules, much less the significance of winning it. How is this for a new twist on your leisure-time ruminations? A game in which the participants challenge one another without knowing what the final prize will be. And if it's some kind of punishment, what then? Wouldn't this be an inversion of the logic that has been so carefully developed over the years? Well, maybe I exaggerate. I'm an impatient man, you know that better than anyone. And all I have to go on is a loose end of Ariadne's thread, a maze of unknowns, and I find myself reluctant to forge ahead, what with all the darkness Germany seems mired in. I'm talking about—of course—a secret mission, and presumably I'm not to breathe a word of this to anyone, but I have decided to take that risk in writing to you.

I return, then, to my initial dilemma. Klingsor. Does this word mean anything to you? I still don't know if this amounts to anything more than trickery or if, on the contrary, one of those dossiers might lead me to something of real importance. All I can say is that it supposedly refers to the code name of a German scientist who, according to some, was a very important figure in the Reich. A kind of spy, part of Hitler's fifth column in the German scientific community. Is this just another of the many rumors swirling around Adolf? I doubt it. In any event, military intelligence has placed me in charge of the case and naturally I intend to get to the bottom of it. All right: Now you know that I am about to ask something of you, so I will dispense with the niceties. I need your guidance. Despite my previous work, I simply don't know where to begin. I anxiously await your response.

Princeton, New Jersey, 9 November 1946
To: Lieutenant Francis P. Bacon
From: Professor John von Neumann

My dear Bacon:
It was a great pleasure to receive word from you, specifically because it means you are alive. A reasonable inference, I suppose. I hadn't heard news of you since we last saw one another in London a thousand years ago. What an extraordinary age we find ourselves living in! Why, it's as if time was accelerated just for the benefit of us men of science. Of course, I don't mean to be insensitive: I know the tragedies have been devastating, perhaps more so than at any other time in the history of humanity. But I am convinced that we had no other option. The war had to end. The bad part is that one was barely over when another began: Now it's us against the Russians, and they could turn out to be worse than the Nazis, mark my words. I lived in Hungary under the Reds, and it was hell, my boy. So here we are once again, applying our game theory to win this round against Stalin.

My dear Bacon, I, too, have wanted to tell you about dozens of interesting things that have transpired in the last months of the war, specifically regarding research being carried out in New Mexico. But I am extremely tired these days, and as you might guess, it is expressly forbidden for me to discuss that work with anyone. In that case, I shall answer your question.

Good news, my friend! Luck is on our side. Now, you should know that I have had to move heaven and earth on your behalf, but I have the feeling that it was worth the trouble. I spoke with some friends in Washington and London, and even made contact with a few people close to Patton and Eisenhower. At first I got no response, just as I had suspected. Nothing more than impenetrable silence. I pressed them. "We're sorry, Johnny," they all said, "but we don't have any idea as to who this Klingsor could be." I pressed them again. "We're tired of you, Johnny! You and your Klingsor." But I told myself that I wouldn't stop bothering them until they came up with something—for God's sake, I'm a national security adviser. Every day I would make my calls and every day they would answer my queries with the same silence and the same objections . . . bureaucracy is the same everywhere. A bureaucrat will never answer your question the first time around, that's rule number one. First you must get authorization from his superior, who then has to get it from his superior, and on and on until you get to the secretary of defense, the secretary of state, or the president himself. I told you once, if we wanted to beat the Germans, what we really needed was patience. Anyway, just as I predicted, a door finally opened.

Now, don't get carried away here. This isn't monumental, it's just a little crack in the wall. But it's a start. Follow the path of elementary particles, my friend, because that's what the universe is made of. This is the story: In 1944, a group of German army officials decided to do away with Hitler. Their idea was to assassinate him, stage a coup, and purge the Nazis from the government. In the best of all worlds, this maneuver would enable them to sign a peace agreement—or so they thought. Dreamers! They went ahead with their plan, and in July they placed a bomb in one of Hitler's bunkers. Unfortunately, something went wrong. Hitler emerged unharmed and Himmler and the SS—experts at this sort of thing—thwarted the coup with unprecedented force. Now, this is nothing new, although this particular episode has been practically forgotten by now. The plot involved a general in the German army, the diplomatic corps, and even extended into civilian circles. Himmler ordered the arrest of every last person who had even the remotest connection to the people involved in the coup attempt. He detained them, accused them of conspiracy to overthrow the government, and had them executed. From August to December of 1944, hundreds of people were imprisoned, the majority of them shot or sent to concentration camps.

This is where it gets interesting. Among the detainees, there was a mathematician, a friend of a certain Wehrmacht official, who had participated in the coup attempt. Along with many others, he was accused of high treason and had to appear before a Berlin court, but for some reason *he never received a death sentence. Instead, he was sent to prison and subsequently transferred around to various different locations until he was finally liberated by an Allied squadron a few days before the war ended. There would be nothing noteworthy about this story if it hadn't have been for two coincidences that appear to have worked in our favor. The first is this: During an interrogation, an American official questioned him about the reason for his arrest, and his response was that it was all Klingsor's fault. When the official said that he did not understand, the only thing our man offered was a description of his role in the July 1944 conspiracy. The second coincidence, however, is even more astonishing. I knew him. That's it, dear Bacon. The mathematician we are talking about was a friend of mine from before the war. His name is Gustav Links.*

He was a modest man with an astounding mind. I first met him in Berlin; it was around 1927, when I was still studying with Hilbert at Göttingen. He was almost as young as I was, but he had already created a stir on the mathematics conference circuit. He was obsessed, if I recall correctly, with Cantor's continuum hypothesis. He had earned his degree at the University of Leipzig and then did doctoral work in Berlin. We stayed in touch until about 1936; after that I never heard from him again.

How does that grab you? Luckily, he is still alive and he's still got the finest credentials. He's our man. Where can you find him? Simple: The same place you'll find all the scientists who were lucky enough not to have remained in the Russian-occupied zone. In Göttingen. He won't be hard to find.

I wish you the best of luck in your new game, dear Bacon, and I do hope you will keep me abreast of your progress.

Nuremberg, 28 November 1946
To: Professor Gustav Links
From: Francis P. Bacon

Dear Professor:

My name is Francis P. Bacon, and I am a physics graduate student at Princeton University. I am currently in Germany, on a research assignment for the United States Army, and a mutual friend of ours, Professor John von Neumann, suggested that perhaps you might be able to assist me with something. I would be glad to come to Göttingen to discuss this with you, if you would be willing to meet with me. Thank you in advance for your attention.

Of what use could I possibly be to a physicist who, as he so indiscreetly mentioned, was working for the United States Army? What could he want from me? And moreover, why would Von Neumann assume that I could help him? Was my torture never going to end?

After my liberation in 1945, my chances for a normal life were slim. Germany was in utter ruin and the Allies had carved up and parceled out its remains as per the conferences at Yalta and Teheran. Unlike the physicists who had been working on the atomic project, I was just a simple mathematician. I had worked with Heisenberg on different facets of the program, but my participation was quite marginal, and that was what saved me from the fate that awaited the other members of the *Uranverein:* I was never considered part of the spoils of war, and I never went to Paris or to Farm Hall. Quite the contrary, in fact: Mine seems to have been a far more humble destiny. After confirming my identity and corroborating my opposition to the Nazi regime, the Americans simply let me go. A few months after the war's end, I managed to get transferred to Göttingen. I took what few personal belongings I could carry with me (ever since Marianne's death, material things mattered little to me) and I retreated to that somber university town inside the British-occupied zone.

Compared with the French and American troops (who displayed a rather exaggerated animosity toward the Germans) and the Russians (who only centralized the German scientific investigation to serve their own interests), the British seemed the most compassionate of the Allied forces. Inspired by their antiauthoritarian traditions, they believed that the future peace and stability of Europe could be established if the German territories under their control were granted a relative degree of autonomy. Basing themselves on this notion, they decided to turn Göttingen into Germany's new scientific capital. The only inconvenience, perhaps, was its location: Göttingen was only a few kilometers away from the Soviet zone.

By the time I arrived in Göttingen, I was a broken man. I didn't care about anything. I didn't want anything. I was nothing. The only thing I could think about was the futility of my previous life. Numbers, formulas, theorems, and axioms—they seemed so trivial now, but they had condemned me to living inside a vortex of silent complicity. In 1946, a German scientist was about as important as a fly on a wall. Who cared about such scum when the world was in ruins? What possible service could such an animal offer? Rather than laying bricks, this creature dedicated himself to studying their shape, calculating their measurements, and defining the laws which proved their existence. I was more than useless, I was superfluous, redundant. If literature became useless after Auschwitz, as a certain philosopher said, it is only because any kind of happiness was impossible after Auschwitz. And if poetry was impossible, then where did that leave mathematics? Who could possibly care about Cantor or the continuum hypothesis when millions of human beings had been annihilated? How could I even hold my head up as I walked down the street?

I moved into one of the many ramshackle buildings on the outskirts of the city, where the neighboring apartments were occupied by entire families who piled themselves into cramped, shabby quarters. I didn't know what to do with myself. Otto Hahn had just received the Nobel Prize for his discovery of fission, and near the end of February he and Werner Heisenberg arrived in the city to rebuild the Kaiser Wilhelm Institutes of Chemistry and Physics, respectively. The project, which had been approved by both the British and American governments, conferred a special distinction upon the city, but it did little to alleviate my lethargy. In those days, my spirit was ripped to shreds, and I operated like an automaton, accepting a professorship in mathematics at the university simply because it seemed the easiest and least demanding way for me to earn a living. In any event, I was totally uninterested in spearheading any kind of research projects or participating in any of the usual academic activities.

Meanwhile, the Allies had already begun an accelerated program of de-Nazification that was to affect all public life in Germany. All German citizens had to fill out forms stating whether or not we belonged to any associations or groups affiliated in any way with the Nazi party. Those who did had to appear before the military courts, and anyone discovered to have been a member of the party or any related organization was then barred from the civil service. In Germany, the university professorships had always fallen under the auspices of the central government, which meant that many professors had joined the Nazi party so as not to lose their jobs. As a result, hundreds of distinguished scientists were unable to return to academic life after the war, and many second-tier professors—simply because they had not been Nazi party members—were granted positions that would have been far beyond their reach under any other circumstances.

Several people knew that I had kept my distance from the Nazi party and testified on my behalf when I was summoned to state my case. Thanks to these *Persilscheine*—the popular term for these declarations of innocence, derived from the soap brand Persil, whose slogan was "Not just clean but immaculate"—I was named professor extraordinarius of mathematical logic at the venerable Georgia Augusta University of Göttingen in October of 1946.

The moment I read Lieutenant Bacon's letter, I knew that it was a sign of some sort, a message from Providence. At first, I tried to brush it off; I wanted to think that it was just another routine investigation that was so typical in those days. But the mention of John von Neumann strongly suggested otherwise. Old Johnny was not going to dig my name up just so some rank-and-file soldier could complete some bit of bureaucracy. No: Between those lines there had to be something far more important. The question was, however, did I want to participate in whatever that something was? Did I want to immerse myself once again in all the pain of the past, in the protracted anguish that had only just come to an end after twelve years of Hitlerian threats? Wouldn't it be better to put it all behind me? That was what everyone around me was doing, acting as if there was some ironclad law against actually naming the particular hell in question.

According to Aristotle, the cause of the cause is also the cause of the effect. Could I really blame Von Neumann for all that would soon happen, just because he had found himself in the unusual circumstance of recommending my name to someone? Or, worse yet, could I hold him responsible for writing a simple letter—perhaps in a rush, perhaps somewhat distractedly—to one of his students? Old Von Neumann, the reigning expert in chance, had now become a protagonist in its deliverance.

When Lieutenant Francis P. Bacon appeared in my cold office, he was dressed in his American uniform—something I interpreted not only as a sign of disrespect but as an attempt at intimidation. For the first time, I will allow myself a physical description of him—that is, of how I saw him back in Göttingen. He was tall, though not too tall, and had a permanently tight look on his face, as if especially conscious of his ill-fitting uniform. His back was slightly stooped, and his limbs rather long—when he greeted me I noticed that his shirtsleeve rose halfway up his forearm—although on the whole, he wasn't unattractive. His eyes never rested for long on any one thing—in fact, I wondered if he was trying to memorize the objects in my office in order to write up a report on them. But his intelligent face was filled with an energy that seemed to compensate for his rather clumsy movements. I estimated that he couldn't be more than thirty years old—with a margin of error of +/- 2, it turned out to almost exactly accurate—or approximately fifteen years younger than myself.

He still possessed that classic arrogance of young scientists who think themselves eminently prepared to make great discoveries, as well as a suspicious friendliness—like that of someone who thinks himself superior to the majority of the people he meets, but who is clever and cynical enough to hide his true feelings. I found his tense gestures slightly unsettling, though I suppose that my own apparently passive ones had a similar effect on him. He had clearly shaved before coming to my office; tiny, garnet-colored nicks dotted his chin and neck. A nervous tic just above his left eyebrow revealed an obsessive quality, as did the blackheads lodged among the too large pores on his face. In contrast, his arresting, dry lips looked as though they had been drawn with an intentionally dramatic flourish, giving him a certain rough sensuality which, I suppose, couldn't have gone undetected by women. His angular nose and broad, strong temples gave off a distinctively "Hollywood" impression—in the worst sense of the word. That first day, the sum total of these features led me to define Francis Bacon as "a man who might be capable of murder, but who would never do so for fear of the guilt he would suffer."

From the moment I laid eyes on him, I knew that behind his sincere, proud demeanor there hid a timid, introverted boy, and that frightened me—much more, in fact, than if he had been one of the rough soldiers who came by regularly. He may not have known it at the time, but that inner weakness actually gave him a strength and determination that could have easily intimidated someone less indifferent than myself. He introduced himself in a very officious manner—as if I didn't know who he was—and then I invited him to sit down. He poised his arms on my desk, and went straight to the point.

"Were you a member of the Nazi party?"

Obviously, he already knew the answer.

"No."

"Were you ever affiliated with any organization related to the Nazi party?"

"I have answered this question a thousand times. Moreover, you have already read my dossier," I said, trying to defend myself. "No, I never belonged to any of those organizations."

"Why, then, have you chosen to remain in Germany?"

"This is my country. Would you have done any differently?"

"I don't know. Not under the conditions that existed here, with Hitler."

He listened to me rather disinterestedly, as if this were a simple formality that he wished to get through as quickly as possible.

"You simplify things. Perhaps I shouldn't say this to you—I'm tired of trying to convince people of this—but in the beginning, things weren't as clear as they seem now. In 1933, Hitler didn't have a sign on his forehead saying 'I'm a murderer' or 'I'm going to start World War Two' or 'I think I will kill millions of people.' It was never that simple."

"But people knew of his plans, people knew that he intended to rearm the country, and that anti-Semitism was a basic pillar of his program. Don't try to tell me you didn't know."

"It matters very little to me whether you choose to accept my observations or not, Lieutenant. I am not attempting to defend anyone, least of all myself."

"Very well."

He was such a child. Von Neumann had sent me a little boy! He continued:

"So then why didn't you ever protest openly against Hitler?"

"*Openly?*" A scornful grin came over my face. "If I had openly protested, right now you would be interrogating another mathematician instead of me. In Hitler's Germany, 'open protests,' as you call them, were punishable by death."

"Even so, you were thrown in jail and found guilty."

"Let's try to be clear from the very beginning," I said. "You have already conducted a thorough investigation of me before coming here. Is this an attempt to get me to corroborate the information in my dossier?"

"That wasn't my intention."

"Yes, I was made a prisoner at the end of the war, after the failed coup of July 20, 1944. Scores of my friends, guilty of nothing more than privately criticizing Hitler's atrocities, were less fortunate than I and did not live to tell about it. The most important people in my life are now dead. What more would you like, Lieutenant? Would you like every single German who survived to ask the world's forgiveness for Hitler's mistakes? I'm afraid you have everything mixed up. You don't realize that nothing is one way or another. Hitler had just as many victims in this country as he did in Poland or Russia."

"I apologize. I know it's an uncomfortable topic."

"*Uncomfortable?*"

Our conversation was becoming more and more hostile. But I couldn't allow myself to be intimidated. If we were to have any sort of relationship, I needed to set down the rules; it wouldn't work otherwise. I tried to soften my tone of voice.

"How can I be of help to you, Lieutenant?"

"Professor Von Neumann said you and he were friends."

"That's true," I lied. "Although obviously we haven't seen one another in a very long time."

"What is your field of specialty?" This was the moment when I first sensed that the mind of a scientist lay hidden behind this professional military man.

"Number theory. At least that is what I *once* worked on."

"Professor Von Neumann tells me you were an expert on Cantor," he said.

"I still have some of it in me," I admitted, though I always found it annoying to talk about science with soldiers, whether they were Nazi bureaucrats or learned members of the profession. "I never could stray very far from my passion for infinity."

"Infinity?"

I nodded, not understanding why he seemed so shocked. He looked as if he had just heard me say that I spent my time studying the bone marrow structure of baboons.

"Do you think that's a bad thing?"

"No, no, on the contrary," he said, trying to sound agreeable. "I think it's very interesting, actually." His German wasn't hopeless, just a trifle limited.

I settled deeper into my chair. Taking out a pen, I began to sketch something on a sheet of paper.

"One day, I would very much like to see some of your work," he said.

"Thank you for the compliment, Lieutenant, but I can't imagine that was your reason for coming to Göttingen."

"No, of course not." He had that habit—copied from the American movies, I am sure—of drawing out suspense with long, boring pauses. "As I told you in my letter, I came to request your help."

"And how can a mathematician be of help to you?"

"I haven't come here to consult you in your capacity as a mathematician."

"How, then? As a prisoner of war?"

"As someone who understands the scientific panorama of this era, Professor." He was trying to make his voice sound steely and resilient. "I only want to listen to you."

"What is it you want from me?"

"Your voice, your history, the history of science in Germany."

"I don't understand," I pressed him. "In all sincerity, Lieutenant, to find what you're looking for, I hardly think you need a German mathematician to reveal his secrets to you. In our territory, your country can do whatever it pleases. I'm not complaining; that is simply the reality and one must accept it. With that uniform and the appropriate conduct you can gain access to archives from Göttingen to Munich. What do you need me for?"

"Please believe me—if I didn't need your assistance I wouldn't have come all this way to ask you for it." Then he counterattacked: "And I would like to emphasize the last part of what I just said to you: ask you for it. This is not an order or a command. I am coming to you as a friend, as a colleague. I need someone I can trust, that's all."

I felt my blood boil as it surged into my cheeks.

"Are you looking for me to be your informant, Lieutenant?"

"Of course not!" He was sincerely taken aback. "My intentions couldn't be more different. I don't want to incriminate anyone. I simply want to do my part in helping to bring the truth to light. I am simply looking for the truth."

At this point, I was intrigued. Lieutenant Bacon, in spite of his arrogance, seemed to have a spark in his eyes, and I was drawn to it. I saw something of myself in him—or at least something that resembled the person I used to be. It was the same spirit, the same youthful enthusiasm that I no longer felt. In some way, the insolent Lieutenant Bacon was my doppelgänger, a kindred soul. If I had been born in America fifteen years later, perhaps I would have found myself in a situation similar to his. But now, if I didn't help him, that would be my problem; he would continue to pursue his objective, the goal that had been laid out for him.

"I'm afraid I may not have been clear in stating my purpose," he said. "I apologize. Might we start over?"

I liked his directness; there was something innocent about it. Go ahead, Professor Bacon, Lieutenant Bacon, Frank.

"My main concern is that we trust one another. I can't imagine that is going to be easy. Our countries have been enemies for too long."

"You still haven't told me what I stand to gain from helping you," I said to him.

He looked me in the eye, trying to read my intentions, and then he answered me:

"You have long been a victim of the Nazis' arbitrary rule," he tried. "If you ask me, I think that deep inside you want to help me just as much as I want you to. In short, I am offering you the possibility to do the right thing. To act. The war is over, but that doesn't mean that war crimes should be left unpunished, forgotten. Not the crimes against humanity committed by the Nazis. Not the crime they committed against scientists like you. I'm not asking you to become involved in a dangerous mission, or with anything that would compromise your reputation. I'm only asking you to guide me through those areas of Nazi history that I am still unfamiliar with. This is your chance to do something for yourself, and for your friends who died."

I had to think about it for a few seconds.

"I understand why you're skeptical of me," he continued. "I would be, too. So this is what I propose: a trial period. Let's see if we can work together."

"All right," I answered him finally.

Bacon cleared his throat. It was clear he loved theatrical moments, drama, police novels. Little by little, I had gotten to know him.

"Very well, then." A stern, officious look came over his face. "Have you ever heard of a very high-ranking scientist, the adviser to the Research Council of the Third Reich, someone known by the code name Klingsor?"

I looked at him, baffled.

"I've never heard of anything like that."

"Apparently, nobody in Germany knew of his existence," Bacon explained, with an irony that I chose to ignore. "Nevertheless, we have reason to believe that he was someone very close to Hitler."

So that was what his visit was about.

"And why is it so important?"

"Please, don't ask me to answer that quite yet, Professor Links," he said as he got up and began to pace around the room, showing off his ability to take control of the moment. "I need you to help me disentangle the bureaucratic chaos of the Nazis so we can find something that might tell us who the devil Klingsor is." He paused again. "I repeat the question, then. You've never heard mention of him?"

He had found me out. Worst of all, he knew it. But I wasn't about to hand myself over quite so easily. Klingsor. How long had it been since I had heard that name? There was a time when I thought I would never hear it again, that his shadow would disappear in the dark night of history like a ghost, a creature from the past, an agonizing spectre. And suddenly here was someone reminding me of his existence. How had he found out? Nuremberg, of course, Nuremberg! The city from where he mailed his letter to me. Someone had opened his mouth, someone had let out the secret. And what was I supposed to do? Tell Bacon the whole story? Guide him, as he was asking me to do, down the paths that would lead him to Klingsor? What was I, an advocate for hatred, for senselessness, for vengeance? Well, fine, if that's how he wanted it.

"Klingsor," I said. "Of course I have heard of Klingsor."

"So why did you deny it just a moment ago?"

"I wasn't certain I wanted to get involved."

"And now you are?"

"I think so."

"All right. I'm listening."

"Under the present circumstances, the subject of Klingsor is still too sensitive, Lieutenant. Especially now that we are embarking on a new era of peace and reconciliation—at least that's what they tell us. Klingsor, I must emphasize, will bring up events that will be unpleasant for a great many people. Important people believe that we should allow the wounds to heal, to rebuild Europe and establish it as a bastion against the Reds. Our old enemies are now your enemies as well. You do understand what I'm saying? The bomb, for example. Nobody wants the Russians to get their hands on the bomb, isn't that right?"

"Klingsor had something to do with the bomb?"

"Klingsor had something to do with *everything*, Lieutenant. That is exactly the problem with your enterprise. He was involved with too many important issues, military officials, and scientists for anyone to want to draw attention to his activities now." Bacon couldn't hide his surprise at this. "And that is that, Lieutenant. Klingsor authorized the budgets submitted for the Reich's special investigations. Nobody knew him, but it was assumed that he was a leading scientist who, from the shadows, from a supposedly apolitical and nonpartisan position, advised Hitler for the duration of the war. All of us scientists wanted to know who he was! In that sense, your investigation is nothing new, Lieutenant. At first, we simply thought it was a rumor. Whenever something would go wrong, or whenever something would go extraordinarily well, whenever a project was either approved or rejected by the Scientific Research Council of the Third Reich, it was said that Klingsor had intervened either for or against it when the time had come to make a decision. He was a kind of demigod who operated behind all the operations that we scientists only saw on the surface; we thought of him as a combination of messenger and spy in control of vast, unknown quantities of information. A man who was all-powerful in his realm and who only responded to Hitler in person."

Bacon was too stunned to speak. I had cracked open a gold mine for him. I was giving him a reason to go on.

"Please continue, Professor Links."

"Klingsor was so powerful that some of us assumed that he didn't exist, that he *couldn't* exist. Theories about his identity began to circulate: that Goebbels had created him as a device to keep the scientific community under control; that Klingsor was actually the code name for a group of scientists working together; that he was an invention of the secret societies that had existed in the Reich. One person even speculated that Klingsor was Hitler himself. Rumors and more rumors, Lieutenant, in a time when it was particularly difficult to discuss such things. The uncertainty was dreadful." I felt exhausted after this long-winded speech. "Would you care to hear my opinion on the subject?"

"Please."

"Unlike many of my colleagues, I think the real Klingsor was one person. Why? It was the way he acted, it was the footprints he left behind, and the string of scientific coincidences that occurred later on—too many of them for Klingsor simply to have been the product of our collective fear. One could almost say that Klingsor's actions took on a personality of their own. Unfortunately, I don't have a single shred of evidence to support these speculations." I paused. "That was why I hesitated to tell you the truth, Lieutenant. I don't have a single definitive argument to support my theory and I wouldn't want you to embark on the wrong path as the result of my error."

By then, Bacon was no longer listening. He seemed to be in a state that seemed dangerously close to ecstasy. He began to perspire.

"Do you mean to say that Klingsor was the person who controlled all the secret scientific investigations undertaken by the Reich?"

"That is correct."

"Then why isn't there any proof of his existence? Why won't anybody talk about it?"

"Do God or the devil provide explicit evidence of their influence over men, Lieutenant? Of course not. You will never find a single document signed by Klingsor, a report of his activities, a memorandum sent to his office, much less a dossier with a photograph attached. But that doesn't mean that he didn't exist or that he doesn't still exist. On the contrary, I think that his invisibility is evidence of his presence among us. Because of the very nature of his activities, every step he took had to be erased; that much is obvious. But those are the facts, Lieutenant. If you observe them slowly and carefully, you will be able to interpret them, and from there, you will be able to reach *him.*"

"I must confess, Professor, that I'm astounded. I don't know what to think."

"Why don't you take it slowly, Lieutenant. Think about it for a bit, and we can plan to see each other again. Then you can tell me whether you think me mad or if you think there may be some truth in what I've said."

"I don't know."

"The only thing I ask of you is that you don't mention any of this to your superiors. Our trust is paramount, you said it yourself. If I held back before discussing my suspicions with you, it was only because I was fearful of having encountered a man less capable of comprehending the situation than you. If our work together comes to light, we will surely lose him, and my future as a scientist in Germany will surely be lost as well."

"But how do you know he's still alive? How do you know he hasn't died or escaped?"

"I don't know," I said. "But I *suspect* it."

"And I should base my investigation on a suspicion?"

"That decision is entirely up to you. I, meanwhile, am willing to help you by dedicating my time and my knowledge toward the goal of revealing the true identity of Klingsor. With only one condition."

"That your name be omitted from all my reports."

"Exactly."

"I can't do that, Professor."

"It is the only way I am willing to help you. I have already had too much trouble. It's a test of your trust in me, Lieutenant. That's what you wanted."

Uncomfortable, Bacon remained silent for a few moments.

"All right, then. You will become my guide," he said, trying not to sound too enthusiastic. "My Virgil."

I liked the analogy. We were beginning to understand one another.

THE QUEST FOR
THE HOLY GRAIL

"Do you know who Klingsor was?"

"If I knew, I wouldn't be asking you."

"No, no, you misunderstand me, Lieutenant. I meant do you know who the original Klingsor was, from the ancient legends."

"I imagine he was one of those heroes from some Wagnerian opera, someone Hitler admired."

Evidently mythology was not Bacon's strong suit.

"I'm sorry to disappoint you, Bacon, but Klingsor was no hero. He was, in fact, a villain, a character in Wolfram von Eschenbach's *Parzival*. Although, yes, Wagner did popularize his myth in the opera *Parsifal*."

"Which, I'm sure, Hitler adored."

"I'm surprised that you are taken in by such common gossip," I replied. "Hitler may have adored Wagner, but *Parsifal* certainly wasn't his favorite. Like Nietzsche, he found it far too Christian."

"Very well, Links." That was the first time he addressed me by name, in such a familiar, exasperated tone. "Tell me the story of that *other* Klingsor. I'm all ears."

"All right. The action takes place, of course, long, long ago in a magical land that some people claim is Sicily, while others believe it to be England (this is the same story as that of King Arthur's knights), and still others say is the Black Forest. Act I. We are in a forest near the castle of Monsalvat—"

"The Mountain of Salvation," Bacon translated. I barely acknowledged his attempt at sounding erudite.

"This is the meeting place of the military-religious fraternity known as the knights of the Holy Grail. The Grail, according to legend, is the chalice that Christ used at the Last Supper. A few days later, a Roman soldier named Gaius Cassius Longinus was said to have pierced Christ's side with a lance (now known as the Spear of Longinus), and the chalice was then used to catch the blood that dripped from Christ's body. Now, then: The sacred mission of these knights is to guard the Grail and venerate it in a ritual ceremony. In Wolfram von Eschenbach's version, the Grail has nothing to do with Christ's blood, while Wagner's tale follows the Christian tradition. So while the medieval troubadour Eschenbach treats it as a pagan celebration, Wagner turns it into something more like a Mass."

"Slightly convoluted, but I follow you."

"At the beginning of the opera, we find ourselves by a lake. There we find Gurnemanz, the oldest of the Grail knights, bent forward in prayer. Availing himself of the familiar device of melodrama—which some people find annoying—the old man recounts the story of the King Amfortas."

"And that way he fills us in on the story."

"Amfortas has an enemy who is something of an evil twin—"

"Klingsor."

"Right. Klingsor. The two men represent two opposing forces. During many years they challenged one another, but to no definitive conclusion. Neither was ever able to declare himself the victor, until finally, after many sly maneuvers, the devil figured out how to conquer Amfortas: by making him commit a sin."

"With a woman."

"Very good, Lieutenant. You are sharper than I thought," I said, slightly annoyed. "That is precisely right. The instrument of evil here is a woman of 'fearsome beauty.' In Klingsor's enchanted garden, not far from Kolot Embolot, his palace, the young woman, a 'flower from hell,' seduces Amfortas. Distracted by her loveliness, he agrees to lend her the sacred Spear of Longinus and she immediately betrays him, delivering it to Klingsor, who then uses it to inflict a wound upon his former master. From that ill fated day onward, the king languishes in agony, slowly losing blood from a wound that never heals. Of course, the only way his illness can be cured—"

"Let me guess," interrupted Bacon. "Is by obtaining the aid of a young maiden, a woman true of heart and pure of spirit."

"Wagner is less generous, preferring to call her 'innocent,' which in his day was more or less a village idiot. This is where Gurnemanz's story ends. At this very moment, a wild swan falls at his feet, the white feathers of its breast stained by an arrow that has pierced its heart. In a matter of moments a hunter appears, in search of his prey—"

"Parsifal."

"Gurnemanz reprimands him for having killed the swan: In the vicinity of Monsalvat, even animals are sacred creatures. At the sound of the old knight's voice, however, a young woman emerges. Her name is Kundry, and she is a maiden who has lived in Monsalvat ever since Titurel,

Amfortas' father, discovered her amid the wooded undergrowth of a forest. The messenger of the Holy Grail, she carries a balsam from the far-off land of Arabia to cure the wounded king. Kundry pleads for clemency on behalf of the hunter, declaring he had no knowledge of the laws which prohibit the felling of wild beasts. The old man asks Parsifal his name, but the young man replies that he does not know. All he remembers is that his mother, Herzeleide ("Heart's Sorrow"), raised him in the cradle of innocence. Gurnemanz meditates on Parsifal's words and begins to wonder if this young hunter might not be the messenger of Providence he has been waiting for. He then invites the young man to *Liebesmahl,* the religious festival celebrating the universal glory of love, to be held that evening in the castle.

"Back at Monsalvat everything is ready for the ceremony. The knights of the Grail, Kundry, and Parsifal gather around the stone altar in which the holy chalice has been placed. On Titurel's insistence, the weakened Amfortas uncovers the Grail to set the stage for the miracle of salvation. All those present are awed by the magnificence of the moment, with the exception of the poor king, who can only lament the pain of his wound and the gravity of his sin. As he watches Amfortas, Parsifal feels no compassion at all for the king's suffering. On the contrary, he feels that he actually *deserves* the pain he is being forced to endure. Gurnemanz loses all hope and orders Parsifal to leave. With this final declaration, Act I comes to an end."

"Thank God," Bacon responded dramatically. "Why don't we go out for a *real* drink before moving on to Act II."

When our conversation ended, Bacon insisted upon taking me to a filthy pub, not far from the university, whose clientele mainly consisted of off-duty American soldiers. The bar was small, but it had a sort of decaying charm. An old bartender and a young waitress (who, if one looked beyond her haircut, was rather attractive) leaned against an old, pockmarked wooden bar counter. I suspect that the waitress was the bar's main attraction. Bacon walked over to greet her, winked at her, and ordered two bourbons. She seemed especially friendly to Bacon, who couldn't take his eyes off her.

"Her name is Eva," he whispered. "Just like Hitler's lover."

We placed our overcoats on hangers and then sat on a pair of tall stools at the bar. It was nice to feel the blast of heat from the wood-burning stove.

"Is that what Kundry's 'fearsome beauty' looks like?" Bacon asked.

"Well, if we changed her hairstyle . . ."

It was clear that the bourbon had an effect on him, as did women.

"Go on about Parsifal and Kundry. I'm listening." His gaze left my face and wandered over to the young woman's breasts. "Did you say Klingsor was some kind of devil?"

"The incarnation of evil, or of perfection, depending on your point of view. The castle of Kolot Embolot is on a tall hill that towered over an enchanted valley. There is one catch, however: In the land ruled by Klingsor, everything is an illusion. Beauty is false, for beneath her facade lies death. And according to legend, that is the reason why Klingsor has castrated himself. He is a demon, no doubt, but an impotent, sterile demon."

"A temptation, then, like the one Christ faced in the desert," noted Bacon distractedly as he signaled for two more drinks.

"Klingsor, being the devil, promises that he will deliver love and truth, but it's all lies. He is made of stone. He is a creature with a deformed, empty soul. In the tower of his castle he does nothing more than stare at himself in an enormous mirror. He is a narcissist incapable of loving anything but himself. But he needs to prove his love, like a jealous husband, by guarding over his own likeness. Or perhaps the image in the mirror is as false as the man reflected in it." I took a sip of my drink. "He is a kind of Mephistopheles, the spirit that denies, an odd child of chaos."

Eva walked toward Bacon. I imagine they were going to have to agree on a price.

"And Parsifal is his opponent, his opposite."

"No," I answered flatly. "Klingsor's true rival is Amfortas, the stricken king. The core of the tragedy resides in him, the man who is dying because he is not permitted to die. Parsifal is merely the hero, the vehicle necessary to break the equilibrium between good and evil in the world. Remember, in this universe there are only two magical lands: the area around Monsalvat, controlled by the knights of the Holy Grail, and the heavenly gardens hidden inside the Kolot Embolot. Parsifal will be the person who will finally put an end to this game that seems caught in a permanent tie."

"Do you like chess?" Bacon asked suddenly, for once turning his attention directly to me.

"I haven't played in a long time."

"Let's play sometime, what do you say? I was crazy about it when I was a child."

"Yes, let's do that," I agreed, and then returned to the subject at hand. "Parsifal is an innocent man. Rather than being the incarnation of human goodness—that is the role of the wounded Amfortas—he represents ignorance. Parsifal is content because he does not know who he is, nor does he care. Gamuret, his father, died in battle. His mother, Herzeleide, has raised him in a world removed from all knowledge of good and evil. He is a new Adam, almost a savage, who is unaware of the primordial struggle that is eternally being waged all throughout the universe. And for that very reason he is the only person who can possibly change the fate of the universe."

BOOK TWO

BOOK TWO

LAWS OF CRIMINAL MOTION

LAW I: *All crimes are committed by a criminal*

The origin of this precept is Aristotelian, although its modern formulation has its origins in Sir Isaac Newton's laws of motion. After all, what is a crime if not a motion provoked by someone, an action that occurs in absolute space and time, an occurrence in which one body escapes paralysis while the other is plunged into it, perhaps forever?

Let's take a look. Sir Isaac says the following: "Every body continues in its state of rest, or of uniform motion in a right line, unless it is compelled to change that state by forces impressed upon it." Is this not the very definition of murder, rape, massacres of all shapes and sizes? Newton would have made a superb criminologist. Human beings tend to remain the same, obeying the inertia of their background, traditions, and temperament, unless they are jolted into action by some external force. Violence is the predominant element that precipitates this sudden change. The average person might have no desire to change, and therefore the only thing capable of startling him, driving him mad, or destroying him is the physical or mental force inflicted upon him by someone else. By killing Abel, Cain sabotages the existing order and lays the foundation for a new civilization based on that one crucial act: murder. He disrupts creation but at the same time allows it to move into the future. If it wasn't for this kind of barbaric initiative, we would still be living in the bowels of dark, primitive caves, praying that nothing would come to disrupt our dark, primitive lives.

Moving on, Newton adds the following: "The change of motion is proportional to the motive force impressed; and it is made in the direction of the right line in which that force is impressed." For a clearer idea of what this concept means, think of a firing squad, or thousands of them, sending their bullets in straight lines toward the shirtless torsos of their adversaries.

In his final law, the physicist explains: "To every action there is always opposed an equal reaction: or the mutual actions of two bodies upon each other are always equal, and directed to contrary parts." Rarely in life will one encounter a statement as perfect or as influential as this one. A thrilling stroke of genius. This sentence does not merely describe the notion of displacement but rather the nature of all the battles that have ever been waged throughout the universe. Every time a human being makes a decision, he is either attempting to surpass his own limits, or he is trying to break someone else's will—and this is true whether his intention is seduction, persuasion, or murder. In each case, he will obey the traditional laws of mechanics.

In this light, the proof of the First Law of Criminal Motion is child's play: All crimes are committed because someone has defied inertia and harnessed his own energy to launch an attack against one of his peers. Whenever a person finds himself before a bloody corpse, a raped woman, or a still-smoking gas chamber, he can be sure that a battle between two opposing wills has taken place—a shocking, frightening drama.

COROLLARY I

What was Klingsor's crime? What was the crime that Bacon, with my help, was trying to investigate? That was the first question the young physicist should have asked himself. In order to hunt down a criminal, the first thing one needs to know is the crime he purportedly committed. Obstinate and irascible, Lieutenant Francis P. Bacon feverishly began his pursuit of Klingsor, treating it as a divine mission or a date with destiny, when, in fact, he didn't know what he was looking for. Such foolishness, such innocence. What had Klingsor done? Why was it so important to catch him? Why did he have to be punished? Why was he so responsible?

LAW II: *Every crime is the portrait of a criminal*

Anyone capable of murder, theft, or betrayal will always try to find ways to justify his actions and create his own barometer of truth so as to measure the effects of his handiwork. By imposing one force upon the other, the criminal both defeats the other person's will and also imposes his own conditions upon the situation. It seems almost pointless to repeat the everyday version of this precept, but the criminal defends his innocence in the same way that, as they say, "history is written by the winners."

Murder and rape are more than physical humiliation, they are more than acts that alter another human being's existence, for they reveal the criminal's desire to make his mark, seal his own brand of truth. Crime victims speak volumes, not so much in uttered words but rather in the unspoken message of their bruises and scars. Dead bodies, bullet wounds, and destroyed lives are the words—the scars—that the criminal uses to express his worldview. Criminals are obsessed with the recounting of their crimes—as much as or even more than the detectives who follow their trail in the hopes of delivering justice. The truth of the criminal is *other;* it is elusive and warped, indifferent and alien to the rigid logic of those who pursue them. Someone who kills—whether he kills one person or millions—will either try to shirk his responsibility by creating a conveniently redemptive version of the facts, or attempt to escape history altogether by disappearing among the anonymous masses who remain silent. But even silence can be truth for the criminal. And the real investigator, just like the real scientist, must study the facts very carefully if he wants to stay on the right track. In each and every case, he must be ready and able to identify all the little signs that hint, imply, or reveal that small morsel of will that the criminal, unwittingly, has left exposed to the world.

COROLLARY II

We could find the identity of Klingsor through the evidence he left behind. But could we ever find out how important he really was? Could we ever gauge his true influence?

Where were we to begin? The kind of world in which fugitives run loose is like a chessboard. The metaphor could hardly be more appropriate. Watching the criminal's movements is like watching a half-finished chess game: One must try and reconstruct the opening in order to map out all the possible endings. But how could we get to him? If the evidence of his existence was not convincing enough, then the only path to him was through his work. Through the influence he exerted upon others, the clues he left behind him as he went, and most especially his theory of the world, which he branded on the faces of each of his victims.

LAW III: *Every criminal possesses a motive*

I should elaborate on this precept: Only the great criminals, the *real* criminals, are willing to defend their actions to the bitter end. Machiavelli was one of these people, and not even the worst of them, at that. The end justifies the means or, in other words, a crime is not a crime but rather an act of revolutionary justice, redistribution of wealth, benevolence, legitimate defense, philanthropy . . . The very worst sins have been committed in the name of the most absurd, abstract ideas—race, religion, political affiliation, national borders.

The true criminal considers himself a man of virtue, and in a certain sense he is. Robespierre, Hitler, and Lenin are only the most prominent examples of a long line of *pure* criminals, a group that includes a host of less infamous names such as Truman, Mohammed, and various popes. These criminals never act out of evil, perversity, or whim, but rather out of a sense of obligation. Their task is neither simple nor particularly pleasant: If they follow through with their objective, it is only because that is their mission in life. At this point in history, it is hard to imagine that Hitler and Stalin actually believed they were doing the right thing, that they were simple redeemers of humanity and not perverse, mad villains who reveled in the torture of others. Nevertheless, evidence suggests that neither the Nazis nor the Soviets considered their actions to be criminal. The inversion of values espoused by Hitler and Stalin was such that the virtuous and the good (which by nature require large amounts of humanly effort) came to occupy the moral position previously ascribed to the most aberrant of behaviors.

This kind of action—motion, as we have said—is no longer selfish, and transforms the criminal into a mystic, an ascetic priest.

COROLLARY III

We ask ourselves whether Klingsor was a "pure" criminal. Did he really believe that his purpose was to save humanity, as Hitler did? Was he just another of those mystics of desperation who walked around in the black uniforms and insignias of the SS, willing to commit the vilest acts in the service of a loftier goal? Was he, like all "great men," a custodian of faith?

Allow me to frame these questions in another manner. Does God need a reason for his actions? An interesting question, one that fascinated the subtle minds of medieval doctors. Does God have any reason to be good? Is God benevolent for *something*? The theologians' response is negative. God is goodness itself, and needs no motive to bestow his grace. If this were not true, he would be cheapened, he would become utilitarian and human, all *too* human.

And is the devil wicked for any specific reason? This is a slightly more complicated issue. Does the devil sow his evil freely and indiscriminately? Or does he have a specific objective? Here is where the theories branch off in every direction. Some people assert that, yes, in effect, his intention is to sabotage the designs of Creation, that his job is to foment bedlam, to lead the universe toward chaos. We could call him the lord of entropy. And why does he do all this, why does he insist upon delivering us to death? Easy: to prove that he is every bit as powerful as his adversary. Of course, there are demonologists who feel otherwise. Satan, they say, has no reason for being evil; if there were a reason for his evil, then we would have to admit that he isn't quite so terrible. We would be forced to admit that something logical, perhaps even understandable, is behind his desire to control the cosmos, and consequently there would exist a reason to grant him forgiveness on Judgment Day. On the other hand, if we believe that evil has no foundation at all, then we can be sure that we are facing the ultimate horror: the irrational, the arbitrary. Lucifer, the fallen angel, not only governs hell but the rules of chance as well. Hitler and Stalin were, of course, incarnations of the first theory: minor demons. They acted according to their objectives, they thought they were doing the right thing and, even worse, went to their graves believing this. Theologically, they cannot even be classified as heretics. But Klingsor?

MAX PLANCK, OR
A LESSON IN FAITH

If Lieutenant Francis P. Bacon's mission was to be judged by the kind of office he was given by the authorities of the Quadripartite Commission in charge of governing Germany, one could only assume that his project was, at best, a third-level priority. That is, of little or no importance at all. The building that housed his office, miraculously, had remained intact; it was as though the Allied bombers hadn't bothered to destroy an edifice that would most likely fall to pieces on its own. Before the war it had been a printing plant and later on, to the surprise of the American pilots, it was converted into a munitions warehouse.

"Compared to my new apartment," Bacon said as I walked in, "this is a palace."

I snickered and sat down on a wooden bench in front of his desk. To make things even worse, it appeared that the Army Corps of Engineers had not managed to repair the heating system, because the chill inside his office was close to arctic.

"Any progress, Lieutenant?" I asked him diplomatically, shivering.

"I'm afraid not. It's all so very vague, Professor." Bacon seemed especially nervous today, and two dark purple circles framed his eyes. "There are too many loose ends, there's too much information, too many possible places to begin. And this is a real problem, because the Klingsor mission consists of a staff of two: you and me."

"Don't your superiors feel this to be a relevant project?"

"They still aren't sure if it's worth the effort. And until I produce conclusive results, they won't give me another dime." The lieutenant pounded the table with his fist. "There are hundreds of archives, hundreds of index cards, hundreds of possible players. . . . During the Alsos mission, almost twenty of us worked for over three years to gather all the available information relating to science and the German scientists. We are talking about thousands of pages that I am going to have to look through and review all over again."

I cleared my throat.

"As far as I see it, they should be happy that you have so many good leads."

I rubbed my hands together, trying to get warm.

"The maintenance personnel tell me that the heat will be fixed in a few days," Bacon said apologetically. "Although based upon what the other staff in this building have told me, they've been promising that since October. Very well. All right, I can tell from your expression, Professor, that you have decided upon our course of action."

"Very good, Lieutenant," I said. "Now, in the first place, Klingsor most certainly existed, and in the second place, he was of vital importance to Hitler. These are the two postulates of our new faith. All the hypotheses and theories that we develop from this point on must derive from these two axioms. As you know, the best way to prove that a given statement is false is to first assume that the statement is true. If it isn't, the contradictions will surface quickly enough."

"A reductio ad absurdum."

"Just as in any respectable investigation, the first step is to define the problem. Then we can map out a theory. Or several, depending on the situation. In our case, this means that we must identify a handful of suspects." I was starting to like my job as a detective! "First we need to come up with a list of possible names, gather the necessary biographical information, and reconstruct their activities under the Third Reich. Only when that is accomplished will we be able to eliminate some names and focus in on others until, with a little luck, we identify our man. At that point we can begin to assemble the necessary incriminating evidence. By the way, I've even come up with the perfect cover for you: You introduce yourself as an American official writing a book about Nazi science. This way, we will be able to gain access to many of our potential suspects; they won't be able to refuse us!"

"And I suppose you have already selected our first candidate?"

"I have thought of something even better, Lieutenant," I admitted, unable to contain my pride. I had to show him that my hunches were more than mere flights of fancy. "In a normal court of law, a man is innocent until he is proven otherwise, but we should employ the inverse of this method. All of our suspects are guilty until we can prove their innocence." The lieutenant's eyes widened like saucers. "Don't misunderstand me, I'm not suggesting anything illegal. After all, you and I are not judges, just simple investigators. We are not going to hurt anyone."

"We should mistrust everyone?"

"With one exception." Now I took the ace out of my sleeve. "There is one man who knows the history of German science better than anyone else. He knows the story of its protagonists, its evolution, its glory and its tragedy, because he, in fact, was one of its most respected forerunners. He is beyond good and evil. Admired by one and all, he is a man of great moral integrity. Not only do I believe he can help us, but I think he just might become our touchstone. He is an old, tired man, but I am sure he can do something for us."

"Aside from Einstein, I can only think of one person who fits that description: Max Planck. How old is he by now? A hundred?"

"Really, Lieutenant. He's eighty-eight."

"And you think he will want to help us?"

"He might. In any event, I should remind you that he is a man who has suffered greatly in recent years. One of his sons died in battle. Another was sentenced to death for participating in the July 20 coup attempt—and as if he hadn't suffered enough, his house in Berlin was destroyed in a bombing raid."

"I see."

"He lives here now, in Göttingen. He's ill and as far as he sees it, he no longer has any reason to live."

"And therefore, according to you, he also has nothing to lose. Let's get to work, Professor. I will remit an order for us to solicit a meeting."

"No, no, that's not the way to do it. We should approach him as two men of science, his disciples. In some way, all living scientists are his students, don't you think? We owe him some respect. This is what I propose: Give me a few days to try and get him to agree to see us. If it doesn't work, then you can try it your way."

The following day, we met in his office again. Everything was the same except for the brown folder sitting on Bacon's desk. Max Planck's dossier. Bacon began reading out loud:

Report #322-F
Planck, Max
Alsos
170645

Max Planck was born on 23 April 1858 in Kiel, Schleswig-Holstein, to a family of lawyers and theologians. Though his early years were spent at the University of Munich, for the majority of his career he was in Berlin, at Friedrich Wilhelm University, where he was first named professor in

1889. In 1912 he was appointed permanent secretary of the mathematics and physics sections of the Prussian Academy of Sciences, and in 1913 he was named dean of the University of Berlin. At the end of World War I, he was made director of the German Science Emergency Fund, an organization whose job was to finance the majority of the country's scientific research projects. In 1930, he became the president of the Kaiser Wilhelm Society, and in 1918, he was awarded the Nobel Prize for physics, for his work on black body theories, something that Wilhelm Wien* had already begun to research. Planck had discovered a new universal constant, a principle of nature previously unknown to man. Without realizing it, he had shaken the very foundations of classic mechanics, paving the way toward a new kind of physics. "Planck's constant" (identified by the letter h) demonstrated that energy is not released randomly, but rather in uniform quantities that are whole multiples of h. Planck named these little "packets" of energy *quanta*.

"Did you write up this report?" I dared to ask Bacon.

"To be honest, I can't remember, but from the style I'd have to say no." Bacon's head jerked up with a start. "I know it's not the most accurate report in the world, but the OSS wanted us to write in a style that the military officers could understand."

"It reads like an encyclopedia entry on German science," I joked. "Perhaps one day you might become an author of a fashion book. I assume the asterisk refers to a cross-references."

Bacon seemed miffed by my comments.

"We didn't just compile an 'encyclopedia,' as you call it, with entries for all the preeminent scientists of our time, but a succinct pocket science dictionary. As hard as you might try, sometimes you have to realize that it will be impossible to explain the difference between an electron and a positron to an army general." Bacon slapped his cheeks lightly, trying to wake himself up.

"Go on, Lieutenant."

Politically, Planck was never sympathetic to democracy. In fact, he was among the group of scientists who signed an open letter of support for the Kaiser during World War I. Later on, although he would never become a real champion of democracy, he did demonstrate more of a willingness to work under the newly formed Weimar republic. (Of the German physicists, Einstein* was the only one who was a vocal supporter.)

When the Nazis rose to power, Planck was faced with the same dilemma. Should he actively protest the new government? Just like most of his colleagues, the only thing he cared about was science. He believed that politics and science should remain separate. His job was to continue working on his research projects irrespective of the political regime in place. For this reason, he never thought twice about remaining in Germany, despite the Nazis' ever-increasing excesses.

In 1933, as acting president of the Prussian Academy of Sciences, he was forced to request the resignation of his old friend Albert Einstein (who was in the United States at the time), to avoid further conflicts with the Nazis. Einstein obliged, but even his resignation was not enough to satisfy Bernhard Rust, the new education minister of the Reich (*Reichs-erziehungsministerium*, REM), who considered Einstein a symbol of Jewish power. In a public statement made at the behest of Rust, Ernest Heymann, the secretary of the academy, declared that the academy was not sorry at all about Einstein's resignation, and in fact, was overjoyed at the announcement.

When Planck and the other academy members met to discuss the recent turn of events, they were cautious in their support of Heymann's statement. As Einstein's longtime friend Max von Laue* noted, the transcript stated that no other member of the German scientific community had been consulted in the matter. Planck was truly saddened that Einstein's political activities had obliged the academy to take such a stance, but years later he would publicly acknowledge Einstein's contributions to the academy, and he even stated that Einstein's achievements were of a magnitude comparable to those of Newton and Kepler.

Planck endured the Nazis under the Third Reich simply because it was his only way of maintaining any independence. The Führer and his ministers, however, were growing more and more interested in personally supervising the scientific life in their country. On one occasion, Planck actually had a private meeting with Hitler, but their conversation never had any kind of concrete, practical outcome. Planck tried using his influence to prevent a number of Jewish scientists from losing their jobs as a consequence of the Law for the Restoration of the Professional Civil Service, but there was little he could do. His influence within the academy had begun to wane, something that became all too apparent when men like the mathematicians Ludwig Bieberbach* and Theodor Vahlen (both staunch supporters of the Nazi regime) became members. In 1938, Vahlen was elected president of the academy, thanks to REM's direct intervention in the matter. By this time, Planck was eighty years old.

"I'm sorry, I can't stand it anymore, this room is an icebox," I exclaimed. "We are going to have to install a heater in here. In any event, I have a surprise for you, Lieutenant. Thanks to the efforts of Max von Laue, Planck has agreed to a brief meeting. Friday at noon."

I shook his hand and hurried downstairs as quickly as possible. I walked away from the building, slowly and deliberately, watching the icicles that had formed on the eaves of the windows. The day was dull and gray, and right at that moment what I needed more than anything was a nice glass of warm wine.

It was barely seven in the evening, but it was already dark, and a thick fog had rolled in over the city. The near-empty streets that Bacon had to cross in order to reach his apartment were ethereal and ghostly beneath the glow of the streetlights. Normally he whiled away his afternoons in his favorite bar, flirting with Eva the waitress either until he got tired or (worse) she invited him to spend the night, but today was different. Today he went directly to his apartment, where he planned to go straight to bed.

In a foul mood, Bacon entered his building and climbed the dusty, rickety stairs. The place was in even worse shape than the remains of that old printing house where his office was. This building *had* been damaged by the Allied bombing raids, but that hadn't stopped dozens of families from piling into the rooms that hadn't crumbled to pieces. Each time he walked up those wobbly stairs, surrounded by those dark, damp walls, he would feel a growing pressure against his temples, as if he were walking the path to hell itself.

Distracted, Bacon was rummaging for his keys when he crashed into a young woman with a baby in her arms. Lost in his thoughts, he hadn't seen them coming at all.

"Excuse me! Are you all right?" was all he could think of to say as he reached out to grab the woman's arm.

"Don't worry," she said. "He's still asleep."

"Please, allow me . . ." Bacon insisted, and he walked her to an apartment at the other end of the hallway.

After a minor struggle to open her front door, the young woman sped into her apartment to place the baby in his cradle. Bacon remained at the vestibule, awkward and watchful, as if this were his first time seeing a mother with her child.

"Thank you," she said. After a pause, she added: "My name is Irene."

"Frank," he said, flustered. He proffered his hand.

She looked him straight in the eye.

"I should go, otherwise Johann will wake up." Then she closed the door.

Talking to Max Planck was like coming face-to-face with a ghost from the nineteenth century. His shriveled face was peppered with pockmarks and scars, little emblems of wisdom, pain, tranquillity, and rage that reminded Bacon of an ancient relic, or the cross-section of a tree trunk whose circles of age are exposed for all to see. The iron will of this immortal man had staved off the end of an era, whose last remaining vestiges were the hollow cheeks and heavy bags underneath his eyes. The great physicist's facial expression revealed no hatred, only a profound disenchantment at the world he still found himself living in. Educated during the glory years of the German empire, Planck had reached middle age during the Great War and had grown old under the Third Reich, and seemed to embody the very spirit of Germany itself, destroyed over and over again, and now reborn out of the ashes of its past. By now, his weakened arms and legs and withered body had relegated him to his bedchamber, but his formal manners and direct gaze had not fallen prey to the passage of time. His diminutive pupils still radiated the same terrible disdain with which he looked upon the chance-filled universe he himself had helped define. And in spite of all the disappointment and bitterness, the pain and the solitude, he was still alive, tenacious and strong, one of the few remaining reference points that could guide his compatriots toward the future. Max Planck, still alive in 1946, seemed to have remained on earth as a symbol of the *other* Germany—the rational, scientific Germany that had coexisted with the ferocious, bellicose Germany which had first won out before falling into utter self-destruction.

In Göttingen, Planck was seen as a kind of phoenix. As long as he lived on, the vast, desolate wasteland of German science had a chance for resurrection. This is why despite his great pain—or perhaps because of it—Planck continued on, undaunted and indifferent to the decaying of his skin and the slow disintegration of his memory. Behind the funeral mask his face had become, there was a mind at work, a mind still capable of encouraging the fallen, the beaten, the guilty. If anyone possessed sufficient moral fiber to prove that human reason did not lead inexorably into an abyss, it was Max Planck.

"Thank you for your willingness to meet with us," I said to him.

Absent and alone, Planck remained seated in his ample easy chair, covered with blankets like a child wracked with fever.

"Speak up, he doesn't hear well with his left ear," advised the matron who supervised him. She was a wide, stocky woman with long blond braids, straight out of a German folktale.

We sat down on a pair of chairs brought in from the dining room. The apartment was comfortable in an artificial sort of way, as if someone had decorated it to remind Planck of his home in Berlin. His study was off to one side of the drawing room, though it was obvious that he had little use for it anymore. A broad mahogany desk dominated the room like a sarcophagus: shiny and well preserved, with no sign of human activity upon its surface. Framed photographs sat in a pile on a large bureau; some of them, surely, were of his dead son. The windows were covered with thick linen curtains which didn't completely block the sun's rays, but at least alleviated their force upon the old man's weakened eyes.

"I hope we're not disturbing you," said Bacon.

The old sage coughed with difficulty. He wore a traditional black suit with a tie, despite the fact that he no longer went outside. It would have been beneath his dignity to receive us in a bathrobe. Despite his rather absent expression, he was freshly shaven and his large white mustache looked like a small bird perched upon his lips.

"I haven't received any visitors in quite some time. I know you, don't I?" he asked in an almost inaudible voice, as he turned to look at me.

"That's right, Professor. Gustav Links. Mathematician."

"Yes, yes." He paused, trying in vain to remember the last time we had seen one another. Giving up, he continued: "Would you like something to drink? Coffee? I think there's coffee, isn't there, Adelaide?"

"Yes, Professor," she answered.

"Thank you," said Frank. He was clearly nervous; in his hands he held a book and held his pencil in a viselike grip that would have cracked a walnut.

Adelaide left us alone. Bacon introduced himself. In a tremulous voice, he explained to Planck that he was a graduate student in physics at Princeton University. He spoke of Einstein and Von Neumann, and then told Planck that he was truly honored to have been granted the opportunity to meet him.

"I wouldn't want to be guilty of suspicion," Planck said, coughing again. "But something tells me this is more than a courtesy call."

"Professor Bacon is preparing a monograph on the history of science in contemporary Germany," I interjected. "And I thought that you might be able to clarify a few confusing bits in his research."

"Yes, I wanted to speak with you about an issue that I thought you might know something about, Professor," Bacon stammered.

"I haven't known much of anything for a long time now," said Planck, laughing at first and then collapsing into a sneezing fit. "Like Socrates . . . well, why don't you tell me what it is you're looking for."

"Although my project isn't strictly scientific, Professor," Bacon said, handing me the pencil and notebook, indicating that I should take notes, "I do try to apply the same scientific principles to all my work. I consider myself, more than anything, a researcher. And now I find myself here, in Germany, facing you in person, and I realize that in some regard I am doing what I've always done—formulating hypotheses, performing practical experiments, testing my results, developing theories. They aren't scientific theories but rather—how shall I put it?—theories about people, theories about the truth of certain real-life events that, in fact, don't disobey the rules of scientific research."

What nonsense! I thought to myself. Naturally Bacon was frightened by the prospect of meeting Max Planck face-to-face and I knew he had a tendency to wax philosophical at times. As such, I was all prepared to jump in and apologize for him, until I realized that Planck was actually interested in what he was saying.

"I think I understand," he said, fiddling with the plaid blanket that covered his legs. "Science is a bit like religion. I hope you don't find the comparison shocking. Both science and religion pursue their objectives with the fiercest sort of determination, in the hopes of convincing their believers of the inherent goodness of their respective enterprises. But I'm afraid that churches fall short of providing the spiritual backbone that people search for. And that is why people look elsewhere. The main reason religion has difficulty in attracting believers stems from the fact that its 'calling' requires a spirit that already believes." Planck smiled. "Faith. Amid the general skepticism that surrounds us, that particular calling receives no response."

"Do you think science is a substitute for religion?"

"Not for a skeptic, because science also requires a spirit that believes. Anyone who has seriously studied a scientific subject knows that there is a sign above the entrance to the temple of science which says *You must have faith.* Scientists cannot ignore that. Anyone who analyzes a series of results obtained through a scientific experiment must be able to imagine the law he is seeking to prove. Then, he must bring it to life with an intellectual hypothesis." By now I was lost; I had no idea where Bacon had led him nor where he was headed.

"Do you mean to say that hypotheses are like acts of faith?"

"Exactly." Planck's eyes glittered, as if the words that fell from his dried lips had granted him a new lease on life. "The ability to reason, on its own, will not help you move forward, because order cannot emerge from chaos without the intervention of the mind's creative faculty, which is able to build a kind of order through a systematic process of elimination and selection. Over and over again, the imaginative plan upon which that order is based will be foiled, requiring you to go back and try it again. That ability to fuse vision and faith is indispensable to achieving success in the end."

"Are you saying I should trust my instincts?" Bacon seemed bewildered. "In this process of attempting and then correcting, should I allow my faith to guide me?"

"Science alone is unable to solve the ultimate mystery of nature. And that is because we ourselves are part of that nature, and therefore part of the mystery we are trying to solve." Planck cleared his throat, and then immediately returned to his train of thought. "In some respects, music and art are efforts to understand or at least express this mystery. In my opinion, the more progress we make in these fields, the closer we come to achieving harmony with nature."

Bacon contemplated this for a few moments before responding. I, meanwhile, continued taking notes.

"Nature will never cease to astonish," Bacon said. "Science can help us to understand it, but quite often it falls short. There will always be something that eludes us."

"Yes," agreed Planck, implacable. "Time and again we come face-to-face with the irrational. Otherwise we would never be able to have faith. And if we didn't have faith, life would become an unbearable burden. We wouldn't have music or art. And we wouldn't have science, either, not just because it would lose its principal attraction (that is, the search for the unknowable) for those of us who study it, but because it would lose its foundation: the human perception of life as an external reality."

"The mysteries are there for us to solve. To give meaning to our existence," Bacon interjected.

"As my old friend Einstein said, a man cannot be a scientist if he doesn't believe that the world really exists. But that understanding is not the result of any kind of reasoning. It is a conviction that comes directly from nature, and for that reason it is quite similar to our convictions about faith. It is a metaphysical faith—"

"Let me see if I understand," Bacon interrupted. "If I *think* that there is something in this world worth investigating, a mystery that needs to be solved, is that enough?"

"If it satisfies the requirements of your method, yes. If you have the faith that some part of the world deserves to be investigated, use your faith to find your way there. You might stumble, or not find anything at all, but it wouldn't be the first time that's happened to a scientist. If you still believe there is something to be uncovered, begin again from a different angle— that is how all great discoveries have been made." Planck seemed exhausted but satisfied.

"Now tell me," he continued. "What is this situation in which you have so much faith? What are you searching for?"

Bacon paled, as if revealing the true motive of his visit would somehow cheapen the theoretical discussion they had just had. He looked back at me for support; I offered nothing more than a slight nod of the head.

"Klingsor."

An ominous, dark silence descended upon them, impenetrable. We had gotten where we wanted, though I never imagined Frank would present the question so bluntly.

"I don't understand."

"Do you know who he was, or is? A man who responded to the code name Klingsor?" Our inquirer remained silent for a moment. "This is the focus of my suspicions, Professor. I think there is a mystery hidden behind that name, and it is a serious matter that I need to resolve. I am hoping that you can help me do that."

Planck's face suddenly changed color, and a violent spasm interrupted the flow of conversation.

"Adelaide!" he barked. "My medicine! Please!"

The matron returned with a small bottle and a spoon. She opened the bottle and poured a few drops onto the spoon, which she then brought directly to the professor's mouth. Before leaving the room, she glared at us suspiciously.

"I'm sorry, I haven't been well lately," coughed Planck. "I'm afraid we are going to have to continue our conversation on some other occasion. Please forgive me."

"Please, won't you just answer me? Do you know who Klingsor was?"

Planck took a moment to consider the question.

"Take your time, Professor," I said.

"My dear man, the name you have just uttered is a most terrible one," said Planck. His voice now sounded sinister and distant, as if he were speaking from the bottom of a tomb. "If it isn't absolutely necessary, I'd rather not discuss it."

That was it! Old Planck had confirmed my suspicions.

"It's extremely important," Bacon insisted.

A grimace of pain clouded Planck's face.

"It brings back too many painful memories. And I'm not sure it's worth it."

"Why does everyone refuse to talk, Professor?"

"I've already tried to explain this to the lieutenant," I offered. "I've told him that this was simply a rumor, nothing more—but he wanted to see you to confirm that."

Planck looked at me, baffled.

"If Professor . . . Links . . . has told you what he knows, what do you need me for?"

"The scientific method, Professor. I need confirmation."

"Confirmation? Of what?"

"Of whether Klingsor existed, or exists."

Planck fell silent again.

"Please, tell me one thing, Professor: Do you have any idea who he is? Is there any way you can help us find out? Anything you could add would be most valuable, even if it's only speculation, even if it's nothing more than a hunch."

"That, gentlemen, is the awful thing about this matter. I have my suspicions, but can you imagine what my conscience would do to me if I were mistaken? The tiniest slip in my memory could incriminate a good man, a good scientist—and I can't take that risk, gentlemen. Not at this stage in my life."

"I'm not asking you to incriminate anyone, I was simply hoping that you could shed some light on this. Not a name, just a little something, a hint, to guide us."

"If he truly existed," said Planck, who clearly did not want to mention him by name, "he would have to be an accomplished scientist, someone familiar with quantum mechanics, the theory of relativity, subatomic particles, fission . . ."

"What are you trying to say, Professor?"

"He was one of us," Planck lamented. "He knew us down to the last detail. He lived with us. And he fooled us all."

Planck's voice broke, as if he suddenly realized he had said too much. Then he began to shake uncontrollably, unable to calm the chest spasms that attacked him once again. Adelaide came bounding toward him with a glass of water. The old man took a few, painstaking sips.

"You must leave," Adelaide said. "The professor is not well."

Bacon got up from his chair, but wouldn't let up.

"Who was he, Professor. What was his name?"

"I hate to disappoint you," Planck said apologetically, "but nobody knew him by his real name. Nobody ever witnessed him at work. He could be any-one. Any one of us . . ."

"Gentlemen," insisted Adelaide.

Bacon and I walked toward the door.

"Is that all you can tell me?"

"You're a physicist, aren't you? Study the methods of your colleagues! Klingsor is as elusive as an atom." Planck's voice reemerged from the cav-ernous walls of his chest. "Learn from your predecessors! That is the best advice I can give you. And hold on to your faith, my son, for that is the only thing that will save you."

Planck's words echoed in our ears long after we left the house. His con-fession had succeeded in confirming my own suspicions, but his words had a far more profound effect on Bacon, who suddenly realized that Klingsor was no illusion but rather a tangible—and very dangerous—reality.

Much later on, Bacon would try to recall exactly what it was that had attracted him so strongly to that woman, the one he had crashed into the previous evening. For some reason, he couldn't get her out of his head. Just like that, like a whim, one decision among so many others, a coin tossed into the air, Bacon felt compelled to meet her, to know her.

Night had fallen, and the city sprawled out before Bacon like a lonely gray lake. He walked in circles, his footsteps leading him nowhere. It was as if he were trying to fool the passage of time, or perhaps escape from the labyrinth he was creating, a puzzle made up of Klingsor, Planck, and that woman. It was nearing the end of the year, and though he had long since stopped believing in God (and had promptly forgotten about the faith the German physicist kept insisting on), he felt the need to cleanse himself.

A fine layer of snow covered the rooftops of Göttingen, and Bacon reflected upon how lovely it was that for once the skies had seen fit to reflect his mood. He turned up the lapels of his coat to cover his chest, trying to protect himself from the frigid winds. And that was when he saw her. If he had taken another route home, if he had gone back to the office instead of wandering through the winter streets, if he had been a few minutes faster or a few minutes slower, if he hadn't come to Europe, if he hadn't worked at Princeton, if he hadn't studied physics, he would never have found her there, standing before him, at that very moment. Right then, it seemed that every single decision he had ever made had led him to her.

The street was narrow and obscured by shadows, but Bacon recognized Irene's slightly disheveled figure instantly, as if he had known her all his life. She wore a flowered dress and a slightly threadbare coat, and she stood there in the middle of the street, staring at the snow, impervious to the cold. She seemed unbothered by the freezing wind, like a statue accustomed to the inclement weather and the indifference of the passersby. Her fingers were interlaced, but she didn't tremble at all. Suddenly, she began hunting through her pockets and produced a rumpled, broken cigarette, which she placed between her cracked lips. She struggled to light it with a match. In a different setting, she could have easily appeared to be threading a needle. No longer enraptured by the skies, she focused on this task as if her life depended on it. Her slender hands tried to provide shelter for the flame, but time after time the wind blew it out.

Bacon watched as a weak flame tenaciously resisted the gusts of air swirling around it. Irene smiled. In the middle of the vibrant burst of colors that went from blue to light yellow and red and orange, she had sealed her destiny. In that small gesture of satisfaction, Bacon imagined years of hardship, hours and hours tending to a sickly or frightened Johann, endless gray days like this one, countless empty nights. . . . That one brief miracle—the conversion of mass into energy—seemed to epitomize her entire existence, common yet proud. And just like the match that implored the shelter of her clean, white hands, her body seemed to call out for his protection. How many sorrows were buried in Irene's embrace? How many tears, how much heartache? Wasn't that senseless act of preserving the fire in the middle of that blustery cold just another manifestation of the human will—the same will he saw alive in Max Planck—attempting to survive and to endure, to defeat adversity and create the cosmos from nothing? Bacon approached her silently, careful not to scare her, as if she were a bird dragging a broken wing. He couldn't let her escape. His figure was easily lost in the shadows; he could almost smell her clean, windburned skin, feel the breath that smelled of heavy, dark wine. Right now, she seemed lovelier and more vulnerable than ever.

"What are you looking at?" she greeted him.

Her eyes. The same eyes from the night before, yet now they were different, transformed into two burning embers, far more intense than any flame Bacon could have imagined. That was why she had lit the cigarette: nostalgia for her igneous origins.

"You," he replied.

Irene laughed. Then she took a long, deep drag from her cigarette, which looked ready to disintegrate between her fingers.

"Are you really that cold?" she asked.

"I'm freezing."

"Well, then, you could use a cup of tea."

Together they raced toward the building and climbed upstairs.

"Don't make any noise," she warned him before entering. "Johann is sleeping."

The room seemed bigger than Bacon had envisioned, and was far cozier than his. Still, the high ceiling and the top part of the walls were decorated with those telltale idiosyncratic signs of ancient apartments, the idle artwork left behind by years of dampness and mildew. A large table sat in the center of the room; near it was a tall armoire that almost reached the ceiling. The kitchen, consisting of a sink and a stove, was at the far end of the room. Two additional doors led to the bathroom and the baby's bedroom.

"Johann doesn't give me much time to rest," Irene said as she placed water to boil in an ancient pot on the stove. She removed a tiny bag of dried leaves from the armoire and dropped it in the makeshift kettle.

Suddenly Bacon no longer saw her as a wounded bird, but rather like a squirrel, hoarding all sorts of useless objects. After a few moments, Johann's cries rang through from the bedroom.

"I woke him up."

"No, no, he's just hungry," Irene explained. "He's always hungry."

She went into the other room and returned with little Johann in her arms. She heated a bit of milk on the stove, and quickly poured a small glass of milk for the baby.

"Can you check on the tea?"

Bacon nodded, slightly taken aback. He poured the water into two cups and placed them on the table.

"How old is he?" asked Bacon, just to break the unbearable silence.

"You certainly don't know much about children." She laughed. "He's two."

Bacon felt a visceral repulsion when it came to children. He was simply incapable of understanding them: The diminutive perfection of their little arms and legs seemed more monstrous than miraculous. His needs taken care of, Johann burped and he fell back into a peaceful sleep in his mother's arms. Irene put him back in the little cell that was his bedroom.

"What did you do? Before the war, I mean," she asked when she returned, taking a sip of tea. "This tastes awful, doesn't it?"

"It's fine," said Bacon.

"So, then . . ."

"I was a physics student."

"Physics?" Irene's eyes lit up for a moment. "I've never met a scientist before. Is that why they sent you to Göttingen?"

"I suppose so, yes. And you? Where are you from?"

"I've always lived in Berlin, but I was born in Dresden. Have you ever been?"

"I'm afraid not."

"Well, you're lucky," she said, without a trace of sarcasm in her voice. "Because Dresden doesn't exist anymore. The bombing didn't leave a single stone unturned. And now the Russians are there."

"It's been so terrible, hasn't it?" offered Bacon.

"It was the most beautiful city in all of Germany. The Zwinger, you know? Such a magnificent palace, and the opera house, and the cathedral . . ."

"And you?" Frank tried to change the subject.

"Me?"

"What did you do before the war?"

"Before the war? Nothing very special." Her voice revealed no nostalgia whatsoever. "I worked as a teacher in an elementary school. And then in a factory, if you can believe it."

"And Johann's father?"

"I'd rather not talk about him. Another day I'll tell you about it. More tea?"

"No, thank you. I should be going, anyway. Tomorrow I have to get up early."

"Well, thank you for the company," she said, and offered him her hand.

"Another new idea, Professor Links?"

This was how Bacon greeted me when I arrived at his office to review what Planck had told us.

"I've been thinking about something Planck said: 'Klingsor is as elusive as an atom.' I don't think it was just some kind of *boutade*. I rather think he was tossing out some kind of clue," I said.

"What do you mean?"

"Remember what the old man said. The notion that all things in the universe are made up of the most basic, elementary particles—why, the idea is almost as ancient as humanity itself. It can be traced at least as far back as ancient Greece. Nevertheless, it wasn't until a few years ago that physicists were able to prove their existence. Rutherford's atomic model is only from the beginning of this century!"

"So . . . what are you getting at?"

"Planck was trying to point the way for us, Lieutenant, encouraging us to forge ahead! Right now Klingsor is nothing more than a name to you and me, but we have the wherewithal to prove his existence and turn him into a man of flesh and blood, just as Thompson, Rutherford, and Bohr did with the atom. I don't know if we can extend the analogy quite so far, but at least in the past this approach worked."

"A map," Bacon said, starting to get excited. "What we need to do is draw up a map, with Klingsor in the center. Like Rutherford's atomic model. That's right. Now I understand. Very good. Let's think, then. What are the particles we should be focusing our attention on? What route shall we take to arrive at that elusive goal called Klingsor?"

"The German physicists and mathematicians and their work. We need to draw up a great blueprint, elaborate and detailed, that shows how they are all connected: all their activities, all their connections, and their various relationships to the Nazi authorities."

"All right, then, let's get to work," Bacon exclaimed.

I stopped to think about this.

"What would you say if we began with the most obvious suspect?" I said to him, knowing this would attract his attention. "I am thinking of a first-rate physicist, winner of a Nobel Prize, a man who supported Hitler from the beginning, when Hitler was nothing more than a poor Austrian conspirator stuck in Munich. Johannes Stark."

"Well, like you said, it's too obvious. Einstein and Heisenberg's arch-enemy?"

"Think about it: a man with considerable power in Nazi Germany, an ardent anti-Semite, a party member since the 1920s."

"He's the first person anyone would suspect. Don't you think that's reason enough to cross him off our list?"

"Just like that, without even testing him? What kind of scientist would you be if you refused to perform an experiment simply because the conclusion seemed self-evident? Are you satisfied with 'mental experiments'? If Stark is innocent, it should be easy enough for us to prove it. You asked me where to begin, and I gave you a logical answer. Lieutenant, I don't think you fully understand what I'm saying. I am not suggesting that I believe Stark might actually be Klingsor, but what I *am* saying is this: I am absolutely certain that someone *just like* Stark must have had a close relationship with

Klingsor. His activities, his access to the Führer, his privileged status in the Reich scientific community—all of this leads me to believe that their paths must have crossed, not once but many, many times. In the long run, perhaps Stark will only be a reference point that will lead us toward Klingsor. Think of it as a kind of working hypothesis."

Bacon took a moment to ponder this, though it felt like an age. Didn't he want to follow my intuition? Hadn't he called upon me for my advice, for someone to point the way for him?

"I'll call for his dossier," Bacon agreed.

As the last rays of light battled unsuccessfully against the windstorm that preceded the sunset, Bacon found himself facing the only challenge—outside of Klingsor, of course—that meant anything to him these days: the ancient walls that separated him from Irene. He ran to her as if each minute apart were an eternity. His breathing was labored, and he had to take a moment to catch his breath before ringing the doorbell. Irene answered the door wearing a black housedress, a shawl wrapped around her shoulders. She didn't seem surprised at all to see him.

"Come in," she said in a tone of voice that seemed animated, at least to Bacon. "Tea, yes?"

"Yes, thanks."

Frank was following the predetermined routine, the kind of routine that keeps people together: He took off his coat, looked around the room, walked over to Irene, looked into her dark eyes and her freshly washed blond hair. He inhaled the scent of her body. She offered him the steaming cup of tea and they sat down close to one another.

"Johann?"

"He's with his grandmother for the afternoon."

Bacon smiled.

"Maybe we can go out for a little bit," she proposed shyly. "It's a rare occasion for me to have an afternoon free."

"Let's go," Bacon announced, grabbing his coat.

After running a comb through her hair, she grabbed Bacon's arm, like a little boy eagerly awaiting his trip to the circus. It was dark outside, but the afternoon wasn't particularly cold. The dirty snow, piled up on the sidewalks and on the tree branches, was like an ugly blemish on the landscape of the city. High above, however, the majestic expanse of sky opened up toward the heavens, illuminated by a tiny sliver of moon.

"He died in the war."

"What?"

"Johann's father," Irene explained.

"I'm so sorry."

There was something about Irene's face—a new sparkle, a childlike energy that made it hard to envision her as the mother of a little boy. They continued walking until they reached a small tavern.

"Don't worry," said Irene. "By the time it happened we weren't terribly close. I don't mean that I wasn't sad, just that I don't really miss him."

They walked inside the tavern and found seats toward the back, where the heat was intense but welcome.

"Yes," Bacon mused. "Sometimes routine can kill love."

"What do you mean?"

"I think that love begins to go awry when you can begin to predict your lover's behavior, when you grow certain that he loves you, and will continue to love you."

"That's terrible," Irene said, pausing to order two glasses of hot wine.

"Maybe I'm not explaining myself very well," Bacon improvised. "What I'm trying to say is that, when you know a person, sooner or later you can predict their reactions to things. I don't mean to say that love necessarily has to be boring, just that inevitably it becomes predictable. The quest for love is a long road, and once we finally arrive at the goal, the reward can sometimes be a letdown. When you are searching for something so desperately, the worst thing that can happen is to get what you want right away."

Irene cast him a scornful glance.

"I don't look at love as a horse race. And what if the purpose of love is to transform a boring, insignificant moment into a life-filled experience?" Suddenly this taciturn young woman had become quite eloquent.

"You know, I think we're saying very similar things, although from two different angles," said Frank, taking a sip of wine. "If I love a woman, I want it to be different every day."

"Interesting problem," she said sarcastically. "So I guess that means you need either an actress or an escape artist. Or, better yet, a schizophrenic."

"Don't make fun of me."

"Forgive me for saying this, but I don't think you've ever been in love." Her cheeks suddenly became flushed with an intense red. "You want every woman to be a harem, and that's not possible. When you love somebody, you don't want them to change. Unless both want to change, together."

Bacon's head was spinning from the alcohol. He loved how passionate she was, how she contradicted everything he said. He didn't really know what he was talking about, but her fiery retorts inspired and emboldened him to put up as good a fight as he could.

"I like the image of the harem, but I think you've misinterpreted what I said. I don't want a different woman every night, but rather a kind of Scheherazade who is able to invent a new story every night. The *Thousand and One Nights* is a perfect example. When Scheherazade is unable to create a new story for the sultan—that is, a new chapter of her love for him—he has no choice but to have her killed. It isn't an act of cruelty, but rather an imperative which is imposed upon them by the game they have both agreed to play. An imperative of the game of love. And the moral, of course, is the following: If your love can't be continually reinvented, then it is better to let it die."

"What a typical comment for a man to make."

"No, you're wrong again: My opinions apply to men as well as women." Bacon was now trying to synchronize his bodily movements with those of Irene. "The sultan and Scheherazade were constantly trading roles."

"But what if one doesn't have sufficient imagination necessary for this kind of game?" Despite the seeming humility of this question, Bacon found something unbelievably arrogant about it.

"It's a question of will, not of imagination. I'm not asking my companion to recite novels or write poems for me, I simply ask her to accept the plurality that exists in all of us and allow it to take its course. It has nothing to do with pretending or acting, but rather transforming the love so that each day it can be renewed. A bit of uncertainty never did anyone any harm, Irene."

It was the first time he called her by name. He felt a sweet rhythm accompany the syllables as he uttered them.

"I don't think you have the courage to admit that you want to be with lots of women at once." Irene was doing her best to catch him in his trap. "There's nothing wrong with it. Perhaps what you want isn't love but *diversity.*"

"I'm hurt that you would think that of me. We're talking about love. I'm not asking for different personalities or different women—I'm not trying to be some kind of monogamous Don Juan. The only thing I reject, that I simply cannot accept, is a woman who loves me (or says she loves me), but then isn't willing to change once she knows I love her, too. If there's one thing I can't stand it's conformists—especially the kind who think they've found love and then fall into that complacent bliss, so certain that they have found something permanent, eternal. I believe one should always continue searching."

"And what guarantee do you have that this interminable search won't lead to indifference? Or to the realization that you aren't in love after all, or that you love someone else?"

Bacon pondered this for a moment.

"It's worth the risk. It's painful, but sometimes love dies or fades precisely because the people in question haven't made the effort to keep searching, the way they did in the beginning. Just when a person *has* something (in the sense of being its owner, its proprietor) is when he is most likely to lose it."

"That is horrible," said Irene, clearly outraged. "If that is the case, how can we ever know that the person who loves us isn't fooling us, or that we aren't fooling the person we believe we're in love with?"

"We can't!" Bacon's voice rose to a shout. "That's the point. We trust the other person, and moreover we trust our own intuition. Everything goes back to trust. What is trust if not the confidence to believe in another person—without the guarantee that they are telling us the truth? Anyway, it always works out like that. We have to be realistic, Irene. We can never be sure of other people's intentions. Never."

"You make it sound as though love is a game between two people, each person trying to take advantage of the other."

"That's an excellent definition. Except love is the kind of game in which there are no winners or losers, in the long run. Of course, one of the two might decide not to play the game anymore, and then it's all over."

"But how can you know if the game is over if one person still wants to play?"

"That's not so hard, Irene. There are clues everywhere. Hundreds of little details begging to be interpreted. External acts that we can associate with their corresponding romantic significance." Bacon took a napkin and raised it to his lips. "A love letter, a conversation, a flirtation, a date, an act of revenge, a fit of jealousy. Each one of these acts is no different from a pawn or a rook being moved from one spot to another on a chessboard. I say, 'I love you.' And you say, 'Well, I don't love you.' And you go on from there, until you manage to convince yourself that, behind all these myriad combinations, the other person feels a wide range of emotions for you that can be identified as 'love.' Good lovers are nothing more than good readers: men and women with the experience necessary to decipher the encoded messages which others send them."

"Why do you insist on treating love as a kind of competition? I always thought it was something far more spontaneous."

"Well, your idealistic approach is not entirely inapplicable to my theory," replied Bacon politely. "But it doesn't have anything to do with the strategy people use to fall in love. To show our love. To need love. To complain about love. To want more love. To run away from love. To recapture lost love."

Bacon knew that he had won the game. This time. But he didn't want to leave Irene empty-handed. Before dropping her off at the doorstep of her apartment, Bacon held her in his arms for a few brief minutes, though to him they felt like centuries.

REASONS FOR
DISCOURAGEMENT

BERLIN
MAY 1937

It was a hot Sunday afternoon, like so many others, and we had gone for a walk near the Wannsee. We strolled around the lake, contemplating the undulating reflection of the trees in the shallow waves, the two of us locked in an uncomfortable silence which we had been maintaining for a few months now. Marianne was still angry with me for not allowing her to visit Natalia and Heinrich, and she used every opportunity to remind me of how she felt.

"She's always been my friend—I can't imagine the rest of my life without her."

All I offered was an apology. "Well, her husband was my friend, too, but under the circumstances, I simply can't have anything to do with him. It's his fault, not mine."

Marianne didn't understand my reasoning, and so this became the focal point of all our arguments.

"I married you, not them," I replied angrily.

As a form of revenge, she would refuse to allow me to hold her at night, and the anger she felt would come out in her dreams. In her sleep she would repeat her friend's name over and over again like some kind of mystical incantation. Of course, this wasn't our first or only problem, but it was one of the more recurring ones.

The hot sun deposited light drops of sweat upon Marianne's cheeks and upper neck. The truth is, she was still beautiful, even though I didn't realize it then. She wore a tailored white dress and a little mauve-colored cap. As if she were the picture of Dorian Gray, I would admire her reflection in the water, only for the lake to give her back to me as a blurry, impertinent beast.

"I've made up my mind, Gustav."

"What?" I asked, trying to provoke her.

"You know perfectly well what."

"I told you it's out of the question."

"She's my friend, not yours."

"She's the wife of a man who is my enemy, and therefore yours as well."

We continued walking.

"Let's go back."

"Yes, why don't we?"

We walked back toward Bismarckstraße, and got ready for the trip back to Berlin. The silence that engulfed us felt as vast and deep as the ocean. We stopped for a moment in front of the grave of the poet Heinrich von Kleist. I shivered at the coincidence between the two names. After several failed suicide attempts and countless allusions to that effect in his poetry and prose, Kleist and his lover killed themselves. She had been terminally ill, and together they had made a pact.

"Since you won't allow me to go and visit her at her house, I've invited her over for tea."

Suddenly, I just didn't want to disagree with her anymore. Even the most perfunctory kind of disagreement required a level of energy that I didn't have anymore when it came to Marianne.

"Do what you want."

"I already have," she said. I knew she was as surprised as I was by the words that had just come out of her mouth.

"It doesn't matter. You never obey me, anyway."

"Never."

"Never."

When was the last time I'd seen Natalia? The same time I'd last seen Heini, about three years earlier. Somehow, the idea of seeing her in my home, next to my wife, didn't bother me at all.

"She's to come over tomorrow at five, in case you don't want to be there."

"It's my house, too, isn't it? I have the right to be there whenever I please."

"I only said it because I thought her presence might upset you, that's all."

"What upsets me is that she insists on defending a Nazi, Marianne. Don't you see? He betrayed all of us."

"I'm not sure who has betrayed who, Gustav."

"What is that supposed to mean?"

"By treating your friends the way you do, you become something worse than a Nazi."

"There is nothing worse than a Nazi, Marianne."

"Oh, yes, there is, Gustav."

Johannes Stark, or
a Lesson in Infamy

Once again, Lieutenant Bacon began to read aloud:

Report #650-F
Stark, Johannes
Alsos
110744

Some people consider him the prototypical Nazi scientist. He was one of the pioneers of *Deutsche Physik,* a movement created to fight the "degenerated science" practiced by Einstein* and other Jewish physicists. He received his first professorial appointment from the University of Aachen in 1909, and around that time is said to have been at the center of a bitter dispute with Arnold Sommerfeld,* professor of the University of Munich and a proponent of quantum theory. The friction between the two men grew worse when the Dutch physicist Pieter Debye,* one of Sommerfeld's students, was appointed chair of the physics department at the University of Göttingen, a position Stark had long since coveted. Furious, Stark declared it a conspiracy plotted by the "Jewish and pro-Semitic club" whose "general manager" was Arnold Sommerfeld.

In 1917, Stark transferred to the smaller University of Greifswald, and it was there he received word of the Germans' defeat. This milestone only intensified his already nationalist tendencies, and some close friends managed to coax him into launching an antisocialist campaign, in response to the socialists' increasingly strong hold on local political life.

In 1919, he was awarded the Nobel Prize for the discovery of what would then be called the "Stark effect," or the splitting of spectral lines produced in an electric field. He was then invited to work at the University of Würzburg, in Bavaria. In April of that same year, he founded the German Professional Community of University Physicists, which was an attempt to challenge the more liberal-leaning German Physics Society, dominated by the more cosmopolitan and theoretical physicists in Berlin. In Stark's opinion, the Berlin scientists discriminated against the professors who worked at the universities in the provinces. Stark, however, was unsuccessful at rallying his colleagues' support in this effort, and when the German Physics Society held elections for their new president, the winner was Wilhelm Wien, a former member of Stark's group. Devastated by such a blow, Stark's association folded.

Before Stark, another German physicist had spoken out against "Jewish science." In 1922, Philipp Lenard,* Nobel Prize winner and professor at Heidelberg, published a manifesto in which he called for the acceleration of the country's "Aryan science" programs, and accused the German scientific community of betraying its racial legacy.

"In 1920, a meeting was held by the Association of German Natural Scientists for the Preservation of Pure Science, in the hall of the Berlin Philharmonic," Bacon announced. "The 'Anti-Relativity Company,' as Einstein called it. From that moment on, the attacks against him intensified."

"That group never really existed. It was a fantasy dreamed up by Paul Weyland, one of Einstein's archenemies. He only created it to generate attention for himself," I answered. "But it was enough to generate a response among many physicists who, until then, had remained somewhat indifferent to the politics of the times. Einstein attended one of the meetings of the association and, later on, wrote a response to the Anti-Relativity Company in the *Berliner Tageblatt*, which caused a major uproar."

"Did they hate Einstein simply because he was Jewish, or was it the relativity theory?" Bacon asked me.

"I think that at first, his Judaism was less important to them, Lieutenant," I began. "His political stance was what made him dangerous. During the Great War, the majority of the German scientific community had supported the Kaiser and his generals, but Einstein became a Swiss citizen and a pacifist instead, something that the Germans viewed as a betrayal. He emerged as one of the few consistent public supporters of the Weimar republic, partly the result of his friendship with Walther Rathenau, a fellow Jew who was also acting foreign minister at the time. Einstein's public image was too volatile. Not only was he devoted to revolutionizing the world of science, but he also insisted upon supporting the chaotic republican regime that had accepted Germany's defeat. For many people, that made him doubly despicable." Bacon sunk deeper in his chair. "And the hatred for him grew and spread as quickly as his scientific renown. Soon he became the emblem of a kind of internationalism that the German nationalists abhorred. In those days, we all thought politics should be kept away from science. One shouldn't dirty one's hands with reality, we said."

"Like Einstein did."

"His detractors tried to prove that relativity was a farce, and they did this with rational arguments. They worked hard at sounding convincing and serious in the articles they published—after all, they didn't want to become a laughingstock. At first, they avoided the anti-Semitic arguments at all costs. The German scientific community, don't forget, was a stiff bunch. But then Einstein's supporters began to claim that his Judaism was the root of the attacks against him. They were the first ones to use the word and to turn the scientific discourse into a racial affair."

"I see. *You* were the ones who brought politics into science, *you* were the ones whose methods were not strictly scientific, *you* were the ones who made public declarations. They must have thought Einstein was some kind of monster."

"He undermined all the protocol and etiquette that German physicists had observed for generations. Even Planck was rather scandalized. Geniuses are always a bit bothersome, but Einstein really crossed the line. He never held back his opinions—in fact, he handed them out as freely as if he were a deputy of the Reichstag."

"At Princeton I always got the impression he hated politics."

"Maybe that's how he was in America, but not here," I said. "In Germany he was always involved in politics and never hesitated to share his opinions with the press."

"His portraits. His newspaper interviews. The front page of the *New York Times*. The public fanfare over relativity. Of course." Bacon smiled at the sudden flash from his past.

"Philipp Lenard had nothing to do with the conferences in Berlin," I noted. "Nevertheless, Einstein decided to mention him in his response. This infuriated Lenard, and he began to attack Einstein simply because *he* felt attacked, a victim."

"Some victim!"

"Well, maybe he wasn't a victim, but he acted like one. The atmosphere was ripe for it: Everywhere you went in Germany it was bedlam. Revolutions, murders, sackings. Everyone wanted just a little bit of peace and stability, and Einstein's positions seemed to encourage only conflict and chaos.

If my memory serves me right, Rathenau, Einstein's friend, was assassinated in 1922. On Lenard's orders, the flags at the University of Heidelberg did not fly at half-mast that day. An infuriated mob attacked and booed him, which made him even more furious."

"Hmm. Let's get back to Stark.

In 1921, one of Stark's most beloved students, Ludwig Glaser,* presented his thesis on the optical properties of porcelain to the *Habilitationsschrift*. Glaser, in addition to editing his own journal on technical aspects of physics, had his own laboratory, and the previous year, he had participated in one of the antirelativity conferences held in Berlin. The judges felt that Glaser's thesis did not shed any new light onto the field of physics—in fact, some even went so far as to make fun of him, calling him "Dr. Porcelain." They rejected his thesis, but there was a story behind it. Einstein's supporters had been known for harboring a certain hostility toward the young physicist, and in response to this incident Stark resigned from the University of Würzburg, accusing the judges of conspiracy.

After winning the Nobel Prize, Stark used his award money to start up various enterprises. He also tried to get appointed director of the Imperial Physical-Technical Institute, but once again the advocates of relativity denied his candidacy. By now, Stark was more than angry; he was furious and he was bitter. Suddenly he found himself ostracized by the academic world he had so badly wanted to be a part of. To make matters worse for him, in 1921 Einstein won the Nobel Prize, which only enhanced his already rising international celebrity.

That same year, Stark published *The Crisis in Contemporary German Physics*, a book that denounced the dogmas and excessive formalism of the relativity and quantum theories. According to Stark, Einstein's science was nothing more than mathematical speculation without any real, tangible meaning. Stark went further, claiming that Einstein's supporters acted as a bloc, as if they were endorsing a political ideal, instead of encouraging the open discussion of its principles. In a very special way, Stark criticized the manner in which Einstein's theory had been disseminated: According to him, Einstein's supposed physics "revolution," widely acclaimed by the nonacademic media and in conferences all over the world, was nothing more than an act of political propaganda.

That was the moment in which everything changed in the controversy surrounding the relativity theory. In the beginning, relativity's detractors had tried to confine themselves to purely scientific arguments, yet Einstein's defenders insisted upon dragging politics into the discourse. Now, however, Einstein found himself bombarded by personal accusations and anti-Semitic attacks. In 1922, Lenard and Stark—who by now had cultivated a most cordial relationship—joined forces to defend the so-called *Deutsche Physik.* Their objective was to eliminate all the "Jewish elements" from German science—that is, its dogmas, its mathematical abstractions, and their corresponding uselessness—in favor of an "Aryan" science more concerned with practical results than metaphysical speculation. The initial nucleus formed by Stark and Lenard quickly grew as a large number of ultraconservative, anti-Semitic, nationalistic physicists joined their cause in the belief that the relativity supporters were enemies out to marginalize them from academic life.

In 1923, Lenard and Stark began to move closer to Hitler's circle. They were among the first scientists to publicly support him during the Beer Hall *putsch,* and they remained in contact with him during his two years of incarceration. Stark did not join the party until 1930, but in fact he had been working on its behalf since 1924, when Hitler was released from Landsberg Prison. Later on, as a reward for this loyalty, he would earn the moniker "Old Fighter," and when Hitler became chancellor, Stark began to exercise considerable influence upon the scientific politics of the Reich.

"The rage," I said to Bacon. "Do you realize that rage is what transformed a normal scientist, a respected scientist and Nobel Prize winner, into the aider and abetter of criminals? This was the question you asked me the other day, isn't it? Rage and envy. Did it really matter whether relativity was valid or not? I doubt it. There was a war in the middle of all this, and just like any other war, each side was prepared to do anything to defeat the other. Blood, threats, betrayals. Stark and Lenard would do whatever it took to finish off Einstein."

"Are you saying that truth and science were the least of it?"

"What I'm saying is that during such turbulent times, truth sometimes is a lower priority after other considerations," I corrected him. "If one could just stick to the evidence, the issue would be much simpler, wouldn't it? It would have been enough to prove scientifically that Einstein was right and the others were wrong, or vice versa. But that didn't happen. Science was no longer clear or precise. One group believed one thing, and another group believed something else. That's all. One group presented its evidence, and the others rejected it—they claimed the results had been manipulated, or weren't conclusive. It was all *politics,* Lieutenant. Physics had practically nothing to do with it."

"So, then, if Hitler had won the war, relativity might not even exist in Germany."

"Right. Or else it would have been reinvented by someone inside the Nazi regime. That's how it is, as unbelievable as it sounds. The validity of any given idea depends on how able you are to assert its truth. And if people believe what you say, the experimental evidence will follow soon enough. Science had become so ambiguous that people had begun to interpret things according to their own whim. Perhaps that was why Einstein was so skeptical of quantum theory: If a measurement is incapable of reflecting a complete truth, then it becomes sort of a half-lie, doesn't it? And then who knows what that would lead to," I finished dramatically. "Of course, Einstein was sharp enough to realize that he had laid the foundations for his own defeat. He hated the concept of randomness because he knew that in a truly relative—not relativistic, but relative—world, some authority could eventually demonstrate that *he* was wrong. In the spirit of the great cynics of classic antiquity, lover of paradoxes, Einstein thought that if all movement was relative, well, then, so was relativity itself."

Frank could still feel the bittersweet taste of Irene on his lips. They had been saying good-bye, with that vague, skittish hesitation that builds up after so much unconsummated flirtation, when she suddenly decided to plant her face in front of his and wait for him to make the first move. For a second, Bacon hesitated—it had been so long since he had felt anything for any woman. But finally he bent down and kissed her delicately. It was a brief encounter, but it was enough to make him feel connected to Irene.

From that moment on, his daily routine followed a mathematically precise pattern. In the mornings he would go to his office, where he would review archives and documents, and type up memos and reports. He would check in with his superiors occasionally, or wander through the old printing presses that were still standing in the building, like the bones of prehistoric animals. Then he would go out for lunch, always alone, and return at around three in the afternoon. I would arrive at four o'clock, we would have tea together and then work on Klingsor until seven, when Frank would say good-bye and hurry off to spend a precious few hours with Irene.

As always, she would greet him with a hot cup of tea; sometimes they went out for drinks but inevitably the evening would wind down in Irene's small living room. There they would lie down in her easy chair and talk for long stretches. Every so often Johann would spend the night at Irene's mother's house.

"Tell me about you," she said one day.

"I'm afraid I'm not a very interesting topic of research."

"You're so secretive."

"I'm just cautious."

"So what are you running away from?" Irene asked.

"I'm not running, I'm searching. I'm a researcher. I used to research science and now I research human beings." There was an undeniable hint of melancholy in his voice.

"It doesn't sound as though you like it."

"Well, I can't complain."

"Would you rather work in a laboratory?"

"To tell the truth, I never have," Bacon said, laughing. "I know that's the classic image of the scientist, concocting all sorts of potions and pouring them into beakers and bulbous glass jars, like medieval alchemists. No, before I enlisted, I worked in a place where our only instruments were blackboards and chalk."

"And what did you do?"

"Think," Frank said. There was no pride in his voice. "Or at least try to. May I have another cup, please?"

"I can't even imagine it. Thinking all day long, my God. I couldn't do it. I would go crazy."

"I couldn't either. And you're right, in the end it drives people mad. That's why there are so many scientists like Einstein—absentminded, isolated, removed from the world. Although not all of them are like that, of course."

"Did you ever meet him?"

"I saw him a couple of times," Bacon lied. "He was better-looking than they say."

"A job that forces you to spend all your time thinking," Irene repeated robotically. "For me, that would be torture."

"Torture."

"And so what did you think about?"

"Atomic particles: electrons, neutrons, protons . . ."

"But it didn't give you time to think about yourself."

"I don't follow."

"Atoms were all you had to keep you busy? Where were *you* in the middle of all that?"

"Running circles around physics, like an electron. Attracted and repelled by the energy of women." He laughed. "My mother, my fiancée, my lover . . . does that shock you?"

"Well . . . I didn't realize you were such a ladies' man."

"I'm not—I'm just objectively describing a certain phenomenon, that's all. Women are like stars: They glitter and they dazzle you, but what they're really doing is drawing you to them with a force far more powerful than gravity: infatuation. Men, on the other hand, are like tiny asteroids: They revolve around the stars, pay them tribute, obey their laws. But we all know that if the gravitational field of women were not as strong as it is, men would escape at the very first chance. And do you know why? So they could fall into the orbit of yet another star."

"That's pathetic. I think the opposite is true, actually. Women are the forces that have no other choice than to fight the gravitational field that men want to subject them to."

"Have you ever been in love, Gustav?"

The question took me by surprise. It was a bit of a non sequitur, and, anyway, what did he care?

"I suppose we all have at some time or another," I said flatly, hoping to go back to the topic of Klingsor.

"Love, Gustav. They raised us to believe it's the most important thing in the whole world. As far back as the New Testament we have a God who loves us. *Love one another*, he said. And then they inundated us with novels, poems, radio programs, movies. Love affairs as far as the eye can see. Isn't it rather shocking? The union of two people is the fundamental force which drives our culture."

"Nonsense," I answered. "You said it yourself: They raise us to think that way, even though we know in the end it's just a pretense. Love is an illusion. We all realize it sooner or later."

"Do you speak from experience?"

"We've all been through it, Lieutenant. We all fall in love and only when it's all over do we realize that we've been cheated. Unfortunately, by that time it's almost always too late for apologies."

"I used to think like you, Gustav. Especially at the beginning of the war."

"But not anymore?"

"I don't know. Sometimes I want to think that love is important. It's something so irrational, so elusive . . . it only exists because we insist upon believing in it."

"Like religion."

"Like religion. Or science. So what was her name?"

"Whose name?"

"The woman you were in love with. Or women, whatever the case may be."

"My wife was named Marianne," I replied.

"And were you in love with her?"

"I loved her."

"I didn't ask you that."

"She was my wife."

"I don't know why I say this, but I sense some discomfort on your part, Gustav. What happened with Marianne?"

"She died at the end of the war."

"Oh. I'm so sorry." Bacon was embarrassed now. "I didn't mean—"

"Don't worry, it's over now. Now tell me, are you in love?"

"I still don't know."

"What is her name?"

"Irene," proclaimed Frank, enraptured.

"Be careful," I advised. "German?"

"Yes, from Dresden."

"Even worse. I'd be very careful if I were in your shoes. Love is just bait women use to get us to do what they want."

"I know." Bacon laughed. "But if it were any other way, it wouldn't be worth trying for. Every game entails certain risks. And in the game of love, the person who falls in love first is always at the other's mercy."

"May I ask how you met her, Frank?"

"She's my neighbor."

"Your neighbor," I mused. "You just met her and you think you might be in love with her?"

"Let's drop it."

"I have good news, " I said. "Max von Laue has agreed to see us today, to discuss the Stark case."

A few hours later we found ourselves sitting before the old physicist.

"When Hitler was named chancellor, Stark and Lenard were ecstatic," Von Laue began. "Because it seemed that their moment had finally arrived. In a letter of congratulations to Wilhelm Frick, the new Nazi minister of the interior, Stark plainly stated that both he and Lenard were ready and willing to be of service to the Reich, as soon as was necessary. Lenard even managed a one-on-one meeting with Hitler."

Max von Laue was a tall, fastidious man, like granite. His symmetrical, severe features did little to soften the cold, hard expression on his face. His mustache, eyebrows, and hair were that ash-blond color that could only belong to someone descended from a long line of German nobles. Yet Von Laue was something of a rara avis among the German physicists of his generation, for he was never a Nazi sympathizer. In fact, he was one of the few scientists who openly opposed the regime, and he maintained this stance as long as it was possible without endangering his own life. He won the Nobel Prize in 1914, right at the start of the Great War. He was friends with Planck, and had been very close to Einstein at that time. And although he was not part of the German atomic project, he was captured by the Alsos mission along with the rest of his colleagues. Unbelievable as it seemed, Von Laue was taken into custody and transferred to Farm Hall as "His Majesty's prisoner," along with the rest of the physicists, but Bacon never had the opportunity to meet him there. Now, just like the other German physicists living in the British zone of occupation, he had been transferred to Göttingen, the new heart of the German science community.

"Those vultures saw to it that all the important scientific posts came under attack," he continued. "The Imperial Physical-Technical Institute, the Emergency Foundation for German Science, the Kaiser Wilhelm Society. In 1933, during a meeting of the German Physics Society, held in Würzburg, Stark behaved like a mini-Führer, acting like a little dictator of all the physicists. His idea was that the Reich needed a general editor to oversee all the scientific magazines and journals, a person who would have to approve all articles before publication."

"Exactly what Goebbels did with the newspapers and magazines," I said.

"He was trying to take his revenge on all of us for the isolation he suffered during the republic years. Stark insisted that German scientists would ultimately have the freedom to research whatever they wanted, but in the logic of those times, those words meant precisely the opposite. I felt I had no choice but to stand up and speak my mind. 'You want to judge the theory of relativity the same despicable way the Catholic Church condemned Galileo for defending Copernicus' heliocentrism!' I exclaimed. 'But, just as the Italian physicist said, *eppur si muove . . .*'"

"That must have infuriated him," Bacon noted.

"I wasn't afraid of a confrontation," Von Laue added, excited now. "The whole world knew we were enemies, and so the only dignified thing to do was to spit the truth out at him."

"And how did he react?"

"Like always. He said I was a Jew lover. In any event, my protests had little effect. Stark got his wish: In May of 1933 he became director of the Imperial Physical-Technical Institute, a position he had coveted all his life and which Hitler deigned to award him. Stark transformed the institute into a microcosm of the Nazi party. The scientists who worked there had to obey a very specific hierarchy: They were to respond to their superiors like soldiers, never questioning the chain of command. His plans were truly megalomaniacal. He wanted the institute to become the center of German scientific investigation, in charge of supervising the finances and even the defense of the Reich. Shortage of funds was the only thing that prevented him from reaching his goal. The education and defense ministries eventually realized that his objectives were in fact rather vague, and it wasn't long before they rejected his proposal."

"Did he lose influence after that?"

"Little by little, people began to realize that the only thing Stark cared about was himself, his ego. And in the Nazi scheme of things, that was unacceptable. The politicians all fought among themselves and one man could not be allowed to build such a strong power base. Not long after that Stark was proposed for membership in the Prussian Academy of Sciences—"

"Which you protested vehemently."

"I simply felt it would be an outrage for a man like that to be admitted into the academy," said Von Laue coolly. "He would try to turn it into another Nazi puppet organization, just as he had done with the Imperial Institute. But Stark had more powerful enemies than me, and in the end membership was out of the question."

"So you won out," Bacon said.

"Let's just say that within the academy the necessary environment was created to frustrate his possibilities for membership. But Stark wouldn't give up so easily. In 1934, he tried to gain international prominence by sending a long article to the English magazine *Nature*, in which he explained the scientific politics of the Reich. His arguments and theories were an absurd mixture of everything from preposterous accusations to outright lies. In the piece he contended that the new regimen actually promoted the scientific freedom that the Weimar republic had limited."

"And he was careful not to attack the Jews."

"Naturally. Stark simply repeated the same excuse as always: Hitler is not after Jewish scientists, he simply is trying to reform the civil service to make it more efficient. If Jewish scientists are being dismissed from their jobs, it's because they don't deserve the positions they occupy. In response to the many scathing letters to the editor of *Nature,* Stark counterattacked with a new barrage of nonsense and lies. This time, he was bold enough to mention the 'defenders of Jewish science' by name: Planck, Sommerfeld, and, of course, me."

"How did you respond to the attacks?"

"By exposing his lies, as always. But then he tried another *coup d'effet.* At the behest of a high-ranking official in the Ministry of Propaganda, he tried to gather the signatures of twelve Aryan Nobel Prize winners as a way of mustering support for Hitler. Most of us refused."

"Weren't you afraid of reprisals, Professor?"

"Well, politics and science were not supposed to mix. We had said it a thousand times; it was our only line of defense. Stark had to admit his failure to Goebbels himself."

"In any event, Stark was named director of the German Research Foundation, the new name of the Emergency Foundation for German Science." I was trying hard to direct the conversation toward something more substantial.

"Bernhard Rust, the education minister, had fired the foundation's previous director, Schmidt-Ott, and was ordered by Hitler to replace him with Stark. And can you guess the first thing Stark did as president of the foundation? He canceled most of the funding for projects related to theoretical physics, and those funds were then channeled to military programs."

"I have here an article by Lenard which appeared in the *Völkische Beobachter,* the Nazi party newspaper. In it, he congratulates himself on Stark's recent appointment," I said, and then read a few sentences from the article. "'Einstein is our most prominent example of the harmful effect Jews have had on the natural sciences. Active theoreticians occupying relevant positions should have monitored these developments more carefully. Now Hitler has decided to do so himself. The game is over; the foreign elements are voluntarily fleeing the university and the country itself.'" Then, in a less pompous tone, I added: "It wasn't long before the battle began over the position Arnold Sommerfeld was about to relinquish at the University of Munich."

"Sommerfeld detested Stark as much as I did. In 1934, when Arnold announced his retirement, the most obvious candidate to fill the post was Heisenberg, one of his most brilliant students—he had just won the Nobel Prize, in fact. But as soon as Stark heard the news, he did all he could to sabotage Heisenberg's candidacy. From that moment on, Heisenberg became Stark's scapegoat."

"But why did he become so fixated on Heisenberg?" asked Bacon.

"Well, for all his celebrity, Heisenberg was still very young. And moreover, he had never held an important position in the academic world. He was just another professor from Leipzig. The perfect target."

"I was in Leipzig then," I said. "The Nazis worked hard to create a thoroughly oppressive atmosphere. I remember it well—in fact, if I'm not mistaken, Stark actually called Heisenberg a 'white Jew' in an article that appeared in the *Das Schwarze Korps*."

"Stark didn't write that article, one of his followers did. His name was Willi Menzel, a physics student," Von Laue corrected me. "But it might as well have been signed by Stark. Heisenberg a Jew! You'd have to have quite an imagination—or quite a sick mind—to say such a thing. Please don't misunderstand me: I'm not referring to his religious beliefs or his race, just the methods he employed for tackling physics problems. Heisenberg was the prototypical German physicist. Since there was no way Stark could accuse Heisenberg of being a poor physicist, the best he could do was accuse him (and the rest of us) of practicing 'Jewish' science."

"What were the consequences of the attack, Professor?"

"Stark was a snake. In those days he was feeling more powerful than ever. In 1935, Lenard published a book on the *Deutsche Physik,* which stated that race was the underlying foundation of all human activity. Of course, science was no exception to this rule. Jews, then, had their own physics, totally different from German, Aryan, or Nordic physics, as he called it. So what was the basis of this distinction? Good question. In reality, all Lenard said was that Jewish science was what he and his colleagues *said* Jewish science was. It was that simple. There was no rational argument. As if that weren't enough, that very same year the new physics institute at the University of Heidelberg was baptized under the name of Philipp Lenard. Stark spoke at the inaugural ceremony, and took full advantage of the opportunity to launch even more attacks. His verdict was crystal-clear: Einstein's relativity, Schrödinger's wave mechanics, and Heisenberg's matrix mechanics were all considered paradigms of Jewish science and, as such, were to disappear from German science altogether. These very statements appeared in Menzel's article. Of course, neither Schrödinger nor Heisenberg was Jewish."

"Heisenberg tried to defend himself," Bacon noted.

"What else could he do? He sent a response to the *Völkische Beobachter.* This infuriated Stark, who answered Heisenberg himself, accusing him of poisoning the youth of Germany with his defense of Jewish physics. As far as he was concerned, relativity and quantum theories were nothing more than unintelligible mathematic formulas, useless 'mental gymnastics,' and this opinion was echoed by Alfons Bühl, Rudolf Tomaschek, and the rest of the disciples of *Deutsche Physik*."

"So what did Heisenberg do then?"

"You know, I have never known a man who loved his country as much as Heisenberg did," said Von Laue, though his voice was utterly unsentimental. "Stark had vilified him, but he wasn't going to leave Germany just because of that. Instead, he chose to fight to clear his name. And he did so using the only avenues the regime made available to him. It was a slow, rough battle, and by the time it was over, Heisenberg was broken from the effort."

"But in the end Heisenberg won," I observed.

"A Pyrrhic victory, Professor Links. Yes, he got the Nazi authorities to agree to prohibit Stark from attacking him anymore, and he was even permitted to respond to Stark with a new article, published in the *Völkische Beobachter*, but in the end he never did get the position at Munich. Stark and Lenard were responsible for this injustice, as well as countless other blows that German science endured during those years."

"Do you think their power base was broad enough for them to control the scientific life of the entire country?" asked Bacon.

"Germany was an intricate web of offices and bureaus, all of which carried out the same tasks, which meant they were always in stiff competition with one another. Naturally, with the Imperial Physical Technical Institute, the Research Foundation, the Heidelberg Institute, and the many university physics departments under their control, Stark and Lenard had considerable influence. But it was kept in check by other Nazi agencies that were also involved in scientific investigation: Rust's education ministry, Himmler's SS, Frick's Ministry of the Interior, and, of course, Goering's Scientific Research Council. To say nothing of the efforts of the many, many physicists working independently, myself included."

"Even so, would you say that Stark was the physicist closest to the Nazi command center? That Hitler considered him his personal scientific adviser?"

"Without a doubt."

"Despite the groundswell of opposition?"

"Yes, despite all that, he was the most powerful physicist in all of Germany."

I met with Bacon the day after our encounter with Von Laue. The sour expression on his face was not a promising one, and his suddenly peremptory attitude deflated my spirit.

"No matter what Von Laue said yesterday, there is absolutely no way Stark can be Klingsor," he scolded me as I walked in. "Remember what Planck said: 'He was one of us.' The majority of the scientific community thought that *Deutsche Physik* was nothing but hogwash—a smoke screen for politics, cheap vendettas, and petty chicanery."

"But Von Laue assured us that Stark was the most important scientist in Germany then," I reminded him, suddenly the devil's advocate. "Hitler protected him."

"Maybe not, though," Bacon remarked skeptically. "We have a new element to consider. I don't know if you knew this, but just before the war broke out, Stark was nearly expelled officially from the party."

Bacon left his office for a moment and returned with a young officer struggling beneath a heavy pile of papers in his arms.

"By pure coincidence, I found out that Sergeant Johnson here is transcribing the Nazi party archives that were used during the Nuremberg Trials." Bacon paused for a moment. "Sergeant, I'd like to introduce you to Professor Gustav Links."

"It's a pleasure to meet you," said Johnson in a high-pitched voice. He sounded just like a little boy; he couldn't have been more than twenty years old. He still had a few stray pimples scattered across his otherwise smooth, hairless face, and his stiff gestures indicated that he wasn't fully at ease in civilian company.

"Sit down, Sergeant," Frank said, and the young man sat down on the other side of the desk. "Read us your report, if you would."

Johnson cleared his throat, but it didn't have much of an effect on his delivery. He had difficulty speaking, even though he was obviously quite a brilliant boy. Whenever he got tongue-tied he would fumble through the mimeographed sheets in his trembling hands, as if reciting the *particella* of some opera.

"It all started because of a certain man named Endrös," Johnson began. "A dishonest man, not unlike the many little Hitlers who, from 1933 on, had assumed positions of power in Germany. Endrös was friendly with a man named Karl Sollinger, a con artist linked to Adolf Wagner, the *Gauleiter* (party leader) of Traunstein, the same region where Stark lived. Stark envisioned himself as something of a spokesman for the area's residents, and had no qualms about marching up to Sollinger and Wagner and confronting them about their ethical infractions and crimes, which he claimed tarnished the party's image. But Wagner was not about to be humiliated, and so he accused Stark of betraying the party."

"Take a few breaths, Sergeant," I said, trying to ease his nerves.

"Don't you see, Professor? Stark thought he was omnipotent, a special envoy to Hitler, and then suddenly a trivial, small-town political leader manages to make trouble for him," Bacon interrupted.

"Hitler actually enjoyed causing conflicts among his subordinates, Lieutenant," I insisted. "But Stark didn't lose his scientific influence because of that."

"I don't doubt that, Professor," Frank said. "But there are other important facts I want you to know about. Please go on, Johnson."

"Finally," continued Sergeant Johnson, "the matter was settled by the party tribunal in Berlin, with Stark and Wagner ending up in a kind of technical tie. But the most devastating thing of all was the effect the controversy had on Stark. In the end, after a heated dispute with the Ahnenerbe, the SS's department of scientific research, it cost him his position in the Reich's research foundation."

"As if he didn't have enough trouble, Stark now had to confront, of all people, Himmler," Bacon explained. "And the outcome was nothing less than disastrous."

"The Ahnenerbe was priority number one in the Reich," Johnson concluded. "For that reason they absolutely had to procure Stark's resignation. Once Himmler publicly exposed one of the more disastrous projects approved by Stark's administration, Stark had no other choice than to accept the following compromise. He would give up the presidency of the foundation but would be able to remain in charge of the Imperial Physical-Technical Institute. No matter how you looked at it, his influence had clearly been diminished. In the several letters he wrote to Philipp Lenard during this time, Stark complained incessantly, for he felt he had waged a long, hard battle against Nazi bureaucracy, but in the end, found himself beholden to it."

"Thank you, Sergeant. Your work has been extremely helpful to us."

"At your service, Lieutenant."

Johnson excused himself with a military salute and quickly exited the office.

"All right, Frank, you've convinced me," I admitted. "So what are we going to do now?"

"That's what I was going to ask you," said Bacon. "Once again we find ourselves facing a dead end."

"We could arrange for an interview with Stark," I suggested.

"That won't get us anywhere, I don't think."

"I agree."

"So?"

"You're asking me?"

"Yes," Bacon replied. "Only you know, Professor. So I'll ask you again. Where do we go from here?"

"Perhaps Stark isn't Klingsor, as you suggest, but we shouldn't be sorry. We should be glad, in fact."

"Explain."

"I told you before. From the beginning we suspected he wasn't our man, but we also knew that given the nature of the work, Klingsor and Stark must have been in contact with one another. It was inevitable. So if Klingsor was not one of the *Deutsche Physik* disciples, then he would have had to have been on the other team. You just said so yourself. The logical consequence, then, of this part of our investigation is—"

"That Klingsor was one of Stark's enemies," Bacon finished.

"This is what I suspect."

"What you suspect is horrifying."

"But inevitable, Lieutenant."

"And who do you have in mind, Professor?"

"Consider this, Frank," I said, trying to calm him down. "Who was Stark's worst enemy during all those years?"

"Heisenberg?"

"You said it."

"Do you love me?"

How long had it been since Frank was last forced to answer that question? How many years was it since his ill-fated engagement to Elizabeth? How long had it been since he had last heard news of Vivien? Unlike his courtship with Elizabeth, things with Irene felt completely natural; there was no pressure at all. And unlike his affair with Vivien, the words he and Irene exchanged were just as meaningful a part of their relationship as the union of their bodies in bed. Irene was lively and intelligent, and she seemed truly interested in Bacon's work, his progress, the new turns his investigation was taking. Bacon had begun to think of her as a confidante and friend as well as a lover—something he had never felt with Elizabeth, much less Vivien. And every day he would be restless with impatience, counting the minutes until he could see her again.

Irene had been careful not to overwhelm Frank with too many personal questions, but now that she was reasonably certain of his feelings, she felt able to muster the courage to talk to him seriously. Bacon was more than a source of comfort and support for her, someone to confide in when she was lonely or feeling low. In Irene's eyes, Bacon embodied the possibility of a new and happier way of life, a world away from the hardships of her past. This was why she could no longer remain silent, hiding her doubts in an effort to maintain the comfort and security that had become so indispensable. At some point she had to take the chance, and the sooner she did it, the better. She had no desire to corner Frank, nor did she wish to be like the other German women who so desperately chased after American soldiers in those days. She simply wanted to know how he felt about her.

"Do you love me?" she repeated the question.

He sat up for a moment and then fell back down against the pillow, in an attempt to buy some time. He was afraid to open his mouth because he simply didn't know the answer.

"I think I do." Bacon was trying hard to find the right words. "I'm sorry . . . it's just that this has all happened so fast."

"So you say you think you love me, but for me that's not enough. Is it that you don't know if you love me? I need a real answer, Frank, that's all."

Did he love her? How could he know for sure? The signs are generally obvious enough, he thought: a physical sensation, as identifiable as a headache, a fever, nausea . . . The body reacts to it just as it does to a sudden illness or fright. But was he in love with her? That was a question exceedingly closer to faith—and, hence, disillusionment—than conviction.

"Yes," declared Bacon, in the firmest tone of voice he could muster, and he proceeded to wrap his arms around Irene.

"Say it again."

"I love you, Irene."

He began to kiss her, on her temples, her nose, her eyelids. He climbed on top of her, taking over her body, and his mind drifted off, lulled by the rhythm of the creaky bed. Bacon's caresses were more like little nips, subtle pleas for silence, his wordless way of saying *please, let's not talk anymore.* Once their equilibrium was restored and their rapture subsided, she brought it up again.

"Are you sure?"

Good Lord, this was torture! How many times was she going to make him say it? Frank was exasperated by now, but tried to assuage her doubts by repeating his declaration in the same assertive tone of voice as before, as if expressing a self-evident truth.

"Yes, I love you. *I love you . . .*"

"All right, then. I want you to promise me something."

Irene now looked him straight in the eye; Frank could feel her gaze piercing his pupils, burning him with the fury of a fiery goddess.

"What else?"

"If you really love me," announced Irene, grabbing Bacon's shoulders and placing her forehead directly against his, "you have to promise me something, Frank. Promise me that you'll always trust me."

"Is that all?" Frank broke into a smile. "I was beginning to get worried."

"Promise me, Frank," she implored him.

"I promise, I promise, all right?"

"Know that I love you," she whispered, as tears slipped down her cheeks. "I'm not saying it to trap you, or so that you love me . . . I'm just saying it because it's the truth. I want you to know that."

"I love you, too—I've already told you, haven't I?"

"Will you always believe in our love?"

"Always."

This time she climbed on top of him. Slowly her hands traveled across his face and neck as she caressed his legs with the tips of her toes. Then she pressed her lips against his, almost biting him, as if to seal their promise in blood. As Frank felt Irene's breasts sliding back and forth across his chest, and her hips pounding hard against his, he imagined they were acting out some kind of heady erotic ritual, an ancient Germanic ceremony that she celebrated to express her adoration for him. He had never seen such devotion, such tenderness, and he wasn't surprised, just exhilarated. Like an inert body or a corpse, Frank surrendered in full to his beloved's whims. At this moment she was the only force in the universe, the living incarnation of movement, the harmony of the spheres. Deliberately, forcefully, Irene took command of his fantasies and imposed her will upon every last muscle of his body, eliciting both pleasure and pain from the most unexpected places, reducing her lover to pure desire, pure energy.

"I love you," Frank gasped before she cast her final spell.

It was the first time he had really meant it.

"Don't waste your time requisitioning his dossier," I said to Bacon coolly. "I'm sure that I can tell you more about Heisenberg than anything you'll find in your files."

"How long were you working as his assistant?"

"His assistant! I was never his assistant—I am a mathematician, remember. I worked *with* him. I never worked *for* him."

"I'm sorry, I didn't mean to—"

"We worked together on the atomic project from 1940 to 1944."

"When you were arrested."

"Exactly. But our ties go much further back than the war. We've known each other, you could say, almost since childhood. I was born in Munich in 1905, on March 21." (I mentioned this so as to be as exact as possible, and also to remind him of my birthday.) "Heisenberg was born in 1901 in Würzburg, though his family had already been living in Munich for quite some time. We were only about four years apart—he could have been my older brother, Lieutenant."

"Were you friends?"

"Well, I wouldn't go so far as that. To a child, three or four years' age difference can be an eternity." I laughed, trying to keep an angelic expression on my face. "Naturally we knew one another; the city wasn't that big. Even then I looked up to him. He was like a hero to me."

"Come on."

"No, that was quite the case," I exclaimed. "Young Werner was a model child. Handsome, intelligent, studious, a good musician, a born leader, from a good northern German family. How could I not admire him, Lieutenant? His father was a professor of Greek, one of the few experts in Byzantine art in Germany."

"Oh, yes, the very image of perfection."

"Laugh all you want, Lieutenant, but those are the facts. Ask anyone: Nobody will ever say a bad word about him. In fact, he still has that same mask of perfection that he always had. Werner the Great! Ever diligent, ever attentive, able to do no wrong! The living picture of virtue and moderation."

"Why do you say *mask?*" Suddenly Bacon's interest perked up. "Was he not as good as everyone said?"

"Did I say that? I had no idea, Lieutenant, my goodness . . . well, in any case, what's said is said. But don't misunderstand me. Werner is a curious person. Why not find out for yourself? You've seen him here, haven't you? In Göttingen?"

"Well, not here," Bacon answered vaguely, suddenly distressed.

"But you agree with me, then, don't you? That he seems to have discovered the fountain of eternal youth? He always looks the same, and always has, as far back as I can remember. Blond from head to toe, chiseled features, the complexion of a schoolgirl—a child, Lieutenant. Still a child prodigy at age fifty." Even I was surprised at the accuracy of my own description. "Nevertheless, on the inside he was exactly the opposite: always an adult. Mature, responsible, and dead serious from the moment he uttered his first word. . . . Tell me, Frank, am I not mistaken in describing him as an old man in the body of a wide-eyed adolescent?"

"Do you mean to say that he was never restless, never rambunctious, he never played tricks like other little boys?"

"Never. Or maybe he was just clever enough to behave that way without anyone realizing, perhaps by pinning the blame on others."

"Do you remember anything else from those days?"

"Well, it was an especially difficult time, Lieutenant. You can imagine: the end of the Great War, the economic crisis, the shame and the bitterness of our defeat, the communist protests in the streets. Well, Werner had to face the same indignities as the rest of us. Don't forget, he was a bit older: When the war ended, he was seventeen, a difficult age. By that time he was already a star physics student, and he was fascinated by philosophy as well. And when he was not occupied by his studies, Werner devoted his free time to one activity in particular that served as an escape from the oppressive society that we all hated so much. This activity, moreover, allowed young Werner to immerse himself in the ancient traditions of his homeland, channel his adolescent rebelliousness, and cultivate his leadership qualities. The youth movement."

"Kind of like the Boy Scouts?"

"You could say that." Suddenly I realized that I sounded like an anthropologist talking about a long-extinct era, a bygone age that had been all but wiped out. "Nevertheless, there was something about Werner that was a trifle uneasy. Behind that perfect exterior, there was a void, a secret, terrible shyness, an inability to really communicate with those around him. I know that might sound like a typical Germanic temperament, but even so, Werner took it to the extreme. Despite his youthful looks, he had a deep melancholy about him, and it was plain to see, in his face and in the things he said."

"And what do you attribute that to?"

"I'm not a psychologist, Lieutenant. I can only tell you what I see, not what I imagine or believe to be true. However, I will venture to propose a theory, just to keep you satisfied. My guess is that souls like Werner were never able to accept the devastation that befell us. Like so many of us, he longed for the medieval heritage, the stability, the serenity and fortitude of our legendary heroes. In short, he despised the chaos of modern times. Anything that interfered with the completion of his activities was despicable. He never did adapt to the new world."

"Did you ever talk to him about these things?"

"When we were teenagers? No, no . . . To him I was always just one of the little ones, a student he could teach things to, not someone he could talk to about truly important things." I shook my head scornfully. "In any event, Heisenberg moved to Göttingen in 1922 to continue his studies under Max Born, while his mentor in Munich, Arnold Sommerfeld, went on an academic tour through the United States. I only saw him once, when he returned to Munich to go on trips with his youth group or his family. Even when he was battling the most profound, perplexing physics problems, Heisenberg would count the moments until he could escape to the mountains with his young charges. It was an absolutely basic element in his life, the only opportunity he had to guide and shape a perfect little miniature society, his own happy little world."

"A physicist who insists upon remaining a Boy Scout, someone who resists growing old, who yearns for the past, for his childhood, for innocence, for security . . ."

"Just remember, though, our idyllic image of children isn't necessarily a very accurate one."

"True. Children can be quite cruel."

"Yes, far more cruel than any adult. *Infinitely* more cruel."

"I know I am taking liberties by saying this," said Frank. "And maybe it's overly obvious, or a meaningless generalization . . ."

"Go on, Lieutenant."

"Well, all this affinity for uniforms, for hierarchy, for German heritage, the desire for guidance, for a leader of some sort . . ."

"I know exactly what you're thinking: Do you see in the youth movement the same characteristics exhibited by members of, say, the SS or the Gestapo?"

"Yes."

"You are far from the first person to notice this, you'll be glad to know. That's exactly it, Lieutenant. In Germany the conditions were ripe—and had been for some time—for a movement like Hitler's to take hold. Even those of us who opposed the regime have to admit that it was no aberration, but rather a somewhat radical consequence of our vision of the world. I worked with Heisenberg, Lieutenant, and I can assure you that behind that young, idealistic facade there lurked a tyrannical, greedy man with an indomitable will and a character of pure steel. He was a real boss, a potential Führer himself."

"But he was never a Nazi sympathizer," Bacon insisted. "In fact, he had more than a few conflicts with them."

"Did you read that in your dossier?"

"He was forever battling with the *Deutsche Physik* scientists. Just like Von Laue told us, he was on Einstein and Bohr's side, and so that made him a natural enemy of the nationalists. Didn't Stark call him the 'white Jew?' "

"Yes, Stark did attack Heisenberg unfairly in several articles, and it's also true that Heisenberg defended himself to the end. But tell me, who ended up the winner of those little skirmishes? Our friend Werner, of course."

"Are you suggesting that Heisenberg—"

"Let's not get ahead of ourselves, Lieutenant," I said, cutting him short. "We've only gotten up to 1922, and we shouldn't lose track of things because then we'll just have to go back and correct our hypothesis. Stark didn't launch his offensive, you'll note, until ten years later, anyway. We need to look closely at the facts that led up to it if we want to understand what happened afterward."

Frank nodded, slightly miffed. My comment, however, had the intended effect. The idea was now planted in Bacon's mind, like a virus, a doubt that would gnaw at him little by little from that moment on. I had to lay the groundwork in preparation for the moment when he—on his own accord—would see the truth.

"In 1922, Göttingen was one of the scientific capitals of the world. Richard Courant, David Hilbert, and Lev Landau, the authorities in my field, were all at the Mathematics Institute. And then some of the greatest names in physics were at Göttingen as well: Pohl, Frank, Born . . ."

"But you didn't study in Göttingen, if I remember correctly."

This time he succeeded in unnerving me.

"No, Lieutenant, I wasn't quite so fortunate. Göttingen was a mathematician's Mecca, although in this case the chosen ones were a select few. Unfortunately, I was not among them. While Werner went to Göttingen, I made my way to Leipzig."

"Nineteen twenty-three was another critical year, Lieutenant. In another one of his typical non sequiturs, Max Born grandly announced that the entire field of physics had to be reformulated, the scientific equivalent of dropping a bomb on the Reichstag. A few weeks later, Heisenberg returned to Munich to complete his *examen rigurosum* under the watchful eye of Sommerfeld, who had just returned from the United States. On July 23—I remember it well because I was there—Werner earned a three, the equivalent of cum laude, despite the fact that Willy Wien, his tutor in experimental physics and Sommerfeld's old enemy, failed him. Without even pausing to celebrate, Heisenberg quickly returned to Göttingen, arriving just before Hitler's coup d'etat in Munich. Heisenberg stayed in Göttingen until the middle of 1924, and toward the end of the year received an invitation from Niels Bohr to visit Copenhagen. From that point on, they became close allies, and Bohr came to consider Heisenberg his four-star general. From their base of operations at the Institute for Theoretical Physics in Copenhagen, they launched a powerful scientific offensive, establishing themselves as the pillars of the new physics. . . .'"

"Tell me." Her voice was even, smooth. "What you do is important to me. *You're* important to me."

"I don't want to bore you, Irene," Frank mumbled.

She shivered for a second or two, just enough time to recover from that strange, wonderful sensation Bacon had aroused.

"Please, Frank," she wheedled. "Tell me about that friend of yours, the mathematician," she insisted. Then, ever so lightly, she began to run her fingers along his belly, traveling downward, as if she barely noticed what she was doing.

"Links?" asked Bacon, arching his back in response to this last bit of sensual provocation. "He's eccentric, that's for sure, but no more so than any other scientist I've ever known. If you knew what some of those characters were really like—Von Neumann, my mentor, or Kurt Gödel—you'd think Princeton was nothing but a gallery of maniacs, obsessives, and neurotics. A psychoanalyst would have a field day there. . . . Yes, right there, that's it, that's it . . ."

Irene stopped in her tracks.

"Do you like him?"

"I think so," Frank said quickly, hoping Irene would resume her fondling. "For all his eccentricities, he's still an awfully intelligent man."

"What kind of eccentricities?"

"I don't know exactly how to describe it," Frank exclaimed, once again basking in the pleasure received at his lover's hands. "He just seems, I don't know . . . I still don't fully understand him."

"And you trust him, anyway?" Irene asked.

"I wouldn't worry about it," snapped Frank, condescending and impatient. "I don't think it has anything to do with our work. It must be something from his past."

"Maybe he's tormented by some sad, long-lost love affair," she said teasingly.

"Whatever it is, he doesn't want to tell me about it. His personal life is totally off-limits. There are days we can go on talking for hours, but I always seem to do most of the talking."

"Tell me what you do together," Irene said as she took Bacon's member in her hands. "What are you investigating?"

"We're after a scientist, someone who, it seems, was very close to Hitler and who managed to remain anonymous, hidden away behind a facade of respectability," Frank confessed.

"Was he a physicist like you?"

"We think so. The only thing we know for sure is his code name: Klingsor. Have you ever heard of it?"

"No."

"He's a character from Germanic mythology. A demonic figure. Irene! . . . I do adore you. . . . He also appears in a Wagner opera, *Parsifal* . . . !"

She paused again. She parceled out pleasure as if it were a mind-altering drug.

"Go on . . ."

"All right, all right," he said, and she resumed. "If we guessed right, then Klingsor was responsible for deciding the amount of money to be budgeted for all the scientific investigations undertaken by the Third Reich, including the atomic project, the experiments on prisoners, all those things. But, unfortunately, that's about all we know. See what I told you? It's not very interesting. Links is helping to guide me through all of this."

"Him?"

"Yes, *him*," Bacon whispered, his voice straining. "He knows the history of science in this country better than anyone. He worked with Heisenberg, and he's given me some invaluable clues . . . without his help, I'd still be in the dark." Finally, the lieutenant was making some sense. "It was a miracle that I even found him. . . . Yes, he might be a bit grim, a bit obsessive, but without him I'd be nowhere. We're moving ahead slowly but surely. Twentieth-century physics, seen through his eyes, seems more like the history of a conspiracy. Suddenly, the world's greatest physicists all look like criminals to me . . . any one of them could be Klingsor."

"And who are you leaning toward now?"

"Well, I can hardly believe it myself, but all our research seems to be pointing toward one person. Heisenberg."

Frank was just on the precipice of arriving at that heightened moment of self-discovery that some people call revelation, others, religious ecstasy, and still others, rather boorishly, orgasm. That was when Irene stopped cold.

"Irene, what on earth is going on?"

"I'm thinking."

"Thinking?"

"Yes," she said. "This is just fascinating, Frank! Do you think there's any way I can help you?"

"To do what?"

"To solve the mystery."

"I don't see how."

"Trust me," she begged, trying to cajole him. "Woman's intuition . . . Let me help you, Frank, oh, please. From now on, you'll tell me all about your discoveries, all right? I can help give you ideas."

"I didn't think any of this interested you."

"Oh, you're wrong! On the contrary! I think it's fascinating," she whispered, and in place of her hands, her head traveled down along her lover's body until her lips found themselves hovering upon Frank's impatient penis. Finally, she was ready to finish what she had started.

·

THE GAME OF WAR

In his *Mein Kampf,* Hitler declared that unless Germany became a world power, there would be no Germany. And he was prepared to go to any length to fulfill this prophecy. *Tertius non datur,* there was no third option: It was either supremacy or ruin. In 1939, this meant, inevitably, the beginning of the hostilities. In reality his main objective had always been to eradicate the Soviet Union—as well as all the Jews—and he had announced his plans as such. In the latter part of 1939 the Führer decided to deploy one of his most brilliant strategies. On August 20, he sent a telegram to his Soviet counterpart, requesting a meeting on behalf of Joachim von Ribbentrop, his eccentric foreign minister. When Stalin agreed, almost immediately, Hitler achieved far more than a mere diplomatic triumph. The last piece of his puzzle was now in place, and Germany was finally poised to take control of Europe.

Hitler's plan was simple: Germany and the Soviet Union would carve up Poland before the expectant, shocked eyes of France and Great Britain. Once this mission was accomplished, Hitler would quickly turn against Stalin, his new ally, and crush him. And when his victory in the East was more or less certain, Hitler would turn his attention to the West.

On August 23, Ribbentrop and Molotov, the Soviet foreign minister, announced their recent signing of the German-Soviet nonaggression pact. Great Britain and France felt utterly betrayed by the Soviet leaders, but the greatest blow of all was to the communists, who had been actively protesting fascism for years. Suddenly Stalin was telling them not only to surrender but to cooperate with the enemy.

One week later, on September 1, Hitler's troops crossed the Polish border, with the full knowledge and support of the Soviet Union. The Soviets, meanwhile, quickly took control of the territories on the eastern border of Poland, which they had been granted by a secret clause in the pact. And just as the Führer had predicted, France and Britain declared war on Germany.

Some two weeks later, Poland was declared an occupied zone, and Hitler, in one fell swoop, wiping away both its history and its identity, renamed it with the more neutral-sounding *général gouvernement.*

The swift conquest of Poland was followed by another equally successful Blitzkrieg, with Denmark and Norway falling under the command of the Third Reich. Nobody seemed able to defy Hitler's plans. It was finally the right time to turn to the West. After a period of tense calm known by the French, in a rather macabre display of humor, as the *drôle de guerre,* Hitler ordered his troops to invade France. On May 10, 1940, an intrepid convoy of armored tanks under the command of General Hans Guderian crossed the Ardennes, accomplishing in a few short weeks something that could have easily taken years: the siege of Paris. And on June 22, barely six weeks after the start of this spectacular campaign, France signed the armistice. The historic moment was sealed in the same railroad car at Compiègne that had witnessed the German defeat in 1918, and which had been especially refurbished for the occasion. Hitler had wrought his revenge.

When the war broke out, Heinrich was called to active duty, and after the invasion of Poland he went on to fill various positions, first in the occupied zones and later among the troops that made their triumphant entry into Paris. In the space of a year, he was granted only two leaves of absence to return home to his wife in Berlin. Aside from those two brief visits (during which I naturally refused to see him), he was more or less permanently away, and Natalia was forced to take care of herself.

On the surface she appeared strong, but in reality Natalia was nothing more than a helpless little girl. She seemed to fancy herself a kind of Gretel, mute and lonely, abandoned by her loyal Hansel. As you could imagine, her visits with Marianne became more and more frequent. From that moment on, in fact, Natalia often came running to our house, as if we were her only source of comfort in the world. I would try to talk to her and calm her tears, but she always ended up crying her eyes out in my wife's arms.

Who would have guessed that during these moments of caring friendship and sisterly support, Natalia and Marianne were nurturing an unspoken passion? Who would have guessed that behind the tears and the hugs, the gentle pats and the gestures of affection, lurked the most unspeakable rapture? Who would have guessed that Natalia's misery was caused not just by Heinrich's absence but, in large measure, by this terrible, private torment?

Not me, for one. Despite our many nights of youthful gallivanting, in which our sexual liaisons often skirted the limits of propriety, the four of us had long since become adults. Model members of our Hitlerian society, we had become serious and responsible people, careful observers of the standards of courtesy and honesty with which we had been indoctrinated. For example, despite the fact that I had lost all interest in Marianne, I still considered myself a loyal husband. After all, who would blame me for a few meaningless nocturnal escapades? For that reason, I was altogether baffled by the complex, contradictory emotions that bubbled to the surface at the beginning of the war. Had something changed, or broken, or gone so bad between us that we could just shamelessly abandon our customs and mores, and live as if each day were our last? Do war and the imminence of death have the power to free us from our obligations, our convictions, our fears?

I can hardly find the right words to describe how it all began. The memories are still so painful, like a cut that hasn't fully healed. Perhaps if we had let it pass, or if we'd pretended a little while longer, or if we'd been more stoic, or more certain, nothing would have happened. But all of us—Marianne, Natalia, and I—surrendered to our desires, creating our own little world, governed by a different set of rules and regulations. In our desire to live purely on instinct, we stopped caring about the opinions of others. Unfortunately, though, we also stopped caring about our own opinions, as well. We were no longer social beings, distinguished and proper, but primal forces at battle, unleashed, unidentifiable sources of energy thrown into hostile, unfamiliar terrain.

It all began in July of 1940, on an afternoon that was like any other—hot, dry, and uninspiring. Natalia and Marianne were in the library as usual, discussing the same things they always discussed—war, fear, death. I, meanwhile, was in my study. For days I had been struggling with a series of tedious mathematical problems, and was desperate to finish them. All of a sudden, I looked up and found myself enveloped by a disconcerting silence. All noise had ceased—absorbed by a rather ghostly calm. I could have heard a feather drop from the highest spot in the ceiling. I felt uneasy, flushed, and intrigued by that midday tranquillity.

Careful not to break the silence, I proceeded to the library, preparing to surprise Natalia and Marianne. I tiptoed all the way to the door, opened it ever so slightly, yet, as is wont to happen in situations like this, the surprise was mine. At first, upon seeing Marianne embracing Natalia so tenderly, I assumed that I had just interrupted another one of Natalia's crying jags. But then as my eyes focused on the scene before me, I realized the two of them were stretched out upon the sofa, their fingers intertwined and their lips locked in a passionate kiss.

My eyes had not deceived me: their lips, their tongues, their labored gasps, were easy enough to see. Suddenly and without warning, I found myself veritably knocked over by this pure, simple, self-evident truth. I felt a numbness in my stomach. What should I do? Leave the room and act as if it had never happened? Alert them of my presence, thereby opening the door to an exceedingly unpleasant situation and unpredictable consequences? The worst part of it all, I must admit, was that I found myself highly aroused by what I was seeing, like an accidental voyeur. I couldn't help it—my body disobeyed my mind, just as theirs appeared to be doing, as well. The three of us were now held together by a secret complicity, and it was a tie far stronger than love or fraternity or guilt. Before they could notice me, I withdrew from the room, disturbed and afraid. That afternoon, Natalia said good-bye to me just as she always did, but I couldn't help but see her in an utterly different light. It was as if she had suddenly grown up, a real woman who was finally in control of what she did and how she felt— a fearless, unapologetic rebel.

"I'm glad we can do something for her," I said to Marianne, without a trace of irony in my voice. "At least she knows she can always count on us."

From that moment on, our life would never be the same, though at the time I was the only one who knew it.

WERNER HEISENBERG, OR
A LESSON IN SADNESS

Less than two years had passed since Bacon had last laid eyes on him, but it felt more like centuries. An entire universe seemed to stretch out between this frigid winter day and that bright, luminous morning when the members of the Alsos mission had finally located and arrested Heisenberg in his home outside Urfeld. Today, Bacon summoned the courage to knock on the door to Heisenberg's office at the Max Planck Institute, Göttingen's newly inaugurated physics center and successor to the old Kaiser Wilhelm Institute. Bacon had no idea whether Heisenberg would recognize him as the soldier who had taken him into custody at the end of the war, and he felt a twinge of shame about the incident, as if he had violated Heisenberg by treating him like a common prisoner of war, taking him away from his family and sending him off on a long, grim journey through the devastated precincts of Europe. Perhaps this was the reason Bacon forgot to tell me that he had made an appointment with him.

I had told Bacon that Heisenberg seemed to have tapped the fountain of youth, but Bacon saw only how the ravages of time had left their mark on Heisenberg's soft features. His white-blond hair was the same, but his face seemed to have grown old overnight, like that of a small child who falls gravely ill. Profoundly affected by the hardships of war and the German surrender, he had endured an additional blow when he learned that the Allies had beaten him in the race to build the atomic bomb. By the time the war was over, something had died inside him—confidence, perhaps, or that sense of being one of God's elect. If before the war he seemed introverted and taciturn, now it was virtually impossible to get anything out of him—a confession, a hint of personality, even the most minimal spark of spontaneity. He was proper and courteous, dry and direct, and never, ever friendly. Any attentiveness he demonstrated was inspired only by obligation and irreproachable politeness, never the desire to please his inquirers. His small blue eyes, half open, had become the incarnation of gloom: Lifeless and unfocused, they couldn't help betraying the terrible melancholy he felt in his heart. A less severe, less proud, or less brilliant man would have long since surrendered to desperation or apathy, but Heisenberg's iron will—so very *Germanic*—kept him where he was, working toward Germany's future with the same blinding determination that had fueled his efforts for Hitler. And this was how, in accordance with his duties, Heisenberg received Bacon in his office without a word. Neither of them dared to acknowledge that this was hardly their first meeting.

"You studied at Princeton."

"Yes, Princeton University first, and then at the Institute for Advanced Study," Bacon confirmed.

"A marvelous place, yes," remarked Heisenberg, not without a hint of nostalgia.

There was a time when he had toyed with the idea of remaining there, of pursuing his research in the United States, far from Hitler and the war. He had received several offers, and many of his expatriate friends had tried to convince him, but in the end he held out. Germany was his home; it was where he belonged. He couldn't desert his country, and he had nothing to fear there.

"What a privilege to be among such men—Einstein, Gödel, Pauli . . ."

"I never got to meet Pauli," Bacon admitted. "He arrived after I enlisted. But the others I did. Yes, a great privilege. My tutor was John von Neumann."

Heisenberg said nothing, as if the mere mention of those names was enough to silence him. Anything he said could be used against him.

"Professor, I hope to inconvenience you as little as possible. As I've mentioned, I am a physicist, but the nature of this visit is more . . . historiographical. I am gathering research for a monograph on the scientific developments that have taken place in Germany during the past twenty years." Bacon's choice of euphemism couldn't have been clumsier or more obvious. He might as well have just said "during the Nazi regime." He continued: "And, naturally, any discussion of the subject would be incomplete without first coming to you."

"I'm happy to help you, Professor Bacon. As you know, I am a busy man, but I can always make the time to answer any questions you may have."

"Thank you. This isn't exactly easy for me. I've always admired your work, and never imagined that I would come to know you under these kind of circumstances."

"Don't be concerned. It was nothing either one of us could have helped."

"I do want to emphasize, though, how very much I appreciate your understanding, Professor." Bacon's manners were growing exaggerated. "If you don't mind, I'd like to begin by talking about Professor Stark."

"I'm sorry, but I've already told you everything I know." There was a perceptible note of arrogance in Heisenberg's careful choice of words. "I served as a witness during his trial. I can read the minutes if that would help you."

"I've already done that, Professor, and I truly don't mean to be a bother, but what I'm interested in is *your* version of the story. That's the reason I made this appointment with you."

"Is it absolutely necessary?"

"I'm afraid so."

Heisenberg leaned back in his chair and began rubbing his hands. How many times had he told this story? How many times had he been forced to talk about his battle with Stark?

"Why don't you ask the questions and I'll try to answer them as best I can," he said.

"All right." Bacon took out a pencil and a notebook, which he studied for a few moments before he began. "When did you and Stark first become enemies?"

"You mean when did Stark first consider me his enemy."

"Yes."

"I've thought a great deal about that. At first I thought it was something personal. He attacked me so often, and so viciously, during a time in which his disapproval could create quite serious problems for someone." Heisenberg was trying to remain composed, dispassionate. "An accusation from him, published in a Nazi newspaper, was tantamount to a death sentence. Suddenly, doors were being slammed in my face, and my family and I became concerned for our safety."

"But you don't think so anymore."

"Now I think that Stark's rage was directed against anyone who didn't think the way he did. The truth is that after winning the Nobel Prize he became something of a second-rate physicist. After that initial success, his career went from one failure to another. That was when he joined the party and began to support Hitler. Just like all the Nazis, he despised the people he felt had placed Germany in danger. And who were those people? For Stark, it was simple: the physicists working in the new sciences, in quantum theory. That is, a field that he couldn't understand and which, naturally, he could never control."

"Do you think, then, it was a simple case of resentment?"

"It was spite. And bitterness. But there was something else as well. His vision of physics didn't jibe with ours; Stark felt that the model proposed by Planck and Einstein—and those of us who followed their lead—was nothing but a bunch of mathematical abstractions that didn't accurately reflect the natural world. The reality of it, though, was that he didn't have enough of a background to understand it."

"Was he a bad scientist?"

"No, he was a bad person." He paused, stunned by what he had just said. "The Nobel Prize was proof that he had talent. But that talent, unfortunately, had to compete with both his ego and his mediocrity. In his zeal to revive experimental or practical physics, as he called it, he decided to condemn those of us who were making strides in theoretical physics, which for him was simple dogma. And then there was the subject of his anti-Semitism. That was how that ridiculous *Deutsche Physik* movement came about."

"In July of 1937, in an unsigned article published in the *Das Schwarze Korps*, you were insultingly referred to as a 'white Jew.' Stark quickly followed this with a series of articles: 'Science has failed politically,' 'White Jews in Science,' and 'The Pragmatic and the Dogmatic Spirit in Physics,' this last piece published in the English journal *Nature*. What effect did they have upon your career?"

"At the time, I was working as a professor at the University of Leipzig, but it was no secret that I coveted the position at the University of Munich that had recently been vacated by my old mentor, Arnold Sommerfeld. Stark's attack effectively wiped my name from the list of contenders, and he won out in the end: Wilhelm Müller, a member of the group that embraced *Deutsche Physik*, received the appointment. But more than that, I suddenly found myself under tremendous pressure. My reputation was marred, and everything had become so uncertain. The SS launched an investigation of my activities. It was hell, Professor Bacon."

"So what did you do?"

"The only thing I could do. Protest. Defend my case. Clear my name."

"And finally justice was served."

"For once, yes."

"Due to the fact that Himmler intervened on your behalf."

"Due to the fact that for once in the history of the world, a government bureaucrat got wind of injustices that were being committed under his command."

Bacon decided it was time to change the subject. He hadn't wanted to ruffle Heisenberg's feathers quite so quickly.

"During the period of 'de-Nazification' after the war, Stark claimed that he deserved full exoneration of all guilt. Nevertheless, the denazification court at Traunstein condemned him to four years of hard labor. Stark went before a Munich court and appealed the decision, defending himself against three accusations: the first, of carrying out political activity in the Traunstein region; the second, of supporting Hitler and the Nazis before 1933; and the third, for his activities as president of the Research Foundation and of the Imperial Physical-Technical Institute. The appellate court threw out the first two accusations for lack of evidence, and so the only remaining charge was the third, the scientific issue. You testified as a witness in this case, as we discussed. Might you tell me, Professor, what you said?"

"Didn't you say that you read the testimony?" Heisenberg suddenly snapped, an irritated look on his face. Then, just as quickly, he softened. "It doesn't matter. I'll tell you again. They questioned me about two issues in particular. The first question was if the distinction Stark made between dogmatic physics and theoretical physics was in fact rooted in anti-Semitism. The second issue I was asked about was whether Stark had a principal role in the suppression of the relativity theory during the Third Reich. To be truthful, I felt obligated to respond that in my opinion, Stark was not a rabid anti-Semite, just a man mad with power."

Bacon checked his notes. "I have noted here that the court heard testimony from Einstein, who also admitted that though Stark was indeed paranoid and an opportunist, he was not an anti-Semite."

Heisenberg said nothing; he had nothing to add.

"But why?" Bacon pressed the issue. "Why would you and Einstein defend him like that, Professor?"

"Because he *wasn't* an anti-Semite, just a megalomaniac; that's what he really was. And he was an expert at painting himself as a victim."

"Victim of whom, Professor?"

"First of the Jews and then the Nazis, whose case he never ceased to defend. What do you want me to tell you? Luckily, the *real* truth finally came out."

"Meaning that in the end the Nazis turned on him?"

"You could say that."

"But why?" Bacon feigned ignorance. "Did he do something to make them angry? Protest their politics?"

"I think that after tolerating him for a certain number of years, the party authorities realized that Stark was simply not a competent scientist."

"What do you mean by that?"

"He was all talk. The *Deutsche Physik* was just a lot of rhetoric."

"And they wanted results."

"Exactly."

"So they decided Stark was useless to them, and they simply dropped him."

Heisenberg nodded.

"And that was when they turned to your group, Einstein's supposed 'disciples,' to replace Stark."

"There is only one 'real science,' Professor Bacon. In the long run, anyone would have realized that we were in the right, not Stark."

"That is, his failure was scientific, not ideological."

"Exactly."

"Paradoxically, the Munich Court of Appeals decided it wasn't fit to settle a scientific debate, and lightened Stark's sentence to a fine of one thousand marks," Bacon added.

"Yes, I heard that."

"Thank you for your time, Professor," Bacon concluded. "I hope this hasn't been a great inconvenience."

The waves, as high as a castle tower, crash against the rocks like an army of water molecules trying to crush a coastal fortress. Millions of molecules, hundreds of millions of atoms, rage mercilessly against those walls that stave off the invasion despite the gusts of wind and rain. The ocean is a vast, inky mystery that spills out to the ends of the earth; upon its waters sits a steely gray sky, slightly bloated and trembling, contemplating the never-ending battles waged on the cliffs below. It's no wonder this watery maelstrom is so often associated with the siren's song. Sliding through caverns and rocky promontories, the choppy waters crash down on steep slopes whose contours seem cut by the hands of a giant, and the blasts of wind wail with an almost human cry.

The lower Saxony coastline extends far beyond the eye of this furious, fast-moving thunderstorm. The island trembles like a toy boat on the verge of capsizing, despite possessing the same foundations as all terra firma. Its eternal enemy, the sea, has never consummated its full assault, sliding around this isolated, wild corner of the world. A weak, leaden ray of light, little more than a thread woven together by microscopic quanta, falls upon the ocean mist, illuminating a landscape of lost ships, wandering ghosts, bloody monsters, and errant pirates. Helgoland suddenly seems like the stomach of an enormous amphibious mammal, a gentle giant that braves the elements and lives silently, nourished by plankton and algae.

The storm slowly begins to ebb, absorbed by the nautical currents, and the equilibrium of the universe is slowly restored. The two colossi—land and sea—retreat to their former positions, having agreed to a truce in order to tend to their wounded. Like the gesture of a benevolent god indicating his approval, the storm clouds suddenly separate, and a reddish sunset emerges, exploding across the sky in a blaze of color just above the very center of the water. A bleached-white, exhausted sun rests in the crystalline arms of twilight, near death.

On closer inspection, the silhouette of a man emerges. Sitting high atop a craggy cliff, he looks like an absurd night watchman stationed there to guard the skies. Or perhaps this raincoated young man is here to serve as a witness to the miracle that has just taken place before his eyes. He is an observer who watches, impassively, the bitter combat and then the serene reconciliation that unfold in the course of these few, brief hours. Summer has just begun, but dark shadows still dominate the island at twilight. The young man rubs his icy hands together; anyone observing him would think he was offering a prayer to the gods. His goal, however, is far more pedestrian: He exhales deeply into his cupped palms, producing a tiny cloud of warm dew that evaporates quickly in the cold air. Far off, the sun has disappeared again—who knows if it will ever come back?—and as compensation for his patience, the dark, nighttime underworld is suddenly aglow with a blanket of tiny, timid lights. Soon the young man will be able to count thousands of them, expectant and slow, twinkling in the sky. How could it be that we are all made of the very same matter? That in the center of each star little electrons dance to their own celestial music? That the harmony of the heavens is found in the transformations and mutations that work their magic in these giant, volatile heavenly ovens?

A mysterious smile slowly creeps onto the face of the young man, whose childlike features reveal his identity as that of Werner Heisenberg, the wunderkind of Munich. This is his last day on the island and, despite his slight sadness, he feels he has done his job. He, too, has won a war after confronting demons as powerful as the subaquatic angels that now surround him. Inside his head—a rather uncomfortable metaphor—a transmutation has occurred, similar to the one he has just witnessed. A star has died and in its place, hundreds of others, smaller but even more beautiful, have been born. For ten days, Heisenberg has been at war with his worst enemy, the one he faces each time he peers into a mirror: his own impatience. Just like the hermits of old, he has spent these ten days as far as possible from the temptations of the twentieth century. Saint Simon Stylite lived out his days on the top of a pillar and Saint Jerome chose the company of lions over human beings because they both knew that the greatest revelations come in the intimacy of total solitude. On this diminutive island in the North Sea, dozens of miles from the nearest human being, Heisenberg has retreated from civilization to unravel the sublime enigmas of physics. Here in this island sanctuary, which has been both prison and paradise, he has finally cracked the mystery.

An epiphany? He would never venture to call it that, but in his heart he knows that is the word. And the secret catalyst of this epiphany is nothing but the harsh light found in this part of the world. The solution to the giant puzzle of creation has finally arrived: Every piece fits, all the loose ends disappear as if they never existed at all, as if they were mere errors in perspective, flawed interpretations of the laws of nature. Could there be anything more thrilling than the moment when one comes to *know* something?

They were days and nights of dizzying mental activity. Ideas raced through his brain like a cerebral cyclone, or a raging virus that turned his brain into a well-oiled thinking machine. He didn't sleep a wink; he couldn't stop thinking, examining and reexamining the universe, fighting with the banal yet magnificent spectral lines of the elements, testing his ideas on a thousand and one mathematical models in the hopes that one of them might enable him to organize everything into a single, concise vision of the cosmos. And precisely when he thought he could take it no more, wearing the same sweaty shirt he had been wearing for the past week, his hair flying in every direction and his face unshaven, he finally reached the end. He had triumphed. He might very well have been on the verge of a nervous breakdown, but he had gotten it.

Now Heisenberg laughs openly and out loud, as he would never do in the presence of another human being. He is doubled over with hysterical laughter, possessed by the notion that his investigations in fact have a purpose, possessed by the realization that he has been rewarded with the very treasure he has been searching for since childhood. Some people may see it as a mere mathematical excuse, a stroke of luck, or a rather ordinary, imperfect formula, but he knows better. He is certain that this is something far more profound, something perfect.

Slowly he walks back toward his cottage at the southern tip of the island.

There is no rush. Not until tomorrow, when he will begin the long trip back to civilization, will he feel the urgent need to communicate his discovery to the world. After all, what is a prophet without an audience to hear him? Before returning to Copenhagen, Göttingen. or Munich, he will stop in Hamburg to visit Pauli, whom he hopes to convert as his first disciple, a disciple of the prophet of matrix mechanics. In the meantime, he will settle in to his last night in Helgoland. A final evening in his narrow bedroom, sheltered from the gusty nocturnal winds. Safe.

"It was something of an impulse, Gustav," Bacon said. As he continued to apologize for his deplorable behavior, I continued to play the role of the insulted friend. "Please remember, the last time we saw each other was when I arrested him. I had to keep my distance then—I didn't say a thing, I condemned him with my silence. I had to see him alone this time, as a kind of apology, I guess, for the way I acted then."

"I don't think you have anything to apologize for, Lieutenant," I said sincerely. "What's done is done. May I ask what you talked about?"

"I didn't want to alarm him with our suspicions."

"So what did you talk about? The weather? Or physics?"

"We talked about Stark," Frank replied, ignoring my provocation.

"I suppose Werner told the same old story. That Stark, Lenard, and their *Deutsche Physik* cronies were the only scientists in Germany who worked directly for Hitler. That the rest of us just did our work, kept out of politics."

"I detect disapproval in your voice, Professor. Do you have some other version of the story?"

"I think that the truth is far more dangerous than lies, Lieutenant."

"Are you and Heisenberg still friends?"

"If you must know, I haven't spoken to him since my arrest. At least not like before."

"May I ask why?"

"Why don't I explain with a mathematical simile," I said, smiling. "After two lines intersect at a right angle, they will never meet again no matter how far you extend the lines."

"Unless they inhabit a sphere, Professor," Bacon replied wryly.

"Perhaps that isn't the best metaphor," I admitted. "But you understand what I'm saying."

"And he never sought you out, either?"

"Werner? No, of course not. He'll do everything he can to distance himself from the past, he's so uncomfortable with it."

"Why do you say that with such mistrust?"

"The mistrust isn't in my words, Lieutenant. Look at the facts in the conduct of each individual. Go ahead. Trace the irreproachable Professor Heisenberg's conduct during the war and you'll see what I'm talking about."

"Why are you being so vague, Professor? I thought we promised to trust one another."

I cleared my throat. I didn't want to answer that question.

"Did Werner tell you how it all ended?" I asked after a pause.

"Yes, I asked him about it, and he admitted that Himmler had helped him out. He said it was one of those rare cases in which a disturbed individual commits an act of justice, something like that."

I fell silent. I wanted the magnitude of that statement to speak for itself, without the addition of another sarcastic comment from me.

"Please, just tell me the truth, Professor," Bacon pleaded, with a voice that appealed more to our friendship than to his superior rank. "Do you think Heisenberg has something to hide?"

I weighed my words carefully. "Frank, we all have something to hide. Even you. Or me. A secret, a past mistake, a wrong we tried to redress secretly, a bit of guilt that we tried to bury away. And Werner? In all honesty, I think he has a *lot* of things to hide."

"Well, tell me about them, then! I need to know."

"Ask him yourself, you have access."

"Gustav, please."

"I've told you everything I know, Lieutenant," I replied coldly. "I have to go now. I can't spend all my time chasing ghosts."

"I just don't understand him, Irene." Frank was stretched out on the bed, facedown, nude. Irene, meanwhile, was massaging his neck and shoulders.

"I don't like that Links, I've said it to you before," she said.

"He was really furious at me for going to see Heisenberg without telling him. As if I had to ask his permission!"

Irene wrapped her fingers around Bacon's neck, rubbing it harder.

"What did he tell you?"

"He insinuated that Heisenberg had something—many things—to hide."

"He's just trying to provoke you. He's upset with you because you slighted him."

"No, it's not that. If you had seen Links's face that moment, you wouldn't have thought he was lying. I think something happened between him and Heisenberg. Maybe around the time Links was sent to jail."

"Are you thinking that Heisenberg betrayed him somehow?"

"Could be. Goudsmit, my old boss, felt the same way. That behind his image of honor and decency, Heisenberg was actually a fearful, cowardly man who couldn't stand up to the Nazis."

"Do you really think he could be Klingsor?"

"I don't know, Irene."

"Why don't you talk with someone else? Some other physicist who can tell you something about Heisenberg and his connection to the Nazis."

"Are you thinking of someone in particular?" Bacon asked.

"Well, you told me that there was another physicist who discovered quantum mechanics at the same time as Heisenberg did."

"Schrödinger. For a long time, he was Heisenberg and Bohr's worst enemy. A competition developed between them to see whose theory would win out. Heisenberg had discovered matrix mechanics in Helgoland, and Schrödinger, only a week later, discovered wave mechanics in Arosa. It was a battle to the death whose final outcome was decided in the strangest way. Precisely when the controversy was at its peak, Schrödinger, like some kind of scientific Solomon, discovered that their two theories were in fact equivalent, the same idea simply formulated in two different ways. All of a sudden the war seemed to be over. Schrödinger, however, soon began to run into trouble with the Nazis, despite the fact that he wasn't Jewish. After an endless string of complications, he was granted permission to leave, and he moved to Dublin, where he established a research institute similar to the one in Princeton."

"Is he still there?" A devilish smile crept over Irene's face as Bacon turned his body around. She looked deep into his eyes before allowing him to penetrate her.

"What are you suggesting?"

"I've never been to Dublin."

"To where?" I asked Bacon, horrified.

"I just told you. Dublin."

"That's crazy," I said over and over again.

"I know it is, Professor, but it might be worth a try."

"Do you really think Schrödinger has anything worthwhile to tell us? You don't even know him."

"I don't know, but we're going to try." Bacon was transparently, annoyingly, stupidly in love. Even so, he did add: "Would you like to join us?"

"What do you mean, 'us'?" I asked, shocked.

"Irene and me."

"Lieutenant, I don't mean to be a bore, but this is an official mission. I'm not sure it's at all appropriate for you to bring someone who isn't directly involved with the investigation."

"Answer the question, Professor. Do you want to join us or not?"

"Well, if that's the way it is . . ."

"If you have other work here, I won't hold you to it," he said slightly threateningly.

"No!" I said, surrendering. "I'll go with you. The *both* of you."

"All right then. I'll work out the necessary details."

The Dangers of Observation

Berlin
July 1940

One of the more baffling consequences of quantum theory was the new relationship it established between the scientist and the physical world that the scientist studies. In the realm of classic physics, this issue had never created any conflict: On one side of the wall was the world with all its mysteries, and on the other side was the meticulous physicist who tried to solve them. What could be simpler? One side's role was to measure, calculate, predict, and solve, while the role of the other side—that is, the physical universe—was basically passive. All it had to do was allow the scientist to carry out those measurements, calculations, predictions, and solutions. *E tutti contenti.*

Beginning in 1925, this system began to break down. According to the discoveries of the quantum theorists, it was now necessary to completely reformulate something that previously seemed innocuous and stable: the measurement of the physical world. According to this new physics, the relationship between observer and observed was no longer "independent," as the laws of Newtonian mechanics stated. The physicist could no longer simply admire the subatomic world, since it was now abundantly clear that his very measurement transformed the object he was trying to measure. In other words, as the scientist explored reality, the reality itself changed, such that it was different after having been measured. The scientist was no longer innocent: His observation alone was enough to alter the order of the universe.

Every three days I was subjected to the same torture: Natalia and Marianne's visits in the library. There, indifferent to my presence in the house, they exchanged muffled words and whispers as they surrendered to their private desires. At first, I thought that what I had seen that afternoon could be attributed to an innocent, capricious indiscretion, an anecdote in the friendship that they had shared for so many years. In times of war, and amid all the adversity it brought about, people occasionally confused their emotions, their actions, their ability to handle things. But soon I realized I was mistaken. I would sit at my desk and try hard not to spy on them, but it was nearly impossible. Twice I burst into the library claiming I was looking for some book or another, and both times all I found was the two of them chatting away, sitting several centimeters apart on the sofa. They acted as though they didn't even notice my intrusion, and so I resolved to act as though I hadn't seen them either. Nevertheless, as I concentrated on my numbers and formulas, all I could do was imagine what they were doing a few short meters away from me.

A couple of times I dared to leave my room and tiptoe over to the library, where I would hide behind a column to eavesdrop, either on their conversation (did they whisper sweet nothings to one another?) or their guilty silence. Yet again, I was unable to confirm my suspicions. They spoke in hushed tones, of course, but that wasn't enough to incriminate them. What could I do? I tried hard to be consistent with Marianne, though I don't know how successful I was at that. We lived in a dizzying age of ups and downs. Our armies were currently reporting victories on all fronts, and perhaps this explained why she wasn't particularly bothered by my sudden, violent mood swings. How could I admit to her that my worries and my insomnia had nothing to do with the war? That Hitler and his glorious discourses had long since ceased to concern me? During that period, I was scarcely capable of adding up a simple string of numbers.

What happened next was my idea, which, I now know, makes me responsible for the consequences. One day Marianne casually suggested that we take a trip, a little escape from Berlin. At the time, I was so agitated that I barely even acknowledged the suggestion and brushed her off. It wasn't until a few hours later that I realized what a perfect pretext it would be.

"Marianne," I blurted out, unable to contain my excitement, "that's a splendid idea."

"You mean the trip?"

"Yes. Let's go to a spa, or some quiet, peaceful place."

"Well, I'm happy you agree," she said, pleased at my enthusiasm. "It will do us a world of good."

I waited a few seconds and then, acting as if it had just dawned on me, sealed my fate: "Why don't you invite Natalia? Heini still has another few weeks at the front, and she seems to be going through a difficult few days. I would hate to leave her here all alone."

"Gustav . . ."

"She'll say yes, I know she will. We're like family to her. No, in fact, we *are* her family," I declared. "Call her, see what she thinks."

"I don't know if that's such a good idea, Gustav. I thought you wanted to get away from all that. For it to be just you and me."

"I think it would be selfish of us not to bring her along. In fact, if she says no, then we won't go at all. She's your best friend, and my differences with Heini aside, I've grown to love her. I won't take no for an answer."

"Well, all right," she said tentatively.

Just as I expected. It took her a few minutes, but Marianne managed to convince Natalia to join us. All she needed to do, she said, was write to Heinrich (she liked to keep him informed) and then she would be ready to leave when we were. I planned the excursion with painstaking detail, with the meticulous precision of a spurned lover planning his suicide. I sent off a letter to a spa in Bavaria, obtained permission for leave from my superiors, and made sure that the location had the amenities I required in order to carry out my plan.

We left at the end of June. To assuage Marianne's initial reservations, I worked hard at fostering a cordial atmosphere, a camaraderie that would dispel any last bits of tension between us. I wanted to create the ideal conditions for my experiment; any disagreement or unpleasantness would ruin everything, so I did what I could to eliminate all obstacles. I think I succeeded, because neither Marianne nor Natalia ever suspected the true motive behind our little jaunt. Leaving Berlin was like traveling back in time to the days of our misspent youth. And for some reason, the ominous specter of Heinrich never once crossed our path, perhaps because by then we had grown accustomed to his absence. Of course we remembered him, and I even managed one or two agreeable words about him so that Natalia would have something nice to say to him. All of this fell perfectly within the framework of my relaxation tactics.

The spa was a lovely, restful retreat, with a decadent, fin de siècle charm. The building's facade was dripping with German Art Deco details. And just as I had suspected, given the time of year and the wartime circumstances in which we found ourselves, the hotel was practically empty. It was the perfect place to disconnect from the world or, if one preferred, to create a parallel world. The two spacious, beautifully appointed rooms looked out onto a small garden and were connected by an interior door that was normally kept closed, but luckily it had neither lock nor key (I took care to double-check beforehand).

Our first day was spent in a whirlwind of lively discussions and forays into the surrounding countryside. In the distance, the still-snowy peaks of the Bavarian Alps protected us like the stone walls of a giant castle, but the brisk weather got the best of us and so we retired to the warmth of the fireplace in the main salon, where we played cards with an elderly couple we met there. They were the only other guests aside from the three of us, a minor detail that made me feel as though all of this was happening somewhere outside of normal time and space. The restaurant, fortunately, still served excellent food. Our only contact with the outside world was an old radio that the spa manager turned on each afternoon to keep up with the war news.

Amid the chats, the jokes, and the eventual laughter, I paid close attention to the two women, trying hard to discern a slip, a complicit gaze or a furtive caress, but I came up with nothing. I refused to concede defeat. The afternoon of our third day was a decisive one. The chilly weather had abated and I announced my intention to go for a walk, knowing that they wouldn't want to come. They hated going for walks after lunch. And just as I predicted, they said they would stay in and rest for a while. Just the moment I had been waiting for.

"I'll be back in a few hours, then," I replied, and I even took a voluminous book with me to indicate that I planned to be gone for a good while.

I walked only about one hundred meters from the inn. Once I was certain nobody had seen me, I returned to the hotel via the back road and crept into the empty room next door to Natalia's. It wasn't long before the two women returned from the sitting room. Were they aware of the trap I had laid? Apparently not, I deduced from their muffled laughter. They entered the room and at first just talked about all sorts of things. The conversation, however, eventually and inevitably came to a halt. Aha! I waited a few minutes before opening the door that separated us. And what I saw before me was one of the most traumatic, extraordinary spectacles I had ever witnessed in my entire life.

Slowly, deliberately, Marianne was removing Natalia's clothes. My wife was standing up and my friend's wife sat on the bed, both of their backs to me. As she unbuttoned Natalia's dress, Marianne paused to kiss her friend's hair. She caressed Natalia and her moist lips traveled down the white nape of her neck. Natalia, meanwhile, took Marianne by the hand and, as far as I could see, returned her lover's kisses. Next, they changed positions and now Natalia unbuttoned Marianne's blouse. They didn't undress completely—a precaution, perhaps, against the possibility of my sudden return—but instead just loosened their clothes.

There is no way to describe the feelings that washed over me: rage, arousal, jealousy, tenderness . . . What else can I say? I was the one responsible for staging this scenario, like a theatrical director or laboratory technician, so I couldn't take issue with the results. One thing was certain, however: I would not dare interrupt them and ruin the marvelous tableau I was admiring. For the remainder of the week I did everything I could to make sure that they reenacted the scene each afternoon. As the days passed, my uneasiness grew—but so did my delight, for I was the person who made this miracle possible. All I had to do was look at Natalia—her bare back, her wild mane of red hair, her dewy skin, and her hands resting on my wife's breasts—and I found myself transported to a state that I can only describe as ecstasy. How could I not marvel at the two of them? How could I not celebrate this capricious union, this strange coupling that, to a large degree, I myself had created? But at the same time, how could I not feel like the most miserable of men, doubly cuckolded before my very own eyes? How could I not feel like a masochistic voyeur?

It's safe to say that by the time we returned to Berlin, we were different people. How could any of us have possibly been the same as we had been the week before? Maybe Marianne and Natalia had kissed before, but I knew that they had never experienced the level of erotic freedom they enjoyed during our time in Bavaria. As for me, I was profoundly affected by those afternoons of silent observation. I wasn't sure what my next move would be, but I suspected it would be something drastic, a decision that would radically transform my view of the world and profoundly change the course of my life to come.

Erwin Schrödinger, or
A Lesson in Desire

Dublin
March 1947

All Bacon managed to come up with was a rickety old American military plane, which delivered us to Dublin, en route from Hamburg to the United States. It was a monstrous thing, grimy and ugly, though according to the cabin crew it was the very best of the fleet, having logged relatively few hours in the air during the war.

"And why would that be?" I asked. "Do they have a surplus of contraptions like this one?"

"No, no, on the contrary." The young attendant laughed. A raging case of acne had rendered his face a veritable minefield. "It's just that each time before takeoff, there were always last-minute problems with this plane."

Wonderful. Such a comforting explanation sent me into a nervous panic, another reminder that I never should have agreed to come. My nausea reached its peak just when Bacon and Irene arrived at the plane.

"Professor, I'd like to introduce you to Irene," said Bacon enthusiastically.

"*Enchanté*," I responded—only out of obligation.

I can hardly even attempt a physical description of the woman, for I could hardly stand to look at her, she was so vulgar and common. Except on the few occasions in which we were obligated to exchange a word or two, I avoided looking at her entirely. The only thing I can say with any certainty is that she wore an exceedingly cheap perfume—a gift from Frank?—and that her accent sounded more Slavic than German.

"This is Professor Links, the man I've talked so much about," Bacon said. "He is the brain behind this mission."

The woman inspected me from top to bottom, not unlike someone appraising a herring in a fish market—no doubt a task she was more than familiar with.

"How do you do?" she mumbled, offering her hand, which I had no choice but to shake.

Once we were inside the plane, I tried my best to move as far as possible from the happy couple, but the cabin crew insisted that we all sit together, side by side. Inside, the plane looked like some kind of abandoned factory: There were no real rows, just a few seats lined up on either side of the plane, which was shrouded in a rather depressing penumbra. In a surprising gesture of deference, Irene decided to sit between me and Bacon.

"How long is the journey?" I asked. What I really meant, of course, was "How long am I going to have to tolerate this woman sitting next to me?"

"Around four hours."

Maybe they could give me a sleeping pill. Well, I had brought a copy of Pascal's *Thoughts* with me; I could at least leaf through it for the duration of the trip. My vertigo permitting.

"I understand you have a little boy," I said to show I didn't have anything against her.

"Johann," she said with false pride. "I had to leave him with his grandmother. I'm going to miss him so."

Thank goodness I had Pascal.

The engines soon began to roar, creating a terrible racket, and the plane began to move. I felt as though a team of locusts were marching through my stomach.

"Do you have a fear of flying?" Irene asked.

"I manage," I replied.

Irene and Bacon spent the entire four hours chatting affectionately, holding hands like a couple of newlyweds on their way to a honeymoon paradise. Each time I lifted my eyes from my reading I had to confront the spectacle of their intrepid tongues and their wandering hands, which explored an unseemly array of body parts. Was this what love meant to them? Heavy petting at high altitudes?

We arrived in Dublin at around eight in the evening. Someone from the institute met us at the airport and took us to our hotel. As my miserable luck would have it, my room was next to Bacon and Irene's, and the wall separating us was wafer-thin, which meant I had to endure all-night vigils of yelps and moans from the other side, turning me into a de facto—though most unwilling—voyeur. All my efforts to sleep were frustrated by their deafening outbursts of ecstasy—how could Frank not realize that those moans *had* to be fake? And when I managed to drift off, I was rudely awakened by Irene's grotesque cries indicating she had finally reached the peak of her carnal pleasures. Suffice it to say that the following morning I was a walking zombie with a cadaverous white mask of a face, and in no condition to join in the discussion with Schrödinger.

Erwin Schrödinger was born to an old Viennese family in 1887, making him fourteen years older than Heisenberg. As fate would have it, he also happened to be Heisenberg's polar opposite. An engaging, charming womanizer, he was a dandy and bon vivant whose philosophy of life might best be summarized by the Strauss waltz "Wine, Women, and Song." If Heisenberg was the stoic of the physics community, then Schrödinger was its Bacchus. Their respective careers had taken quite different shape: While Schrödinger spent his youth blissfully unaware of the new quantum theory, Heisenberg had practically grown up with it. And while Schrödinger was a simple professor at the University of Zurich when he first began publishing his scientific discoveries, Heisenberg already had a reputation as a kind of boy wonder, cosseted and protected by the great physicists of the world ever since his teenage years. So while Heisenberg was a twenty-five-year-old celebrity, Schrödinger was already pushing thirty-eight.

Schrödinger visited Princeton in 1934, but Bacon had been able to attend only one of his lectures. As a professor he was clear and concise, but at times his reputation preceded him. It was common knowledge, for example, that he traveled in the company of both his wife, Anny, and his lover, Hilde March (the wife of an ex-student). For his entire stay in the United States, moreover, he did nothing but complain about the American way of doing things. In Princeton, they put Schrödinger up at the Graduate College, an old building not unlike an Oxford college, complete with common rooms and a grand old medieval-looking dining hall, but the professor was said to be suddenly indisposed—apparently he found the food abominable, and it wasn't long before he returned to England, where he had been living previously. Upon his return, he summed up his experience in the United States by saying he was constitutionally incapable of living in a country where fifth-rate wines were considered superior.

In spite of this, Bacon remembered Schrödinger as having been one of the best lecturers he had ever listened to, light-years beyond the paralyzingly dry academic discourses to which he was accustomed. For this reason Bacon was truly chagrined when Schrödinger, near the end of his U.S. trip, declined the job offers he received from Princeton University and the Institute for Advanced Study. After that, Bacon lost track of the professor's career.

Schrödinger remained at Oxford until 1936, when he made the most unfortunate decision to return to Austria to accept the chair he was offered by the University of Graz. When his country was annexed by the Reich in 1938, Graz was among the cities that demonstrated the most enthusiastic support for the Nazi troops. At that point, Schrödinger—accompanied by his ample and extended family—made the slow, tortuous journey over land until he was finally able to set sail for Great Britain.

A timely invitation from Eamon De Valera, the prime minister of Ireland, presented Schrödinger with a new professional challenge: the establishment of an Institute for Advanced Study in Dublin, in the image and likeness of the one in Princeton. Schrödinger, naturally, would assume the directorship of its scientific division. He made it out just in time to escape the war, arriving in Dublin on October 7, 1939. The institute had had its fair share of opponents, who saw the project as an egocentric indulgence on the part of De Valera, all the more objectionable considering the difficulties Europe was going through. The institute was established, however, and from then on, Schrödinger enjoyed a measure of peace that few of his scientific colleagues would know during those years. Despite the usual hardships and fears, Ireland kept itself out of the conflict, which meant that the now mature physicist could spend his time reading the Vedas, drafting articles on physics and philosophy, enjoying the company of his increasingly motley family (which now included Ruth, the daughter Hilde bore him, equally doted on by Anny), and planning his sexual conquests.

In the first act of Mozart's opera *Don Giovanni*, the title character's obedient servant Leporello recounts the story of his master's romantic victories.

> *Madamina, il catalogo è questo,*
> *delle donne ch'amò il padron mio.*
> *Un catalogo egli è che ho fatt'io.*
> *Osservate, leggete con me.*

How many women had Erwin conquered between the sheets? Could he, like Leporello, compile a catalog of his exploits? Such an ugly, skinny little man, with giant round eyeglasses that obscured half his face, yet he was the undisputed Latin lover of the modern scientific world! He was a rogue disguised in a genius's clothes, a satyr with the manners of a country gentleman, a sexual obsessive who hid behind a veil of anodyne normality. Looking at him, one wondered how he found the time to have so many love affairs and how he managed to drive so many women wild. One wondered, also, what it was that enabled him to fall in love with every one of his female conquests. My choice of words is deliberate: Erwin could have sworn up and down that he felt a most affectionate love for all (or at least most) of the women he had seduced. Two in one month? Why not? Three? Naturally. How about four? At one time he even got up to six.

His first lover bore the conspicuous name of Felicie. Felicity, happiness. Nevertheless, she appears to have been the only woman who ever denied his advances. Erwin was in Vienna, in the early years of his career, when he first succumbed to the delights of this discreet, aristocratic young woman. His passion for her had reached such heights that at one point he declared himself willing to renounce even physics if doing so would win her love. But his loss was physics' gain, as the young woman's parents had very different plans for their daughter, and they expressly forbade her from seeing him. Like any other romantic soul, Erwin fought with all his heart to overcome the social obstacles that stood in his way. And in the spirit of the best romantic novel, our hero transformed his defeat into a tragedy of epic proportions.

After heartbreak came revenge. After a few weeks of romantic mourning, Erwin decided to dedicate a healthy portion of his time to the study of the female soul. Ladies and maids, virgins and whores, fat and thin—if it wore a skirt, it was good enough for Erwin, who added any name he could to the statistical analysis he was carrying out on the female gender. From this period, only two names survive: Lotte and Irene (interesting coincidence, wouldn't you say?).

In 1920, shortly after the end of the great war, at the age of thirty-two, Erwin began to show signs of settling down and married a woman who was not young, not pretty, and who many people say was neither nice nor particularly sharp. Annemarie Bertel was her name, though he always called her Anny. You might ask, then, why he married her. I should warn you that the reason may not seem especially heartwarming: He did it to maximize his opportunities with other women. Anny, however, proved to be far more astute than anyone could have imagined. Upon discovering her husband's infidelities, she decided not to do a thing.

Now, Erwin was not exactly known for his discretion. He was never satisfied with merely conquering a woman, for a great part of his pleasure was derived from admiring her (or at least pestering her) in public, for all the world to see. It wasn't long before his flirtations became legendary among Erwin and Anny's friends in Zurich, where they made their home. Anny, meanwhile, took a leaf from her husband and she, too, broke the weak vows of marriage they had taken, falling in love with one of Erwin's colleagues. At first, Erwin pretended not to notice the affair—an eye for an eye, as they say—but after a time he could no longer ignore it, and by 1924 he was seriously considering the possibility of divorce. At the time, neither of them could have known that 1925 would be a magical year.

Hoping for a respite from the endless battles with his wife, that year Erwin decided to spend Christmas in one of his favorite places in the world, a mountain hideaway in the valley of Arosa, in Switzerland. From the very beginning, there was something special about this trip. Instead of staying at the small house next door to Dr. Otto Herwig's villa, where he usually stayed, Erwin stayed at a cottage tucked away in the mountains, far away from everyone and everything. And there, he had a revelation that would revolutionize contemporary science, not unlike that of Heisenberg only a few months previously. Invigorated by the snow-covered pine trees, the clear blue sky, the warmth of the fireplace, and an ample selection of wines, Erwin suddenly realized his life's mission. For a few ecstatic moments, the solution to the baffling puzzle of science became eminently clear to him. If Planck, Einstein, and Bohr were responsible for smashing the notion of classic physics into a thousand little pieces, Erwin's job was to put them back together.

Erwin was not nearly as aloof as Heisenberg, his nemesis, and in this case we can be almost certain that he was not alone during those moments of exceptional genius. The problem is that, given the vast number of women in his life, it is virtually impossible to determine which of his female companions was with him during his time in Arosa. When an interviewer asked him to elaborate on this topic, Erwin simply responded that he had indeed entertained a visitor, a mysterious woman of fearsome beauty whose unprecedented talents deserved the credit for his amazing discovery. According to him, wave mechanics were the product of an act of erotic imagination. And the rest was history: Erwin then wrote several articles that came to be considered among the most influential works of contemporary science, and he became an overnight sensation. Everyone seemed to want a piece of his celebrity, and he and his followers quickly found themselves embroiled in an acrimonious battle with Heisenberg and the disciples of his matrix mechanics. There was, however, a special bonus that came as a result of Erwin's discovery: His newfound fame opened the door to an even wider range of potential romances.

After his retreat at Arosa, a few months was all Erwin needed to patch things up with Anny, who promptly—and rather curiously—decided to introduce her husband to a pair of fourteen-year-old twins, Ithi and

Roswitha Jünger, for mathematics and physics tutoring. Needless to say, Erwin fell in love with both of them, although in the end he settled on one to serve as his inspirational muse: Ithi. From that moment on, he courted her tirelessly. Poetry, it seems, was one of Erwin's lesser-known (though undeniably intriguing) talents, and he quickly put his lyrical gifts to work on Ithi. The following lines were dedicated to her:

> On Herr Professor Schnitzer's traces
> With algebra and three-cornered races
> He ran Ithi-bitti almost to death—
> The poor little kid was quite out of breath.
> Of Zurich there is much more could be told
> But about such things I won't be so bold.

Perhaps he wasn't bold enough to "tell" of certain things, but *doing* them didn't seem to be a problem for him. When Ithi turned sixteen, the mature Erwin had already done just about everything he could think of to get her in bed, but she had always denied him. But if there was anything that fired his passion, it was a challenge. He refused to give up, and one day while visiting Salzburg, where Ithi lived with her family, he snuck into her bedroom, and for a few precious moments he basked in the glow of her slender, youthful body, which seemed like the fountain of eternal youth itself. Yet despite his insistence, she stubbornly refused to surrender the one thing he wanted. For another of her birthdays, Erwin sent Ithi yet another poem, the inner meaning of which hardly requires the services of a psychoanalyst.

> When they unfolded your diapers the very first time,
> The bells on your cradle did joyfully chime.
> The king of the fools gave his scepter a shake
> And bid you in life every happiness take.

This anecdote might seem mischievous, or even charming, if it hadn't ended (as so many of these stories do) quite so sadly for Ithi. For seven long years she had been the one object of Erwin's impossible desires. Finally, toward the end of 1932, Ithi took a trip to Berlin, where the professor found himself alone. Anny had been called away unexpectedly, and on this occasion Ithi finally succumbed to her teacher. Like a sheep that willingly follows her pastor to the slaughterhouse, Ithi threw herself into wave mechanics without knowing that Erwin had already fallen in love with another woman,

Hilde March. The situation went from bad to worse a few weeks later, when Ithi discovered she was pregnant. Petrified, the young girl sought the help of a doctor who could rid her of this terrible disgrace. But the tragedy did not end there: The procedure was unsuccessful and Ithi, sweet Ithi of those dulcet verses, was torn to shreds. She would never be able to get pregnant again. Nevertheless, she would always remember Erwin with great fondness.

How many had there been by now? Who cared? Erwin was in love again! Hilde would eventually become one of the most devoted and stable figures in his life and, unlike Ithi, bore him a daughter, Ruth. So first there was Ithi, then Hilde, and after Hilde it was on to Hansi, an old friend of Anny's who visited them in Berlin in 1931.

Erwin wasted little time after arriving in Dublin. Despite the presence of both Anny and Hilde, Erwin quickly succumbed to the charms of Sheila May, a popular actress at the time. He dedicated an endless amount of poems to her, and he even dared to publish them in book form.

When Lieutenant Bacon, Irene, and I arrived at the Institute for Advanced Study in Dublin, Erwin introduced us to his latest amour: a pale young woman who worked in some government office. She was twenty-seven years old, and he, only sixty.

It was all too apparent from our first meeting with Schrödinger that we had arrived at the worst possible moment. That day, the look on Erwin's face would have awakened a dead man. I've never been a particularly good judge of masculine looks, but I can say this: Erwin was not handsome, but like so many Viennese men, he carried himself with a distinguished, almost priestly dignity.

Despite the fact that his discovery of wave mechanics was crucial to the rise of quantum physics (and the fall of Newtonian principles), in his heart, Erwin was a kindred spirit of Planck and Einstein. At the end of the day, he was still an aristocratic, reactionary man of Vienna, and after the revolution he helped start, he returned to the more stable, familiar territory of traditional physics. From the beginning of the war onward, he locked himself away in his office at Dublin's Institute for Advanced Study and became Einstein's newest ally, joining the great physicist in his battle against the defenders of randomness. And just like Einstein, Erwin had one single objective: to conceive of a unified field theory that could explain away the universe, encompassing all the forces found in nature: electromagnetism, gravity, and atomic theory.

For several months now, Einstein and Schrödinger had maintained a correspondence regarding the unified theory. Though less determined than his colleague, Einstein was still obsessed with the notion of unifying gravity and the electromagnetic force in some coherent manner.

On January 27, Erwin wrote to Einstein announcing that he had finally figured out a way to solve the problem. "Today I can report a real advance," he wrote. "Maybe at first you will grumble frightfully, for you have explained just recently why you don't approve of my method. But very soon you will agree with me." Erwin was so convinced of his achievement that he ignored Einstein's reservations and presented it as soon as possible before a session of the Royal Irish Academy. As if this weren't fanfare enough, he announced it to the Irish press in the following manner: "I have the honor of laying before you today the keystone of the Affine Field Theory and thereby the solution of a thirty-year-old problem: the competent generalization of Einstein's great theory of 1915."

The next day, Erwin's news was splashed across the front page of the *Irish Times* as well as other Irish newspapers. When one of the reporters dared to ask him if he was absolutely certain of his theory, Erwin replied: "This is the generalization. Now the Einstein theory becomes simply a special case. . . . I believe I am right. I shall look an awful fool if I am wrong." Without knowing it, Erwin sealed his fate with these words.

When the news of his "discovery" crossed the Atlantic and Einstein caught wind of it, he flew into a rage. Infuriated, he wrote an article for the *New York Times* in which he asserted that in the best-case scenario, Schrödinger's theory represented only a minor step forward. "The reader gets the impression that every five minutes there is a revolution in science, somewhat like the coup d'état in some of the smaller unstable republics. In reality one has in theoretical science a process of development to which the best brains of successive generations add by untiring labor, and so slowly lead to a deeper conception of the laws of nature. Honest reporting should do justice to this character of scientific work."

To Schrödinger's fiery temperament, this was tantamount to being doused with a pail of cold water. Every last international wire service ran Einstein's comments next to Erwin's unfortunate observation, "I shall look an awful fool if I am wrong." When Erwin read the newspapers he fell into a deep depression. On February 2, 1947, scarcely a month before our visit to Dublin, Einstein sent Schrödinger one final letter with respect to the issue, saying that if he made any significant advance he would write to Schrödinger to let him know.

The "Einstein mess," as Schrödinger referred to it, was not among the topics we discussed during our meeting. Still, the pain and embarrassment of it all were in his eyes, like a terrible reminder of that disastrous time. As we would later see, the entire episode had had an extremely humbling effect upon him.

"Thank you for agreeing to see us," Bacon said, unable to come up with a more original conversation starter.

What I couldn't comprehend was why Bacon insisted on having Irene tag along with us to Schrödinger's office.

"My pleasure," said Erwin in a mollified tone of voice. "It's been a long time, hasn't it, Links? Are you as obsessed as ever with Cantor and the infinite?"

"You could say so, yes."

That was the sum total of the attention Erwin paid me; his eyes were instantly and intently focused on the legs of our female companion.

"What is your name, miss?"

"Irene," she said knowingly.

"A very good choice, young man. The world would be far too boring a place to live in without a woman to share it with, don't you agree?"

Frank blushed, but even worse, our Don Juan's comment made Irene's preening even more intolerable.

"As I mentioned in my letter, Professor," Bacon stuttered, "I am preparing a paper on German science during the Third Reich. You were one of the preeminent figures from that period."

"Why don't we start out with the early days of wave mechanics, Erwin?" I added, trying to seem less formal. "Why don't you start with 1925, the *annus mirabilis*?"

"A truly marvelous year," Erwin agreed, nodding nostalgically. "Until then, the world of science (and the world in general, I might add) was mired in a terrible, interminable chaos. We all knew that the old rules of classic physics were kaput, but nobody knew how or where to find the new ones. Everywhere people were trying to figure it out; there were little steps forward and giant steps back, but nothing that was able to effectively replace the clear and necessary principles Newton had laid out." Erwin focused his discourse on Irene, who couldn't have understood more than three words of what he was saying. "Everyone had an opinion on the matter, and there were very few solid answers to go on. Planck's quanta, Einstein's relativity, Bohr's atomic model, the Zeeman effect, the problem of spectral lines—it was chaos. The mystery could be cracked only if someone came up with a quantum theory that could explain the behavior of an atom."

"What do you mean by that, Professor?"

Was I hearing things, or was that actually Irene's voice?

"Technicalities," I interrupted. "It would be too complicated—"

"No, Gustav, I think the young lady has a right to understand what we're talking about," Erwin admonished me. "Let me try to explain it a little better."

How many hours were we going to have to waste so that Erwin could flirt with Irene? Was Bacon going to do nothing at all to save us from this preposterous waste of time?

"As your friends surely remember," Erwin began, adopting his old lecturer's tone of voice, "the first person to shed light on the matter was Prince Louis de Broglie. We have him to thank for the brilliant observation that matter could be studied just as one studies a ray of light. That is, using a method similar to the wave optics system that optometrists use to grind lenses."

"Before him," I jumped in, determined not to be left out, "the laws of classic Newtonian mechanics governed the study of bodies in motion."

"This simple hypothesis was enough to turn science upside down for the next twenty years," said Erwin, regaining control of the discussion. "You might ask why, young lady, and I'll tell you. It's because, without meaning to, De Broglie had hit upon the precise tool that was so desperately needed to study the atom! Imagine the scenario, if you will: All over the place physicists are driving themselves mad trying to figure out a method that can assimilate the new physics, and all of a sudden this French aristocrat—De Broglie—appears on the scene, telling everyone that the missing link they've all been looking for has been right under their noses the whole time! They just didn't know it, he said, because their methods were all wrong."

"Right about then both you and Heisenberg came out with your theories, at practically the same time," Bacon pointed out.

"That's correct."

"Could you talk a bit about what Heisenberg proposed?" asked Bacon.

"The main problem with Heisenberg's mechanics was that the mathematics he used were all but incomprehensible even for the majority of us physicists. Werner was a child prodigy, doted on by the likes of Bohr, Sommerfeld, and Born, but he ended up creating more problems than he solved." Schrödinger fell silent for a moment after casting this none-too-subtle aspersion on his adversary's reputation. Then he resumed speaking: "Please don't misunderstand me. Heisenberg's discovery was extraordinary. Instead of directly examining the various possibilities of an electron's position, he worked out a method that allowed scientists to reasonably predict (that is, according to the rules of probability) the locations to which the electrons might migrate. The idea, I repeat, was extraordinary. The icing on the cake was how he put it into action. To make it happen, Heisenberg had to deploy a highly complicated mathematical system which Kronecker had discovered toward the end of the nineteenth century."

"Kronecker being Cantor's archenemy," I added, unable to contain myself.

"To summarize, Heisenberg had made great progress, but very few people could understand it." Erwin's hands flew to his head upon the realization that, try as he might, there was no getting around the difficult terms that our dear, sweet Irene had never heard before in her life. "Even later on, when the phlegmatic Paul Dirac reviewed Heisenberg's conclusions, he declared that no better results could be produced."

"And that's when you arrived."

"Well, I don't mean to seem vain, but, yes, I was able to shed some light on the matter."

"Unaware of what Heisenberg and Dirac were doing at the very same time."

"There was no way I could have known. I've told the story a thousand times. They all worked in teams, in Göttingen, in Cambridge, in Copenhagen, sharing ideas and writing long letters back and forth to one another. I, meanwhile, was more or less isolated in Zurich." Erwin paused for a moment or two, happy to be able to describe, for the umpteenth time, the discovery which had made him so famous. "During Christmas of 1925, I decided to take a vacation alone, at a spa in the small town of Arosa. A lovely place, Irene. You should tell your friend to take you there. There, in the middle of all that snow and solitude, all my thoughts came to a head. I had read Louis de Broglie's papers and knew they had been well received by Einstein, and I had a feeling they would make a good starting point. My idea was simple: apply a quantum perspective to De Broglie's wave mechanics. You might ask exactly what my contribution was. And I'll tell you again: putting the puzzle together."

"And putting the world to work," Irene observed.

"A friend of mine at the time, a young woman whom I tutored in mathematics, said something of the kind: 'In the beginning you never thought that so many logical things would come out of this.' Yes, it was something like an explosion. But the process was extremely exhausting. In 1926, I published six articles on the topic, until I finally caught the attention of the great ones, that is, Planck, Einstein, and company. Suddenly they all began ringing me, asking me to deliver lectures on my discovery."

"A much more overnight success than Heisenberg's," I noted.

"I told you already: Heisenberg's mathematics were simply too complicated."

"But he felt that he was the true father of quantum mechanics."

"A question of semantics," Erwin replied. "Ultimately, the important thing was that physicists finally had a practical method at their disposal for studying the atom and, thanks to its mathematical simplicity, the method they opted for was the one I had devised. As soon as they realized that my system was much simpler than Heisenberg's, all the physicists began to use it. Even Pauli, who was Heisenberg's friend, was enthralled by the elegance of my formula. Unfortunately, not everyone responded with the same level of intellectual honesty," Erwin added. "Naturally, it was too good to be true. Egged on by Bohr and Heisenberg, everyone was suddenly skeptical of the idea that a Viennese arriviste could have made their own projects go sour."

"What exactly did Heisenberg think, Professor?"

"He was very standoffish with me. He wrote that wave mechanics were 'incredibly interesting,' but that they didn't add anything to the work he had already done."

"And did Heisenberg have a point, or was it just sour grapes?" I ventured to ask.

"Listen, I don't like to speak badly of people. Yet I do think the competitive spirit strongly affected his judgment. Remember, up until then, he thought he alone held the key to the truths of modern physics."

"But were your perspectives that radically different, in reality?"

"Well, at the time, yes. Heisenberg and Born remained wedded to their positivist line of thinking, saying it was impossible to visualize atomic motion, whereas I saw it the other way: According to my theory you could practically see what was going on inside the atom."

"A real paradox," Bacon interjected. "For years, physicists had been complaining that they had no system to effectively describe atomic behavior and suddenly they had not one but two theories which, moreover, were apparently at odds with one another."

"That's the key right there: *apparently*," said Erwin, clearly enjoying his lecture. "In May of 1926 I published another article which proved they were basically the same theory, despite their being articulated via two different kinds of mechanics. Heisenberg's followers took this as an affront. They were infuriated; it was as if I had insulted them personally. Not only had I dared to solve the same problem in a different way, but now I was proving that my system could do everything theirs could, only with fewer headaches. Now, if both theories served the same purpose but one was better, why stick with the lesser one?"

Bacon glanced back at his notes and began reading: "Heisenberg then said to Pauli: 'The more I think of the physical part of the Schrödinger theory, the more abominable I find it,' and later on he said (please forgive the language), 'I think it is bullshit.'"

Erwin let out a devilish cackle.

"It was war. Heisenberg, Bohr, and Jordan were on one side with their matrix mechanics, and I was on the other side with my wave mechanics. And even if the two were ultimately the same, neither side would ever dream of caving in, because the battle, ultimately, was about dignity. Our dispute had become the nerve center of the entire scientific community, because its outcome would determine who would be the dominant players in quantum physics for years to come."

"Was it a power struggle?" Irene asked.

"You might call it that, young lady. I wouldn't disagree with you."

"Some people have said that Heisenberg's envy, ambition, and snobbery were the real cause of the problem," I added.

"I've heard people say that."

"And what happened next?" Irene asked. "Who won?"

"Naturally, things had a way of working themselves out. Little by little, physicists began using my method for their research even though they still publicly supported Heisenberg's model," Erwin said with another sly smile.

"And that was what gave way to your direct confrontation."

"In July of 1926 Sommerfeld invited me to present my findings at his *Kolloquium* at the University of Munich. I accepted, happily. When my lecture was over, a tall blond man arose from his seat and began criticizing me, and then asked me if I thought that the rest of the great questions in physics could be resolved by using my theories. Naturally it was Heisenberg, who *just happened* to be passing through Munich at the time. I scarcely had time to answer him, because right then Willy Wien, the moderator, said to him in a thunderous voice that I can still hear, 'Young man, Professor Schrödinger will certainly take care of all these questions in due time. You must understand that we are now finished with all that nonsense about quantum jumps.' Heisenberg was furious, and stormed out of the lecture hall like a scolded child looking for his older brother to defend him. And he immediately dashed off a letter to Bohr telling him what had happened."

"And what did Bohr have to say?"

"What he usually said." Erwin shrugged enigmatically. "He wrote me a letter, inviting me (you might say obliging me) to pay him a visit in Copenhagen."

"And did you accept?" Irene asked.

"Well, what else could I do, my dear?" Erwin said, chagrined. "It was one of the most exhausting experiences of my entire life. Bohr is a charming man, but not when you have to be around him all the time. When he becomes obsessed with something, he is unstoppable. He put me up in his house and treated me like a prisoner, doling out bread and water until he was finally through with his interminable interrogation. He became an utterly ruthless beast, refusing to give me a moment's rest as long as I disagreed with him."

"Was it really that awful?" asked Irene.

"I can assure you, my dear, that I wouldn't wish that appalling episode on my worst enemy. I told Bohr what I thought, and Bohr rejected my opinion over and over and over again. Finally, I became so exasperated that I simply exploded, saying I was sorry that I had ever gotten involved with quantum mechanics in the first place. Only then did he calm down a bit and try to make peace with me, saying, 'We, on the other hand, are grateful you did. Wave mechanics, with its mathematical simplicity and clarity, is a great step forward,' and other such things."

"Did you ever arrive at any sort of conclusion?"

"We kept on talking, day and night, but we never got anywhere," Erwin answered, exhausted. "In the end, Bohr succeeded in driving me to distraction. I got horribly sick from the whole thing, and if it hadn't been for the efforts of the lovely Margrethe, I would have wanted to die right there and then. I had a raging fever at that point, and it was a struggle simply to remain conscious, but that didn't stop Bohr from planting himself at my bedside to continue tormenting me. 'But Schrödinger,' he said, 'you have to understand . . .' Those words still send me into a cold sweat. It was pure torture. By the end I didn't know if I agreed with him or if I still believed what I believed. Whenever I talked with him, everything would become so vague and confusing, so *philosophical,* that I couldn't understand anything anymore."

"All right," I exclaimed. "I hardly think our dear Professor Schrödinger deserves to be subjected to another experience like that. Why don't we go for a bite to eat and continue our chat tomorrow?"

"That's the best idea you've had all day, Links," said Erwin. And then, turning to Irene, he added: "Anyway, I have a few questions for you. After all, I wouldn't want the young lady to think that all I'm interested in is physics."

Erwin got up from his chair and offered his hand to Irene.

"Follow me, gentlemen, if you please," he said, grabbing on to Irene's arm. "The institute has prepared a little lunch for you. Right this way . . ."

After enduring another exhausting night of moans and sighs that wafted over from the room next door, I arrived the next morning with Bacon and Irene at Schrödinger's office, ready to pick up where we had left off. The atmosphere was decidedly more relaxed now, perhaps because we knew one another a little better. Irene was less impertinent, and I was less concerned about her pretentious posturing and calculated innocence. Erwin, meanwhile, had realized that she was not about to become another of his conquests—Frank had managed to make this abundantly clear—and so he, too, was more subdued.

"Now, according to what you described yesterday, it sounds as if your relationship with Heisenberg was always somewhat strained."

"We were rivals, Professor Bacon, competing for the same prize," Erwin agreed somewhat dismissively. "To a certain degree, his attitude was to be expected. As you yourself know, a physicist can spend years—his best years—studying one single topic, one single goal, without any guarantee of success. Heisenberg had spent years and years on the same set of problems and he thought he had solved them. And then someone came along and dared to insinuate not only that Heisenberg was wrong but that he was on the wrong track altogether. I don't think he had anything personal against me, he just reacted out of frustration. It was understandable, really."

"The two of you received the Nobel Prize in the same year."

"Not exactly. It wasn't awarded at all in 1931, so in 1933 they gave two prizes, one for that year and one for the previous year. For some reason, the Swiss Academy felt that Heisenberg's was for 1932, while mine—which I shared with Paul Dirac—was for 1933. It was a wise decision."

"What is your impression of Heisenberg now?"

"What a question. Without a doubt, he is among the great scientific minds of this century. A brilliant, astute, severe man."

"Ambitious, too," I added.

"And who isn't in this field, Links?"

"But how far was he willing to go to get what he wanted?" Bacon asked.

Erwin paused, and smiled conspiratorially.

"I'd love to say that he was a kind of Faustian figure, willing to sell his soul in the name of . . ."

"Glory? Immortality?"

"No. Knowledge. Never once did I think of Heisenberg as weak; his goals were never petty. On the contrary, from an extremely young age, from the very beginning of his career, he knew that he was one of the 'chosen ones,' one of a very few human beings the good Lord had blessed with a special talent to solve his mysteries. That was the reason for his arrogance. Yes, I suppose he would have done anything to get closer than the rest of the world to the *truth*."

"*Anything?*" I insisted.

Schrödinger ignored the question.

"Heisenberg was obsessed by uncertainty. He was perfectly aware—perhaps *too* aware—of his own abilities, and that was why he was so very anxiety-ridden about the future. Quantum mechanics was his mission in life—he wanted a monopoly on truth, and for that, he would have to disprove theories like mine. To me, it all seems like one man's desperate effort to make some sense out of the world he lived in. I know it sounds paradoxical, but a man who so meticulously studied the notion of uncertainty, the physical *impossibility* of ever possessing all the information on a given system—why, that is the kind of man more desperately in need of concrete answers than anyone else."

"In that case, Professor, do you think that the *uncertainty* established by quantum mechanics was Heisenberg's way of celebrating free will somehow?" asked Bacon, suddenly philosophical.

"That was what Pascual Jordan, one of his colleagues, believed. And Jordan, you'll recall, was an ardent admirer of the Nazis for many, many years. Jordan thought that given the indeterminate quality of the natural world, it was man's obligation to go around filling in the holes that nature left empty. How, you might ask? Through the force of will. It is an ancient and, I'm afraid, rather tyrannical notion. Since the universe is vague and unclear, truth is on the side of the fittest. The difference between good and evil, right and wrong, should be determined by those who have the power to do so—that is, men who possess an iron will."

"Let me see if I understand this, Professor," Bacon said, taking a deep breath. "According to this philosophy, the origins of free will can be found in the randomness of the quantum, relativistic universe."

"That's what they believed. That the cosmos is made complete by our acts of will."

"You don't agree, do you?"

"Absolutely not!" Erwin exclaimed, horrified. "I find this attitude completely intolerable and utterly irresponsible on a moral level. I am not good or evil because things happen randomly. On the contrary: My decisions are motivated by a wide variety of factors, from the most petty to the most noble. They are not made in a vacuum. Quantum mechanics may assert that certain aspects of the universe will always be impossible to determine, but it also makes statistical predictions which are absolutely not based on randomness."

"What conclusion have you come to, then?"

"In my opinion, the best thing to come out of this controversy has been the reconciliation between free will and physical determinism. After so many false starts, we have finally realized how mistaken it is to use the randomness of the physical world as a basis for ethics." Erwin sounded like a scientific pope, defending his neodeterministic dogma. "To make a long story short, quantum physics has no relationship whatsoever to free will."

"Nor, then, does physics have a relationship to the moral quality of our actions," volunteered Irene.

"The scientific view of the universe doesn't say a single thing about our final destiny, nor does it care in the least about God. Far from it. Where do I come from and where am I going? Science is utterly incapable of answering such a question. Men like Jordan (and perhaps Heisenberg as well), however, believed that quantum physics was proof that we could never fully *know* the reality of things. And, as such, only human will could establish the parameters of human behavior. For me, this is a wholly perverse idea that can only lead to perverse behavior."

"In an indeterminate world, then, where good and evil don't exist in and of themselves, things like concentration camps and atomic bombs could be considered 'normal,' " Irene ventured.

"If we follow that line of thinking to its ultimate consequences, that would be correct, my dear."

"You were one of the few leading physicists who did not participate—even indirectly—in the development of the atomic bomb, on either side," said Bacon.

"I was never asked to, and if I had been, I would have refused."

"Why, then, did so many scientists, both in the United States and in Germany, voluntarily participate in these sorts of projects?"

"It was a great challenge," Erwin replied.

"Are you saying that it was a decision based on personal pride?"

"Absolutely. Any physicist would have been overjoyed to show that his theories had some practical use. My dear friends, we scientists—and theoretical physicists in particular—are by definition perverse beings. We spend all our time studying things and calculating formulas, so naturally the prospect of a direct application of our theories is extremely tantalizing."

"And the ethical and religious considerations?"

"Given that the universe is relativistic (not in the Einsteinian but the Protagorean sense) and indeterminate, a physicist must distance himself from it. If he simply does his job, keeping himself far removed from any extrascientific consideration, he can live with a clean conscience. For someone who thinks that way, the radioactive mushroom of an atomic explosion is nothing more than proof that he was right."

"That's all?"

"That's all. Why else do you think so many men were more than happy to participate in the atomic projects? Patriotism? That was the least of it, although there may have been some of that mixed in. It was pride! *Vanitas*, Professor Bacon! Physicists fight their own wars, the kind that have nothing to do with armies and governments. Every one of them wanted to be the first to build an atomic bomb; to do so would mean the unequivocal defeat of the other team. The consequence of the explosion was the last thing on their minds; the important thing was to humiliate the other side. And that's what happened. And as fate would have it—if you'll excuse my saying so, Professor Links—Heisenberg's team lost the battle."

"I can't believe it," exclaimed Irene, suddenly the moral conscience of the group. "They couldn't care less about the lives that would be sacrificed just so long as they won their scientific battle. I think that attitude is far more sickening than Hitler's."

"We scientists have never been a flock of white doves," said Erwin cynically. "I'm sorry to disillusion you. You're not living among the best this world has to offer."

"Millions of people perished just to prove a theory."

I was growing more and more uncomfortable, but there was little I could do about it. Schrödinger was provoking me.

"To them it was a game," Erwin insisted. "Like poker or chess. Mathematically, at least, it was no more relevant than that—as you well know, Links. The objective was to defeat the opponent. That was the main thing."

"That was why, by the end of the war, Heisenberg was so destroyed," Bacon said, thinking out loud. "Not because the Germans lost—he had gotten over that months before. But to discover that the Allied physicists had achieved what he had only thought was the remotest of possibilities. That was why Gerlach, the director of the German project, cried when he heard about Hiroshima."

"It's disgusting," Irene snapped, her whiny voice sounding like that of an indignant crow. "He shed tears of vanity; he didn't give a damn about the victims."

"I must remind you that none of that would have been possible if it hadn't been for the intervention of the military and the government, miss. As despicable as a physicist might be, he cannot build warheads unless either of these entities empowers him to do so. The dangerous enemy here is the government, any government. The abscess of fascism has been eliminated, but the idea is still kept alive in the minds of those ruthless enemies. . . . I shiver just thinking about how far we could take this. In fact, we've gone way too far already."

A squalid military plane delivered us back to Hamburg. From there, we took the train to Göttingen, and the railway corridors were witness to a most uncomfortable discussion between me and Irene.

"Didn't you find him simply brilliant?" I said, referring to Erwin.

"Sharp, no doubt about it," said Bacon.

"Well, I think he was pathetic," announced Irene, incensed. She only wanted to be contrary.

"I'm sorry to disagree with you, but I think you're mistaken," I said. "I don't mean to offend you, I'm just telling you what I think. Honestly, I think Schrödinger is just carrying out a practical reductio ad absurdum of his theories."

"Explain what you mean, Gustav," Bacon goaded me.

"It's very simple," I began. "I'm sure you can both remember the famous scientific example of Schrödinger's cat."

"The professor told us about it over lunch," Frank reminded Irene, though I'm sure it had gone way over her head.

"If we follow the paradox to its final consequences (despite Professor Schrödinger's objections), each time one carries out a measurement of some quantum phenomenon, the universe splinters into a variety of possible outcomes."

"And what does that have to do with Professor Schrödinger's romantic life?" Irene retorted.

"Simple. On a quantum level, each decision we make forces us to choose one path over another, even though we might know that a part of us (or the 'other us,' as it were), within our universe, goes in a different direction. And what is love if not the greatest of all the decisions we make? Each time a man *decides* to love a woman, he is ultimately opting for only one possibility, effectively eliminating the others. Doesn't that seem like a terrifying prospect? With each decision we make, we lose hundreds of other possible lives. To love one person means not to love so many others."

"I don't think that our notions of love have anything to do with one another," Irene snapped.

"But of course they do, young lady. What I'm saying is hardly a revelation. You have chosen this fine young man," I said, gesturing toward Bacon. "And upon doing so, you have eliminated the possibility of loving anyone else. Professor Schrödinger, for example, or me."

"That's just luck."

"That's it!" I exclaimed, ignoring her irony. "You see, you agree with me. To choose one thing is the same as losing hundreds of other possible worlds. And if what we find is a dead cat, then there's no turning back; our observation condemns us to remain in *this* world. The same is true of love. The famous *what if?* That's the frustrating thing."

"I think that a person should take responsibility for his decisions."

"My dear Irene, I admire your principles, but not everyone sees things that way," I said, laughing. "Human beings tend to be fallible. Perhaps not you, but the majority of us make mistakes, and we often regret the things we've done. And that is when those magic words appear: *what if?* I think Professor Schrödinger is one of those miserable souls who wishes he could have lived a thousand different lives. Erwin is a man who has tried to live several different lives in one lifetime. That's why he can have a wife and a lover and live with both of them."

"I don't think he loves them all, even though he said that," Irene countered.

"If you'll excuse my saying so, I think he does. Or at least he thinks he does, which is enough."

"Either he loves or he doesn't love, Gustav."

"You're wrong, Irene. I'll say it again: In a world where absolute guarantees do not exist, not even love can be exempt from doubt. Let's say that he considers it highly probable that his love is true. That is the best anyone can hope for. As far as I'm concerned, then, Erwin loves (or thinks he loves, which is all the same to me) many women at the same time, in an attempt to escape from the bondage of making decisions. Why limit oneself to one single universe when there are so many? Convinced of this idea, he throws himself into several different lives simultaneously. Erwin is not a Don Juan or a Casanova: He doesn't chase maidens for sport, to add a notch to his belt or to deceive them. Exactly the opposite. He is trying not to put a limit on his love, or on his possibilities. Live with a wife, a lover, and a daughter all together? I don't think that's such an easy thing, or very much fun, for that matter. As I said before, Erwin doesn't do it because he wants to have a good time, but rather because he doesn't want to regret only having chosen Anny, or Hilde, or the girl from the radio. This way, he has them all!"

"You are as despicable as he is," Irene spat, furious. Bacon, who remained silent throughout this conversation, tried unsuccessfully to calm her down. "To use science as a justification for immaturity. What does he do to avoid the doubts and the regrets that are part of every decision in life? He doesn't decide at all! That is the worst act of cowardice I have ever witnessed in my life. To me, freedom is a virtue precisely because it entails risk. Naturally, there is always the possibility that something might go wrong, but that doesn't make the risk less worth taking. That's what makes us genuinely human, Gustav. You and Schrödinger take the easy way out, which is to take all the roads, all at the same time. You always want to win, but I think that in the long run, you're mistaken. The one advantage of being defeated, of being wrong, is that you have a new opportunity to try again."

"How much longer is it to Göttingen?" I asked.

THE LAWS OF ATTRACTION

How long could Marianne, Natalia, and I have gone on like that, trapped in our roles by the force of our own inertia? While the two of them continued their secret love affair, I continued spying on them in silence, hidden behind the walls like a cautious, timid scientist gingerly carrying out his experiment from a distance, nestled in the comfort of his macroscopic world. Perhaps if I had been less fascinated by the idea of this unprecedented experience, we would have emerged unscathed by the chaos we had created for ourselves. So I ask myself again: How was it that such a tiny little snowball turned into such a tremendous avalanche, dragging us down with it? And once in motion, would there have been any way to stop us?

Six months had passed since our return from Bavaria, and the situation was the same, each one of us playing our respective roles in the miserable little game we had created. Marianne was still my distant wife and Natalia's passionate lover; Natalia missed Heinrich terribly, and sought solace in Marianne's arms. I, meanwhile, entertained myself by watching the two of them.

Everything changed in 1940, on the evening of our Christmas dinner, right around the time when Hitler was planning Operation Barbarosa, a surprise attack on the Soviet Union for the following summer. As usual, we had invited Natalia to celebrate Christmas with us, as Heini had not been able to return for the holidays. From Paris, he wrote us a long letter which Natalia read to us out loud, choking back tears. In addition to the typical pleasantries and apologies for not being able to be with us, Heini directly asked me to reconsider my attitude toward him, saying that we might not have many more opportunities to reconcile. I don't know what it was—the time of year, the bitter tone of Heini's letter, Natalia's choked-up voice, Marianne's tears—but suddenly I couldn't help myself, and I finally gave in and said that I was ready to forgive Heini, that I missed him as much as they did, and that as soon as possible I would do whatever was necessary to patch up our friendship. My unexpected change of attitude had a miraculous effect on the atmosphere in the room. Suddenly, we were a family once again.

Upon hearing my declaration, Marianne pounced on me, and Natalia quickly followed suit, kissing and hugging me, and then kissing and hugging Marianne with the same warmth and delight. Once we realized what was going on, the three of us were overwhelmed, filled with a happiness and exhilaration that we hadn't expressed toward one another in ages. Suddenly we were no longer three separate people, but rather three parts of one single spirit. We needed each other more than ever at that moment. The night air outside was frigid and dense and, leaning out the windows, we were reminded of the precariousness of our situation. What were the chances that we would feel that way again, our souls united, in a year's time? Slim at best. In the middle of the fear and the vertigo, we turned into little frightened animals, trapped by the gripping force of our mutual appetites.

Who was the first to make the decision? Perhaps it was me. Yes, I was the one who set off that chain of unfortunate events. But in that instant, it seemed like such a sweet, tender, loving gesture. I kissed Marianne passionately, something I hadn't done for so very long, and at the same time held on to Natalia's delicate hands, intertwining her fingers with mine. And the next thing I knew, it was Natalia's lips I was kissing and, without missing a beat, I pressed my own against hers even harder. I slid my tongue around hers, giddy with the electricity that traveled across our skin, and Marianne began to unbutton Natalia's dress. By virtue of some kind of miracle (a miracle that now seems like a curse), the three of us became one single being: our perspiring, aroused bodies struggled to free themselves of their clothing that Christmas night, like slaves who had finally managed to break free of the chains that had kept us in bondage. We fell to the floor, like beasts devouring their prey, kissing and caressing and tearing and killing and loving one another uncontrollably, endlessly, to the point of total exhaustion. Surrendering our individual personalities, we were transformed into one multiple being, governed only by our heady desire. For that moment, it didn't matter what belonged to whom—legs, eyes, an inner thigh, a few inches of skin—for we surrendered everything to one another in that indiscriminate moment of bliss, which was sustained by the mutual belief that distances and limits have no place between people who truly love one another. *Love one another as I have loved you,* said he whose birthday we were celebrating that day, and we took this commandment to heart. We weren't sinning, we *couldn't* be sinning. If anything, we were possessed by a grace that, for once in our lives, had given us back our innocence.

We ran to the bedroom, where, exhausted and unclothed, we clung to the bedsheets as if they were fishing nets that the Holy Spirit himself had laid out for us. Never before had I witnessed such an abundance of beauty in one place. And rather than two ecstatic women revolving around the one man present, the scene was beyond gender; we were a giant, tangled web that swayed back and forth of its own accord, mystified and awed by its own beauty. Each detail was a work of art: two sets of magnificent breasts that slid effortlessly across one another; my tongue, traveling down the belly of one woman until reaching the back of another; the kisses that went from my shoulders down to someone's feet; my member, in perpetual motion, sliding in and out of two different yet identical vaginas; our six hands, interlaced like six meticulously woven fibers; three voices that soothed, blended, cried out, sobbed, and filled with tender insults, until it was impossible to distinguish one from the other. The universe was born that night with us; it belonged entirely to us. Our embrace was the primordial force in constant expansion; our whispers, the Word; and our mutual exhaustion, the seventh day of rest.

After the storm, calm returned. The three of us lay motionless on the bed like survivors of a shipwreck, floating on imaginary rafts of the mattress, waiting for someone to save us, too tired to call for help. If that wasn't love, what was it? We floated upon ourselves, thirsty and disoriented, staring up at the chandelier that hung from the ceiling as if it were the star of salvation. Were we praying? Almost wordlessly, barely moving our lips, swallowing saliva that tasted of sweet wine, we begged for forgiveness—from God, from Heinrich, from mankind—and at the same time we begged to be granted another encounter like the one we just had. And another, and another, and yet another, to the point of utter damnation. Unto infinity.

THE LIAR'S PARADOX

Locked in an ominous silence, Lieutenant Bacon, Irene, and I arrived at the Göttingen train station at about seven in the evening that Friday. Bacon hailed a taxi and sent Irene to her mother's home, where she was to pick up Johann.

"It's been an awfully rough week, Gustav. Go and rest. I'll see you on Monday."

"Right. Monday, then," I said, still extremely bothered by the disturbing conversation Irene and I had gotten ourselves into.

Bacon, after glancing up at the clock inside the train station, decided to walk home. After so many hours together with us, the idea of losing himself in the sweet anonymity of Göttingen was delicious. At nighttime, the city was different: refreshing, free, and unencumbered by the worries and obligations of the day. The building he lived in looked like a giant sleeping whale, and the light from the streetlamps only barely illuminated its mouth. Bacon entered his apartment like a rodent trying to sidestep the traps laid by his furtive predators. It was midnight. He would take a bath and only then—if at all—would he even contemplate crossing the short distance that separated him from Irene's front door.

He turned on a table lamp and began to undress. As he threw his trousers to the floor, he noticed a white envelope that had been stuck underneath his front door, and for a few moments, he just stared at it. For a second, Bacon probably thought it was a memorandum from his superiors alerting him that his orders had been changed, but that wasn't the standard procedure for such notices. Intrigued, he quickly opened it, only to find yet another white envelope within the first one. He opened that one, impatient now. From there, he pulled out a tiny rectangular card, a note written in large, elegant script whose only notable characteristic was a slight aperture in the formation of a few of the vowels. The message was as follows:

Dear Professor Bacon:

Although you have not requested a meeting with me, I know that sooner or later our paths will cross. For this reason, I have decided to take the initiative. Why? To warn you, my dear friend. You are entering unfamiliar territory. In my day, I did the very same thing, and I lost out in the end. Which is why I now say to you: Be careful! All physicists are liars.

Professor Johannes Stark

A shiver went down Bacon's spine. Was this some kind of joke? How did Stark get his home address? And why would he send such a sinister message? Was he trying to dissuade Bacon from completing his mission? Was he merely trying to warn him? Or scare him instead? Bacon lay down on his bed for a few moments, motionless. Then he got up and did the first thing that came to mind the very worst thing he could have done: He went looking for Irene. He found her, sleepy and surly (probably angry at him for not coming sooner), holding her baby, who refused to go to sleep.

"What's going on?" she asked. "You nearly broke down the door."

Bacon entered the apartment, ignoring Irene's comment.

"Have you seen anyone come near my apartment?"

"No . . . I've been here the whole time since I got back. Why?"

Bacon handed her the note.

"I don't understand."

"I found it underneath my front door," Bacon said.

Irene glanced at it.

"How odd. Why would he send you such a thing?"

"I don't know. But one thing is for sure. He knows exactly what I'm up to."

"That's ridiculous."

"More like treacherous, I'd say."

Irene quickly put Johann in his crib. Then she turned to Frank and hugged him tightly, as if she wanted to protect him from some sort of unknown menace.

A few hours later, Bacon was sitting in a chair in my living room. I looked at my watch: four in the morning.

"This couldn't wait until tomorrow morning?" It was cold, and my nightshirt provided little warmth. "Coffee?"

"Yes, thank you."

"All right, Lieutenant, what's going on?"

He handed me the same slip of paper he'd shown Irene.

"Old Stark sent this to you?"

We went into the kitchen, and as I filled the coffeepot, Bacon told me what had happened.

"We always suspected he was crazy," I snorted, nervous. "And now he's trying to get involved in our game. But why? What can he get out of it?"

"He wants us to know that he's on to our investigation and that he's not concerned. And maybe also . . ."

"What?" I said with a start.

"Well, obviously this is some kind of challenge. Read it again."

" 'Be careful! *All physicists are liars,*' " I read out loud.

"He's establishing the rules for our encounter, as if this were a game of poker or chess. But why would he do something like this? Why is he daring us like this? Wouldn't it have been more prudent to simply say nothing, like he's done up until now?"

"Clearly, Stark thinks we consider him a suspect, and this is his mode of defense. He's trying to get ahead of us."

"It's absurd," Bacon mused. "He can't be in his right mind."

"Maybe not, but that doesn't matter. We have no choice but to move ahead."

"And what should we do now?"

"The same thing we've been doing. Continue with our investigation."

"And his game?"

"Maybe he's just trying to buy time."

"He's playing games with us!"

"Calm down, Frank." I offered him a cup of coffee. "Let's just forget about him. We can't give in to his rules."

"It's too late now," Frank insisted. "We only have two choices: either to play or give up the game. If we decide not to play, Klingsor wins."

"All right! All right!" I said, taking a sip of coffee, scalding my lips as I did so. "Let's play, then. Now tell me, Lieutenant, what do you think the meaning of Stark's letter is?"

"Honestly, I have no idea."

"Do you think he is suggesting that the testimonies you and I have gathered are false? That someone has been lying to us?"

"Yes, that's exactly what I think it means. Someone has been trying to mislead rather than help us with their testimony. And now we have to figure out who the liar is. Don't you see? Stark has managed to plant a seed of doubt. By first implying that we're on the right track and then telling us that someone has been trying to trick us."

"That's what I've said all along. The perverse hydra of uncertainty."

"Worst of all, he's succeeded." Bacon slammed his hand against the table. "We can't trust anyone now, even less than before." He paused, and before I had the chance to say anything, he gathered his belongings and announced: "I'll be waiting for you in the office, Professor. I think I know someone who can help us."

Despite the fact that it was Saturday, the old building that housed Bacon's office was not empty. Here and there, soldiers moved about carrying boxes and dossiers, while a half-dozen civilians sat at their desks filling out forms or reading their mail. I arrived just after nine o'clock. We spent the whole morning sitting in front of a Morse code machine, tapping out a long message which Bacon drafted with utmost care. By midafternoon we had the answer we were waiting for. Once translated, I discovered that our international correspondent was none other than Professor John von Neumann.

> To: Lieutenant Francis P. Bacon
> From: Professor John von Neumann
> Dear Frank,
>
> Wire received. Interesting problem. It reads like a gangster movie. A physicist who likes to play games. Very clever. One day I wouldn't mind sitting down to a cup of tea with old Stark. No doubt he's slightly mad, but at least he has a sense of humor.
>
> The mystery he placed before you is brief but profound. I'm surprised that scientists as competent as the two of you didn't pick up the allusion he made. Perhaps it seems too obvious. It is a paraphrased version of the celebrated Epimenides Paradox. He was a Sophist who loved to poke fun at his colleagues, a healthy tradition that we should certainly keep alive. Invoking his wisdom and valor, this good man (born in Crete) once said: All Cretans are liars.
>
> I don't think I need to elaborate on the logical contradictions that arise out of this statement. Perhaps Stark is as sharp and honest as Epimenides, or our good friend Kurt Gödel. I wish you luck. It sounds as if you need it. Keep me informed.

"How could I not have realized?" I chastised myself.

"I didn't get it either. How stupid: It's the very foundation of Gödel's theorem!" Bacon seemed truly ashamed of himself, though I—a mathematician—was the one who really looked foolish. "Anyway, the important thing is that we've gotten somewhere."

"Just like the statement that all Cretans are liars, 'All physicists are liars' is an innocent enough statement until uttered by a physicist."

"Right. A physicist is telling us that all physicists are liars."

"Exactly," I observed. "It's as if I were to say, 'I'm lying,' or 'This statement is a lie.' If this is true, then the statement is false. And if it's false, the statement seems true; but if it's true, then it's false, and on and on, ad infinitum. A classic recurring paradox."

"A paradox from which, as Von Neumann has so kindly reminded us, Gödel's theorem emerged. Don't you see, Gustav? Uncertainty yet again. Before it was something that gave rise to quantum physics, and now it serves as the nucleus of mathematics. As Gödel himself said, even in the most perfect system there will *always* exist at least one proposition that cannot be verified by the laws of the system. It is neither true nor false but *undecidable*."

"Like Schrödinger's cat, alive and dead at the same time."

"Too many coincidences, don't you think?" added Bacon. "I met Gödel when I was at Princeton. In a way, you might say that it's because of him that I'm here now."

"The message, then, is filled with other messages."

"And they all revolve around the same thing: the impossibility of ever knowing the truth."

"He wants to discourage us," I added, uneasy. "What he's saying is this: If one can never reach any absolute certainty in the areas of science, physics, and mathematics, then why are we so insistent on pursuing this with such determination? The truth is as ambiguous as an undecidable proposition, as fickle as an electron, as uncertain as any paradox."

"In other words, 'You'll never find Klingsor.'"

I said nothing for a few seconds, weighing the various possibilities.

"Something occurs to me, Lieutenant," I said. "Perhaps this missive has simply served to confirm our previous suspicions. Stark was the enemy of all the scientists we've interviewed until now. They were all working against him, and perhaps still are."

"Elaborate, if you please."

"Don't forget the message: *All physicists are liars.* Stark wants us to doubt all the testimonies we've heard. Do you see why? If we accept the hypothesis that Klingsor was in fact one of Stark's enemies, then all those physicists would have been lying to protect his identity, just as they had done before. And what if they were all lying to protect *one of their own?* Heisenberg, for example?"

"It seems like madness not to trust Heisenberg just because of something that Stark said."

"That's it, Lieutenant. Stark knew that we wouldn't believe him; that's why he didn't try to convince us of anything. He's challenging us to prove him wrong. It isn't an accusation but rather, as you yourself said, a challenge. If we can prove that one of our interviewees had lied to protect Heisenberg, we'll be on the right path."

"But that would mean involving the entire scientific community of this country." Bacon was alarmed, although in his eyes I could tell that he was warming up to my idea. "It would be like exposing a conspiracy."

"And if that's what it really was?" I baited him. "Stark is a despicable character, obviously, but maybe for once he's telling the truth. It would be terribly unfair of us to eliminate this theory simply because a somewhat wretched character suggested it. And what if the others are far more wretched than he? I'm not the only one who mistrusts Heisenberg, Lieutenant," I said, inserting my most sibylline provocation. "The whole world knows that in the end, even Bohr turned against him."

"Bohr?"

"That's right, Lieutenant. I don't know the details that led to their falling-out, but it must have been very serious. Why don't you ask Werner about it?"

Frank didn't say a word. He seemed lost in his own world, an ocean away, inaccessible.

"What are you thinking about?" Bacon asked as he looked at her, sullen and reserved, hidden amid the shadows of the bedsheets.

Her body was like a fish tossed upon the sand, exposed to the hot rays of the afternoon sun. Frank slid his hand between her parted thighs, but she jumped with a start, slithering away as if he'd just prodded her with a harpoon.

"I don't think Heisenberg has anything to do with this, Frank," Irene said, popping out from under the sheets. Her breasts, tiny and flushed, stuck out like freshly picked apples.

"I think you're more worried about this than I am," he murmured, tucking his head in her lap.

"I don't understand how you can take this all so lightly," she said, pushing his head away. "You've been working at this for four months, and you have nothing to show for it, don't you see? That Gustav is taking you for a ride. You don't have one solid lead!"

"Well, there's the letter." Bacon sat up and tried to cuddle her, to no avail.

"Right, the letter!" she retorted. "As if we could consider it of any value at all. It's nothing, Frank. In no way does it prove that Heisenberg is guilty. It's all an illusion."

Bacon finally began to lose patience. If I were him, I would have dropped the subject entirely or at least told her to stop interfering in my affairs, but poor Bacon was too timid for that.

"I've had enough, Irene!" he exclaimed. "Now you're taking it personally. I know you don't trust Gustav, but without him I never would have gotten anywhere."

"But you *haven't* gotten anywhere, Frank."

"That's what you think. I, on the other hand, feel that we've made some good progress."

"Such as?"

"Well, with Planck, Von Laue, Schrödinger. And even if Heisenberg isn't our man, it's possible that he could point us in the right direction."

"I repeat," said Irene, as she got up to get dressed. "You don't have a single shred of evidence. All you have are your speculations."

"I don't understand why you're so bothered by all this," he argued. "Where are you going?"

"I'm just worried that you're wasting your time, that's all," she said. "I have to get ready. It's almost seven."

"Irene, please. I have enough problems already. I don't want to fight with you, too."

She chose not to respond. The anger intensified the already troubled look on her face.

The midday sun was white and luminous. As always Bacon arrived on time for his appointment—his obsessiveness, at times, had a way of driving me mad—and Heisenberg was punctual as well. I was beginning to feel more and more uncomfortable in the presence of the obstinate, innocent American. The pretext for this visit was the same as before: the supposed research project on German science.

"I hope this question isn't too untoward," Bacon began. "But why did you agree to participate in the German atomic project? Were you aware of what the consequences would be if Hitler possessed the atomic bomb?"

"I was simply performing my job as a scientist, Professor Bacon." Heisenberg's voice acquired an icy edge. "I agreed to work on the German atomic project because I had no other choice. In such a position I was able to be of service not only to my country but potentially to the entire world."

"What do you mean, Professor?"

"The progress in the atomic bomb research depended on me," he noted persuasively. "And I never would have allowed a weapon of that magnitude to be unleashed upon humanity."

He then fell silent.

"Do you mean that you would have been prepared to prevent the successful deployment of your own project?"

"I said that I would never have allowed such a weapon to have been used, Professor Bacon. That's all."

"Even if it would have been construed as an act of treason against your own country?"

"I would never betray my country, Professor," Heisenberg fumed, nearly exploding before Bacon's eyes. "But I also would never have allowed millions of innocent people to die at my hands. You, on the other hand, have Hiroshima and Nagasaki."

Heisenberg had turned the tables. He had a point, in a way.

"Let's be realistic, Professor Bacon," he added. "In the end, I caused nobody's death. On the other hand, hundreds of my American colleagues did just that, for whatever reason you like: patriotism, a desire to prevent further disaster—I am hardly one to judge. So now, why do you continue accusing me of such things, Professor?"

"I'm sorry, Professor."

"How many illustrious physicists and mathematicians participated in the Allied atomic bomb effort? The list goes on forever. Einstein himself was one of the bomb's very first supporters. Bohr himself was on that list, and now he is the one who criticizes me."

Heisenberg realized he was getting overexcited and was beginning to say too much. So he stopped talking and, cold as an iceberg, buttoned up his rage behind a tight, forced smile.

"Bohr?" asked Bacon, feigning innocence.

Heisenberg hesitated.

"Yes, and many others as well."

"Aren't you friends anymore?" Frank pressed on mercilessly. "I always thought of you as sort of a family."

"Perhaps at the bottom of it all we are," Heisenberg mused cryptically. "I never stopped admiring him."

"But you aren't in contact anymore?"

"No."

"Since when? The beginning of the war?"

"More or less. Since the last time I saw him in Copenhagen."

Bacon knew he'd hit gold.

"May I ask what happened then, Professor?"

"I'd rather not talk about it," Heisenberg snapped, tense and surly. "That is a personal matter that has nothing to do with your project."

"It seems logical that Bohr would have been upset," continued Bacon, ignoring his interviewee's discomfort. "Denmark had been invaded. Perhaps he was offended by your position."

"I suppose so."

"When did you last visit Copenhagen?"

"In 1941."

"Did you visit the institute, like in the old days?"

"No. I had been invited to the city's German Institute to give a few lectures. I thought it would help improve relations among the German and Danish scientists, but obviously I was wrong."

"And you took advantage of the opportunity to visit with Bohr."

"Naturally."

"And what did you talk about?"

"The war, Professor Bacon. And physics, of course. It was a very brief visit."

"And after that you lost all contact."

"Unfortunately, yes." Heisenberg drummed his fingers on his desk. "Are we finished yet?"

"Yes, Professor. For the moment, yes," Bacon concluded, immediately nervous that his tone sounded sarcastic.

"I hope I've been of some help," Werner said. His hands were trembling.

There was one question that German scientists had to answer when the war was over. It was the same question that those of us involved in the atomic project were constantly asking ourselves: *Why?*

Did you participate in the German scientific project that was involved in the development of experimental weapons? *Yes.*

Were you aware that your work could lead to the creation of an atomic bomb? *Yes.*

Were you aware of the potential uses the Nazis could find for such a weapon? *Yes.*

But you say that you consistently opposed Nazi politics and that you never joined the party? *Yes.*

Then why did you do it? Unfortunately, that was not such an easy question to answer. Given that I was something of a victim, I didn't have to rack my brains to think up a convincing explanation—my suffering in prison was sufficient evidence of my repentance. But others, like Heisenberg, were forced to come up with far more elaborate justifications. After the war was over, and for quite some time after that as well, whenever he was asked to explain his wartime activities he would always say, "It was *suggested* I work on it. The government's official slogan was 'We shall use physics to serve the war,' though we changed it around to suit ourselves: 'We shall use the war to serve physics!'"

How many words, how many clever expressions like this one, could we invent to alleviate the terrible weight we carried on our shoulders? At least we had one point in our favor, one saving grace: We had *failed*. After all, by war's end Heisenberg and his team had produced neither a chain reaction nor a real reactor, much less a bomb capable of a mass explosion. They had tried and they had failed. But what if they had been successful? If Hitler had killed millions of innocent people in London or Birmingham, as the Americans did in Hiroshima and Nagasaki, would history have been as kind to Heisenberg then?

He continued to defend himself as best he could. In those days, the historical circumstances were different. He was German, after all. Wasn't it logical, understandable, that he would rather hope for his country's victory than its annihilation? Wasn't it his duty to help defend his homeland? In a normal war, yes, that would have been his duty—that was made clear—but not in *this* one. Hitler was no statesman fighting for the good of his countrymen, he was a criminal. Hadn't that been made abundantly clear in Nuremberg? Nobody—especially a scientist—has the obligation to obey a criminal.

So why did Heisenberg agree to work on the atomic project?

He thought he had found a better excuse: because he wanted to use the war to serve his own scientific interests. From the beginning, he knew that the actual construction of the bomb would be out of his hands, at least for the duration of the war. The only thing he wanted was to do his work, but he never would have handed over a weapon of mass destruction to the Nazis. To him, fission—and the practical use of the energy that was released in this process—was a research topic, a scientific and technical challenge, that was all. Naturally he wanted to be up to speed with the Allies (why not ask them how *they* felt upon hearing that millions of people had died thanks to their efforts?) but there was no crime in that. It was actually a legitimate sort of competition—though, as he insisted, he never would have permitted a genocide like the one in Japan.

Was there, in reality, some truth to what he said? And were his interrogators, in fact, justified in their accusations? Or did they feel even guiltier—and as such, more willing than ever to issue pardons—because their own scientists had not only built war materials but actually put them to use? Weren't the prosecutors as corrupt as the defendants? Heisenberg, meanwhile, deployed one final, definitive argument in his defense: If he and his colleagues had refused to work on the project, then other scientists, far less scrupulous and ethical than they, would have accepted the work. (Was he perhaps thinking of Stark and his cronies?) And who knows what that would have led to? It was far better for a man like Heisenberg to be behind the project, supervising its progress, and even—why not?—slowing things down if necessary.

But could we trust this version of the story? Could we trust someone like Heisenberg? Of course not, Lieutenant. Absolutely not.

"How did it go?"

The ambiguous look on Lieutenant Bacon's face offered no clue whatsoever as to the outcome of his visit. I was dying of curiosity, but attempted to appear casual, indifferent. Frank barricaded himself behind his desk and contemplated the look on my face, as if trying to gauge my reaction.

"Well?" I said.

"I hate to admit it," he confessed, "but I think you were right."

"About what?" I said, startled.

"About Heisenberg. I thought the topic of the bomb would be the thing to set him off, but it wasn't that. It was Bohr that did it. Apparently, they had some kind of falling-out after our friend visited his old teacher in Copenhagen during the war."

"I knew it!" I exclaimed.

"All of a sudden you seem awfully excited by the idea that Heisenberg is our man, Gustav," he said, baiting me. "I still don't understand what, exactly, was the nature of your relationship with him."

"We were colleagues, Lieutenant," I said, without missing a beat. "Although we didn't even work in the same building. I don't even think we crossed paths more than two or three times while the atomic project was under way. They divided us into groups, as an intelligence precaution, you know, to avoid slips in the classified information we were handling."

"Very well, then," he conceded. "But if there's one thing I know it's this: We have got to investigate exactly what transpired between Bohr and Heisenberg in Copenhagen. And if our instincts are right, it must have been something more than just the 'tension' between a ruling country and its conquered territory."

"That's exactly it, Lieutenant. Bohr and Heisenberg were like father and son. They had the closest relationship I've ever seen between any two physicists. So for them to have such a terrible disagreement means it would have to have been extremely serious."

"Let's not speculate, Gustav, please." Bacon's tone of voice was growing more emphatic by the minute; a bit excessive, as far as I was concerned. Obviously it was Irene's noxious influence at work. "Let's stick to the facts, all right?"

"Of course, Lieutenant."

"I'm going to have to see Bohr."

"In Copenhagen?"

"Well, where else would you suggest?" he snapped. I knew he was on edge recently, what with the investigation, but there was no need to get aggressive. "I'll leave sometime in the next few days."

"But that barely gives us time to prepare."

"I'm sorry," he cut me off. "But this time, I think it would be better if you stayed here in Göttingen."

I couldn't believe what I was hearing: Thanks to me he had finally found the lead he was looking for, and now he didn't want to include me in the plan just because his little woman didn't like me! It was insulting.

"Frank, I don't understand," I murmured.

"I'm sorry, Gustav," he said, his voice softening. "Honestly, I'd rather visit Bohr on my own. Anyway, I've taken enough of your time. I don't want you to drop your own projects on my account."

"Don't you trust me anymore?" I asked him.

"Oh, no, it's not that at all," he replied with false sincerity. "It's just that the situation is getting more and more delicate. Every day I'm seeing how more and more people, important people, are tangled up in this. I have to take precautions, Gustav. Please understand, it's nothing personal. I know as well as you do that without your assistance I never would have gotten anywhere."

"It's your decision, Lieutenant."

A heavy silence hung over us for a few seconds as we tried to read each other's intentions. After a while, I couldn't resist the temptation, and asked him the one question that irked me the most.

"Is Irene joining you?" I asked.

"I don't know yet," Bacon said. "Maybe, but it might be too complicated."

"Right."

"You aren't upset with me, are you, Gustav?"

"Of course not, Lieutenant."

"I'm glad. I hope to have some better news for you when I return. Until then, keep thinking about all this. Every one of your hunches has been extremely valuable."

I never liked her. From the beginning I knew there was something diabolical about her, and that clever, obsequious manner of hers. It was there, in every move she made and every opinion she stated, and especially in the way she controlled Bacon. Those big eyes, that sulky attitude, the sullen reserve and hostility she exhibited toward anyone who displeased her—to me, this was sufficient proof that she was not to be trusted. Up until now, I had kept quiet—on many more occasions than I would have liked—out of respect for my friend. I would maintain a complicit, conscious vow of silence to avoid a confrontation that, in the middle of our investigation, wouldn't have done anyone a bit of good—that is, except for Klingsor. But now, more than ever, I knew I had to urge Bacon to be careful with Irene. There was something sinister about that woman, that mother whose tenderness and femininity had so enraptured Bacon. I couldn't allow her to ruin all of our hard work of the past few months.

Two things caught my attention right away. First, the ease with which she had slid into Bacon's professional life. And second, the fact that ever since meeting her, Bacon had never once seen her during the daytime. They always saw each other at night, when he would arrive home. He seemed uninterested in whatever it was she did for the hours that they were apart. Perhaps I was imagining things, given our mutual dislike, but I had to find out what Irene's real motives were.

One morning, instead of going to the institute or attending a meeting in Bacon's office, I woke up earlier than usual and planted myself near Bacon and Irene's building. The day felt morbid and hot; it was as if the sun weren't sure it wanted to show its face. At about eight, I recognized the lieutenant's nervous, hurried gait as he exited the building and rushed down the street to work. Perfect. Now all I had to do was wait for Irene. I had vowed to follow her wherever she went, to keep my eyes glued on her at all times.

The wait was long and tiring. Finally, at about ten, she emerged from the building with the baby in her arms, ready to hand him over to her mother— or at least that's what she told Bacon. From what I could tell, she was not aware that I was watching her, because she carried herself in an agitated, indiscreet manner that made her look absolutely ridiculous. I wasn't at all surprised to see that she wasn't particularly affectionate with the baby—she treated him more like a package she had to lug from one place to another. She never once kissed him or hugged him and, after carrying him for about four blocks, simply handed him over to an anonymous pair of arms that reached out from the inside of a ramshackle little vestibule. Irene didn't even go inside, and without even bidding her son good-bye—that is, if he *was* her son—she turned around and very quickly walked away from the building.

Making sure she didn't see me, I continued to follow her. At 10:15, Irene arrived at the door of the factory where she worked—or where she *said* she worked—and scurried inside, perhaps fearing a reprimand from her supervisor. That was about it for my investigation, I assumed. Still, I decided to continue my vigil and waited around until lunchtime. I hadn't been planning to go to the institute, anyway, and Bacon hadn't wanted to see me that morning, either.

Finally, at 1:10 in the afternoon, Irene emerged. Her movements were as rapid-fire and spasmodic as before, as if some interior pressure was nudging her to move faster and faster. I assumed she was on her way to pick up Johann, or to go somewhere for lunch, but soon I realized that she was heading too far away from the center of the city for that. At 1:30, Irene entered a small church on the outskirts of the city. Hidden behind a column, I saw her exchange a few words with a tall, gawky man dressed in peasant's clothes. She handed him an envelope. This scene was repeated every three days. I wasn't wrong. That man was her informer.

The Dimensions of
Affection

After that unforgettable Christmas of 1940, that night in which we inaugurated our secret society, several weeks went by before Marianne, Natalia, and
I were together again. The rather embarrassing nature of our experience was
enough to put some distance between us, and by the time we were fully
aware of what we had done, we were too confused even to talk about it. The
last thing I remember from that night was that Natalia simply got up, got
dressed, gave each of us a little peck on the cheek, and then left our house
without saying a word.

The situation between Marianne and me wasn't quite so simple. We had
no reason to hurry up and get dressed—we were in our own home, after all—
nor could we hide behind the false illusion that this was just another night
together. We took turns in the bathroom, and then we returned to our rooms,
put on our nightclothes, and went to bed. Neither of us was able to sleep, but
we couldn't talk either, and remained locked in a stubborn, uneasy silence.

Instead of thinking about my own actions and their consequences, I
stayed awake wondering how Marianne and Natalia would react to what
had happened. What were they thinking about right now? Why hadn't
either one of them objected? Why had they, in fact, plunged headlong into
the cauldron of emotions that I had created? Was it a mere aberration that
we should tactfully overlook, or was this the beginning of a new way of life?
I, for one, felt no guilt whatsoever, and I sincerely doubt Marianne did
either—of all of us, Natalia was possibly the only one who might have been
wracked with guilt and remorse. After all, Marianne and I were husband and
wife—an eccentric couple, maybe, but husband and wife all the same. The
fact that we had revealed our sexual fantasies to one another and shared the
mutual object of our desire was, in a way, a symbol of the trust we shared.
From that perspective, Natalia was the only adulterer in the group.

As I realized this, I felt a terrible knot in my stomach. All of a sudden I was gripped by a terrifying fear, an anguish that condemned me to insomnia. Where did it come from? It didn't take long for me to realize: It was the fear that I would never again *suffer*—and I think the term is most aptly employed here—another experience like the one I had just shared with Marianne and Natalia. What had happened between the three of us was nothing less than fascinating: the strangest mixture of impulses, arousal, pain, pleasure, jealousy, happiness, guilt. A concentrated, powerful potion which had penetrated each and every pore of my skin, my bones, my sex. But what if Natalia refused to relive that encounter? Or if Marianne decided she wanted to keep me and Natalia apart? What would become of me then? I couldn't allow it. I would be incomplete, empty. It was the only thing capable of lightening the heavy load of my existence: that painstaking, slow creation of a world which the three of us alone inhabited—our bodies, our desires, our woes, and our frustrations, all together. Scarcely three hours had passed since our interlude and I already felt the pressing need to repeat it.

The next day, Marianne woke up before me. When I woke, I went to find her, and I walked into the bathroom just as she was getting into the shower, already naked.

"What do you want?" she asked, hostile.

"You," I replied.

Without missing a beat, I pressed against her, feverish with the memory of the night before. Showering her body with delicate kisses, I fell at her feet like a slave, until my lips made their way to her sex. I wanted to pay homage to the body that I had previously spurned, to somehow show how grateful I was for the gift she had given me, of sharing her secret lover with me. Marianne wordlessly surrendered herself to me, and the silence which enveloped us was punctuated only by the sound of her faint, almost imperceptible sighs. Afterward, she fell into my arms, crying and begging for forgiveness.

"But there's nothing to forgive."

"How long have you known?"

"I don't know. It doesn't matter."

"I promise—"

"You don't have to promise anything, Marianne. All three of us have to take responsibility for what we've done."

My words calmed her down a bit, although not enough to prevent the numbing listlessness that took hold of her during the next few days.

"What's the matter, darling?" I would ask her, but all she could do was kiss me and murmur some meaningless excuse, a sudden headache or vague stomach pains.

After a while, I began to understand the nature of her reaction—after all, Marianne was a lot like me, although neither of us had the courage to admit it. She missed Natalia, that was all. After that Christmas dinner, their contact had been reduced to sporadic telephone calls. Brief and unsatisfying, they only served to remind Marianne of the void which now lay between her and her old friend. Once I was sure that Marianne wanted the same thing that I did, I resolved to take action.

One afternoon in early March, I arrived unannounced at Heinrich's house, hoping to have a chat with Natalia. A number of troops had already been transferred to the Eastern Front, but Heinrich was still in Paris. When Natalia opened the front door, she seemed unsurprised to find me standing there.

"Come in, Gustav," she said warmly.

I followed her into the living room.

"How is Marianne?"

"Not very well, actually. To be honest, not well at all."

"What's bothering her?"

"I think you know. The same thing that's bothering you. And me."

"Gustav . . ."

"Look, I won't say anything else if it makes you uncomfortable, but we can't go on hiding it. It would be hypocritical of us to deny our feelings. Nobody made us do it, Natalia. That night we all acted out of our own free will, our love. . . ."

"Please, Gustav, I'd rather not talk about it." Natalia's voice broke.

"I just want you to know how the two of us feel. You're not alone, Natalia. All three of us are going through the same agony."

She took one of my hands in hers and squeezed it tight, as if trying to confess something she was unable to express with words.

"I think it would be best if you left, Gustav," she said after awhile, in a quiet, repentant, infinitely sweet voice.

"You always have a place with us, Natalia, I hope you know that."

A few weeks went by before she came to visit us. It was a windy evening sometime in April when we heard the doorbell ring. Marianne and I both knew who it was instantly. Natalia was bundled up in a red dress that revealed the contours of her breasts and matched the color of her curls perfectly. A parasol dangled from the crook of her arm and a pair of emeralds hung from her ears. Her bare lily-white neck was so achingly lovely it was painful to look at her.

Marianne welcomed her with a sisterly hug that lasted ages. Meanwhile, I watched as Natalia's delicate hands clung tenderly to my wife's back, covering her with invisible caresses. There was no need for pretenses. I approached that person with two heads and began to kiss it, alternating from one to the other, reveling in our shared breath.

That evening marked the initiation of a secret ritual that the three of us would perform every time we came together. Our desire and—why should I be embarrassed to say it now?—our love were so great that we could no longer bear to be apart. Whenever the three of us were together, we would be overwhelmed by the need to hug, to touch, to bring pleasure to one another as none of us had ever done before. Passion came to dominate our lives with an intensity we never dreamed we were capable of. Suddenly, as our armies determined the fate of the world—and as Heinrich felt more isolated and lonely than ever—we closed ourselves off, retreating to our special, secret universe, our paradise, our own private utopia. . . . We shared everything, each of us belonging to the others in body and soul, to the very end. In the middle of this madness, we never once questioned our actions. To reflect upon them would have condemned us in advance. We chose to follow our instincts and then say nothing, just as we did in the beginning, pretending that our interludes were no different from those of normal people. Only when our encounters began to take on a sweetly ordinary quality—proof that monotony is inevitable—did I begin to realize the true nature of my feelings. And it nearly drove me insane.

Niels Bohr, or
a Lesson in Will

The building was an imposing stone structure, three stories high and with a gray stucco exterior and a reddish-colored roof. Little ivy vines crept up the walls, as if trying to sneak inside. Above the sober, neoclassical door was the following inscription:

UNIVERSITETETS INSTITUTET FOR TEORETISK FYSIK, 1920.

The day of its unveiling, Bohr had stood contemplating the mass of stone and cement as if it were some kind of metaphor for the science he loved so dearly. Gleefully, he thought back to his first encounter with the political life of his country, in 1916. At the time Bohr was nothing more than a promising young physicist student, and King Christian X, a stern man with military bearing, had granted him an audience. Bohr anxiously awaited the moment in which the monarch would approach him to greet him formally, and when the king finally extended his hand, he made the following remark: "It is my great pleasure to meet such an accomplished soccer player." Bohr, startled by the comment, couldn't resist correcting the king: "I am sorry, but Your Majesty must be thinking of my brother." The king's stewards suddenly descended upon the young rapscallion: *Nobody* was to correct the king during a public audience. Red-faced, Bohr tried to fix the faux pas by saying, "I am a soccer player, but my brother is the *famous* soccer player." King Christian was annoyed now, however, and all he said was "This audience has concluded!"

It was already early March of the year 1921, but the frigid, arctic temperatures continued to blast icy air on the large group of people gathered in front of the door to number 15 Blegdamsvej, a neighborhood of rambling homes and parks, not far from the cluster of Copenhagen hospitals. Niels and his wife, Margrethe, who had been one of the pillars of this project, were flanked by the president of the university, several government officials, and an assortment of academic types. After his brief official speech, Bohr said a few words that were not intended for the select group of Danes that surrounded him, but for posterity. Among the various goals of this new entity, Bohr said, was "the task of having to introduce a constantly renewed number of young people into the results and methods of science. Through the contributions of the young people themselves, new blood and new ideas are constantly introduced into the work."

But the Institute of Theoretical Physics was hardly the inner sanctum of a genius and his disciples, nor was it a hermit's cave, Saint Jerome's cell, or Simon Stylite's column. What Bohr had inaugurated was not a think tank, though it may have seemed like it on the surface. No, what he had built was a castle, a fortress, a trench—a base of operations from which he could supervise, like a decorated military general, the hundreds of soldiers who were preparing to fight in his name, and defend the theories that had come of age in Copenhagen. General Bohr? *Present! Raise arms!* Heisenberg? *Present, sir!* Pauli? *Present, General!* Schrödinger? *I'm sorry, General, he is absent today.* Well, bring him to me right away! He must come and stand guard here, at the altar we have built on Viking land!

For more than twenty years, from March 4, 1921, until the Nazis occupied the institute grounds in 1943, Bohr was the father of quantum physics, its spiritual leader, and, above all, the one man capable of reconciling the myriad battles waged by his disciples. Like a true Viking, Bohr was tireless: He wrote hundreds of letters, organized conferences and seminars, rubbed shoulders with illustrious scientists from all over the world, smoothed ruffled feathers, forged alliances, and blacklisted his enemies, though he had few of those. A humanist? An impartial soul, an arbiter of his times, the moral conscience of the century. He was all of the above, and more.

"Might you talk a bit, Professor Bohr, about the period in which you and Heisenberg were working together?"

They had only arrived in Copenhagen a few hours earlier, and the lieutenant—accompanied by the ubiquitous Irene—had insisted upon interrogating Bohr from the very moment he arrived at the institute. The great physicist gamely accepted the challenge, charmed by the idea of recalling the glory years of quantum physics, the golden age before the rise of Nazism and the war.

Bohr's heavy face resembled that of a bulldog, or a pug. His wide, spongy cheeks hovered dangerously over his nose, as if waiting to pounce on it, barely permitting his weak smile to break through, like a thin plank stuck between two chunks of flesh. His little eyes exuded a childlike exuberance, and the same was true of his mind. He possessed a neurotic temperament— but what scientist does not?—and an obsession for detail, clarity, and simplicity; these last attributes, unfortunately, not terribly congruent with his mode of analysis. Every time Bohr opened his mouth to speak, it seemed as though a pitched battle was raging inside his head, as if the statements he spat out were the result of a painful explosion that had taken place somewhere deep inside his brain.

"The year is 1927," Bohr began, stroking the ample double chin that protruded from his collar. "The battle between Schrödinger's wave mechanics and Heisenberg's matrix mechanics still lingers in the air, despite the recent compromise that has accorded validity to both theories. The atmosphere is charged, and everyone is on pins and needles because we know that we are nearing a turning point in which the atomic model will take a great leap forward and we all want to be the ones to make it happen."

"A collaboration but a conflict as well," remarked Bacon.

"More like a game, my friend," Bohr said.

"And then in 1927, Heisenberg publishes his article on indetermination."

"At that time I was traveling in Norway and was extremely perturbed by the letter he wrote me in which he told me the news."

"Heisenberg declared that it was impossible to know the exact speed and momentum of an electron at any given time," Bacon recited like a distracted student suddenly caught off guard by his teacher.

Bohr took a deep breath, moved by the recollection. He remained seated in his chair, restless and focused. Bacon, on the other hand, was having trouble hiding his nervous energy. Scores of physicists and wise men of all kinds had visited with Bohr in this very room at the Institute of Theoretical Physics in Copenhagen, chatting with him for hours as they dissected the popular questions of the day. How many times had Bacon dreamt that one day he might be one of those visitors? Yet now, in the most paradoxical scenario imaginable, he found himself in Bohr's office, in that sanctuary— though not as an equal or even one of the master's followers. No, he was there as a kind of reporter, a prosaic scientific historian, a mere witness to the professor's greatness. In reality, he couldn't help but feel disenchanted: Fate had granted him the rare privilege of meeting with the pope of physics, but only to make fun of him.

"Heisenberg's statement led to a rather disturbing result," Bohr exclaimed. "Just as he himself used to say, 'Quantum mechanics definitively establishes the invalidity of the law of causality.' With that, he single-hand-edly destroyed three centuries of scientific history."

"And this was what led you to mistrust Heisenberg's uncertainty princi-ple."

"When I returned from Norway, he showed me his article (which Pauli had revised) and I read it eagerly. At first, I must admit I found it brilliant, but in the end I couldn't help feeling slightly disappointed." Bohr's enor-mous eyebrows, like giant hairy worms, seemed to shift from one side of his temples to the other. "It seemed to me that his article contained certain tech-nical errors, even though his conclusions might have been accurate."

"And Heisenberg didn't like that."

"Naturally," Bohr admitted. "We argued about it for weeks, and occa-sionally things got quite heated. It was not an easy time, I can assure you. But, at least then, we managed to come to an agreement. Shortly after, he sent me a letter apologizing for his lack of courtesy. Of course, I thought nothing of it. Science is born of chaos and conflict, not tranquillity and peace."

"Afterward, however, your relationship would never be quite the same," Bacon suggested.

"Heisenberg finished up his work in Copenhagen, and then left for Leipzig, where he had been offered a chair. It was logical that our friendship would deteriorate in some way."

"And it never really recovered."

"No, unfortunately." Bohr seemed truly chagrined, as if Bacon were forc-ing him to talk about an unrepentant prodigal son. "The contact I had with him was extremely stimulating for me. Without his uncertainty principle or the discussions we had during those years, I would never have arrived at the complementariness principle. In those days the one thing I wanted more than anything else was to find a global explanation of quantum physics. A vision of the whole which would supersede the isolated advances we had made up until then."

"A kind of philosophy."

"An explanation, yes . . ." Bohr was having difficulty expressing himself. "For several months, I focused on this subject alone. It was the sort of thing that allowed me to do nothing else at all—not even sleep. I had to find a solution, a rational answer to all our efforts. I don't think I have ever had so much trouble writing an article defending my point of view. I felt as though I was writing some kind of criminal confession."

"But you did it."

"Only after a lot of suffering. Even my beloved Margrethe suffered tremendously during that time—I infected her with my anguish. But yes, in the end I finally got it. I presented it in a position paper I wrote for the congress at Como, which was held in September of 1927 to commemorate the one hundredth anniversary of Alessandro Volta's death. I'll never forget how nervous I was that day—it was a real trial by fire. Sitting before me were the most renowned physicists in the whole world—except for Einstein, who had refused to travel to Italy because of Mussolini. The anticipation was unbearable, for what I discussed that day had the potential to sound not only highly disconcerting but entirely paradoxical. But I knew that I had to do it: 'Our interpretation of the experimental material rests essentially upon the classical concepts.'"

"I imagine it was a shocking declaration, especially coming from such a staunch supporter of the new physics."

"I had no other choice. In classical physics, a theory is proven by comparing it with the experimental results obtained through scales, thermometers, voltmeters, telescopes. And suddenly I realized that the theories coming out of quantum physics were being tested with instruments that were perhaps slightly more efficient, but essentially the same as always, and that had to be acknowledged: Those were objects that were subject to the laws of classical physics."

"But wasn't it possible to see those measuring instruments—a telescope, for example—as subject to the laws of quantum mechanics as well?"

"Possibly," Bohr admitted. "But then we would have to eliminate the limited descriptions offered by the laws of classical mechanics. And the conflict arises when we have to register the quantum properties of the telescope—to do that, we would need *another* instrument that would use the classical measurements, again. Don't you see? It's a never-ending cycle unless, at some given moment, we can accept a measurement derived from classical physics. The notion of observation, then, becomes so arbitrary that it depends on how many objects are considered 'included' in the system under observation." The old man clasped his hands solemnly, content with his explanation of this apparently conflicting vision of past and future. "The only solution is to accept that classical physics and quantum physics are complementary."

"That was how the issue was resolved, but it did not convince very many people at the time, Einstein particularly."

"After Como, I reread my paper at the Solvay Congress, in October of that same year. Einstein was there, and I don't think I did anything but argue with him for those entire four days. Einstein's relationship with quantum physics had always been tenuous—naturally, he had contributed a great deal to its development and had closely followed its progress, but he was nevertheless unconvinced that Heisenberg's matrix mechanics and Schrödinger's wave mechanics sufficiently resolved all the existing conflicts. He was too obsessed with the clarity of classical physics to be able to accept the conceptual challenges of the new era. In 1926 he wrote that famous, reproachful letter to Max Born, who had then just completed his statistical interpretation of Schrödinger's theory. 'Quantum mechanics is very impressive,' he said, 'but an inner voice tells me that it is not yet the real thing. The theory produces a good deal but hardly brings us closer to the secret of the Old One. I am at all events convinced that He does not play dice.'

"Did Einstein maintain that same position in Solvay?"

"As the papers were being read, he was quiet, indifferent, almost, but when we broke into small conversations in the foyer of the hotel, he roared like a tiger," Bohr explained. "Heisenberg and Pauli scarcely even sniffed in Einstein's direction, so I was the one who had to answer his objections. The truth is, I didn't fully understand what his position was. He spent all his time inventing these 'mental experiments' that were supposed to prove us wrong, but never offered any alternative theory."

"As I mentioned before," Bacon interrupted, "I had the privilege of meeting Einstein when I was in Princeton. It was 1935 when they published that article he wrote with Podolsky and Rosen attacking quantum mechanics, and I still remember the uproar they created. The EPR Paradox."

"A distressing issue, yes," Bohr admitted. "From 1927 on, Einstein remained adamant in his belief that quantum theory was still incomplete. He accused us of being dogmatic, though we felt he was, too, in his own way. The EPR Paradox was simply a radical demonstration of his own mistrust." Bohr seemed uncomfortable now. "I don't know, perhaps the randomness implicit in our argument was what bothered him so. Nevertheless, despite all of his objections and a good deal of skepticism (many people, of course, simply declined to comment on the issue), people left the Solvay conference feeling that our ideas on quantum mechanics had presented a serious challenge to the rival theories."

" 'Our ideas,' Professor?" Bacon dared to ask.

Bohr hesitated for a moment.

"Heisenberg's, Pauli's, and mine," he said finally. "That was the 'Spirit of Copenhagen.' It was the three of us against the world, my friend. Us and us alone."

*   *   *

What is an electron, anyway? Physicists see them, primarily, as great criminals. Perverse and canny little subjects who, after committing countless
atrocities, somehow manage to slip away. No doubt these are clever types,
and every effort to track them down only encourages them to perform the
most devilish escape tactics. With the skill of trapeze artists, they are capable of leaping from one place to the other without us even realizing it. They
fire away mercilessly when they see the enemy approaching, and they always
keep an alibi ready to sabotage any investigation. Some observers have even
come to believe that they don't operate alone, but rather in gangs of like-
minded villains. Either that, or they possess something akin to a multiple
personality disorder. The individual electron behaves not as a single entity
but as a team, a swarm of desires and appetites, a storm cloud of violent
emotions that blasts through the wide reaches of space, swirling around the
objective at its mercy.

Until relatively recently, investigators—physicists, I mean—possessed a
well-organized manual that offered various methods for tracking down these
offenders, and its author was a well-known eighteenth-century criminologist
by the name of Newton. For decades, this manual had served splendidly to
help find and punish those delinquents. Unfortunately, however, the electron
is a far more crafty sort of criminal than his predecessors, and the methods
used in the past no longer worked in the effort to capture him. Compared
with him, the old-world criminals were nothing more than school-yard bul-
lies. Unlike them, the electron not only flees and disappears from the scene
of his crime, but in doing so he breaks every law known to man.

Quantum mechanics arrived in the middle of this discouraging scene
like a police chief desperately attempting to modernize his department's
criminal detection procedures. The primary objective of these new tech-
niques, which were developed by a conscientious, veteran detective (or a
couple of them, maybe), was to discover where on earth these electrons were
hiding. While the old method attempted to locate the criminal based upon
the scene of the last crime or infraction, quantum mechanics opted to determine through statistics the likely hideouts the electron would flee to *after*
committing its dastardly deeds. Remember, we are dealing with a suspect of
almost magical powers. In theory, the electron can be in several places at
once, and only during that one brief instant, when someone is able to make
out its silhouette in a dark alley, can its true identity be ascertained.

In any event, one must remember that electrons are always prepared
with false leads: They might reveal their position but will never offer even

the slightest clue as to their subsequent destination, or vice versa. Their goal is to continue leading us into even greater confusion. To be sure, electrons are devious and brilliant characters. Despite our best efforts, we are scarcely capable of guessing their true intentions. They move from one place to another without any apparent motive, continually throwing us off course, until ultimately, we are utterly unable to guess exactly who or what is hiding behind their many disguises. And right when we finally think we've got them cornered, they disappear into thin air, as if they never existed at all. Their sublime intellect is trying to tell us that they are capable of committing the perfect crime. *You'll never catch us!* they seem to be saying as they run for cover after committing another heinous crime.

How can such criminals be caught? Or even identified? How can we find out what their hidden motives are? How can we predict where they are going, when they are already waiting to trounce us again? How can we stop their perpetual motion? I don't think it is any exaggeration to say that, in effect, *Klingsor* could very well be another name for the word *electron.*

"How did it go?"

Quite predictably, Irene had waged a tireless campaign to get Bacon to take her along to Copenhagen. She was unsuccessful, however, in convincing him to bring her to his first meeting with Bohr. The lieutenant explained that for this first visit he needed to be alone with Bohr, to discuss purely technical topics, but he promised he would introduce her to the great physicist later on. Irene reacted angrily to this, but for once Bacon refused to give in to her threats.

"This project has taught me more about my chosen field than all my years in Princeton combined," Bacon sighed in answer to her protests. "Just as I suspected, all we discussed was quantum physics. Even I'm starting to believe my story about the German-science history book." He removed his jacket and took Irene by the shoulders, kissing her on the lips and neck. "Naturally I took advantage of the opportunity to ask him about Heisenberg."

"And what did he say?" she pressed, returning his affectionate gestures.

"That their friendship soured before Heisenberg had gone to Copenhagen in 1941."

"I told you!" she crowed. "I don't believe a word of that story."

"I don't know," Bacon said pensively. "One thing I was able to see, once again, was that Heisenberg is not precisely as calm and mild-mannered as he would like to appear. Every story I hear about him seems to confirm how very vain he was, and how much he craved the recognition of others."

"But that doesn't make him a criminal."

"Obviously not, Irene. Although I don't quite understand why you're so sympathetic to him."

"I could care less about Heisenberg," she said, beginning, no doubt, to unbutton Frank's shirt. "You're the only one I care about. . . . But I told you already: I think Links is taking you down a dead end, that's all."

"But why would he do that?" Bacon asked, sensibly.

Irene was unable to offer a convincing explanation.

"I don't know."

"Don't you see? It's your own prejudice."

"It's intuition, Frank. Listen, every day I'm more and more certain that he's trying to fool you."

"That's ridiculous," he countered. "For God's sake, Irene, he's just a simple mathematician. He spent the last months of the war in jail and was very nearly executed. Why would he want to do such a thing?"

"The only thing I'll say, Frank," she said, without blinking an eye, "is that this hunt isn't leading us anywhere. Something's wrong. I still don't know what it is, but when I figure it out you'll see that I'm right."

After this last declaration, both Irene and Bacon fell silent as they prepared to while away the afternoon together, alone.

The next day, the Bohrs invited Bacon and his "fiancée" to lunch. Margrethe, the scientist's wife, was a living legend—all the men who had ever visited the Copenhagen Institute always had the fondest recollections of her. She was like a solicitous den mother, forever shielding her guests from the caustic comments her husband was known for. A tall and discreet woman, her face was blessed with a subtle smile and a goodness that could vanish at a moment's notice. Bohr dominated the sumptuous meal with an endless lecture (that nobody dared interrupt) on the Cold War, disarmament, and the nuclear threat. Afterward, the scientist suggested they take a walk, something he often did with his visitors. Margrethe demurred, as always, preferring to stay inside. Irene, however, who never obeyed any rules of social conduct, insisted on joining the two men.

In the middle of May, Copenhagen was the picture of serenity. The weather was still chilly, though the weak sunlight was just enough to turn the scientist's wide forehead a robust shade of pink. Bohr, Bacon, and Irene walked through the sprawling hospital district surrounding the institute, crossed the Fredengade over the Sortedams Sø until finally arriving at the rambling, tree-filled botanical gardens, the art museum, the geological museum, and the small Østre Lake. Polite as always, Bohr took care to chat with Irene, asking her all kinds of questions about her impressions of the city, recounting Copenhagen's history, and pointing out some of its secret charms. A few short minutes later, of course, Irene had no trouble interrupting him with her typical impertinence.

"What was it like when the Nazis were here?" she asked without even looking him in the eyes. Bacon's stomach turned over.

"Terrible, madame," Bohr replied courteously. "I know you are German, and I don't mean to offend you. Before the war, our relations couldn't have been better. Some of my best friends are German, in fact. Thank goodness, all that is over now."

"When did you leave Denmark?"

"Nineteen forty-three. Before then, the situation was difficult, but we were at least able to work; the Nazis allowed us a certain degree of autonomy. But when things started going badly for them on the Eastern Front, they became ferocious in the rest of the occupied territories. I'm part Jewish, you know. On my mother's side. I didn't want to leave, but my friends convinced me that my life would soon be in danger. I could do more for my country if I left. . . . I'll never forget that day. On September 29, Margrethe, my brother Harald, his son Ole, and I (and many others) secretly boarded a small boat that delivered us to the Swedish coast. From there I went to England and then to the United States." Bohr seemed to want to drop the subject as soon as possible.

"What happened to the institute while you were gone?" Bacon asked.

"As soon as the Nazis discovered I had left the country, they arrested two of my assistants, Jørgen Bøggild and Holger Olsen, and a troop of soldiers occupied the grounds," Bohr said with a sigh. "The president of the university protested, without success. Later on, he and professors Møller and Jacobsen turned to Heisenberg, in the hope that he could do something to help them."

"And did he?"

"Werner arrived in Copenhagen in January of 1944. Once they had the institute occupied, the Germans decided that the staff would have to make a choice: either they worked on the German war projects or the cyclotron and other instruments would be shipped to Germany. After meeting with Møller and touring the installations, Heisenberg discussed the issue with the Gestapo and argued that the best thing for Germany would be for the institute to keep doing what it had been doing up until then."

"And was he successful?"

"At the time, yes," Bohr conceded. "That very same day, the president was informed that the institute was once again—and unconditionally—under the auspices of the university."

"Rather admirable on the part of Heisenberg," Irene observed.

"I suppose so," said Bohr dryly.

"When was the last time you saw him?" Bacon asked.

"Heisenberg?"

"Yes."

"A few years before then, in 1941."

"And how would you describe your relationship at that time?"

Bohr said nothing, as if he hadn't heard the question. It was all too apparent that Bacon and Irene were making him uncomfortable, reminding him of all sorts of things he'd rather forget.

"I still admired his work."

"And your friendship of so many years?"

"It petered out, I'm afraid."

"Why?"

"Why?"

"What caused the rift?" Bacon persisted. "Politics? The war?"

Bohr shook his heavy head in rueful acknowledgment of all that had transpired.

"Maybe it was a little bit of everything."

"Are my questions making you uncomfortable, Professor?" Bacon walked alongside Bohr, studying the physicist's deliberate movements.

"I don't really have all that much to say," Bohr admitted. "When Werner visited me, no one knew how the war would end. Hitler now controlled half of Europe, France had just fallen, and the German army was moving full speed into Russia, although they hadn't taken Stalingrad yet. How was I supposed to feel when he came to Copenhagen? When all was said and done, he was a patriotic man, and I knew that in some sense he felt proud of Hitler's victories even though he objected to the Nazis. We simply had nothing to talk about. At least not then."

"But Heisenberg insisted on seeing you, isn't that right?" Bacon was trying to corner him. "You were reluctant at first, but he practically forced you into it. Why was it so important to him?"

"Maybe he felt guilty," Bohr lied. "I don't know, I never found out. We spoke for a few minutes, walking, just as you and I are doing, and then we lost all contact until the end of the war."

"What did you discuss then, Professor, if I might ask?" It was Irene, hoping her contrived innocence would convince Bohr to talk about that last encounter with Heisenberg.

"Truly, I don't remember," Bohr said, ever more evasive. "It's been so many years."

"It must have been something extremely important—why else would he have been so insistent?"

"Please, I already told you that the circumstances were awfully delicate at that time," Bohr pleaded. "He had just taken over the German atomic project. Do you understand what that meant? The possibility of building a bomb for the Nazis. I couldn't confide in him, not like before."

"Did you discuss the bomb?"

"We spoke about it briefly, but I never understood exactly what he was talking about." Bohr suddenly stopped in front of an ash tree. "I hope you'll excuse me, but I'm a bit tired. I'm not the man I used to be. Would you mind terribly if we went back to the institute?"

They began to walk back, bound by an uncomfortable silence no one dared break. The streets of Copenhagen were empty, and seemed threatening, ever so slightly alien.

"Professor," Bacon said, hesitating slightly, "do you think Heisenberg would have been willing to build a bomb for Hitler?"

He took his time answering.

"Right now, I would have to say no."

"And back then?"

"Back then I wasn't so sure. How could I have been? I had no idea why he had come to see me. I didn't know then, and I don't know now. If he wanted to ask my forgiveness in advance, if he wanted me to participate in the project, if he had some other, more bizarre intention. . . . It was all a grave misunderstanding. A terrible misunderstanding that we have yet to overcome. Perhaps we never will."

Another walk, very similar to the one just described, only six years earlier. Those six years now feel like centuries, as if everything had happened in the Dark Ages, a time when laws and traditions were nonexistent, an era of fiery blazes and primal fear. Can you even imagine the tête-à-tête between these two men? The old teacher, citizen of an occupied country, and the young protégé who, like it or not, is now on the winning team, sit down and talk for several hours. They argue, they challenge one another, they compete, and in the end there is silence. A silence that doesn't go away, like an old bullet or a painful scar, forever . . .

For months Heisenberg has been waiting for the chance to go to Copenhagen to visit Bohr, but the authorities refuse him over and over again, still prejudiced by the malicious slander spread by Johannes Stark and his *Deutsche Physik* foot soldiers. His wish is finally granted, thanks to the intervention of his best friend at the time, Carl Friedrich von Weizsäcker, his colleague on the atomic project and son of the deputy interior minister of the Reich. Old Weizsäcker is the supervisor of various governmental agencies, including the German Scientific Institute, an organization dedicated to fomenting cultural exchange between Hitler's allies and the occupied countries. At the younger Weizsäcker's request, the institute invites Heisenberg to participate in a physics conference at its installations in Copenhagen. For his lecture, Heisenberg selects a topic that might not be the most diplomatic, under the circumstances: nuclear fission.

On September 14, 1941, Heisenberg boards the night train to Berlin, continuing on to Copenhagen, and arriving in the Danish capital at 6:15 the following morning. He is scheduled to make his presentation at the institute that Friday, which gives him four days to meet privately with Bohr. Heisenberg visits the institute several times over the course of the week, and on one occasion he even agrees to have lunch there, along with Margrethe and a few of Bohr's assistants, although he takes care to discuss the war in only the most general of terms. The atmosphere is stilted; anything he says could be misinterpreted by his hosts—or at least that is the excuse the German scientist offers later on. While chatting with Møller, the Danish physicist, Heisenberg makes the grave mistake of saying that, for the good of humanity, a German victory would be the best possible outcome of the war.

"I think it's a terrible shame that my country has had to invade countries like Denmark, Norway, Holland, and Belgium, but in the efforts against Eastern Europe, I feel differently. I think Germany can make a real positive contribution to their further development. For as far as I can tell, they have not been able to successfully govern themselves."

"Well, as far as I can tell," snaps Møller, indignant, "Germany is the one who has been unable to govern herself."

This bitter exchange reaches the ears of Bohr and Margrethe, who is even more outraged than her husband by what she hears, and declares that Heisenberg is never to set foot in her home again. Bohr appears crestfallen, and doesn't quite know what to do: Despite everything, he still wants to spend some time alone with his old friend, with whom he has fought so very many battles in recent years. With his customary attention to detail, Bohr decides to employ an odd system in order to make a decision. He carefully notes all the pros and cons on an index card and promises himself to reread them after a few days have gone by, when his mind is a bit clearer. Visibly moved, he decides that his friendship with Heisenberg is more important to him than anything else and, defying his wife's objections, invites Heisenberg to dinner at his home. To pacify Margrethe, he promises her that they will not discuss politics. Science will be their only topic of discussion.

The dinner is decidedly tense although relatively uneventful. Margrethe is polite but reserved, and Heisenberg's blood runs cold each time he spies an unidentifiably harsh or reproving expression on her face. Heisenberg, very clearly uncomfortable, asks his old mentor to go for a walk, as they did in the old days. Bohr, even more nervous, nods in agreement.

The cold Baltic wind has begun to whip through the trees, burying Copenhagen in an excruciating silence. The Nazis in their uniforms roam freely through the city streets, like vultures casting out their bad omens as they fly around. Bohr and Heisenberg walk toward the desolate gardens of the Fælledpark, not far from the Institute. They are watchful and circum- spect, as if preparing to determine not only the future of their friendship but the fate of the world itself. Each man must select his words with the utmost caution, careful to use only the most neutral phrases so as not to arouse the other's suspicion. They almost seem to be speaking in code. As much as he'd like to, Heisenberg cannot be direct about things; the very nature of their conversation forbids it. Bohr, on the other hand, does not seem to want to participate in this game at all. He is fond of Werner, but by now he has become far too suspicious of him, a feeling that intensifies whenever he remembers that Heisenberg is in charge of Hitler's atomic project.

The dry chill of autumn penetrates their stroll. The slightest slip of the tongue might be interpreted as a betrayal; the slightest error, a trap; the slightest stumble, an insult. Language seems to have become an obstacle to their communication, as if all those syllables and letters were in fact a bar- rier to all clarification, goodwill, and understanding. Physics is so universal and so simple, yet human relationships can be so very difficult.

Heisenberg, blind to the doubts now harbored by his old teacher, places all his faith in the friendship he and Bohr have shared throughout the years. For Heisenberg, whose facial features and mannerisms still recall those of a child, the most important thing is to gain Bohr's trust, something he hasn't had for quite some time, though he wishes things were different. Bohr, on the other hand, remains guarded: Why has Heisenberg kept insisting that they meet alone? But that is just one among the many questions that have been forming in his mind over the past few years. Why did he decide to remain in Hitler's Germany? And most especially, why was he so willing to work on a scientific project that could lead to the development of such a terribly destructive weapon?

Heisenberg begins in the worst way imaginable. Just as he did with Møller, he starts the conversation by justifying the German invasion of Poland. He declares that Hitler hasn't behaved so terribly with the other countries, like France and Denmark. Bohr can hardly believe his ears. Heisenberg goes on to say that the future of Europe will be far better off under Hitler than Stalin. But this is too much, and Bohr can take it no more. Furious, he refuses to entertain a discussion that he knows will end in the definitive rupture of his relationship with Heisenberg. But Heisenberg insists. All of this, after all, has been nothing more than a preamble to a far more direct proposition. Avoiding the Gestapo at every turn, he has made this trip to Copenhagen and has attended the conference at the German Scientific Institute for one purpose only: to arrive at this moment. He then whispers something to Bohr, something he wouldn't dare say to anyone else in the entire world.

"As physicists, do you think we have the moral right to work on the development of atomic energy?"

Heisenberg's question sends an icy chill down Bohr's spine. Before, he only felt irritated, but now he looks upon Heisenberg with fear.

"Do you think that atomic energy might actually be used before the end of the war?" Bohr asks him, unable to mask his shock.

"I'm sure of it," Heisenberg responds.

But is Heisenberg talking about bombs or just reactors? About the peaceful use of nuclear energy or the creation of weapons of mass destruction? And is he referring to the German atomic project—which he himself is working on—or rather the Allies' parallel efforts, about which Bohr might very well possess valuable information? Heisenberg continues: "We physicists should be more responsible when it comes to the decision about using atomic energy."

Silence.

"We physicists should control the development of atomic energy all over the world."

Silence.

"We physicists possess a kind of power that politicians will never know. Only we possess the knowledge necessary to actually use atomic energy."

Silence.

"We physicists could wind up controlling the politicians if we wanted to.

Together, we could be the ones to decide what to do with atomic energy. That's something only we as physicists could do."

This time, the silence is broken. Bohr's face is red with rage, and his eyes are reduced to tiny black holes, ready to devour anyone that dares lay an eye on him. In all his life he has never felt more furious, more frightened, more betrayed, more unhappy. Without so much as a glance in Werner's direction, he turns around and begins to march back home. He acts as though he hasn't even heard what Werner has just said, as if that conversation never took place, as if he had never had a friend by the name of Werner Heisenberg. Heisenberg, meanwhile, stays where he is, alone in the middle of the Fælledpark, frozen and sad, as he contemplates the magnitude of his failure. The wind lashes across his face as the silhouette of his teacher recedes into the passageways of the garden, sordid and distant as a nightmare, like a ship that disappears into the infinite darkness of the ocean.

"What do you think?" Irene asked Frank, as if he could offer some kind of logical description of the conversation between the two great physicists six years earlier. "What were Heisenberg's real motives?"

"It's hard to say. The situation is awfully confusing. Apparently he spoke in half-sentences, never spelling anything out, hoping that Bohr would understand what he was getting at, but it doesn't seem that he did."

"Or maybe it was just the opposite: that Bohr understood him perfectly and that's why he was so upset," she suggested. "What do you make of it?"

"Let's see," Bacon said, and proceeded to make a mental diagram with all the possible interpretations of the facts that had been presented. "First let's take the best of all possible scenarios: that Heisenberg was acting on his own accord. This leads to two possibilities: (a) that Heisenberg was aware of Bohr's relationship with the Allied scientists working on the atomic bomb, and was hoping to convince Bohr to dissuade them from developing a weapon that could end up destroying Germany; or (b) that Heisenberg indeed suggested that they form a kind of coalition among the world's nuclear physicists to prevent the use of atomic energy in the military arena."

"Both those cases seem a tad innocent," Irene observed. "Could Heisenberg really have thought the Allied physicists would be willing to drop their entire atomic program just because he had asked Bohr to do it?"

"Don't forget, he was in charge of the German atomic project. If that was what he meant, he was effectively telling Bohr that he would stop his own research if and when the Allies promised to do the same."

"Do you think he would have been willing to betray his country with such a maneuver?"

"I don't think it's that illogical: Heisenberg could have justified it by saying he was doing it for the good of Germany. Nothing horrified him more than the idea of his country being destroyed by nuclear weapons."

"Still, it's rather hard to swallow. Yes, to a certain degree he was responsible for the scientific advances that could contribute to the development of the bomb, but he never had the final word on the project. There were all kinds of other people involved: military officers, party bureaucrats, members of the SS. How could he have stopped them all?"

"I don't know," Frank admitted. "Maybe he thought he was the only person capable of carrying out the technical aspects of the bomb. That nobody would realize it if he sabotaged his own work."

"But there's something else about this possibility, something much more delicate. Let's suppose that he did propose to Bohr some kind of truce among the scientists—fine. With the best of intentions. How could he be sure that Bohr would believe him? And, moreover, how could he be sure that Bohr would convince the Allies to stop their research? And that Bohr wasn't going to say yes and then betray him?"

"He had to trust him. Bohr was his mentor and his friend. He had traveled all the way to Copenhagen just to see him. He had to take that chance."

"It's crazy."

"Maybe. But then we have to consider the other possibility. That Heisenberg was not visiting Bohr on his own accord."

"Meaning that he might have been spying for Hitler? That Hitler had sent him to purposely deceive Bohr?"

"Well, we can't just discard the idea a priori," said Frank unenthusiastically. "If that were the case, Heisenberg would have had little to lose."

"Only his friendship with Bohr."

"But if it's true that he was acting as Hitler's spy, if he was Klingsor, he wouldn't have cared. Any doubt he could plant in Bohr's mind would be enough for him. The slightest doubt in the minds of the Allies would give the German atomic project a considerable advantage."

"That is utterly horrifying," Irene declared.

"Well, we still don't know if Heisenberg was really Klingsor."

Bacon fell silent, as if he suddenly wished he were alone in the world. He seemed possessed, lost in his own thoughts.

"This whole situation reminds me of a diagram I used to analyze several years ago with John von Neumann, an old professor of mine," he said, coming back to reality. "It's the same structure. Here, let me show you." Bacon jumped up to grab a pen and a piece of paper, and began to sketch a diagram similar to those he once drew up with Von Neumann:

	Join Forces	Betray
Join Forces	Heisenberg, acting on good faith, convinces Bohr, and both nuclear programs come to a halt.	Heisenberg, thinking he has convinced Bohr, stops his own research but Bohr does nothing and the Allied program continues as before.
Betray	Heisenberg, fully intending to continue with his research, convinces Bohr to halt the Allied research.	Heisenberg leads Bohr to believe he is willing to sabotage the German atomic project and Bohr says he will halt the Allied research, but both continue their respective programs as before.

"Don't you see?" Bacon was practically ecstatic. "From Heisenberg's perspective, the best thing for both sides would be to join forces, but neither side could be sure that the other would comply. The possibility of betrayal kept them permanently at odds. Look at it this way, as if each decision has a numeric value ascribed to it:

	Join Forces	Betray
Join Forces	2,2	1,3
Betray	3,1	0,0

"For Heisenberg," Frank continued with his line of reasoning, "a good outcome would be that of the upper left-hand box, in which both sides would suspend their atom bomb programs. The worst of all possible situations for him is represented by the upper right-hand box, in which he would suspend the German program but the Allies would continue theirs. If he were to betray Bohr, as shown in the bottom left-hand box, Germany would have the advantage. And finally, in the bottom right-hand box, both Germany and the Allies would continue developing their respective programs, thereby remaining locked in a race against the clock to produce a bomb."

"I understand the diagrams, but I don't see what you're getting at, Frank."

"It's so odd. It's as if this game is following me around wherever I go."

"I don't understand. This isn't a game to me."

"But it is, Irene! I swear it is!" he squawked. "It all fits! It's so perfect it almost seems too good to be true!"

"What do you mean?"

"For goodness' sake, Irene, you're the one who made me see it!" Bacon said, giggling nervously.

"What, Frank? You're scaring me."

"He's testing me," Frank whispered, trembling. "He wants me to set up this puzzle so he can play a game with me, not to help me get to the truth. . . . I'm his real rival. He's so clever it's diabolical."

"Who?"

"Klingsor, for God's sake! Klingsor!" Bacon said feverishly. "Was Heisenberg working as Hitler's spy? Or was he Hitler's worst enemy? Was it his homeland or his old mentor he was willing to betray? Did he lie to Bohr or to the Nazi authorities? Is he lying now, as he makes excuses for everything that happened? Or has he been telling the truth all along?" Frank's heart was beating so fast he could barely get the words out. "Will anyone ever know the truth, Irene? No. We can never find out! Because the truth doesn't exist. It's all a game, Irene, don't you get it? And you don't play a game to get to the truth—you play a game to win!"

"Win? Over who?"

"Me," he said slowly. "Me."

With the intense calm of people who feel themselves being swallowed up by the world, they began to make love, seeking refuge in their tender haven, somewhere outside of time and place. Bacon struggled, afraid to stop even for a second, as if the slightest pause would bring this dream to a halt and force him to return to the reality he didn't want to face. Irene, on the other hand, kept herself removed from Frank's suffering. He may have surrendered to her, but she was somewhere else entirely: in the ugly realm of reason. As Frank whispered obscenities in her ear, penetrating her with contrived aggressiveness, she tried to analyze, to think, to resolve the issue in her own mind. Bacon never should have allowed it.

"Frank, calm down," she begged, pushing him off her. "I think I've got it."

"What are you talking about?"

"Klingsor!" she exclaimed, transfigured. "*All physicists are liars.* Stark's message, remember?"

"So?"

"I've been thinking about it, and I think that's the key, Frank. *All of them are liars.* Why didn't we see it before?"

"See what?"

"Heisenberg's lying. Bohr's lying. Schrödinger's lying. Even you have to lie. Stark himself is lying. Don't you see why? Because all of you are physicists!" She burst out laughing.

Bacon got up out of bed, stunned.

"I don't understand, Irene."

"If I'm a physicist and I say, 'All physicists are liars,' I've created a logical paradox," she explained to Bacon in a sudden flash of insight, as if she were an expert on the topic. "You were the one who explained it to me. In this case, there is no way to know if I am lying. But only in this case. Only if *I* am a physicist."

Irene tried to explain her bizarre, absurd theory as Bacon watched her, incredulous.

"Now can you guess how to resolve the paradox? How to eliminate it altogether?"

"I'm listening."

"It's so simple I can't believe we didn't realize it earlier." Her arrogance was bordering on intolerable. "The contradiction only occurs when the person making the statement is a physicist, don't you get it?" Her voice was shaking with malice. "I think Stark sent you that message so that you would interpret it the other way around. Meaning that you should not be looking for a physicist . . . Because you are a physicist—but so is Stark, so therefore neither of you can say the other is a liar. This proposition is . . . what did you call it?"

"Undecidable."

"Exactly."

"So?"

"The liar is *not* a physicist, Frank. It's someone else."

"But it would have to be someone who, while not a physicist, has an intimate understanding of quantum physics, relativity, the basic structure of bombs."

"And how many people fit this description?"

"I don't know. Maybe a chemist like Hahn, or an engineer."

"Have you spoken to Hahn? Or with some high-ranking engineer? Of course not! It has to be someone close to you."

"A mathematician?"

"That's it!" roared Irene. "It's Links! He's the one behind all this, Frank, that's what I think. It's so obvious. The fact is, there's no way we'll ever know if all the physicists we've interviewed are telling the truth. Everything they say is contradictory, it's written in the paradox. We can, however, determine if Links is telling the truth without entering into that logic issue. That's the solution to our mystery."

Bacon remained quiet, mulling things over. Despite his hesitation, Irene's venom had managed to work its way into his bloodstream. He had been my friend, but even so, Irene had been able to infect him with her virus of suspicion.

"But why the hell would Links do such a thing? It doesn't fit."

"I knew you'd say that, Frank, and I've been working on that. He himself has led me to it. Why did you come to Copenhagen?"

"To question Bohr about Heisenberg."

"And before that, why did you interview Planck, and Von Laue, and Schrödinger? Why them, exactly, and in that order?"

"Well, that was how things presented themselves."

"Come on, Frank, dig a little deeper." She was such a witch, the way she cast her spell of lies upon him. "From the very beginning, Links has been spoon-feeding you so that you would arrive at the conclusion that Heisenberg is Klingsor. That's what he's wanted all along. Don't you realize? If you look at every step you've taken, it's never been a normal investigation. This whole time you've been following a path that he laid out for you in advance. He's manipulated you so that, in the end, you discover what he wants you to discover. You yourself said that all this is like some kind of mathematical game. And that the one thing your rival wants is to beat you at your own game. Well, that rival is Links."

"Why accuse Heisenberg, then?"

"For personal reasons. An old account he wants to settle. Clearly, Heisenberg was no angel. His business with the Nazis was always shady. Maybe Heisenberg washed his hands of the issue when the police arrested Links for conspiring against Hitler, and Links never forgave him for it. That doesn't make him Klingsor, but Links would like us to think he is!"

"You're right about one thing," Frank said. "I've trusted him with far too much, never testing our results, never looking at the facts through any perspective other than his." He was dumbfounded now—vexed and frustrated. "Perhaps it's time to review our findings."

"What should we do?" Irene whispered.

"Say good-bye to Bohr and get back to Göttingen as quickly as possible," Bacon declared. "That's where we'll find Gustav and Heisenberg, the two people who can lead us to the truth."

CHAIN REACTION

When did I finally realize what was happening to me? Could I pinpoint the precise moment the disaster began to unfold? I don't know. I didn't know then and I don't know now, forty years later. Back then it was as if I had been reduced to a blind, deaf creature, dead to the outside world, living on instinct. Everything was conspiring against me. I was edging dangerously close to madness, and not only *my* world but *the* world was slipping away from me. Yet despite all that, something very real was slowly building inside of me, something that could save me from danger, restore my sanity and my serenity, redeem me. My love for Natalia.

I fully recognize how foolish and hollow this declaration may seem, but I feel no need to lie about it or justify it in any way. My love for her was true, perhaps the only true thing in my life. It was the only thing I could ever truly believe in, and if it didn't make me a better person, at least it gave me back my humanity in some way, the humanity I thought I had lost forever. I had always liked her. I had always wanted her, as well, ever since Heini had introduced me to her as his girlfriend so many years earlier. I knew from the very moment I laid eyes on that stark, weak expression in her eyes. Only now, in the most twisted of circumstances, did I understand how true that initial reaction, that faint instinct, had been. The only untrue thing in all of this was my previous existence, my ostensible love for Marianne, for my work, for my science. Natalia was the only thing I cared about. And I was prepared to do whatever was necessary to hold on to her.

All of a sudden, our ménage à trois was no longer a subtle, slightly perverted indulgence. It became a form of torture to which I subjected myself just to be near Natalia. At first we were seeing each other twice a week, but little by little I began to limit the frequency with which we celebrated those misbegotten ceremonies. I began to realize that I felt jealous—yes, jealous— whenever Marianne caressed or kissed or seduced Natalia's body, a body that I felt should belong only to me. It was awful: husband and wife in love with the very same person, fighting one another to conquer her, please her, steal her from the other. Naturally, these emotions remained beneath the surface, hidden from view, but that didn't make them any less powerful. At each rendezvous, the three of us would turn into beasts, tearing off our clothing, allowing ourselves to be dragged into the whirlpool created by our own inertia. We were atoms ready to smash and explode at the slightest provocation.

Finally one night, I couldn't take it anymore. Rather than wait for Natalia to make her ritual appearance at our house, I turned up at hers. She welcomed me in with an uneasy smile, which revealed a knowing, guilty anxiety.

"I love you. Only you," I said.

She embraced me tightly, and then allowed me to very nearly rip her clothes off before violently taking over her body and carrying her to the bed she shared with Heinrich. That night, Natalia behaved like a ghost: No matter how tightly I tried to cling to her, no matter how hard I embraced her, no matter how sweet or vulgar or terrible the words I uttered in the hopes of making her mine, she slipped through my hands, as if her skin and bones were made of mercury, nothing more than a luminous extension of my desire, a radiant glow or a hallucination. Yet in the end, she accepted the obvious.

"I love you, too," she sobbed, burying her face in my shoulder.

How could I believe her? How could I believe that her voice was strong and assured, sharp as the blade of a sword, inexorable as our betrayal? How? Yet I did, for anything else would have been untenable, and I was far too weak to imagine that her words might be infused with simple flattery, confusion, or doubt.

"What about Marianne?"

"What about Heinrich?" I replied, impassive and cruel.

After that moment never again did we mention our respective commitments—it was as if a new universe had unfolded before us, just for us. I was now embarking upon three distinct lives, and to carry them off I would have to deceive a countless number of people. Yet from the very instant I realized I was in love with Natalia, I felt saved. I only existed with her and for her. Everything else—marriage, friendships, mathematics, the war—were illusions, violent, cruel circumstances that had nothing to do with me. What could I do? What could Natalia and I do, in the middle of the chaos of those years? Flee? Was there some place we could have fled to? Was there any possibility, any hope, anywhere? Of course not: Our sentence was all but spelled out for us. Our separation and our death were nothing more than two consequences toward which we were hurtling progressively and inevitably closer. And yet it was the happiest I'd ever been.

THE UNCERTAINTY PRINCIPLE

Who tells the truth? And who lies? Do you love me or do you deceive me? Will you keep your promise or betray it? Will you save me, dear God, or will you leave me to perish on this cross? Guilty or innocent? I know, I know. The uncertainty principle is about to undergo the same fate as Einstein's theory of relativity. Thousands of faceless people who don't understand a word of physics, encouraged by hundreds of journalists who understand even less, believe they have understood the deepest meaning of the expression, despite the dire headaches generally produced by the equation, the union of a variable, a number—and that obnoxious Greek letter! Next, with microphone or pen in hand, the reporters get busy spreading the message of science. Suddenly, Einstein's photograph appears in the *New York Times,* and the entire world examines the shoes he wears (without socks) and the tangled mess of hair atop his head. And soon enough, the town idiot arrives on the scene convinced of the wisdom he announces: "Everything is relative!"

Heisenberg didn't fare much better than Einstein. In reality, his uncertainty principle applied only to the elusive realm of subatomic particles, not to the avatars of love, broken promises, or future betrayals. Originally, Werner had only wanted to explain what was a rather abnormal characteristic of quantum physics. While physicists like Schrödinger and Einstein stubbornly defended the classic rules that said an electron should be identifiable schematically, Heisenberg showed that it was impossible to measure both the position and the velocity of an electron at the same time. It was no error, nor was it a flaw in the instruments we used, but rather the inevitable consequence of the laws of physics.

As he himself wrote: "In theory, to observe an electron directly, one would have to build an extremely powerful, high-resolution microscope. To do so one would have to flood the electron with light of extremely short wavelengths. Unfortunately, the quanta of light released would be enough to modify the behavior of the electron under observation . . . for that reason, the more accurate our measurement of the position, the more inaccurate the velocity measurement, and vice versa. And this relationship also holds true for other pairs of variables, including energy and time. And another thing: the limits of the above-mentioned accuracy—imposed by nature—lead to the critical consequence that, to some degree, there are no longer valid laws of causality."

It was that simple. Or that complex. It was, for them, the conclusive evidence that science could no longer provide a full understanding of the universe, and the entire field would now be relegated to a more modest level of importance, for it could only offer an incomplete, minimal picture of the cosmos. And moreover, as Heisenberg noted, this led to the troubling conclusion that classic causality had also lost its preeminence. When he was still working as Bohr's assistant in Copenhagen, Heisenberg wrote a paper that discussed the principle of indetermination. It appeared in the *Zeitschrift für Physik* in March of 1927 and bore the rather uncomfortable title "On the observable content of cinematic and quantum mechanics." Only two weeks later, Heisenberg wrote another long essay based on the previous one, but this second paper appeared in a nonscientific journal, so he can be considered at least partially responsible for the dissemination of his words by less informed minds.

Please forgive me for resorting to this odious simplification, but at the time, I couldn't help but think that Bacon and I were trapped in something akin to the uncertainty principle. Atoms had little to do with our investigation, but so what? Klingsor had conspired to make us feel as though we were lost in a giant vacuum of doubt. Were we on the right track? Was this nothing but a trap? Or were we simply wrong? From there the questions multiplied, becoming ever more probing and ever more discouraging. Could we believe the things other people had said to us? Was Irene a devoted lover? And was Bacon faithful to her? Was I to continue believing in the lieutenant's foolishness and innocence? Was it prudent of him to follow my suggestions? Was I manipulating Bacon to get him on my side, as Irene said? Or was she the one manipulating Bacon? Who was playing with whom? Who was betraying whom? And why? Were we all, in some way or another, Klingsor's pawns? Or worse still, was Klingsor just some kind of mental abstraction invented by our minds, a wild projection of our own uncertainty, a vehicle to fill our voids?

There was no way to know for sure. To believe one person meant losing the confidence of another. To obtain one result would inevitably lead to some erroneous conclusion which would spring up somewhere else like a sudden illness. We all contradicted one another and at the same time, we all swore we were telling the truth. A truth that apparently no longer existed. Klingsor had defeated us with his own weapons and we, as mortals, couldn't hope to fend him off in the vast solitude of the world we lived in.

I couldn't wait for Bacon to return from Copenhagen so I could tell him the truth about Irene. Little did I know that it would be too late. How stupid I was! I should have made my move before they left, thrown the first punch, attacked her by surprise. I could have beaten her, but either my laziness or my negligence—or perhaps it was fate—caused me to make that terrible mistake. How I would lament that error, that trifling bit of indecision! More than forty years have gone by and the rage and anguish still course through my veins, threatening to burst them wide open, until they come pounding through my aging heart. Sadly, I cannot change the past. The arrow of time doesn't point backward—damn entropy!—and I can't hope to do anything but rue the error I committed.

I knew that Irene and Bacon were scheduled to return to Göttingen on Sunday night, and as such there was no way I could visit him that day without his girlfriend suspecting something. The only thing I could do was wait for him to call me, as I normally did when we were apart, and then I would see him alone to fill him in on what I knew. Sunday dragged on like a century of silence, for the much-anticipated phone call never materialized. Bacon didn't want anything to do with me. I spent the entire afternoon in bed, stricken with a terrible headache that I instantly recognized as an omen of the tragedy that awaited.

As usual, I arrived at Bacon's office at ten o'clock Monday morning. And as usual, he extended his hand for me to shake. He didn't seem particularly disturbed, though perhaps he just did a good job of hiding it. There was no way I could know that despite his deep reservations—or because of them, perhaps—he had decided to act as natural as possible with me so as not to raise my suspicions. Without realizing it, we had found ourselves tangled up in yet another game, one more of the countless mental battles that we were waging at the time. This time it was him against me, and the winner would be the one who was best able to hide his anxiety.

"I think Bohr has turned out to be the most surprising one of all," he said, by way of a greeting. "He's not like the others—he doesn't seem like a genius, or at least not like those men who seem to know everything practically from birth. No . . . he seems like someone who has managed to defy his own limitations with drive and patience."

"What did he tell you?"

"Bohr?"

"Yes."

Bacon still hadn't perfected the skill of remaining impassive in the face of a direct question.

"You were right, as always, Gustav," he admitted grudgingly; his performance was improving. "Heisenberg's last trip to Copenhagen ended their friendship. But I'm still not sure why. It's extremely difficult to talk to Bohr; it was as if he was trying to avoid the issue."

"There's something sinister about it, isn't there?"

"Well, yes, I would say so," he said sarcastically. "Whatever Heisenberg said clearly made Bohr angry, but I'm not so sure he was trying to trick him, Gustav. If Heisenberg was acting as Hitler's agent, his mission could only be considered a complete failure. Let's suppose for a moment that that was the case. Werner goes to Copenhagen on Hitler's orders. After several attempts, he finally gets Bohr alone. And what does he do? That, we don't know, but we do know the outcome of their meeting. Instead of agreeing to work with Heisenberg, or accept whatever proposal he makes, Bohr decides that he can no longer trust his former student."

"Perhaps Heisenberg made a mistake."

"Let's try something, Gustav. Why don't we test out the worst-case scenario. That Heisenberg, as the scientific adviser of the entire German atomic program, attempts to convince Bohr that *all* the research on scientific warfare must be stopped. And let's suppose that in doing this, he was carrying out Hitler's specific orders. In the hopes of halting the Allies' atomic program, Heisenberg is willing to betray his old mentor. Very well, Gustav, now you tell me: In the end, what did Heisenberg achieve?"

"What I just said: Perhaps he made a mistake."

"Klingsor? A strategic mistake? I doubt that." Bacon was growing more unreasonable. "Do you know what the consequences of that conversation were? Well, I'll tell you. Instead of trying to stop the Allied scientists, Bohr encouraged them to work even harder. In 1943 he escaped to Sweden, then England, and then finally the United States. And can you guess the first thing he did when he arrived? He went straight to the scientists working on the atomic project and offered to do whatever he could to help them build an atomic bomb! Precisely the opposite of what Heisenberg or Hitler wanted! Don't you get it?"

"A complete failure," I admitted.

"That's right," Bacon said, smiling. "Suddenly our theory breaks apart. I

think this fact alone is enough to remove Heisenberg from our list of suspects."

"Although his failed mission with Bohr doesn't necessarily absolve him
of everything else."

"Of course not, but it *has* managed to introduce some serious doubts
into our own investigation, Gustav."

That was when I realized it: Irene had won him over to her side. I was on
the brink of defeat.

"Well, perhaps I've been a bit hasty in my deductions, Frank," I said in an
almost imploring tone of voice.

"That's an understatement."

"Frank, please. Let's forget about Klingsor for a moment. What I have to
tell you is even more serious, more painful, I'm afraid." I was playing my last
card now. "I know this might not be exactly the best time, since you don't
quite seem to trust me anymore, but this is something you need to know
about." I couldn't seem to find the right words. "I hope you can forgive me,
but I have no other choice."

"Get to the point, Gustav," Bacon snapped. "I'm getting tired of your
stalling."

"It's about Irene."

"Then there's nothing to talk about! Thank you for your concern, but I
don't think I need your advice."

"No, Frank," I said, trying to appear as guileless and contrite as possible.
"This is rather delicate. I know you may not believe me, you may think I'm
just making this up to distract you, but I'm not. I swear it. What I'm about
to tell you is the truth and nothing but the truth."

"The truth?"

"Please, give me the benefit of the doubt. For once, this is not just one of
my hypotheses. I'm talking about something I've seen for myself. I'm talking about a *fact*."

"Go ahead and say it, Gustav!"

"A few days ago, before the two of you left for Copenhagen, I happened
to catch sight of her, from a distance. Irene, I mean. She seemed to be in a
hurry. And don't ask me why, but I decided to follow her."

Bacon jumped up from his chair, enraged.

"Frank, please, don't get excited. . . ."

"You have no right to interfere in my private life!"

For a moment I was afraid he was going to strike me, but he pulled himself together. I think he was actually rather curious about my discovery.

"Please forgive me," I apologized, trembling. "I didn't mean to interfere, I was just following a hunch."

"I couldn't care less what you saw, Gustav. To be honest, I simply don't trust you anymore."

"Just hear me out, please. Then you can decide what you think is best," I said. "I followed her to a church. Once inside, she walked over to a man and gave him an envelope. She did the same thing every three days."

"And so what?" he said with a slight tremor in his voice.

"Let's not fool ourselves, Frank. We both know what that means. I know you love her, and that's why this is so hard. Frank, she's been lying to you from the start." For the first time I addressed him with the familiar *Du* instead of *Sie*. "Don't you think it's odd that she would take such an interest in your investigation? Don't let your feelings get in the way. Think back to the way she's behaved ever since she first met you."

His face suddenly fell, struck by a flash of pain.

"I think she's working for the Russians."

"I don't believe you, Gustav. I think *you're* the one who's trying to side-track me from my real objective—not her."

"Get one of your men, someone you trust, to follow her, Frank," I declared emphatically. "Find out for yourself."

"I'm going to have to ask you to leave," he said to me. "Our work together is finished."

"As you wish, Professor Bacon," I said evenly, and then got up. "You know what's best."

The night seemed like the bowels of a giant whale, an unfriendly, dark place that slowly engulfed him until every last bit of certainty he ever had was lost. There wasn't a single star in the sky, nothing but the empty void of the new moon to cast only the faintest glimmer of hope.

He wandered aimlessly for a few hours before returning to his house and his inevitable confrontation with Irene. As he walked around, he couldn't seem to make sense of all the thoughts running through his head; it was as if someone had robbed him of his ability to reason. No matter how hard he tried, no matter how he struggled to remember every last moment he had ever spent with Irene, he couldn't figure out if she was really in love with him or if she had been pretending all along. For the past few months, Bacon's private life had been reduced to the nighttime visits they shared, which consisted mainly of their lengthy conversations and, of course, their unbridled passion. But outside of that, he had to admit that Irene was a mystery. He had seen her maternal instincts up close, the tender way she took care of Johann, and that had been enough to inspire his trust. But there was more: He loved her. He hadn't been able to say those words since the long-gone days of Vivien, and even so, he said them with great difficulty. And now he realized that all this might be a giant hoax, a diabolical plot against him. He couldn't believe it, he couldn't accept the idea that he had been so wrong. But nevertheless . . .

Nevertheless he felt trapped by uncertainty. After living with Irene for months, looking at her every day, kissing her thighs and stroking the nape of her neck, showering with her and breathing in her mane of hair, drinking in her body and sleeping in her arms, he still couldn't figure out if she had been telling him the truth or not. It was terrible! He couldn't even trust the person he loved most—and even worse, Irene was the one person in the world to whom he had surrendered everything—his science, his work, his confidence, his life.

Unable to wait any longer, he decided to go and find her. He entered their building and slowly walked up the stairs like a man walking toward a gallows. Scarcely glancing at his own apartment, he went straight to Irene's door. He found her there, waiting up for him as she did every night, although this evening there was a flurry of anticipation in the air.

The minute Irene laid eyes on him, the minute she saw his hunched shoulders and pursed lips, the minute she saw the anguish, the rage, and the impotence that cast their shadow upon his face, she knew that he *knew*. There were times when she was able to play the innocent, but she wasn't stupid. She didn't even have to ask. It was time to put Plan B in action. Her opening words: "Forgive me, Frank."

She tried to embrace him, to no avail. Bacon turned away.

"How could you?"

"I'm sorry, I had no other choice."

"Who's paying you for the information?"

"Frank!" she shrieked. "Please . . ." The tears rolled down Irene's face like two tracks of infamy.

"Who are you working for?"

"I'm begging you—"

"The Russians?"

She nodded.

"Why?"

"Why?" she repeated, taking care not to act overly weak.

"You've been lying to me from the very beginning."

"I was supposed to make you fall in love with me."

"Well, you succeeded."

"But then everything changed. Everything started to go wrong, Frank. I began to care about you but I had no other choice. I had to keep on working for them. They want Klingsor no matter what."

"You betrayed me. You sold me."

"No, Frank, no!" Her performance was not improving. "Maybe it started out that way, but I never imagined that I would end up falling in love with you. I swear! Every day was torture. I wanted to tell you but I was too scared. I should have done it a long time ago, before you found out for yourself. I love you."

"Do you actually think I could believe you now, Irene?"

"But it's the truth!"

"I've heard that so many times," said Frank, numb. "I'd like it to be true, Irene. I'd like it more than anything else in the world."

Bacon turned halfway around.

"Good-bye, Irene."

HIDDEN VARIABLES

BERLIN
JULY 1943

Around the middle of 1943, Heinrich wrote me a letter saying that he had to see me. Marianne took this news harder than I did, though the three of us—Marianne, Natalia, and I—barely slept a wink that week. At that moment, none of us had any idea of the meaning of his visit. He hadn't said a thing about it, not even to his own wife, and so we assumed the worst. When he arrived, I welcomed him with a hug and the sheepish gestures of a man who knows he's guilty. Heini's face was lean, almost emaciated, and lined with wrinkles that hadn't been there the last time I saw him. He thanked me for having him over, and after saying hello to Marianne, he asked if we could talk in the library.

"What's the matter, Heini?" I asked him as I poured a couple of glasses of port. "What's all this mystery? We haven't heard from you in months, Natalia barely sees you at all, and now suddenly you turn up with this desperate need to talk."

Heinrich drank his port in one gulp. Then he began speaking in an almost inaudible voice.

"Gustav, I'm terribly grateful for all you and Marianne have done for Natalia," he said. "But that's not the reason I'm here now. After so many misunderstandings, I can't tell you how much I appreciate being able to come here and speak openly with you."

"We never stopped being friends," I lied.

"I know," he said, patting me on the back. "That's why I wanted to come. You've always been an example for me, did you know that? You've stayed where you are, confident and dedicated to what you truly love—science."

"I only wish it were easier."

"Listen, I don't want to drag this out; you'd start suspecting something, anyway," he exclaimed. "What I've come to tell you is an extremely delicate matter. I'm only a kind of spokesperson. Yes, don't be shocked now, I've come here as your friend, but also as an emissary."

"Of whom?"

"Of many people, Gustav. Many people who, like you, have hated all of this from the start."

"I don't understand, Heini. I think we might be better off not discussing this."

"Wait, Gustav, please!" He grabbed my arm, his eyes searching me, imploring me to listen.

"All right."

"There are more of us than you think. We've been making plans for some time, but only now do we feel we have the strength necessary to carry them off. I know you don't understand me or my motives, but the truth is you never gave me much of a chance to explain. I have to admit it—at first I was dazzled by Hitler, like so many others. But it wasn't long before I began to realize what was really going on. When the war broke out . . . you can't imagine the atrocities I have witnessed over these past few years, my friend! And the reason I never told you any of this before was because I didn't want to put you in danger."

"I told you—"

"I know, and I didn't pay attention then. Forgive me, forgive me for my blindness back then." He poured himself another glass of wine and gulped it down. "But I've changed, that's the important thing. And I'm telling you: There are many of us, civilians, military, and we are not going to allow this horror to go on any longer."

"A bit late to start."

"Yes, maybe, but we might still have some time left. We have to at least try, Gustav. I've told them about you. They're very interested in your support, receiving a scientist's support. You would be most valuable to us."

It felt strange to have Heini talking to me with such assurance, such innocence about such a monumental task: to do away with Hitler for once and for all. And what if it was a trap? What if he had found us out and wanted to take his revenge in the most evil way possible?

"I'm sorry, Heini, but I can't agree to this," I said, troubled. "It's too risky and too late. Now, if *you'll* forgive *me*."

"Gustav!" he implored. "You can't abandon us like this. You know we're doing the right thing. I'll tell you all about what we're doing. Come with me to one of the meetings, and if you agree with our basic ideas, you'll join. If not, we'll act as though we never met you."

"All right, Heini," I said finally. "I'll think about it."

"Thank you, Gustav." He got up and turned to embrace me. "I knew that in the end you'd do the right thing, my friend."

Kundry's Curse

When I arrived at his office, I found him sprawled out on his desk. His face betrayed the ravaging effects of insomnia: Two giant circles under his eyes dominated his face, staining his ruddy skin, and his dry lips and guarded expression indicated that the doubts I had planted the previous day had blossomed during the night, becoming a vast forest of shadows.

"What are you doing here?" he spat with exaggerated violence. "I told you I didn't want to see you again."

I ignored that, and sat down slowly.

"Were my suspicions confirmed, Frank?"

"Go to hell, Links!"

"Frank, I still consider myself your friend," I said quietly. "I'm concerned about you, and about the future of your investigation as well."

"Well, I'm not! To hell with the investigation! To hell with Klingsor!"

"Frank," I insisted, "don't be like that. I understand you feel terrible; there's nothing worse than finding out that you've been betrayed by someone you've trusted so dearly."

"Yes, I suppose you would know quite a bit about that."

"I think we should keep going," I said, ignoring his irony. "I still think we're on the right track."

Bacon wouldn't even look at me. His eyes remained intently focused on his hands, as if the secrets of the entire universe were imbedded in the contours of his fingernails.

"Yes, I'll keep going," he said. "I have no other choice. But it will be without your help, Gustav."

"For God's sake, Frank, you can't just get rid of me because I was the one to tell you the truth about Irene. Why, it would be just like executing the messenger for being the bearer of bad news."

"Don't be ridiculous, Gustav!" Bacon's eyes flashed onto my face, trying to penetrate my skin. "I can't trust you anymore. Or anyone else, for that matter. I don't know if everything I've done over the past few months is nothing more than a useless digression or if I actually have come close to the truth. There's no way for me to know and you are largely responsible for that."

"Me?"

"Gustav, this conversation is going to get us nowhere," he declared harshly. "Thank you for your services, but our work together is over. Now leave me alone."

"But, Frank," I murmured, truly pained.

"There's nothing more to say, Professor Links. Good-bye."

"It's not fair," I insisted. "You are still under that woman's influence. You now know she was lying to you and yet you can't let go of the prejudices she planted in your mind."

"That's not your concern, Professor."

"Very well, then. I'll leave," I conceded, uncomfortable. "But before I do, let me tell you a story. Do you remember how, at the beginning of the investigation, I told you the story of the first act of Wagner's *Parsifal*?"

"I remember," he said icily.

"Well, before I leave, I'm going to tell you the story of the second act. I owe it to you."

"I'm not interested, Professor."

"As I told you before, at the end of the first act Parsifal has attended the banquet celebrated by the keepers of the Grail in Monsalvat's castle. Here the hero has witnessed the suffering of Amfortas, the king who has lost divine grace. Parsifal, however, feels no compassion whatsoever in the face of this pain. He fancies himself too righteous, too virtuous, too severe, and feels that Amfortas' suffering is the appropriate punishment for his sins."

"Gustav, I'm not in the mood. Please, just leave me alone."

"At the beginning of the second act, Parsifal has left Monsalvat and is now heading south, for Klingsor's palace." As I recalled this ancient tale, I suddenly felt transported back in time by some peculiar emotion. "And do you know why he makes the journey to these lands? To test himself. Parsifal wants to find out how strong he really is. He seeks to subject himself to the very same temptation that brought Amfortas to his knees. Just picture it: Parsifal, walking through the enchanted country lanes of the Kolot Embolot. Can you guess who he's searching for? The same woman of fearsome beauty who seduced Amfortas. He desires her, Frank, he desires her more than anything else in the world. But he desires her only so he can reject her, to prove that he is stronger than the king. It's a kind of trial, an enigmatic duel with the past. Klingsor, meanwhile, decides to humor him. Getting the one thing you so desperately desire is sometimes the very worst thing that can happen to you. The devil is poised to accept the challenge Parsifal made when stepping into his dominion, and the game can now begin."

"I know where you're going with this, Gustav. Please. I've had enough."

"No, you don't know, Frank. There's no way you can know," I said, and continued. "The cosmic showdown has begun. In one corner, young Parsifal. In the other, the ancient Klingsor. To start it off, the Man of the Mountain sends Parsifal a legion of flower maidens. These lithe young nymphs throw themselves into his arms, trying to kiss and caress him, promising him pleasures the likes of which he has never dreamed. With them, his future would be certain: All he has to do is succumb to their charms to enjoy the pleasures of eternity. And yet Parsifal resists. Can you guess why? He doesn't scorn the nymphs because he is such a strong and powerful man. He doesn't push them away, without even glancing at their smooth white breasts, because he has such strict self-control. This is a test, but it's an easy one for him. Why, it's as if the nymphs didn't exist at all! And do you know why? Parsifal desires *one* woman, and one woman alone. The inebriating embrace of Amfortas' seductress is his sole objective. She is the only woman who exists! The only possible truth, Frank! And he is determined to get her against all odds, at any price."

"A beautiful story, Gustav, but I'm tired. I'm not Parsifal and I'm not so certain that our Klingsor is a devil, if he even exists at all."

"You haven't understood anything I've said, Frank! Anything at all!" I exclaimed. "Klingsor knows what his adversary wants and, as I've said before, accepts the challenge. What Parsifal doesn't realize is that the woman he so fervently seeks, Klingsor's weapon, is none other than Kundry, the young woman he encountered in Monsalvat. The traitor is Kundry. And all of a sudden there she is. The two of them stare at each other, in the middle of that lush garden, that *locus amoenus* of the chivalric tales. Parsifal can scarcely believe his eyes, for she is even lovelier than before. Her naked body takes his breath away, as if it were the embodiment of truth itself. Kundry stands there, like Botticelli's Venus, ready to offer herself to him, to surrender herself forever to our hero. Feverish and aghast, our Parsifal knows that he cannot resist her, that he will succumb just as Amfortas did. He wants Kundry more than anything else in the whole world, more than salvation, more than God.

"Then, a miracle occurs. To begin the seduction, Kundry opens her mouth. Tenderly, she calls out to Parsifal by name (this is the first time he has heard his name since the days he lived with his mother), and she proceeds to tell the story of Herzeleide's agonizing death. And instead of seducing him with her body, she seduces him with her words. Parsifal realizes that he is in love with her, and that he will not be able to deny his desire. Kundry approaches him and kisses him. And Parsifal's will is not strong enough to turn her away. However, this kiss will ultimately conspire against Klingsor and his kingdom of darkness, for it isn't a kiss of desire, lust, and wantonness, but, alas, one of compassion. And suddenly, an image begins to form in Parsifal's mind: Amfortas and his wound.

"This vexes Kundry, and she tells Parsifal about the time she had the chance to see the Savior. While witnessing his persecution, Kundry merely laughed at him. And ever since, only by forcing someone to commit a sin can she be cured of her never-ending laughter. Parsifal, scandalized by such blasphemy, runs from her, and Kundry, now furious, curses Parsifal. From now on, all the roads of the world will be closed to him. Klingsor, from the hills of the Kolot Embolot, casts the same spell, but it's too late. Somehow, some way, Parsifal has won. And what follows is the sequel to his victory: Klingsor goes down to the garden to face Parsifal, but we already know the outcome, for Klingsor has already been vanquished. Nevertheless, he grabs hold of his weapon, the Spear of Longinus, and with it Klingsor tries to destroy his opponent. But the Spear of Longinus shies away from the young man's skin. Now, all Parsifal has to do is simply make the sign of the cross—a mere formality—and Klingsor's giant castle, his kingdom of illusions and ghosts, of laws and predictions, tumbles down. In a matter of seconds, nothing is left of the great realm built over centuries and centuries. It's a kind of apocalypse, Frank, the end of an era, the tragic end of an entire age. Parsifal turns to Kundry and says, 'You will know where to find me again.' And with these words, the curtain falls."

BOOK THREE

BOOK THREE

Laws of Traitorous Motion

LAW I: *All men are weak*

Why are we weak? For a very simple reason: We cannot predict the future. We live in an eternal present, obsessed with deciphering the future. All of us are, in reality, miserable investigators of the unknown. And what do we do, then, to hide our weakness? We invent, we dream, we create. We cling to the notion that some subtle, devious mind has cast us into this vast ocean for a purpose, and that purpose, we believe, is to resolve at least one of these many doubts. Using this as a point of departure, we become detectives in search of a villain hiding away somewhere. We observe reality as if it were a crime, and inspired by this police metaphor, we race to solve it as if it were a hundred-thousand-piece puzzle. The scientist and the astrologer, the shaman and the doctor, the spy and the gambler, the lover and the politician, are nothing more than subtle variations on this same theme.

COROLLARY I

Amid this perpetual state of confusion, there is always someone ready and waiting to take advantage of everyone else's blindness to assuage his own fears. Intent on asserting some kind of superior truth, this person rises above everyone else, as if performing an act of supreme heroism. Fully convinced of his purpose, he toils for the good of his people, his race, his friends, his family, or his lovers (as the case may be), imposing his own faith upon the prevailing uncertainty. All the truth he proclaims is an act of violence, pretense, chicanery. And how does a weak man become strong? Very simple. Any man who can convince other people—other weak people—that he knows what the future holds is a man who will be able to rise above and control his peers. His influence, of course, is based upon an illusion: As Max Weber pointed out, power is nothing more than the ability to predict, to the greatest possible degree of accuracy, the behavior of one's peers.

Hitler was a visionary: a man who could control masses of people thanks to a seemingly divine—or diabolical—gift that enabled him to envision things other people could not. A person has two options in the face of such a phenomenon: escape or silence. For a man like Hitler, the future is as clear and obvious as the present—what an enviable quality for a person to possess! While the rest of us can scarcely imagine what will happen weeks or a few years from now, Hitler thought in terms of millennia. How could he not despise our miserable mediocrity and venerate his own truth?

LAW II: *All men are liars*

If, as stated by Gödel's theorem, every axiomatic system contains undecidable propositions; if, as stated by Einstein's relativity, absolute time and space do not exist; if, as postulated by the rules of quantum physics and as a consequence of the uncertainty principle, science can offer only vague and random approximations of the cosmos—then we can no longer rely on causality as an accurate predictor of the future. And if specific individuals possess only specific truths, then all of us—made up of the same material of which atoms are made—are the result of paradox and impossibility. Our convictions can only be considered half-truths.

COROLLARY II

As hard as we may try, our very nature precludes us from escaping this abominable, vicious cycle. Deceit clings to our minds and our hearts like a parasite living off the body of its host. We tell lies for the most common reasons: to advance our own personal causes and to guard against attacks, to expose and to hide, to injure our enemies and to protect those we love. And sometimes we lie simply out of habit, because we are so immersed in the cosmic void that we don't even know who we are anymore.

LAW III: *All men are traitors*

In order to become a traitor one must possess at least one fact, at least one truth so necessary that he must destroy it. This person's fate is tragic and cruel: The traitor breaks all the rules of his own system, fighting against himself, defying the principles he believes in. Oscar Wilde said the very same thing, albeit in slightly different form: Each man kills the thing he loves. It's true. In the kingdom of eternal darkness, this is one of the few patterns that repeats itself over and over again, one of the few laws that know no exception.

COROLLARY III

Lovers are the most perverse prophets, the most tragic heroes, the blindest sages. They defend their love as if it were the only real truth in the world, the one thing they give a damn about. Love to them is the one true religion, and with the same force and violence exhibited by dictators and executioners, they subject others to this belief. Salvation, they believe, lies in this truth. Their dogma allows them to damage and destroy, wound and paralyze, and ultimately determine the fate of everyone in their midst.

Back in America, in the name of love, Lieutenant Francis P. Bacon lied to the two people who meant something to him: Vivien and Elizabeth. I did the very same thing with Heinrich, Marianne, and Natalia. What we didn't realize was that traitors are born from such absolutes—and love is the greatest absolute of all.

DIALOGUE I: ON THOSE FORGOTTEN BY HISTORY

LEIPZIG
NOVEMBER 5, 1989

"Can you please turn on the light?"

"Of course," he answers. "How are you feeling today?"

How am I supposed to feel? I have been asked this question so many times over the years that it no longer has any meaning. How do you distinguish the days that go by when you live in a kind of eternity? How do you appreciate the subtle nuances, the changes in mood, the deepening pain, the loss of memory and hearing, when every day is identical to the last, when time has been effectively annihilated? Still, this new boy is sweet. Unlike the others who have come to see me, harassing me with their questions, their prescriptions, their advice, and their smooth indifference, Ulrich is attentive and possesses the optimism that is the sole domain of inexperienced doctors doomed to mediocrity. They assigned him to my case only a few days ago, but I get the sense he's out to be more than just a security guard or a memory poacher. For some reason I think he's actually interested in listening to me. Perhaps it's just the way things are nowadays, but it seems that nobody cares about the past anymore, much less the secrets people have kept locked away over the last few decades.

Ulrich is courteous and circumspect: I didn't even have to ask him to address me as "Professor," for he does so naturally, with a mixture of fear and respect. Sometimes he tells me about what goes on outside of here, in that uncharted, wild territory that is the world. He even reads the newspaper to me, his voice brimming with an emotion I can't ever quite feel in my heart. Apparently, the new leader of the Soviet Union (one of the many reincarnations of old Stalin) is preparing to give up their colonies, including this miserable patch of Germany I am currently inhabiting. "A new era has begun," proclaims my evening visitor, but all I can manage is a sarcastic smile that he surely infers as a sign of satisfaction or, who knows, maybe even revenge.

The walls of my room are suddenly illuminated by the reflection of a thousand suns—an effect not unlike that of an atomic blast. Despite the rust and the cobwebs, the walls have never looked so white, or so willing to disguise what they really are: my prison.

"And how are you today, Doctor?" I ask him, imitating his tone of voice.

"Very well, thank you, Professor Links," he says kindly. "Are you still feeling that pain in your side?"

Pain. I don't even know what that word means anymore.

"May I ask you something?" he says, sitting down on my bed. "Who are you?"

Doesn't he know? People's memories around here have been getting worse and worse, but I never thought it would sink to this level—that they would reach the point of hiring people who don't even know what has happened here over the past few years.

"Gustav Links, mathematician at the University of Leipzig," I say with pride. "At least that's what it says in my file. Or haven't you read it?"

Ulrich displays his yellowing teeth.

"No, no, that's not what I mean. I know your name. I also know that you've been here for over forty years," he says apologetically.

"Well, then, what is it you'd like to know?" I ask, sitting up a little.

"The truth."

"The truth! If you only knew how many times I've heard that one," I reply. "The truth. As if it were actually worth anything."

"I only want to get to know you a little better. Know who you are."

"All the answers should be right there in my file," I insist. "Or have they already ordered it destroyed?"

"I want to hear it straight from you, Professor. I'd like to be your friend. Tell me."

How on earth could the facts of my life be of any use to anyone? I don't even think they're of any use to me. For some reason, however, Ulrich's blue eyes inspire trust. For some reason—perhaps it is chance, or his tone of voice, which reminds me a bit of Francis P. Bacon's—I comply. What more do I have to lose, really?

"It's a long story," I say. "Are you prepared to hear it?"

"That is what I am here for."

"How old are you, Doctor?"

"Twenty-nine."

"Have you ever heard about the attempt that was made on Hitler's life, on the twentieth of July 1944?"

I didn't even need to hear his answer. Of course not.

The Conspiracy

1

A hospital, the same blinding light penetrating his eyes. The patient begins to stir, with difficulty, as if emerging not from sleep but from death. In front of him sits Ferdinand Sauerbruch, the surgeon who has saved his life, who watches him with the calm indifference of someone who lives with death day in and day out. Colonel Claus Schenk von Stauffenberg opens his eyes and tries to focus them on the doctor's face. Little by little he comes to, only to find that he cannot move his arm and that a shooting pain pierces his body from one side to the other, as if he were a butterfly pinned to the back of a wooden box.

"How long will it be before I can get up again?" he asks in a tone that will suffer no euphemisms.

"That depends," Sauerbruch says carefully. "The rest of the body has only suffered some minor scrapes, but a lengthy process of rehabilitation will be needed to recover mobility of the arms and the left hand." He could have been talking about repairing a tank or a gun. "I'm afraid that at least two more operations will be necessary."

"How long?" Stauffenberg repeats.

"We don't know," the surgeon responds. "Several months, perhaps a year."

Stauffenberg adjusts his position in the bed, in search of a pose that can effectively frame the severity of his words. He looks straight into the doctor's eyes as if he were his enemy, and with clenched teeth, struggling to withstand the pain that rips through his body, he says: "I don't have that kind of time. I have important things to take care of."

2

"With every day that goes by, I have fewer and fewer doubts, gentlemen." General Beck's voice is subtle, like the wind that constantly crashes against the mountains but, in the end, wins out over them. He was only released from the hospital a few days ago, after several weeks out of commission. "Only if we can get to *him* will we have a fighting chance."

Nobody dares utter his name. Despite the secret plot, a somewhat reverential aura of fear still surrounds the figure of the Führer, though everyone knows exactly whom the Wehrmacht's old chief of staff is talking about.

"We have no choice," says Friedrich Olbricht, chief of the Wehrmacht headquarters in Berlin. "It's our only way out."

"Now we have to find someone willing to do it," Beck announces, carefully avoiding the word *assassin*.

3

On August 10, 1943, another meeting, a *petit comité,* is held at the home of General Olbricht. General Henning von Tresckow, head of the Führer's elite reserve units, arrives on time, and after going through the few formalities plot conspirators still observe, the host and his guests retire to the library. A young, blond, well-dressed man waits for them there, and as they walk in he rises and greets his host with a military salute. Olbricht approaches the young man and, eschewing the traditionally rigid military protocol, places a hand on the young man's shoulder.

"General," he says to Tresckow with a nervous smile, "please allow me to introduce to you Colonel Claus Schenk von Stauffenberg. He's our man."

Apart from his youth and the fact that he had supported Hitler in the early days (like so many other young military officers), Stauffenberg is something of a rara avis in the army. As a teenager, he and his friends were enthusiastic followers of the poet Stefan George—in fact, Stauffenberg was even present at his deathbed. Though he was never George's closest disciple, there was no doubt that the poet had a profound and lasting influence upon young Stauffenberg. "The Antichrist," one of George's most somber, tragic poems, was among Stauffenberg's favorites, and one he would often turn to whenever he found himself at critical junctures in his life.

Without a doubt, this man fits the bill. In 1942, when one of his colleagues asked him how Hitler's style of governing might be improved, Stauffenberg replied in an unaffected, honest voice: "Assassinating him."

4

"We must review the plan from top to bottom."

Today the scene takes place in an apartment in Grunewald. Claus von Stauffenberg and Henning von Tresckow are sitting face-to-face as equals, fully aware that the history of Germany and the history of the entire world (not to mention their very lives) are about to pass before their eyes. At their side is Captain Heinrich von Lutz, who has been in on the conspiracy ever since the beginning. What they have before them is nothing more than a pile of notes written in code and a set of blueprints, but the three men know that what lies behind all the symbols, letters, numerals, and blank spaces is General Olbricht's meticulously engineered plan of action which will hopefully carry out a coup d'etat and overthrow Hitler.

"We cannot permit even the smallest margin of error," insists Stauffenberg. "And I don't care if we sit here for two days straight."

"You're absolutely right, Colonel," agrees Tresckow, slightly taken aback by the fact that his subordinate has gained control of the situation. "Let's go over it again."

"General Olbricht devised this strategy based on an already existing model," Lutz begins. "The main idea is that after the coup, we deploy the contingency plan the Wehrmacht uses in cases of internal unrest."

"Let me see if I understand correctly, Captain," says Stauffenberg. "Are you suggesting that we use a plan that Hitler created specifically to control potential conspiracy plots?"

"It sounds counterintuitive, but, yes," said Heinrich. "Hitler's military command convinced him that some kind of emergency mechanism was absolutely critical in the event that the communists ever managed to revolt, a possibility, given the millions of foreign workers living within the Reich."

"Very well. Proceed," Tresckow says.

"The plan is known as Operation Valkyrie," Heinrich explains. "In the event of a workers' revolution, or any other kind of internal rebellion, everyone in the reserves would be immediately called to arms."

The three officials take a collective deep breath. The future—*their* future—is in the hands of these reserve units. All they can think of is how it will take nothing short of a miracle for these troops to successfully take charge of the situation, since they will be up against soldiers far better equipped and trained than they.

"Olbricht made one small amendment to the plan, one of the most surprising elements of Operation Valkyrie: In the event that Hitler were to suffer a fatal attack at the hands of a terrorist group, a radio announcement written by Olbricht would be broadcast over the airwaves." As he explains this part of the plan, Heinrich allows himself a satisfied smile in response to Olbricht's obvious temerity.

"Truly ingenious," says Stauffenberg with a touch of irony.

"Moving along," continues Heinrich, "the Operation Valkyrie units will then take control of all the government ministries, the party offices, the radio stations, the telephone and telegraph control centers, and the concentration camps. The SS will be stripped of their weapons, and those who refuse to comply will be executed on the spot."

"We're talking about a colossal lie that has to travel down the army chain of command by word of mouth," Tresckow explains. "We need to convince the world that the coup has been orchestrated by foreign agents and that after Hitler's assassination, Himmler and the other party leaders have attempted to betray the country. If we can keep the situation under control for the first few hours, we just might be able to pull it off."

For several minutes, the three men remain silent as they try to work out all the possible variations to their plan. After awhile, Heinrich speaks up.

"As I've said from the beginning, the one major disadvantage to Operation Valkyrie is that General Olbricht does not have the authority to deploy it. According to the regulations, the only person who has that power is Hitler."

"Some paradox," muses Stauffenberg. "The Führer is the only person authorized to announce his own death."

"A classic Hitler-style precaution," Tresckow observes.

"There is one possible exception, however," Heinrich says. "In the event of a dire emergency, General Friedrich Fromm, the commander of the reserve army, is authorized to approve the announcement."

"Well, despite our best efforts to recruit General Fromm, he has never supported our cause," Tresckow reminds them. "If he were to refuse, we would have no other choice but to capture him and leave it to Olbricht to deliver the necessary instructions. Even so, we can never know for sure that the chain of command is going to work as it's supposed to."

"So many weak spots," Stauffenberg murmurs. "So many loose ends. But we have no other choice. We don't have time for doubts."

"Onward, then," says Tresckow, getting up from his seat, carefully averting his subordinates' gaze so as to avoid detecting even the slightest note of fear or vacillation on their faces.

Alea jacta est.

5

On June 6, 1944, the Allies disembark at Normandy, and only a few weeks later the Red Army crosses the Eastern Front between Minsk and the Beresin River, controlled by the Wehrmacht's Central Group. The end of the war seems closer than ever before.

Despite this news, the coup plotters remain focused on going ahead with their plans. Even if the Allies, as they declared at the Casablanca Conference, refuse to negotiate a peace agreement with them, they must show the world that the German nation is willing and able to rise up against tyranny and ruthlessness. They must prove to the world that Hitler does not represent all of Germany, only its very worst side. Perhaps it is a hopelessly romantic, symbolic gesture, but they are convinced that it is worth it. It is the only thing that can rescue them from infamy.

As Tresckow has written to Stauffenberg: "The assassination should be carried out *coûte que coûte*. Even if it fails, we must make our presence felt in Berlin. The practical aspect will no longer matter; the important thing is that the German resistance movement will be known to all the world and can then take its place in history. In light of that, nothing else matters."

6

On July 1, 1944, Stauffenberg is named army chief of staff under General Friedrich Fromm, commander of the reserve army. This promotion represents a pivotal moment in his career as well as a strategic opportunity which will enable him to carry out the coup attempt and Operation Valkyrie. Nevertheless, the prevailing mood among the conspirators—and Germany in general—is rather low. Time is working against them, every day, every hour, every second. Germany is literally bleeding to death.

In his heart, Stauffenberg suspects that Fromm is aware of his plans, but is willing to let him go ahead with them as long as he himself isn't implicated. By appointing Stauffenberg to his team, the old general is hoping to regain some of Hitler's lost confidence. After all, upon reading one of Stauffenberg's memoranda, it was Hitler himself who said: "Finally, someone with imagination and intelligence!"

Nevertheless, all of Stauffenberg's efforts to persuade Fromm to join his cause have fallen upon dead ears, a veritable wall of silence and mistrust. In any event, Stauffenberg's recent appointment has given him more and more reason to feel that he is in the ideal position to place the bomb in Wolf's Lair, Hitler's headquarters in Rastenburg.

7

After several conversations, the coup plotters have managed to convince General Erich Fellgiebel, chief of the Army Signal Corps, to join their cause.

"We can do it," Fellgiebel agrees. "As soon as the bomb kills him, I will make sure that no alarm signal is transmitted from Wolf's Lair." Like all the others, Fellgiebel does not dare to mention the Führer by name.

"Excellent," says Heinrich excitedly.

"I must warn you, gentlemen, we don't have much time. Even if I can suspend the military signals from Rastenburg's communication center, we mustn't forget that the SS, the Gestapo, and the Foreign Ministry all have their own command centers. We also have to be careful not to cut off all communications with the front, so as not to raise any eyebrows. And finally, we must be absolutely certain that the commands we send out to deploy Operation Valkyrie reach their destinations before anyone else has a chance to make contact with them."

"In conclusion, General . . ." Stauffenberg interrupts him.

"In conclusion, we won't have more than one or two hours to take control of the situation. After that, gentlemen, it will be too late."

8

July 15. The big day. Though he tries desperately to act normal, Stauffenberg realizes, to his horror and chagrin, that this will be impossible. He walks around gingerly; each time someone calls him or says hello, he feels as though his heart might explode inside his chest—hardly original hyperbole, he knows—and the abject smile painted upon his lips feels like a premature gesture of pity. Still, nobody seems to perceive his fear. For once in his life, his condition as a cripple is useful for something: A man who has lost his entire right hand and two fingers of his left hand, who trembles as he walks, is the last person anyone would suspect of wrongdoing.

Inside his briefcase, tucked between a few sheets of paper, a couple of books, and a manuscript version of Stefan George's "The Antichrist," Stauffenberg has placed two packets of explosives that are connected to one another by a cable that will detonate a chain of explosions. The trigger can be found on the side of one of the handles, barely jutting out from the gray felt lining of the briefcase. Over and over again, all week long, Stauffenberg has been practicing to ensure that he can activate the mechanism easily.

Wolf's Lair, Hitler's general headquarters in Rastenburg, reminds Stauffenberg of a giant mousetrap: a trap he has entered consciously, not knowing whether death awaits him at the other end. Suddenly, all the faces he sees before him blend into one another: the same menace, the same mistrust, the same uncertainty. Even so, the colonel moves ahead: He knows there is no turning back now. General Fromm is standing next to him, along with one of the officers under his command, Captain Karl Klausing. A few paces ahead, Stauffenberg finds himself facing Erich Fellgiebel, with whom he stops to chat for a few moments. Fromm and Klausing continue onward, ahead of him.

"We have to wait," Fellgiebel whispers in Stauffenberg's ear.

"What?" Stauffenberg exclaims, alarmed.

"The Reichsführer-SS isn't coming to the meeting today," Fellgiebel insists.

"It doesn't matter," Stauffenberg insists. "We won't have another chance to do it."

"We agreed not to carry out the plan without Himmler here," argues Fellgiebel. "Too many of the generals will refuse to cooperate if the Reichsführer is still alive."

"But Olbricht is ready to launch Operation Valkyrie today!"

"We'll take care of telling him that we have to postpone it, Colonel," says Fellgiebel. "We have no other choice."

9

After lengthy debate, the conspirators finally agree upon a new target date: July 20. The days leading up to the coup are filled with last-minute preparations, quiet fear, increasing consternation, and several inconvenient meetings. Stauffenberg alerts his accomplices that he has confirmed an appointment in Hitler's headquarters on that date, and adds that he will not fail to take action on this occasion.

On the nineteenth, Stauffenberg makes contact with General Wagner, the person in charge of the headquarters at Zossen. After a long conversation, the general promises Stauffenberg that an airplane will be sent to Rastenburg to pick him up after the coup attempt and deliver him safe and sound to Berlin. Although many people remain skeptical, everything is ready. The only thing left to do is pray.

10

July 20

10:00

Stauffenberg arrives at the Rastenburg airport, accompanied by his assistant, Werner von Haeften, and General Helmuth Stieff. Immediately the colonel is transferred to Restricted Zone II, carrying a briefcase containing nothing more than the papers necessary for the officers' meeting that afternoon. The briefcase Werner von Haeften carries, identical to that of his superior, contains the bombs that will shortly be detonated. According to the plan, Stauffenberg is to trade briefcases with Von Haeften at some point before his meeting with Hitler.

As Stauffenberg walks toward Restricted Zone II, Von Haeften and Stieff wait for him in the headquarters of the army high command.

11:00

Stauffenberg meets with General Walther Buhle, and after a brief exchange, they walk together to their meeting with General Wilhelm Keitel, the chief of the Wehrmacht High Command, in Hitler's bunker in Restricted Zone I. There, Stauffenberg learns that Benito Mussolini, recently deposed by the Fascist Grand Council, is presently in Rastenburg and will meet with Hitler at midday.

After his meeting with Keitel, Stauffenberg asks Keitel's assistant, Major Ernst John von Freyend, where he might wash and change his shirt. Freyend directs him to the area of Restricted Zone I where the washrooms are located. On his way there, Stauffenberg bumps into Von Haeften and the two men exchange briefcases. Once in the washroom, the colonel activates the bomb. All systems are go.

Just as he is finishing up, Sergeant Werner Vogel enters the washroom unexpectedly. With Von Haeften's assistance, Stauffenberg organizes the contents of the briefcase just in time.

"Major Von Freyend has sent for you," the sergeant explains. "It seems that there is an urgent call for you from Fellgiebel."

Stauffenberg thanks him and follows him out. The interruption, however, has cut into his time, and he has only been able to set one of the bomb triggers in place. He remains calm, thinking that only one bomb will be necessary to end Hitler's life.

12:00

With Major Von Freyend in tow, Stauffenberg rushes out of the washroom toward the high command bunker, where General Walther Buhle is waiting for him. Twice, Stauffenberg refuses Von Freyend's offer to carry his suitcase.

Accompanied by Buhle, Stauffenberg walks toward the Restricted Zone. Before the meeting, the colonel turns to Von Freyend and requests a seat close to Hitler so he can clearly hear everything the Führer says. By the time Stauffenberg and Buhle enter the room, the meeting is already under way. General Adolf Heusinger, rising up from his seat, announces the news from the Eastern Front. Keitel alerts Hitler that Stauffenberg has been called in to deliver a report which will be presented later on. The Führer, distant and severe, quickly extends his hand to the young colonel, a gesture that could be construed as either mistrust or friendliness.

Stauffenberg has finally relented and allowed Von Freyend to carry his suitcase, and he places it between General Heusinger and his assistant, Colonel Brandt. Despite his attempt to sit as close as possible to the Führer, Stauffenberg is stuck sitting at one of the corners of the table.

After a few minutes, Stauffenberg rises, mumbles an unintelligible excuse, as if he has suddenly realized an important task that needs his attention, and exits. Once outside the meeting room, he walks back down the same path he took to arrive there, and leaving the bunker of the high command, he walks to the communications center, where he finds Von Haeften and Fellgiebel.

A dry explosion shakes the walls of the room for a few seconds. It's over. The time is now 12:40.

11

12:45

Now for the difficult part. How do they know if Hitler is dead? Stauffenberg and Fellgiebel stand there looking at each other, feigning a surprise that nobody else can understand.

"What could that have been?" the colonel asks.

One of the other men in the communications office responds calmly: "Someone must have fired a round or stepped on a mine."

A dense pink cloud bubbles up from the barracks. Stauffenberg can only imagine the bits of wood, steel, plastic, and human flesh scattered everywhere. The dead faces of the men with whom he was speaking only a few minutes earlier. The pools of blood gushing forth like an infernal lake. A sudden chorus of cries—*A doctor, we need a doctor!* he hears—jolts him out of his nightmarish vision and brings him back to reality.

Stauffenberg decides it's time to move, and orders Von Haeften to locate their driver. After a few seconds they enter the car, which then takes off in the direction of the airport. Just before leaving the compound, they catch a glimpse of a small group of people carrying a body toward the infirmary. The body is wearing Hitler's uniform. They've done it. The guard stationed at the entrance has taken it upon himself to block the exit, but upon recognizing Stauffenberg he hesitates only a few seconds before letting him exit the gates.

13:00

Stauffenberg and Von Haeften board the plane that General Wagner has left waiting for them, and they depart for Berlin. They still don't know the outcome of the coup.

Meanwhile, Fellgiebel has successfully intercepted the communications line that connects the Rastenburg bunker to the outside world. There is no longer any doubt as to the general's intentions: They are better off keeping the facts to themselves until receiving direct orders either from Hitler or a high-ranking Nazi official. After a few minutes, Fellgiebel finally learns the magnitude of the tragedy: The bomb has gone off, but Hitler is still alive, unbelievable as that seems. The explosion destroyed the assembly room, but the heavy oak table absorbed much of the impact. A few officers—including the Führer himself—suffered some minor scrapes, a burn mark here and there, but there are no deaths to be recorded. Thank God.

Horrified, Fellgiebel telephones the coup headquarters on Bendlerstraße, not knowing quite how to communicate this message. Their carefully designed code contains no key phrase to describe that, yes, the bomb has gone off, but, no, the target was not hit. By the time he finally gets through to General Fritz Thiele, the communications chief at Bendlerstraße (another active participant in the conspiracy), all he can do is say it, plainly and simply: Hitler is still alive. Caught up in his own panic—or is it a death wish?—Fellgiebel adds that the coup will continue as planned.

14:00

Back at Rastenburg, everything seems to point to Stauffenberg as the author of the bombing. Although at first some people suspect the Rastenburg workers, Sergeant Arthur Adam quickly describes how he saw Stauffenberg rushing out of the installations just after the bomb went off. Martin Bormann, one of Hitler's closest confidants, confirms this.

From Berlin, Himmler immediately contacts Ernst Kaltenbrunner, the head of the Reich Main Security Office, and Bernd Wehner, Berlin's chief of police, and has them report to Rastenburg immediately to begin their investigations.

15:00

A direct order from the Reichsführer-SS overrides General Fellgiebel's order to seal off the Rastenburg compound. Hitler, meanwhile, is giving out orders left and right, ready to take control of the situation quickly. First, he wants to go to the radio, to inform the German people about the state of his health, and more important, to deter anyone else from joining the conspiracy. At about the same time, Stauffenberg and Von Haeften land at Tempelhof Airport in Berlin.

Inside the Bendlerstraße headquarters, General Olbricht finally decides to activate Operation Valkyrie. Albrecht Ritter Mertz von Quirnheim, another top-level conspirator who seconds his motion, joins him. A few minutes later, Von Haeften telephones them from the airport to tell them that the bombing was a success, that Hitler is dead, and that he and Stauffenberg have arrived safely in Berlin.

12

16:00

Following Olbricht's orders, Mertz von Quirnheim meets with the top officers of the Wehrmacht. He informs them that Hitler is dead, that General Ludwig Beck will be named the new head of state, and that Field Marshal Witzleben will assume the position of commander in chief of the Wehrmacht. He also orders the deployment of Operation Valkyrie in every military district, in the naval academies, and in the military headquarters of the city.

Meanwhile, Olbricht walks to General Fromm's office.

"The Führer has been assassinated. A bombing in the Rastenburg headquarters," he tersely informs the general. "I have here the necessary documents to set Operation Valkyrie in motion. Please sign them."

Fromm looks like a ghost. He feels as if all the tension in his body has dropped straight through to the floor, and only a miracle will prevent him from collapsing right then and there.

"You're mad," he says to Olbricht.

"No, General, it's true," Olbricht insists. "Please, sign the paper."

Fromm excuses himself for a moment and places a call to General Keitel at Rastenburg.

"Yes, in fact, there has been an attempt against Hitler's life, but thank God he is safe and sound. Oh, and General Fromm," says Keitel, "can you tell me precisely where we can find your chief of staff, Colonel Stauffenberg?"

"He still hasn't returned from Rastenburg," mumbles Fromm. With that, he hangs up the telephone. Now he knows for sure.

He quickly returns to his office, where Olbricht is waiting for him.

"I'm sorry, General," he says with a tinge of sarcasm in his voice. "But the Führer is alive. I cannot sign that document."

A few minutes later, Hitler adds another appointment to Himmler's long list: a new commander of the reserve army to replace General Fromm.

The Bendlerstraße headquarters are in a state of total bedlam. Nobody knows what to think, much less what to do. Following Olbricht's orders, Captain Karl Klausing takes control of the compound with the assistance of four young officers. Klausing's next mission is to take control of the communications center and address the Nazi officials who have already been informed of the coup.

Klausing commands the radio operator to broadcast the following message to all the units: "The Führer Adolf Hitler is dead! The Führer Adolf Hitler is dead! A group of party leaders—traitors—have tried to take advantage of the situation, attacking our combat units at the rear guard in an attempt to seize control of the government. As such, the government of the Reich has declared martial law in order to stabilize the current situation."

"But, Captain," says the radio operator, "this message doesn't contain any of the normal security codes. Do you want us to code it?"

Klausing hesitates for a few seconds. What should he say?

"Yes, yes," he responds.

At that moment, the only four expert codifiers at Bendlerstraße get to work transmitting the announcement of Hitler's death. They will take more than three hours to complete their task.

A few minutes later, Klausing returns to the communications office to inform them of a new message that is to be aired immediately. Throughout the Reich, all of the *Gauleiter,* high-ranking party officials, and the top officers of the SS and the propaganda machine are to be arrested. "The German public deserves to know that our intention is to do away with the arbitrary methods of the old regime," they add to the broadcast.

13

16:30

Finally, Stauffenberg arrives at the Bendlerstraße headquarters. Olbricht greets him, apprises him of the situation, and tells him that despite Fromm's refusal to sign it, Operation Valkyrie has been set in motion. The two men agree to make another appeal to Fromm, in the hopes of recruiting him to their side.

"The Führer is dead," Stauffenberg insists. "I saw the body myself."

"It must have been someone very close to him," murmurs Fromm, feigning ignorance.

"I did it," says Stauffenberg.

Fromm flails his arms about, as if this gesture would somehow confer him more authority in the eyes of his subordinates.

"Well, you should know that I just got off the phone with General Keitel," he shrieks, gasping for breath. "And he has confirmed that the Führer is indeed still alive."

"That's a lie," Stauffenberg answers calmly.

Fromm's rage is mounting with every passing moment, but so is his fear. He is all too aware that his position is far from advantageous.

"General Olbricht and Colonel Stauffenberg are under arrest!" he howls.

"General Fromm," says Stauffenberg, in quiet, measured tones, "I don't think you quite understand the balance of power here. We are the ones who will decide if anyone is to be arrested, not you."

"You are disobeying a direct order, General," Fromm roars, though nobody pays him any mind.

Like a little boy, Fromm pounces on his subordinate. It takes several officers to successfully disentangle the two men and strip Fromm of his weapons.

"Under the present circumstances," he says, "I no longer consider myself in active service." After a tension-filled pause, Fromm adds, "May I request one last favor?"

"Go ahead, General."

"I need a bottle of cognac."

Olbricht orders someone to fetch a bottle, and General Fromm is led, under arrest, to the office of his assistant.

17:00

The new provisional government of the Reich, with General Ludwig Beck at the helm, gathers in Olbricht's office. Among its first measures is the appointment of General Erich Hoepner to the position occupied by Fromm only minutes before. Hoepner requests a written testament of his new appointment and later, when he moves into Fromm's office, apologizes to his former superior. Already somewhat tipsy, Fromm has this to say:

"I'm sorry, Hoepner. I can't accept this. I think the Führer is still alive and that all of you are making a terrible mistake."

17:30

The two contradictory announcements—the coded message from Bendler-straße and the countercommand from Rastenburg—travel to every last military compound in the Reich, in some cases arriving in the wrong order. General Paul von Hase, in strict observation of the Operation Valkyrie guidelines, summons the director of the naval training academy, the director of the explosives school, and the commander of the reserve army to his headquarters at Unter der Linden 1. There, he gives out instructions for taking control of the city.

A few minutes later, troops working for the conspiracy seize control of the Propaganda Ministry and surround the home of Dr. Joseph Goebbels, one of the few high-ranking Nazi officials still in Berlin. On the outskirts of the city, the plan continues its course and the various military units are able to take control of the radio stations, the party offices, and the SS offices without too much difficulty. It is the one moment of the entire day in which the conspirators seem to have gained control of the situation.

17:42

Despite the conspirators' best attempts to block its transmission, a radio message is successfully broadcast across the Reich from the Rastenburg headquarters. The announcement informs the German people of the bombing, and of the serious injuries sustained by party officials Schmundt and Brandt and a stenographer. "Fortunately," continues the communiqué, "the Führer only suffered a few scrapes and he has immediately returned to his official duties."

19:00

Otto Remer, the commander of Berlin's National Guard, initially follows the orders he has received from General Paul von Hase, his direct superior, to block off the area surrounding Goebbels's house, but he suddenly changes his mind. He enters the house, just as the propaganda minister is about to be arrested, and in typical fashion, Goebbels realizes that he just might have found an ally in the tiny, beleaguered figure of Remer.

"The Führer is still alive," he says.

"That's not what we've been told."

"Would you like to speak with him?" Goebbels asks, baiting him.

Remer says nothing, but allows the minister to pick up the telephone and place a call to Rastenburg. After identifying himself and going through the customary greetings, Goebbels hands the phone over to his captor.

"From this moment on, I give you full authority to end the conspiracy." Remer can hardly believe it, for at the other end of the line is the voice of the Führer.

After apologizing to Goebbels, Remer sets him free, and goes about fulfilling his orders.

14

20:00

The majority of the conspirators have acknowledged that the game is up. They begin to receive word of people identified as traitors to the cause, coup operatives who have refused to follow the orders issued from the headquarters at Bendlerstraße. Remer is but one of many similar cases.

A small group of the most avowed conspirators—those who now know their days are numbered—assembles back at Olbricht's office. Stauffenberg, Beck, Mertz von Quirnheim, and Von Haeften are now joined by Count Ulrich Schwerin von Schwanenfeld and Count Peter Yorck von Wartenburg. They issue commands and field telephone calls, they despair and they deny, they shout and they whisper, and in the end they pray for a miracle. A miracle that never occurs.

Suddenly, Field Marshal Witzleben appears at Bendlerstraße. He is supposed to be the new chief of the Wehrmacht, though until now he was nowhere to be found. He has only just learned of the situation and is more furious than ever. His eyes are on fire.

"This is a disaster!" he announces as Beck and Stauffenberg usher him inside, and he heads straight for Fromm's office.

"There were complications from the start, Marshal," Beck says in an attempt to mollify him.

"So I see!" Witzleben appears unwilling to calm his temper. "You could have waited!" As he says this, he slams his baton against Fromm's desk. "A parade of errors, one long chain of mistakes. That is the only thing you have accomplished!"

Although they all know he's right, nobody appreciates the marshal's tone of voice, like that of a father who rebukes his son for falling down a flight of stairs. The last thing that is called for at such a moment.

"But, Marshal . . ." Stauffenberg pleads, unable to finish his sentence.

One after the other, the many attempts to reason with him fail, and soon he and Beck are shouting at each other, neither one listening to what the other is saying.

Witzleben then storms out of the Bendlerstraße compound and returns to Zossen.

"We're going home" is all he says to General Wagner when he arrives.

21:00

With Bertram's aid, General Fromm discovers a secret exit leading out of the office where he has been sequestered. He grabs a telephone (incredibly, nobody stops him from doing this) and manages to contact several officials under his command, and tells them to disobey the orders issued by the coup plotters.

At that very moment, the conspirators learn that the city's reserve forces have betrayed their cause. Suddenly, scores of high-ranking officials begin to abandon their posts. Even those who have been arrested by the provisional government are liberated and begin to leave, and nobody tries to stop them.

22:00

A few members of Olbricht's group who have not been informed of the coup appear in the office of their superior with pistols and grenades in hand.

"General," they say, "are you for or against the Führer?"

Olbricht says nothing.

"We demand to speak with General Fromm," they say.

"You can find him in his office," Olbricht says dully. Everything seems so useless now.

When Stauffenberg bursts into Olbricht's office, the group of officers tries to apprehend him. Suddenly shouts are heard, followed by a violent scuffle and then the sound of shots being fired. One of the young officers has been hit by Stauffenberg, who has since run for cover in Mertz von Quirnheim's office. A thin stream of blood trickles down his shoulder.

15

23:00

The troops loyal to Fromm and the Führer take control of the Bendlerstraße headquarters and begin an exhaustive inspection of the offices.

"Are you for or against the Führer?" is the question they pose to all those who cross their path, and depending on the speed of the reply, those questioned are either added to the ranks of the Führer or arrested.

Finally, a few moments later, General Fromm takes charge of the situation. He remains surrounded by several soldiers and military personnel.

"Gentlemen," he says, "it is now my turn to do with you what you did with me earlier this afternoon. Please surrender your weapons," he says to the principal engineers of the coup: Stauffenberg, Olbricht, Mertz von Quirnheim, Von Haeften, and Beck.

"If you please, I would like to retain my pistol, to use it for my own purposes," Beck dares to request.

"If you have something to do, do it now!" barks Fromm, livid.

General Beck raises the weapon to his temple, and with all the pageantry he can summon from his glorious past, he speaks in the name of posterity:

"I now think back to days long gone," he begins.

"I told you, just do it!" interrupts Fromm, irritated by the display of emotion.

After a moment of silence, Beck pulls the trigger, but only inflicts a surface wound upon his forehead.

"Seize the weapon!" Fromm commands.

Beck resists, and tries to shoot himself again, but without any success. Finally the soldiers wrest the weapon from him.

"Take him to the other room," Fromm barks, exasperated. "And you," he says, motioning to the other men, "have one minute to make a final statement or to write whatever you wish."

The conspirators say nothing. What could they possibly have to say now? Only Hoepner ventures to speak.

"General," he implores, "I swear, I had no idea what was going on. I was simply carrying out my superiors' orders."

Fromm ignores him.

"May I put a few words down in writing?" This time it is General Olbricht, who has remained remarkably calm.

"Do it at the oval table," Fromm replies, suddenly relenting. "Where you used to sit before me."

An officer enters the room with an urgent message for Fromm. The Reichsführer-SS Himmler is on his way to Berlin. Time is of the essence.

"Have the reserves arrived yet?" the messenger asks.

"They're in the courtyard," he replies.

"Gentlemen," Fromm declares, attempting to adopt an officious tone of voice, "I'm afraid your time has run out." Then, in a far more chilling tone, he adds: "In the name of the Führer, I have convened a court-martial that has arrived at the following verdict: General Olbricht, Colonel Mertz von Quirnheim, the colonel whose name I would prefer not to mention, and First Lieutenant Haeften are sentenced to death."

"I alone am responsible for what has taken place," says Stauffenberg in a fruitless attempt to exonerate his accomplices. "The others have only carried out their duties as good soldiers."

After one officer balks at the request, another sergeant obligingly drags out the still-writhing General Beck to an adjacent room, and shoots him in the back of the neck.

16

00:00

A firing squad, composed of ten soldiers, is assembled in the courtyard. Behind the line, a half-dozen military vehicles turn on their headlights, which shine upon the condemned officers. Olbricht is the first to emerge. Stauffenberg is next, but just as the soldiers shoot, Von Haeften jumps in front of him and takes the bullets himself. In a matter of seconds, the soldiers dispose of the corpse. Once again, it is Stauffenberg's moment.

"Long live sacred Germany!" he manages to scream just before he falls to his death.

The last to die is Mertz von Quirnheim. After the executions, Fromm transmits the following message to his superiors: "Failed *putsch* of traitorous generals violently contained. All leaders are dead." On Fromm's orders, the conspirators' bodies—including Beck—are buried in an undisclosed location in St. Matthew's cemetery.

The following morning, Reichsführer-SS Heinrich Himmler orders the bodies to be exhumed and incinerated, their ashes to be scattered in the wind.

17

Unlike the prisoners executed that day, in the following weeks many others are captured, tortured, and subjected to a humiliating trial in the People's Court in Berlin, created by Hitler just for this occasion. The trials begin on August 7, in the great hall of the People's Court. On that day, eight defendants accused of conspiring against Hitler's life are brought before the court: Erwin von Witzleben, Erich Hoepner, Helmuth Stieff, Paul von Hase, Robert Bernardis, Friedrich Karl Klausing, Peter Yorck von Wartenburg, and Albrecht von Haden. They are not permitted to wear ties or suspenders and their own lawyers even urge them to declare themselves guilty. Flanked on either side by two enormous Nazi flags, Freisler ignores their protests, one after the other. Their crimes are so patently evil in nature that any and all declarations are inadmissible. Without flinching, Freisler condemns each of the eight defendants to death. He directs his gaze upon them:

"Now we can return to our life and to the battle before us. The *Volk* has purged you from its ranks and is pure now. We have nothing more to do with you. We fight. The Wehrmacht cries out: 'Heil Hitler!' We fight at the side of our Führer, following him for the glory of Germany!"

On August 8, the prisoners are led to the basement of the Plötzensee prison. Hitler expressly prohibits them from receiving spiritual attention; he wants their souls to suffer as much as their bodies. They are scarcely given time to change into their prison uniforms before being handed a pair of old wooden shoes. In these outfits, they are to walk, one by one, down the long, grim corridors of the prison until they reach the execution chamber, hidden behind a long black curtain.

A cameraman records the spectacle from start to finish. He captures them changing into their prison fatigues, their thin, naked bodies scarred from the torture they endured for two weeks; he captures their gestures of fear, dignity, and horror; their expressions, arrogant and pained; their stumbling as they walk down the hallway. He also films their entry into the gallows, through the heavy black veil that separates them from death. Each one of their movements is recorded with utmost precision, following the strict orders of the Führer, who was not about to concede them the honor of attending their executions. Of course he wants to watch them die, but only in private, and only after they had been carried out.

The scene is set. The first protagonist appears, an unkempt, pale man, his hair disheveled and his filthy slippers stained by the excrement in the prison hallways. In a flash he is brought into bold relief by two powerful spotlights, and the room is suddenly as antiseptic as it was before. His eyes flicker for a moment, blinded by the light, and his face betrays the shame of someone aware that his infamy will not be forgotten. He is surrounded by a small retinue, there to witness his final moments: the prosecutor, the warden of Plötzensee, some aides, the cinematographer, and a half-dozen journalists.

After receiving the signal from the warden, the executioner approaches the condemned man. Another, more talented filmmaker might portray this severe, icy figure in a tense close-up, following him as he tightens the noose—made with durable piano wire—as he prepares to hang his victim. One almost hopes that the inherent drama will inspire this *metteur en scène* to zoom in on the executioner's relaxed, calloused hands or on the drops of perspiration that fall from the corners of the condemned man's mouth. On this occasion, however, there is no Leni Riefenstahl to provide such cinematic flourishes. Instead, they must settle for a sober, flat technique that provides only wide-angle shots, highlighting the insipid hollowness of the room. The executioner unties the prisoner's hands and orders him to step onto a small platform; he then ties a silken sash around the convicted man's neck. For an instant, the prisoner looks like a marble statue. This drama has now reached its climax. A moment of silence heightens the tension; no one moves, no one stirs. They are all waiting for the warden's signal.

With an almost imperceptible gesture, the warden indicates his assent, and the executioner pulls the floor from beneath the first convict's body, which then begins to sway gently in the hollow well. The camera records every moment of these long minutes of agony: first, the horror that burns into the condemned man's pupils; then the brown stains that seep into the fabric around the noose; then the gurgles and the froth of saliva and blood which come bubbling out of his mouth. Then, the finale: the spasms reminiscent of a sturgeon trapped in a net by an expert fisherman. The victim rocks back and forth, like the clapper of a bell swinging through the air.

To the shock—and delight—of the spectators, there is still one final *coup de théâtre*. The hangman, smiling widely, approaches the dead man and, in one sweeping motion, tears off his trousers. The camera devours the victim's flaccid, shriveled member with a pornographic delight, offering this metaphor as a visual testimony to the weakness of all those who dare to oppose the Führer.

18

"Dim the lights!"

With these words, bitter and brittle with age, he is transported back in time, to the cold age of shadows. The silence brings the shadows into bold relief, and for a few moments no one applauds him, no one deceives him, no one insults him. Even the clocks are obedient: They remain silent.

This, he muses, is what death must be like. Only when the echo of his own voice dies down does he realize that he inhabits a universe that is no longer his.

"Start over!" he commands. "I want to see it again!"

The technician immediately rewinds the machine. He cranks a lever and the heavy apparatus slowly comes back to life. The Führer listens closely for the faint hum of the machine, and when he hears it, the darkness disappears, as does his rage. A bolt of light cuts through the room, and he directs his gaze to the screen. Once again the staircase landing, the folds of the curtains, and the silhouette of the theater seats are illuminated, and the screening room is transformed into a firing line, as it is every night.

The particles of light scatter about the room. They find their way into the

walls and floor coverings, they stick to his lips and ears, and eventually settle in the corners of the room. On-screen, the light and the shadows replay
the same faces and the same agony, bestowing a vicarious existence to those
bodies that have long since ceased to exist. As excited as a child listening to
his favorite bedtime story, Hitler once again savors the spectacle before him.

More than mere morbid fascination, this nocturnal routine, the endless
replaying of his adversaries' suffering, is a form of catharsis day in, day out,
like clockwork, with no company other than the SS-Gruppenführer, who
has received the double honor of also being appointed the bunker's film
technician. By now he has memorized every last frame, scene, and sequence,
and when the footage is replayed, he eagerly awaits each movement with the
eagerness of a movie spectator waiting for the scene in which his favorite
actors finally kiss.

"Bravo!" he bellows as the film comes to an end.

This is how he commemorates the production for which he has been
both director and censor.

"Bravo!" he cries again, as the projectionist turns on the lights, hoping
that the session has helped lift the Führer's intense melancholy. Hitler
remains silent, facing the blank screen, indifferent to the bombs that are
presently obliterating scores of buildings across Berlin, high above this sub-
terranean redoubt. Only during these rare moments is he able to forget
about his defeat.

"Start over!"

The lights go down again and the SS-Gruppenführer, using his finest
artillery skills, fires at his objective. He strikes his target as the Führer settles
into his chair.

Dialogue II: On the Rules Governing Chance

Leipzig
November 6, 1989

Was it possible that I was to be granted the privilege of witnessing the conclusion of a century that ended in precisely the same way it began? Was I to witness the culmination of years of fruitless investigations, the finale of this elaborate farce we have lived through, the last remaining link in this senseless chain of aborted events? The death of this monumental mistake we call the twentieth century?

For years I dedicated my entire being to the devious, cunning behavior of numbers, studying them tirelessly in the hope of understanding the nature of infinity. I doggedly followed the trail of Zeno and Cantor, Aristotle and Dedekind, and filled hundreds of pages with esoteric equations that looked like the characters of some arcane, long-forgotten language. I spent hours immersed in the most exhausting meditation, a state bordering on religious ecstasy. That was how I spent my days as a student, a teacher, a researcher. And yet I have learned far more in these forty-two years of incarceration, a time in which I have not sketched a single diagram nor envisioned even the simplest of mathematical sets. Locked away here, my own life has become infinite, unfathomable. That is, unthinkable. I am the living dead, a kind of Lazarus who has risen only to die over and over again, ad infinitum.

"Now. About the story I told you yesterday. About the attempt on Hitler's life. Fascinating, isn't it?" I ask Ulrich.

His face shows almost no emotion, as if he can't quite believe what I described for him.

"Yes, fascinating," he repeats, although I can't tell if he really means it, or if he is just saying so to humor me.

"And yet, these days, who remembers Count Stauffenberg? Or General Beck? Or Heinrich von Lutz? Nobody. And do you know why, Doctor?

Because their enterprise failed? I'm afraid not. The history books have forgotten them because they were defeated by a regime that was also defeated. Two-time losers, nobody cares enough to vindicate them. Nevertheless, the story of the July twentieth coup attempt is one of the greatest stories ever told."

"Why?" asks Ulrich. If he weren't so sweet, such a question would be unforgivable.

"Simple: because it is the story of a colossal failure." The surprise that registers in his eyes is almost amusing. "Don't you understand? Go back to the story, and you'll see how a chain of the most trivial errors brought down the plan—and, as such, eliminated the possibility of any other ending to the greatest story of our time. A group comprised of no more than twenty people was poised to alter the lives of millions. And because of an oversight, one of those circumstances that we call chance, for lack of a better word, their great plans never became reality."

"But things always turn out like that."

His innocence was now beginning to grate on my nerves; it was like trying to explain quantum physics to a six-year-old.

"No, not always," I said curtly. "Look closely at the details, at the carefully crafted mechanisms that, when touched off, brought down the coup. Or consider this: There were two bombs in Stauffenberg's briefcase, but he was able to activate only one of them. Do you remember why? At a certain moment he received an untimely call from General Fellgiebel, one of his fellow conspirators. This cost Stauffenberg time, and in his rush he was only able to activate one of the bombs. A telephone call, Doctor! What if Fellgiebel hadn't interrupted him? Or if he'd done so a few moments later? The explosive force of the two bombs put together would have been exponentially greater and, beyond a doubt, everyone in that room with Hitler would have been dead on the spot. A telephone call!"

For the first time, Ulrich's expression indicated a hint of agreement.

"That was the first twist of fate," I said, continuing where I left off. "But there was more. What if Von Freyend, instead of depositing Stauffenberg's briefcase under the table, had placed it right next to the Führer? Or, fine, let's assume that all of that occurred exactly as it did; it doesn't matter. Stauffenberg leaves the assembly hall, runs from the headquarters, and heads for the plane that is to deliver him straight to Berlin. Meanwhile, Fellgiebel, the communications chief at Rastenburg, discovers the bitter truth: The bomb has gone off and the Führer is still alive. So what does he do then? Telephones the base of operations at Bendlerstraße and, who knows why, announces that the Führer is alive *and* that the coup must continue according to plan. Two propositions that, by nature, are mutually exclusive. This, in turn, leads to utter chaos and bedlam that will inevitably end in disaster. What if, for example, he had simply said that the coup should go on, without mentioning anything else? Or consider the reverse: What if he had said that the Führer was still alive, and that the coup would have to be aborted?"

"I understand what you're saying," Ulrich says condescendingly. "But tell me, did you participate in the conspiracy?"

"I did not directly witness the events that took place that day, but, yes, I was a member of the group," I say, my voice transparent, ashamed of nothing. "I was—I *am* a simple man of science. I sympathized with them, but there was little else I could do. Heinrich von Lutz, my best friend at the time, asked me to join the cause. He, too, would have played a much more important role in the events of July 20 if it hadn't been for another twist of fate. On July 19, merely one day earlier, he was transferred from General Olbricht's team to that of General Stülpnagel, in Paris."

"And when were you and your friend arrested?"

"What do you mean?"

"When were the two of you arrested?" The doctor tries to play innocent, but he can't fool me.

"After what happened on July 20, Himmler ordered a persecution the likes of which no one had ever seen before," I said. "Thousands of people were arrested. The next day Fellgiebel and Witzleben were arrested, and Popitz, Canaris, Oster, Kleit-Schmerzin, and Hjalmar Schacht quickly followed. General Wagner committed suicide, as did many others. Schlabrendorff, Trott zu Stolz, and Klausing turned themselves in, in the end. And all of them were subjected to the cruelest kinds of torture. Hitler had said, 'I want them hanged, strung up like butchered cattle!' and Himmler was determined to fulfill his orders. Heinrich was arrested during the first few days in August. A few weeks later, I was."

"Do you think he turned you in?"

"I would like to think not," I say, suddenly sad. "The torture was brutal, but he was very strong. Perhaps it was someone else. Someone who would have felt closer to safety with me in the middle. Someone who didn't want to be associated with the coup plotters."

"Are you thinking of one person in particular?"

"Yes, in fact, I am. I've been saying it ever since the first damned day I got here. Heisenberg. Werner Heisenberg."

THE BOMB

1

In 1934, the Italian physicist Enrico Fermi presents the hypothesis that beyond uranium—the last known element in the periodic table—new, heretofore undiscovered metals might be obtained by bombarding uranium with "free" neutrons. Basing their research on this assumption, the chemist Otto Hahn and his assistant, the physicist Lise Meitner, carry out a series of experiments at their laboratories in the Kaiser Wilhelm Institute in Berlin, with this as their goal. Meitner is Jewish, but she has evaded the Hitlerian purges until now, thanks to her Austrian citizenship. However, after the Anschluss, she is forced to flee to Sweden. At this point, Hahn hires a new assistant, Fritz Strassmann, with whom he continues the experiments he began with Meitner.

Finally, in the fall of 1938, on separating the results of his uranium bombardment experiment, Hahn discovers that high levels of radioactivity appear in the barium that he is using as a catalyst. When he describes his findings to Niels Bohr, the Danish physicist believes that such a result is impossible. In desperation, Hahn turns to Lise Meitner, who has resettled in Stockholm, and asks her opinion. With the aid of her nephew, the physicist Otto Frisch, Meitner reaches the conclusion that Hahn is absolutely right: By bombarding uranium with neutrons, the element splits, and a barium nucleus plus a whole other array of elements are created—in the same way that a drop of water can be split in half, to use Bohr's metaphor. Part of the remaining mass is then converted into energy, just as Einstein's formula $E=mc^2$ predicts. On New Year's Day, 1939, Frisch travels to Copenhagen to tell Bohr about the discovery, and Bohr is stunned. "What fools we've been!" he exclaims. "It's been sitting right in front of us all this time! It's exactly how it should be!" Hahn and Meitner have just discovered atomic fission: the beginning of a new era.

A few days later, Bohr departs for the United States, where he will spend the next few months. He has been invited to give lectures at various universities, and also plans to meet with Einstein at Princeton to continue their ongoing debate on quantum physics. But suddenly, Hahn's discovery becomes the focal point of his trip. Bohr is anxious to spread the news in the United States, although he has promised Hahn he will wait until the findings are published. On January 6, Hahn's article on fission finally appears in *Naturwissenschaften,* and Bohr is now at liberty to discuss the topic at the various stops on his American tour. The news of nuclear fission generates a wave of consternation throughout the world, and physicists everywhere— in America, Copenhagen, Paris, Berlin, Moscow, Munich, Leningrad— begin to reproduce Hahn and Strassmann's experiments.

Why all the attention, why all the commotion? Any competent physicist could tell you: For several decades, it was believed that the universe consisted of tiny particles of matter, held together by that special glue we call energy. Later on, Einstein proved that matter and energy were merely two different manifestations of the same essential component. Now, for the first time, it was possible to observe the transformation of matter into energy: that resplendent, glowing energy that explodes into action when uranium atoms are smashed. The most troubling aspect of all this, however, was the practical application of this energy—the creation of chain reactions, the construction of nuclear reactors, and, in the worst-case scenario, the development of weapons whose capacity for destruction would be unlike anything anyone had ever imagined.

From the outset, this last possibility frightens Hahn to the point of contemplating suicide. At a meeting among friends at the Kaiser Wilhelm Institute, he suggests that Germany dump all its uranium reserves into the sea, to eliminate the possibility of ever building such a destructive weapon. Things get worse: One of Hahn's colleagues informs him that following the invasion of Czechoslovakia, the Reich seized the uranium mines of Joachimsthal, the richest of their kind in the entire world. The scene seems to be set for the Apocalypse.

2

From the moment Bohr begins spreading the word about fission in the United States, hordes of scientists mobilize their efforts to test the feasibility of bomb construction. Their goal: to convince the American government to establish a massive atomic study in the hope of arriving at real results before the Germans do. Several physicists who have fled Hitler's Europe are among this group, including Edward Teller (who, incidentally, obtained his doctorate alongside Werner Heisenberg), Leo Szilard, and Eugene Wigner. Eventually, they manage to convince the more prominent scientists working in the country—Fermi, Bethe, Von Neumann, Oppenheimer, and, of course, Einstein—to launch a relentless campaign in favor of a large-scale atomic program. In a letter dated August 2, 1939, written on Wigner's behest, Einstein says the following to President Franklin D. Roosevelt:

> *In the course of the last four months it has been made probable . . . that it may become possible to set up a nuclear chain reaction in a large mass of uranium, by which vast amounts of power and large quantities of new radiumlike elements would be generated. Now it appears almost certain that this could be achieved in the immediate future.*
>
> *This new phenomenon would also lead to the construction of bombs . . .*
>
> *In view of the situation you may think it desirable to have more permanent contact maintained between the Administration and the group of physicists working on chain reactions in America . . .*
>
> *I understand that Germany has actually stopped the sale of uranium from the Czechoslovakian mines which she has taken over. That she should have taken such early action might perhaps be understood on the ground that the son of the German Under-Secretary of State, von Weizsäcker, is attached to the Kaiser-Wilhelm-Institut in Berlin where some of the American work on uranium is now being repeated.*

Roosevelt thanks Einstein for the missive and promises to assign army and navy personnel to study the matter. However, it isn't until October of 1941 that the president grants his final approval to begin work on the Manhattan Project. In any event, the rules of the game and the final objective—to create the most powerful weapon of mass destruction in history—have been established. Whoever wins this race, without a doubt, will also emerge as the decisive victor of World War II.

3

In early 1939, Abraham Esau, the director of the Reich Research Council, receives the German scientists' initial reports discussing the possibility of using Hahn's discovery for military purposes. Simultaneously in Hamburg, the physicists Paul Harteck and Wilhelm Groth bring up the very same issue with Erich Schumann, the director of the Arms Research Council, who immediately assembles a working group to study the matter. The team includes, among others, Kurt Diebner and his assistant, Erich Bagge.

Shortly after the war begins, Bagge approaches his fellow physicists and members of the so-called *Uranverein*—the Uranium Circle—with the suggestion that they invite his old professor from Leipzig, the illustrious Werner Heisenberg, to join their efforts. On September 26, 1939, Heisenberg, Otto Hahn, and Carl Friedrich von Weizsäcker attend the *Uranverein's* second meeting, at the German Army Weapons Office, located on Hardenbergstraße, across from the Berlin Polytechnic Institute.

Only three months after this initial meeting, Heisenberg sends the *Uranverein* a copy of his first theoretical paper on the topic, entitled "On the possibility of technical energy production from Uranium Splitting." In this report, Heisenberg offers a summary of the scant contributions that have been made in the field, and also mentions an idea developed by Siegfried Flügge, one of his students: that basic uranium is composed of two isotopes, Uranium-238 and the far rarer Uranium-235, though only U-235 can be used to form chain reactions. Finally, Heisenberg explains one of the great challenges of atomic theory: the "critical mass" essential to the formation of chain reactions. This is a mystery that, in the end, the German team will be unable to crack.

By the end of 1939, Germany is the only country in the world that possesses the necessary foundations to begin to work in earnest on the atomic project, thanks to Heisenberg's report. The governments of the United States and Great Britain, meanwhile, show little interest in the topic.

By the end of 1940, the Army Weapons Office decides to centralize all the uranium research in the Reich, and takes the following measures: First, Abraham Esau is stripped of all authority; and second, Erich Schumann and Kurt Diebner are appointed directors of the Kaiser Wilhelm Institute in Berlin, thus centralizing the decision-making structure. Heisenberg, putting aside his rivalry with Diebner, agrees to work in two of the study centers that fall within Diebner's jurisdiction: the Kaiser Wilhelm Institute and the Leipzig Physics Institute, which he himself has supervised for several years.

4

In 1942, the course of the war changes drastically. The Germans suffer decisive defeats on the Eastern Front, which threaten the Reich economy, and the Führer is forced to reorganize the internal structure of his government. One

of his first decisions is to appoint Albert Speer—the architect largely responsible for the beautification of Berlin—as his new armaments minister. Amid
the court of miracles that is Hitler's cabinet, Speer emerges as perhaps the
only normal person in the entire lot—in addition to his great intelligence, he
is a tall, elegant figure, and might just be the most astute of Hitler's advisers.

Heisenberg has finally achieved his long-overdue political vindication.
After the long, hard years of fighting Johannes Stark and his pack of wolves
in the *Deutsche Physik,* the Reich scientific authorities finally come out in his
defense. And just as Himmler promised him months earlier, he receives a
double appointment in Berlin the following April. First he is granted a chair
at the University of Berlin and, shortly following that, he is named director
of the physics department at the Kaiser Wilhelm Institute, replacing the
Dutch scientist Peter Debye, who has refused to participate in the Nazi war
effort. In June, Heisenberg signs a contract which will make him both the
director of the institute and the scientific director of the German atomic
project.

Shortly after Heisenberg has settled into his new role in Berlin, Albert
Speer summons him to his offices. From the very beginning, the armaments
minister has been fascinated by the possibility of developing a weapon with
the potential to change the course of the war. During their meeting, Heisenberg complains bitterly of the scant attention paid to the development of
nuclear research.

"In the United States, such a project would receive immediate attention,"
he goads Speer.

The architect seems to understand, and asks the physicist for some more
information on atomic energy and its potential military use. Heisenberg,
with the same patience he exercises in his university seminars, explains the
rudiments of nuclear fission, reactors, and chain reactions to the armaments minister.

"Very well," exclaims Speer enthusiastically. "Let's get to work. What do
you need to move ahead with the project?"

"The necessary budget to cover the construction of a uranium machine,
a cyclotron."

"I'm going to be very direct with you, Professor," says the premier architect of the Reich. "Is it possible that atomic energy could be used to eventually build a bomb?"

"I think so," replies Heisenberg, confident. But then he quickly adds:
"Although I'm afraid that I wouldn't be able to have it ready before the end
of *this* war."

"And do you think the Americans could build one before we do?" Speer presses, growing alarmed.

"I sincerely doubt it," Heisenberg answers, sure of himself. "We all face the same obstacles. While it might be possible to put together a theoretical model for the bomb in a matter of months, the same, I'm afraid, would not be true on the practical side of things. It will be several years before the practical obstacles can be overcome."

"Then what would be the point of supporting this research?" Speer asks.

"Well, in the long run, whoever controls atomic energy will also control the world," says Heisenberg.

5

When the Nazis "peacefully" invaded Denmark in 1940, they did not even need to raise arms. All they did was cross the border and create a kind of protectorate which, in theory, would not affect the political life of the nation. At the time nobody was concerned, for example, that Niels Bohr (half Jewish on his mother's side) might not keep his position as director of the Institute for Theoretical Physics at the university. Despite his aversion to the Nazis and the several offers he received to move to Great Britain and the United States, Bohr chose to remain in his homeland as long as possible.

But in the fall of 1942, less than a year after Heisenberg's unhappy visit to Copenhagen, the situation changes drastically. The king leaves the country and Hitler decides to incorporate Denmark into the territory of the Reich. An SS officer, Dr. Werner Best, is assigned to replace the civil governor, and overnight the situation changes. Until now, the Danish populace has been treated cautiously, but under Best they are subjected to far harsher conditions. Angry and indignant, the Danes establish a resistance movement to sabotage the efforts of the Nazi authorities. Enraged by this sudden act of rebellion, Best declares martial law and executes a plan for the annihilation of all Danish Jews by way of a massive raid, which is carried out on October 1, 1943.

In mid-September, Bohr receives a coded letter from diplomatic sources in Sweden, informing him that all Danish Jews will soon be arrested. For the first time since the Nazi occupation, Bohr's life in Denmark is in serious danger, and he has little time to make a decision. That very same day, the physicist makes contact with several Danish resistance leaders, who immediately offer him their assistance in finding a way out. On September 29,

Bohr and his wife quietly leave their home and make their way to Musickby, the musicians' neighborhood, located near the area of Sydhavn, where they join a group of twelve people who hope to cross the Øresund for Sweden. In addition to Bohr and his wife, the band of fugitives includes Bohr's brother Harald, his nephew Ole, and Edvard Heidberg, a well-known architect and militant communist.

Around ten o'clock in the evening, the group heads for the beach, where a small fishing boat awaits them to make the journey. An hour later, the fourteen passengers board a slightly larger boat, a freighter, which sets sail under cover of night for the Swedish bay of Limhamn, and the passengers disembark on Swedish soil in the early hours of September 30. From there, the exiles travel by land to Malmø. That same day, Bohr boards a train for Stockholm. There, he is welcomed by Professor Klein (a former student of Otto Hahn and Lise Meitner), who has offered him shelter in his home that night. The operation to bring Bohr and his family to safety is complicated and difficult. He is kept under constant vigil, as various officials, police officers, and soldiers take turns guarding him.

Bohr then meets with King Gustav V, the crown prince, and various Swedish authorities to solicit their aid in protecting the Jewish population in Denmark. And then, on October 4, he leaves for Great Britain, boarding an unarmed Mosquito plane sent expressly for this purpose by His Majesty's government. On October 7, he flies to London, where he is met by the Secret Service and Professor Chadwick, one of his old English friends. Despite the assumption that this entire operation is to be carried out with the utmost secrecy, the *New York Times* gets wind of the news and publishes the following article on October 9:

Scientist Reaches London
Dr. N.H.D. Bohr, Dane, Has New Atomic Blast Invention

LONDON, Oct. 8 (AP)—Dr. Niels H.D. Bohr, refugee Danish scientist and Nobel Prize winner for atomic research, reached London from Sweden today, bearing what a Dane in Stockholm said were plans for a new invention involving atomic explosions.

These plans were described as for the greatest importance for the Allied war effort.

In London, Bohr meets with Sir John Anderson, who is not only the chancellor of the Exchequer, but a career physicist and chemist and, on

Winston Churchill's direct command, the head of the British atomic project. To Bohr's surprise, Anderson begins to update him on the progress of the Allied atomic project:

"After several scientists—including Einstein—wrote letters to President Roosevelt, on October 9, 1941, the president finally authorized the construction of an atomic bomb, which would build on the work developed by Enrico Fermi in Chicago."

"I didn't know that the Americans' interest in atomic energy ran so deep," says Bohr, both surprised and troubled by the news.

"I must tell you, Professor, that we also had our own atomic program back then, known by the code name of Tube Alloys." A note of pride is detectable in Anderson's voice as he describes his project. "The project was led by professors Frisch and Peierls, who you must know well from your days studying under Heisenberg."

Bohr would never have guessed that the Allied atomic efforts would have reached such proportions. He had always assumed that the British and American scientists were working on it, but he had never imagined that they could have gotten so far in the last few months.

"From 1941 on," continues Anderson, imperturbable, "the British and American teams began to coordinate their efforts, and that summer, a joint team put together a meticulous report on the Uranium-235 that would be necessary to build a bomb. In July of 1942, I put together a memorandum for Prime Minister Churchill, proposing the merger of the British and American atomic programs, such that the bomb would be created by both countries, on American territory." Clearly Churchill was far from enthusiastic about the idea, though he never said so explicitly, and Anderson refrains from mentioning this particular point. "On August 19, 1943, during a conference in Quebec, Roosevelt and Churchill signed an agreement of mutual accord between the United States and the United Kingdom regarding the Tube Alloys plan."

As if this weren't enough to provoke Bohr's consternation, Anderson launches into a description of one of the program's greatest achievements: On December 2, 1942, at the University of Chicago, Enrico Fermi's research team carried out the first sustainable chain reaction. This exceeds all of Bohr's expectations.

"Since then, various atomic piles have been built, in several different locations throughout the United States, with the goal of finding the one which offers the best conditions for producing an atomic explosion."

"Amazing, amazing" is all Bohr can think to say.

"Starting this year," Anderson adds, "all the experiments relating to the atomic project will be carried out in a new, secret laboratory located somewhere in the New Mexican desert. The head of that project, in fact, is an old acquaintance of yours: Oppenheimer."

That same week, Bohr receives a letter from the British government inviting him to act as a scientific adviser to the Tube Alloys project. Only days later, General Leslie Groves, the military manager of the Manhattan Project, invites Bohr to join the Americans' advisory team. In a grand display of impartiality, Bohr responds to both letters proposing a joint appointment, and both Britain and the United States agree.

On December 6, Bohr and his son Åage arrive in the United States, where they change their names for security reasons: From then on, they will be known as Nicholas and James Baker. During their time in America, the Bakers do not become permanent residents of the Los Alamos National Laboratory, but they do make several lengthy visits to the installations.

Soon after, a pivotal discovery is made. By now, it is common knowledge that U-235 can be used as fuel for a nuclear bomb. However, one of the following elements on the periodic table, known as plutonium (one of the "transuranics" predicted by Hahn and Fermi), is discovered to be easily fissionable. In fact, one of its isotopes, Plutonium-240, does so spontaneously, unaided by neutron bombardment. The project chiefs waste no time in building a bomb with Plutonium-240, in addition to the U-235 bomb they are already working on.

6

Heisenberg's status in Germany is far different from that of Bohr. In November of 1942, he is invited by the Prussian finance minister, Johannes Popitz, to join the Wednesday Circle, a prestigious, decades-old discussion group whose members gather each week to discuss scientific and—it must be said—other topics of a less lofty nature.

The Wednesday Circle meetings are held on a rotating basis, traveling to a different member's home each week. In accordance with the meticulously established ritual, each host offers his guests a light dinner and a brief lecture on his particular scientific specialty. Professors Eduard Spranger, Wolfgang Schadewaldt, and Jens Jessen, as well as Ambassador Ulrich von Hasen, Dr. Ferdinand Sauerbruch, and General Ludwig Beck, are among the more notable names in the roster of the twenty-eight-member group. Needless to say, several of these men will be key figures in the July 20, 1944, plot against the Führer.

The circle members, more or less, share a common political ideology: fierce nationalism, moral rectitude over any and all practical considerations, and an unspoken hatred for the Nazis. They spend a good deal of every meeting complaining incessantly about the excesses of *Schimpanski*, their code name for the Führer.

On the afternoon of July 5, 1944, Adolf Reichwein, one of the conspirators, appears unannounced at Heisenberg's offices. He has met Heisenberg a few times now, thanks to his friendship with Ludwig Beck, Ferdinand Sauerbruch, and other Wednesday Circle members. Ignoring all formalities, Reichwein asks Heisenberg to join the coup they are planning to stage sometime in the next few days. The physicist, who possesses an odd talent for getting out of the most uncomfortable situations, wishes him luck but respectfully declines to participate in the effort. His excuse: He is not a man of violence. A few days later, Reichwein and the other members of the Solf Circle are detained by the Gestapo. Nobody knows who turned them in.

The night of July 12, 1944, marks the last meeting of the Wednesday Circle. It is Heisenberg's turn to host. In an attempt to make the evening as pleasant as possible, he decides to hold the meeting at the Kaiser Wilhelm Institute, in the Harneck Haus, where he is currently staying. In honor of his guests, the physicist has prepared a lecture that focuses on two rather different topics. First he will speak about the structure of stars. This, in turn, will lead him into his second subject, an exquisitely crafted explication of the nuclear fission that takes place inside stars. He will then discuss the possibility of artificially reproducing this phenomenon.

Of the ten circle members who attend, there are at least four who will have a difficult time understanding the laws of the firmaments: Jens Jessen, Guido Beck (brother of the general), Ferdinand Sauerbruch, and Ludwig Diels. A few days later, they will all join the front lines of the conspiracy.

7

On July 19, Heisenberg suddenly leaves Berlin to go to his family, who are impatiently awaiting his arrival in Urfeld. The next day, in Urfeld, he learns via the radio of the failed coup.

Beginning on July 21, sweeping arrests are made. Himmler's sole objective is to eradicate every last bit of subversiveness that remains in the Reich. Thousands of people are arrested for the simple crime of being distant relatives or acquaintances of the conspirators. Virtually all the members of the Wednesday Circle are detained, interrogated, arrested, and, later on, either relocated to concentration camps or shot on the spot. All but Heisenberg, who enjoys the protection of Himmler, Speer, and Goering. All but Heisenberg, whose loyalty to the Reich is beyond question.

As Hitler and his cronies revel in the trials of the coup plotters and, most especially, in the executions of the condemned men (carefully recorded on tape for the Führer's private enjoyment), in an effort to escape the insidious, omnipresent tension, Heisenberg directs his full attention to the work at hand. A tall order, as the work he is performing—the preparations for an atomic reactor—will only serve to strengthen the power base of Hitler, a man who has executed many of his friends.

8

Heisenberg's influence on Nazi atomic policy is growing with each day that passes. Only one year later, in the summer of 1943, he convinces Speer to relieve Abraham Esau of his position as chief of the physics division of the Reich Research Council and the Reich's Plenipotentiary for Atomic Energy, and replace him with Walter Gerlach, an experimental physicist from Munich far more sympathetic to Heisenberg's perspective than Esau. Then, after he gives a lecture on the topic at the Academy of Aeronautic Sciences (of which he is a member), the German atomic project is awarded "urgent" status. This change in status will guarantee the continued financing of the atomic program, even in the most difficult of wartime circumstances.

9

Technically, Heisenberg is the principal brain behind the German atomic program, and as such the person responsible for establishing the parameters of the Reich's scientific research. Therefore, he is rather surprised to learn that Kurt Diebner, working in the experimental laboratory at Gottaw under the auspices of the Imperial Physical-Technical Institute, has begun to obtain more conclusive results in his experiments to achieve the anxiously awaited chain reaction. Ignoring the guidelines established by Heisenberg,

Diebner has decided that instead of filling his atomic pile with the usual sheets of uranium oxide, he will replace them with small uranium cubes floating in heavy water. On his first attempt, the number of neutrons produced versus those absorbed is greater, by around 36 percent, a percentage far higher than any obtained by Heisenberg to date. In a second experiment, performed sometime in the middle of 1943, Diebner raises this figure to 110 percent, getting closer and closer to achieving a chain reaction. Though he is still far from his objective, Diebner is well on his way to achieving the critical mass necessary for a chain reaction when a sudden Allied bombing destroys the Degussa factory where his uranium particles are manufactured. This puts an end to his research efforts.

By the middle of 1944, the harsh wartime conditions complicate things for the atomic experiments, and the Nazi authorities decide to concentrate the lion's share of their research in a secret bunker in Berlin, a bomb- and radiation-proof building with two-meter-thick cement walls. Inside, there is a spacious laboratory, a workshop, air and water pumps, tanks of heavy water, and a variety of electronic instruments for handling the radioactive elements, a miniature Los Alamos, if you will.

Heisenberg's team moves into the new installations, as do some of the people working for Walter Bothe (previously in Heidelberg) and Karl Wirtz, who until now has been working in Berlin. Nevertheless, by the end of 1943, the constant bombings make research impossible, and while the bunker is completely disasterproof, the generators and the scientists' living quarters are not.

In the fall, on Gerlach's suggestion, Heisenberg sends one third of his men to Hechingen, a small village in the Black Forest, and the staff from the Kaiser Wilhelm Institute move into an old textile factory nearby. In December, Wirtz and Heisenberg perform another experiment with uranium oxide plates, though this time—for the first time—they use graphite instead of heavy water as their moderator, just as the Americans have done. Using this technique, they achieve a neutron level of 206 percent. Nevertheless, they are still far from producing the long-awaited chain reaction.

Three months before the end of the war, in January of 1945, Wirtz decides to give it one last try. Here, in the Kaiser Wilhelm compound, he will perform his most ambitious experiment yet: a pile of hundreds of uranium tubes, suspended by aluminum cables inside a cylinder, which is filled with the institute's remaining ton and a half of heavy water. The cylinder, coated with a layer of pure graphite, has been submerged in a tank of water in the antiaircraft shelter. However, just when Wirtz is poised to begin the experiment, Gerlach orders all the equipment in the installation to be dismantled at once. The Red Army troops are advancing toward Berlin, and if they manage to capture the nuclear scientists, the situation will be devastating. Immediately, Gerlach, Diebner, and Wirtz leave for Hechingen, where Heisenberg will be waiting for them.

10

In February of 1945, only two months before Hitler's suicide and the German surrender, the nuclear scientists are still as determined as ever to build a reactor. Transferred to the small village of Haigerloch, not far from Hechingen, they attempt to assemble yet another reactor, this time inside a small cave, the *Atomkeller*, which has been set up as a makeshift laboratory. Following the orders of Goering, Speer, Himmler, and Bormann, Gerlach and his men install their equipment though they have only the faintest hope of achieving their objective before the final bloodbath. At this point their only goal is to produce some test results that might help the Germans negotiate some kind of conditional surrender.

The mood among the scientists is something like that of men preparing to descend into hell— or, if you prefer, of men traveling back to the origins of civilization. Thousands of years ago, a human being would have been scratching bison and snakes on the ceilings and walls of this cave, yet they also would have been stoking the fire—that other source of energy—in as meticulous and reverent a manner as these men now supervise the details of their atomic reactor.

Yes, Heisenberg thinks to himself, we are a feeble tribe, the last inhabitants of this earth, every bit as obsessed with fame and immortality as prehistoric man. Why else would we bother testing an atomic pile in the last days of a war which, months ago, we already knew was lost? Why this one final effort, this one last sin of pride? Why? So we can declare that in this battle, at least, we bested our enemies? A swan song, a last gasp before meekly accepting the death of our civilization.

"Experiment, Series B-8," Wirtz says, like a sorcerer summoning the spirit world in a desperate, stubborn attempt to save the life of his tribe.

The long metal cylinder stretches out before them like a magic wand. These are the men entrusted with the task of laying on the ritual elements, in accordance with the laws passed down from generation to generation. Of course, the toads and bats' wings—they couldn't think of better ingredients—are replaced with elements bearing the most eccentric of names, like uranium oxide or heavy water. For a split second, Wirtz and Heisenberg stop what they are doing to ponder their feelings at this moment, and to observe the faces and gestures of their assistants. A common spirit unites them, similar to the nervous energy of the gambler betting his last dime, the anxiety of a man risking his last possessions—his home, his family—with the weak hope of winning one more chance.

With the same careful attention of priests handling consecrated wafers, the scientists remove the reactor's graphite covering, anxious to marvel at the wonders soon to be produced in this magical piece of equipment. Hundreds of tiny votives—particles of that material known as uranium—sway to and fro in this Gothic sacristy, like First Communion pendants hanging from their slender aluminum filaments. Next, they empty the heavy water with a large, circular cup. *This is the cup of my blood, the blood of the new and everlasting covenant,* some of them think.

Precisely: a Grail, the trophy Heisenberg has coveted for so many years, the final result of a lifelong search. How could he not have seen it before? Of course! The giant reactor, the uranium, the heavy water: the divine elixir that would make him wiser, stronger, nobler. In the middle of the Atomkeller, that atomic cave carved out of the earth, they are ready to consummate a ritual that he has dreamed of since childhood, the symbol he has desired ever since his days as a *Pfadfinder* in the youth movement. It is the prize sought by every knight-errant that ever lived. He likes to think of his actions as heroic, or some similar quality that brings him closer to his youthful idols—most especially with the young man who defeated Klingsor and was blessed with the grace of God.

"All right," he whispers.

Total silence fills the room, like the expectant stillness of true believers waiting for a miracle or of the Grail keepers, gathered in the castle of Monsalvat. All eyes are glued to the chalice, all spirits contrite. They all pray, they all hope for salvation. Little by little the heavy water begins swirling around the uranium atoms, caressing them, inciting them, giving them breath, inciting them to grow and multiply, to explode, to crash into one another, to bounce, to jump, to multiply again, to live . . . Slowly the reaction starts. Yes, there it is! The miracle they have been praying for! The miracle of salvation! Suddenly, Wirtz realizes that they have taken none of the security precautions that will protect them if the chain reaction actually occurs. The emotion, the fury, and the desperation have made them forget the most obvious, the most basic safety measures. Perhaps without quite knowing it, they are willing to sacrifice their lives as long as this invention works and brings them immortality.

Wirtz approaches Heisenberg and advises him that they have only one small bar of cadmium—a substance that absorbs neutrons rapidly—in case something goes awry. He isn't certain they have enough to stop a reaction, which would be the most extreme case. Heisenberg frets for a moment, but then dismisses it—he is too nervous and busy calculating the magnitude of the energy generated. *Yes, go on, yes, yes, a little more, a little—*

Suddenly, the process stops cold. Nothing. Are the Grail keepers allowed to break down in tears? Heisenberg reviews his calculations. When he speaks, the echo in his voice is mortal, catastrophic.

"Six hundred and seventy percent," he says, and then falls silent.

"The highest percentage ever achieved," Wirtz notes.

The highest, perhaps, but what use is it? The experiment is a failure. Another colossal failure. And their last.

"We would need another fifty percent of uranium and heavy water to reach critical mass," Heisenberg whispers.

"Maybe we can still get the material left over from Diebner's laboratory in Stadtilm," says Wirtz.

"Yes. Maybe."

But they both know it's a lost cause. The American troops have penetrated nearly all of Thuringia by now; getting through to Stadtilm would be virtually impossible. On April 8, they learn that Diebner has been forced to abandon his laboratory. Time has run out. There is nothing left. Heisenberg orders his men to prepare for departure, and he leaves immediately for Urfeld to locate his family. There, on May 2, he will be arrested by Colonel Pash of the U.S. Alsos mission.

Five days later, on May 7, in the city of Reims, General Jodl, chief of Operation Staff of the High Command of the Wehrmacht, and Admiral Hans-Georg von Friedeburg, submarine commander, sign the document declaring Germany's unconditional surrender.

11

In Trinity, New Mexico, not far from Los Alamos, the first nuclear test ever to use a plutonium-charged prototype is performed on July 16, 1945. Less than a month later, on August 6, a massive radioactive mushroom cloud rises above the rubble of the Japanese city of Hiroshima. This is the conclusive proof that the U-235 bomb indeed works. Three days later, on August 9, the plutonium bomb is given its moment of glory as it destroys the city of Nagasaki.

In Farm Hall, Scotland, the Nazi atomic scientists woefully mourn the events. But how many of them are crying for the dead?

DIALOGUE III:
ON THE SECRETS OF DESTINY

LEIPZIG
NOVEMBER 7, 1989

"There are so many questions, aren't there, Doctor? I never understood how they could continue defending a man who, to the very end, did everything he could to build an atomic bomb for Hitler," I say. "And what if Heisenberg's team had succeeded? If the Germans had had an atomic bomb at their disposal during the first months of 1945? What would have become of the world then?"

"But that didn't happen."

"Well, in any event," I insist, "it's not the only thing he's guilty of. I'll be honest with you. I think Heisenberg was the one who turned in his friends from the Wednesday Circle, the ones involved in the conspiracy. He was the only one who managed to avoid an accusation."

Ulrich remains perched at the edge of my bed, to my right. Behind his eyeglasses, a curious sparkle lights up his eyes. In his hands he carries one of those little clipboards for writing down the medications to be administered to his patients. He takes copious notes as I talk.

"But do you have proof to support those accusations? What were his motives?"

"Isn't it perfectly clear, Doctor? Heisenberg was much closer to the Nazi authorities than anyone realizes. Look, for years people made fun of him but he also aroused real anger among scores of scientists and party bureaucrats who considered him, to use Johannes Stark's terminology, a 'white Jew.' Then suddenly, starting in 1942, he becomes Hitler's most loyal servant. Overnight."

"Perhaps in Hitler's eyes, his results began to prove more useful than those produced by his rivals," Ulrich responds.

"Very sharp," I answer ironically. "Believe me: By 1939, Heisenberg was one of the most hated men in the Third Reich, a kind of spy working for the

371

Jews. And in 1944, when scores of conspiracy plotters, some of them his very own friends, are arrested and shot, he isn't the slightest bit ruffled. And to top it off, a few days before the coup he actually invites some of its top men over for dinner. After the coup attempt, Himmler launched the most merciless rampage, killing scores of people guilty of nothing more than being related to the conspirators. And nobody thinks about Professor Heisenberg . . . isn't that rather interesting? I was arrested and sentenced. The only thing that saved my life was a stroke of dumb luck. And Heisenberg, meanwhile, was awarded every last honor the Nazis—and, later on, the British—could think of. They absolved him of everything, as if being a genius somehow made him *innocent*."

"It is odd, isn't it," Ulrich replies, and then adds quietly, "But the fact that he went free doesn't make him directly guilty for what you suffered, Professor Links."

"Don't try that one with me, please," I say, growing impatient. "Haven't I told you enough? Heisenberg never gave a damn about what happened to his friends; all he wanted was to feed his ego, to know that he was the best and that his discoveries would enable him to negotiate special treatment from the Allies. All he thought about was himself. Heisenberg never looked out for anyone but himself."

"There's a qualitative difference between action and omission," the doctor observes. For a few seconds I begin to doubt his good intentions.

"Is that so?" I snap, furious. "You know, I simply can't understand why you insist upon defending him."

"Let me see if I've understood this correctly." Despite his youthful enthusiasm, Ulrich is still rather quick to resort to the clichés of his chosen profession. "Do you blame Heisenberg for your misfortune?"

"I don't know," I say, nonplussed. "The one thing I am sure of, however, is that he is the central link in a long chain of events that have no explanation other than some kind of conspiracy. Hundreds of things that occurred, one after the other, that conspired to do me in. Thousands of plots hatched against me, all of them connected by one common thread: Klingsor."

THE REALM OF THE OCCULT

1

Klingsor. To what point can I blame this one single name for all the misfortunes that have befallen me? Don't the syllables themselves ring of hexes and curses? Am I condemned to being the one person who thinks and talks of Klingsor ad infinitum? Very well, then, here is the evidence I have to prove his existence. This is everything I know.

2

In 1946, during the Nuremberg trials of the Nazi officers, the name Klingsor is uttered in public for the first time by Wolfram von Sievers, president of the Society for German Ancestral Heritage and director of a branch of the Ahnenerbe, the secret scientific research division of the SS.

1. When the prosecutors question him, Von Sievers testifies that the SS would periodically send him "Jewish-Bolshevik" skulls so that his laboratory might carry out genetic investigations. This business was made possible by an agreement Von Sievers had previously signed with the Reichsführer SS Heinrich Himmler.
2. When asked explicitly if he knows how the SS obtained the skulls, Von Sievers replies that they were those of former prisoners of war on the Eastern Front, who had been killed expressly for this purpose.
3. When pressed by the judges, Von Sievers talks a bit about phrenology and the physical evolution of ancient races. He mentions the Toltecs and Atlantis, the superiority of the Aryan race, and cites the names of magical realms like Agartha and Shambhala. He then states that his assignment was to determine the inferiority of the Semitic people on the basis of their physiological development. He notes that his perspective was purely eugenic: His task was simply to find out how to eliminate defects.

4. When questioned as to how his experiments were underwritten, Von Sievers responds that the SS supplied all the necessary financing, which was provided via the Research Council of the Reich, an entity under the supervision of Reichsmarschall Hermann Goering.

5. As a final note, Von Sievers adds that all "special" projects were to be approved by the Führer's scientific adviser, who operated under the code name of Klingsor. Later on, he will deny having said this.

3

Who is this Von Sievers? A very good question. For practical purposes, he was just another member of the Ahnenerbe, though it is worth mentioning that he was also a discreet member of the Thule Bund, a society whose roster also included Alfred Rosenberg, Heinrich Himmler, and Adolf Hitler himself, among others.

And what was the Thule Bund? According to ancient legend, Thule was a long-lost island in the waters of the North Atlantic, home to a race of "superhumans" who were ancestrally linked to modern-day Germans. Founded by Count Heinrich von Sebottendorf, the Thule Bund served as a branch of the German Order, one of those secret, ultranationalist German societies which had been in existence for more than a century—its members fought against Napoleon in the 1800s and had managed to survive during the reign of Kaiser Wilhelm. Von Sebottendorf's real name, however, was Rudolf Glauer, a German adventurer who had been living in Turkey since 1901, thanks to the lenient Turkish laws, and was adopted by the real Count Von Sebottendorf.

The raison d'être of this secret society was to determine the true origins of the German and, generally speaking, Aryan race. Its headquarters were located in Munich, where Heisenberg and I both lived, as did the forty lifetime members who comprised the sole decision-making body within the society. At the beginning of the century, two names in this group stood out: Dietrich Eckart and Karl Haushofer. It was rumored that the members of the Thule Bund practiced black magic and demonic arts, but most of all they were devoted to studying—and glorifying—the spiritual foundations of the pre-Christian Germanic peoples.

The end of 1918, with the Great War reaching a close, was one of the worst moments in German history. Around this time, the Thule Bund allocated a substantial sum of money to two men: Anton Drexler, a former locksmith for the railway company, and Karl Harrer, who until then had been a sports journalist. With this money, Drexler and Harrer were to establish a new political party that would fight for the restoration of the Reich government. On January 5, 1919, the German Workers' Party (DAP) was established, its platform a blend of fierce nationalism mixed in with some socialist tendencies. According to its basic operating principles, the party was to be an organization without class divisions, with only German leaders at its head.

On the invitation of Dietrich Eckart, one of his only friends in Munich at the time, Adolf Hitler attended one of the first public meetings of the DAP, held near the Sternecker brewery. In those days, the DAP had only forty members, just like the Thule Bund previously. By the time Hitler joined its ranks, the party had swelled to about one hundred and fifty.

Eckart, who had translated Ibsen's *Peer Gynt,* was perhaps the first poet of national socialism. One of his poems trumpets the arrival of a national savior (later identified as Hitler), and another coins the term *Deutschland erwache*—"Germany awake"—which would later become the Nazi battle cry. The Austrian Guido von List, another member of the Thule Bund and Hitler's compatriot, would be the first to use the four-armed swastika as a symbol of purification. Later on, it would be adopted as the party's official emblem.

On February 24, 1920, the DAP became the German National Socialist Party, and hundreds of unemployed workers joined its ranks. In July of 1921, Hitler became its president, and on the twenty-ninth of that same month he was first identified as "our Führer" in the *Völkische Beobachter.*

During this time, several men who would soon become extremely prominent party figures joined the ranks: Alfred Rosenberg, who would become the official Nazi party philosopher; Erwin von Scheubner Richter, Hitler's close friend at the time; Walther Richard Rudolf Hess, a political science student at the University of Munich and a favored disciple of Karl Haushofer, geopolitical expert and member of the Thule Bund; and Ernst Röhm, future organizer of the party's storm troopers, the SA (Sturmabteilung). Later on, in 1922, Hitler would make the acquaintance of several other men who would ultimately follow him to the bitter end: Hermann Goering, the legendary commander of the Richthofen squadron during the Great War, decorated with the Order of Merit for his heroic acts; and Dr. Joseph Goebbels.

In 1923, Eckart became one of the first martyrs of the Nazi cause. It happened during the time when the communists, led by the Jewish Kurt Eisner, attempted to establish a Soviet-style conciliar republic in Munich. A wave of terror and violence quickly swept through Bavaria. Eckart was the captain of one of the many paramilitary groups fighting for control of the city, and after several attempts, his battalion managed to corner Eisner and kill him in a shoot-out on the streets of Munich. But Eckart would not have long to savor the victory. That December, he would die of complications resulting from having ingested mustard gas during a confrontation with the police. They say that the last thing he said before dying was "Follow Hitler! He dances to the melody that I wrote! Don't cry for me: for my influence upon the course of history will be far greater than that of any other German alive!"

4

When Hitler finally took control of Germany, he called upon Himmler to create a secret research division whose job would be to undertake scientific studies in three specific areas: the study of race and human genotypes (based on Rosenberg's theories); the study of racist geopolitics of Haushofer; and finally, Hörbiger and Wessell's *Welteislehre,* also known as the "eternal ice" doctrine, which stated that, at one time, Europe was completely encased in ice. This division would fall within the aegis of Himmler's ample security structure, better known as the SS.

This research division, a branch of the SS known as the Ahnenerbe, was under the direct supervision of the Reichsführer-SS, and its staff included scores of biologists, pathologists, historians, sociologists, psychiatrists, and physicists. Hundreds of experiments—many of them with human subjects—were performed by this department throughout the course of the war. The majority of them failed, however, or at least that is what they say now.

The Ahnenerbe's financial resources came out of the Reich Research Council, controlled for several years by the physicist Johannes Stark. After Stark fell from grace, his position was initially filled by the minister of education, Bernhard Rust, but he was later replaced by Reichsmarschall Hermann Goering. For the entire duration of the war, the various council officials and the Ahnenerbe were almost constantly locked in a bitter battle of wills. Stark was a man committed to the Nazis, but he was also an illustrious physicist, a Nobel laureate. And not only did he regard the Ahnenerbe experiments as low-priority and irrelevant, he also considered them scientifically inadmissible. In large part, his dismissal from the RFR could be construed as a consequence of his "lack of sensitivity" in the allocation of resources to the SS.

Later on, the Rust and Goering administrations faced the same conflict, which was more or less amicably resolved toward the end of the war. To resolve the issue, Himmler decided to appoint a scientist—approved by Goering—to serve as a general adviser to the RFR. According to the agreement signed by the two men, this adviser's job was to decide how much money would be allocated to each new project presented before the council. The honorable character, the ideological commitment, and the personal prestige of this individual were such that his judgment was considered beyond reproach. After several meetings, Goering and Himmler finally came to an agreement as to who should occupy this most privileged position. To ensure the smooth execution of this special assignment, they decided that the scientist's name should remain a secret. However, his great power and influence led the members of the council to refer to him by the code name Klingsor.

Dialogue IV:
On the Death of Truth

A physicist—a pure soul, dedicated to revealing the mysteries of the universe, a person removed from all earthly concerns and focused entirely on the purity of his theoretical world, yet one who aids in the extermination of millions of men and women. The notion of Klingsor—of the countless Klingsors that have ever lived—is troubling, for this rather shocking contradiction. It seems like some sort of anomaly, a genetic error, an unforeseeable aberration.

I, however, find the connection between science and crime perfectly natural. Allow me to explain. Science, by definition, does not know ethical or moral boundaries. It is nothing more than an elaborate system of signs that allows man to comprehend the world around him and to act upon it. For the physicist—for *all* physicists, and for mathematicians, biologists, and economists as well—human death is simply one among the thousands of phenomena that take place every single day in our universe.

"Klingsor." I enunciate the syllables with fear, with reverence, with disgust. "He is the one responsible for my being here, Doctor. And who else but Heisenberg would have thought to hide behind that name? He, too, was born in Munich, where the Thule Bund and the Nazis came of age, and despite his initial rejection of the National Socialism movement (inspired, to a large degree, by his hatred for Stark) he eventually became the golden boy of both Himmler and Goering, who, as I mentioned already, lavished him with all sorts of special privileges, grooming him to become the scientific mastermind behind the German atomic project. It all fits, Doctor."

I know Ulrich is trying to be friendly with me, but I can't help detecting a peculiar twitch on his face. All psychiatrists have it, it's a universal occupational hazard: The minute someone mentions the word *conspiracy* they immediately think *paranoia,* with that useless, textbook reasoning of theirs.

"Klingsor is the reason I am here," I repeat to Ulrich, to ensure that my accusation remains clear.

"And how is that?" he asks me, indulging me for a moment.

"It's a very painful story, Doctor, brought about by an even more terrible, uncontrollable chain of events."

I try to sit up a little, but I can only hold my neck up for a few seconds at a time.

"I'm listening."

"I was married, you know. To a marvelous woman named Marianne. I met her through Heinrich, who was married to a friend of hers named Natalia. None of this was very simple, Doctor. You know how it is: Families are never very simple, are they?"

My tongue makes a great effort to slide through my mouth, touching all the broken teeth I have left, until it finally manages to move in the direction I wish it to. My voice sounds like a howl, a capitulation, a death sentence.

"Klingsor took her away from me."

"Who? Your wife?"

"No, Natalia."

The Betrayal

1

The first, most important thing I should say—well, perhaps it won't seem so to you, but to me, it is the only transcendent thing in all of this—is that I loved her. I loved her more than anything, more than myself. Of course, more than my country. More than God. More than science. More than truth. And, logically, more than my friends.

I would have done anything to be with her. Anything. And I don't regret it. It is the only thing in my life that I don't regret.

2

"What's going on?" That was Marianne's voice, the morning shortly before I was scheduled to meet with Heisenberg at the Kaiser Wilhelm Institute.

She hadn't been herself for months, but it wasn't because she suspected anything about my relationship with Natalia. No, it was Heinrich—now that he was so close by, she was wracked with guilt about everything. Her face had acquired a yellowish hue, she had lost at least fifteen pounds, and two giant circles framed her eyes, making her look eternally exhausted, which was probably the case.

"What are you talking about?" I didn't want to talk to her; I took a quick gulp of coffee and got up to leave.

"With all those meetings." An accusatory pause followed. "With Heinrich."

So that was it. She wasn't really worried about what was discussed at those meetings—she was worried that our lover's husband was spending so much time with me. Poor Heinrich: attentive, grateful, and utterly unaware of the little get-togethers his wife, Marianne, and I had enjoyed in our house for so many months. I was in no position to criticize her, but this tiny display of pettiness made me despise her even more. Once you decide to be an unrepentant sinner, the last thing you want is to tolerate someone else's guilt or weakness.

"It's better if you don't know." I had thought that answer out carefully, leaving it deliberately ambiguous just to torture her a little bit more.

"I'm worried," she insisted.

"We all are, Marianne. We're in the middle of a war, we're being bombed twice a day, we're lucky just to be alive."

"You know what I'm talking about," she needled me. "You're making me worried. So is he."

I was reaching the end of my rope. What did she think? That because of my rekindled friendship with Heinrich, I was going to go and confess everything? Tell him that all the people he loved the most had conspired to deceive him all this time?

"Don't worry," I answered. "My relationship with Heinrich is strictly professional."

"Professional?" It wasn't the right word, of course, but I couldn't think of any other way of saying it.

"Polite, nothing personal at all," I added. "We get together with friends, never alone, always to discuss other things."

"What things, Gustav?"

"It's not your concern, Marianne," I said, ending the discussion. "For your own good, it's not your concern."

3

It is still hard for me to figure out how I managed to see Natalia during that time. Ever since being transferred to General Olbricht's staff, Heini had moved back home to Berlin, and even though most of his time was taken up by his professional obligations, he did try to spend his free moments with his wife, who now seemed painfully distant. She had no other choice but to respond to him. After all, she was still the long-suffering wife of a military officer, the eternal Penelope awaiting the return of her Ulysses each time he completed another tour of duty.

"I have to see you," I said to her, forsaking all decency, decorum, and basic precaution. "I have to see you today."

"But, Gustav—"

Natalia would always protest at first, but usually she would eventually give in and agree to see me. I would leave work at the most unthinkable times, mumbling something about a secret meeting—one of the few advantages of my position—and I would run to her house, throwing all caution to the wind. On a subconscious level, maybe I wanted people to find out what was going on between us—something she pointed out to me on one occasion.

Be that as it may, we enjoyed nothing more than a few brief moments of glory which were followed by hours and even days of anguish and torment for the both of us. I needed her more and more all the time: the scent of her skin, the aroma of her saliva, the insistence of her kisses. Compared with her, my wife was nothing more than a sorry reminder of paradise lost.

"When can the three of us be together again, like before?" Marianne would ask me in our occasional moments of intimacy, pressing herself against my chest—I really didn't know how to get rid of her—and crying silently for a while before begging for my forgiveness.

"There's nothing to forgive," I would say, and I was basically telling the truth though she interpreted the comment as condescending. "I'm as guilty as you are."

"Maybe it's better that way," she would say after a few minutes, calming down a bit. "To act as if nothing ever happened, as if it were all just a crazy fantasy, some kind of impossible dream, don't you think?" I would say nothing. "In a way, things have fallen back into place: Natalia and Heinrich, you and me . . ."

We both knew that was an abominable lie, but we did all we could to cling to those illusions, as if we had decided to surrender and obey the rules of the hypocritical society we had been born into, the society we had once tried to defy.

"Yes," I lied. "Yes," I lied again. "It's for the best."

4

"What if someone finds out?" Natalia trembled at the mere thought.

"Like who?" I asked rather cynically.

"Either one of them," she said, kissing me on the neck.

I despised talking about it, but by now, it was practically our only topic of conversation.

"It wouldn't be so terrible if Marianne were to find out," I commented cruelly.

"Why?"

"She would never have the nerve to tell anyone. And even if she did, it wouldn't be too hard to change her mind—we could just invite her to join us one day."

"You're despicable!" Natalia cried, furious, and moved away from me.

"Am I? Heinrich is the real problem, and you know it."

"I know," she moaned. "I know he is. That's why he can never find out, Gustav. *Never.*"

Although I knew Natalia was right, it was still painful to acknowledge my role in the situation, obvious as it was. It's funny; at the time I was the one who wanted to hide, to keep Heini from finding out about us, yet I was nonetheless tormented by the fact that Natalia could never truly be mine. First I had to share her with Marianne and now I had to share her with Heini. I was sick of it.

"Do you love me?" It was unfair but I asked it anyway, despite the black-mail and cowardice inherent in such a question.

"If I didn't, I wouldn't be here with you" was all she said, in a stony voice. "I think you should go now."

5

It was the beginning of 1944, and the months raced by, swift and merciless, a constant reminder that the war was a lost cause. Or, to be fair, that the wars I was waging—my affair with Natalia, the conspiracy—were doomed to failure.

"What do you do? What do you and Heinrich do in those meetings?" Just like Marianne before her, now Natalia was the one who dared to ask the question.

"We're part of a study group." Natalia was harder to lie to. "We discuss lots of different issues. Each night one of the guests lectures on a specific topic and the rest of us listen and then comment on it," I lied.

"Tell me the truth, Gustav," Natalia said listlessly. "I beg you."

"I already told you," I insisted. "We talk about things, that's all."

"About killing Hitler, for example?"

Natalia's sarcasm hit me like a bucket of ice water.

"If Heinrich told you that, he's an idiot!" I exclaimed, jumping up. "Don't ever say such nonsense again, Natalia."

"He hasn't said a thing, Gustav."

"That's even worse," I said, dumbfounded.

She began to cry. I hugged her tightly, but it didn't help. She hadn't quite said as much, but she now knew that the two men she loved most in the world were in serious danger. A clear and present danger, far worse than any battles or bombs.

"I'm sorry," I said, trying to console her. "I didn't mean to talk that way."

"It's all right." She wiped away her tears with the back of her hand. "Really . . . I guess I should feel proud—" Her voice broke. "It's just . . ."

She started to cry again, unable to finish the sentence.

"I understand," I lied.

"Forgive me," she said, then paused before speaking again. "When will you do it?"

"Please, it's better if we don't talk any more about it."

"I just want to know how much more time—" She suddenly stopped herself, realizing what she was about to ask. "Forget it, Gustav. I'd rather not know."

6

Perhaps it was fear, or mistrust, or a sudden change of heart, or indifference, but one thing was for sure: Around March of 1944, my attendance at the conspirators' ritual meetings grew spotty. There hadn't been any kind of falling-out—I just slowly began to distance myself from them, the way you do with someone when you fall out of love, or lose interest in a cause you know is already lost.

But that doesn't mean I dropped out of the plan entirely: I had given them my word, and I fully intended to honor it, though whenever possible I would do what I could to get out of those interminable nighttime meetings. Instead of listening over and over again to the civic and moral arguments against Hitler's rule, instead of getting involved in heated debates about the kind of explosives to be used, or the proper procedure for staging Operation Valkyrie (for which I was useless, anyway), I would retreat to Natalia's warm embrace, even if only for a few minutes.

"I can't go today," I apologized to Heinrich. "I have a lot of work, and if I don't hand my reports in on time, people will start asking questions about what I've been doing."

"Understood," he said tersely. "Don't worry, I'll let you know about any decisions we make."

"Thank you, Heinrich. I'll see you next week, then."

And then, as he was apologizing to his friends on my behalf, I would slip in between the sheets of his bed. That unspeakable betrayal afforded me the most airtight of alibis: I could tell Marianne that I was with Heinrich, and at the same time I could be sure that he would be out of his house for a few hours, at least. It was the perfect opportunity; I couldn't pass it up, as much as my conscience objected. God bless Stauffenberg, Olbricht, and Tresckow for giving me the chance to enjoy a few hours in the arms of the woman I loved.

7

"Why don't you try?" insisted Heinrich.

"Heisenberg is a coward," I retorted. "He won't lift a finger for us. The only thing he wants is to be left alone."

"I think you're being hard on him. People tell me that he's actually a very reasonable man. And from what I've heard, he's had his own problems with the Nazis."

"Maybe so," I tried to explain. "But that's ancient history. It's been years since Johannes Stark and those *Deutsche Physik* lunatics, those Nazi fanatics, went after him. Things are different now. It took awhile, but Heisenberg has been reeducated—otherwise they never would have given him the Kaiser Wilhelm Institute or the chair at the university. Don't you read the newspaper? He gives lectures all over the place—Denmark, Hungary, Holland—he's like some sort of German cultural ambassador they send around to the occupied territories."

Images swirled around in my head: the photographs of the German boy-wonder in the company of his foreign colleagues—with Møller in Copenhagen after taking over Bohr's institute; with Kramers in Leyden after the Nazis shut down the university and arrested hundreds of students for protesting the deportation of the Jews.

"No," I insisted. "I highly doubt he would ever agree to help us."

"But General Beck sees him every week at the Wednesday Circle, and he says that Heisenberg talks about Schimpanski in the worst possible terms." I, meanwhile, allow an incredulous expression to come across my face. "You're the one who works with him—at least give it a try."

"All right," I finally say, reluctantly. "I'll try."

8

"Marianne telephoned me this morning," Natalia said abruptly.

"What does she want?" I felt a sudden rage come over me, as if she had done something wrong.

"She asked me over to your house."

"Now Marianne's the one trying to take advantage." I practically spit out the words.

Natalia got out of bed and began to get dressed.

"She asked me to come over this afternoon," she answered calmly. "She said she would try and convince you to get out of work for a few hours. She wants the three of us to be together again—a farewell, she called it. She didn't sound well, Gustav. I think she needs us."

"She needs *you.*"

I couldn't believe it. Marianne had gone behind my back. Did she really plan to call me? Or would she just tell Natalia that I hadn't been able to get away from the office so that she could be alone with her?

"What did you say to her?"

"That I didn't know if I could make it," Natalia said. "I told her that Heinrich sometimes comes home unexpectedly, and that I want to be home just in case."

"How did she take it?"

"Badly, I guess." Natalia was clearly at wits' end; she had simply had enough of all the risks and all the pressure. "She's my friend, Gustav. I miss her."

"She loves you," I said, furious.

"I know."

"But you don't love her."

"Not in the same way."

"Because you love *me,* isn't that right?"

9

The Allied invasion of Normandy arrived like the fulfillment of a curse foretold. It was the beginning of the end. Only a few weeks later we would realize that the sheer number of British and American troops—not to mention the French, who had recently joined their cause—would be impossible to fight. Defeat was imminent, we all knew it—ministers, generals, soldiers, women, everyone. And anyone who thought otherwise was just blinded by

Hitler's rhetoric. "The Führer won't allow Germany to sink: he'll turn the war around," they said. But how? "With one of his *Wunderwaffen*," replied the most gullible of his followers. "With bombs that can destroy whole cities!" If they only knew what sorry condition the *Wunderwaffen* was in! If they only knew that by now it would be impossible to build a reactor, much less a bomb.

I tried to approach Heisenberg on several occasions, to talk with him in private, but somehow I would always invent some excuse to postpone our meeting. He wasn't my friend—I don't think he was capable of friendship, really. Of the few occasions we had ever met in the past, we had discussed only the most trivial of matters. In a sense, this meeting would have been much easier if we hadn't known one another at all.

"Might we chat for a moment?"

"Certainly, Links. What can I do for you?"

"I'd rather speak to you in private, if you don't mind."

"I'll wait for you in my office at noon," he said suspiciously.

"Thank you, Professor."

At twelve noon on the dot, I appeared at his office.

"We have several friends in common, Professor," I began as I sat down in front of him. I felt like a student taking an oral exam. "General Beck, Dr. Sauerbruch, Mr. Popitz . . ."

I was hoping that this list would be enough to establish a certain rapport, but Heisenberg didn't seem to get the message, or else ignored it.

"Yes, I know them" was all he said.

"Well, I'm here today on behalf of them, in a way," I went on.

"They asked you to come and see me?"

"Well, not exactly, Professor." I couldn't seem to find the right words.

"So . . . ?"

"I'll try to be direct. You hate the Nazis as much as we do."

Heisenberg's normally sedate hands flew up, as if jolted by a sudden electric shock. Obviously, he was not interested in discussing this sort of thing with someone he hardly knew.

"Excuse me, Professor," he said curtly. "I don't know what you want from me, but I'm not interested in discussing this topic any further."

"We have to do something for our country," I insisted. "This might be our last chance, Professor. We need to be able to count on you."

"I don't know what you're talking about, Professor Links," he finished. "I am going to act as though this conversation never happened. You are an able mathematician and I am glad to have you working with me, but I prefer to stay out of politics. We are scientists. The only thing that should concern us is science, the future of science in our country. We will be performing a far greater service to our nation if we continue to work toward this goal and not get involved in any other kind of activity. Now, if you'll please excuse me, I must return to my laboratory."

That was it. A few days later, Adolf Reichwein decided to try again. He, at least, had become friendly with Heisenberg through the Wednesday Circle. Heisenberg admitted to him that he supported the conspiracy on a moral level but that he could not get involved with any violence. That he was a scientist, etc.

Shortly thereafter, as I mentioned previously, Reichwein was detained by the Gestapo.

10

"Gustav, do you have a second?" It was Marianne.

"What do you want?"

"I called Natalia this morning."

"Did you? What for?"

"I told her we wanted to see her. To come over one of these afternoons. For a kind of farewell. You could ask special permission, or something."

"Or something," I repeated.

"What do you think?"

"So now you've decided what I should do with my life," I reproached her. "Is that right?"

"I thought you'd be glad."

"And how did she respond?"

"She said she'd think about it. Heinrich—"

"Right, Heinrich!" I shouted. "Don't you realize you're putting her in danger? That you're making her take risks she shouldn't take? Heini is with her now, here, in Berlin. They sleep together every night. They're husband and wife. Don't you get it?"

"But I thought—"

"You're so selfish!" I screamed, utterly unrepentant, without a shred of pity for poor Marianne. "And you call yourself her best friend, you say you love her? If you really loved her you'd leave her in peace."

"I'm sorry, Gustav." Once again those damned tears began to roll down her cheeks. "I didn't mean to . . ."

11

The next morning, Heinrich came to find me in my office, something he'd never done before. As soon as I saw him there, as soon as I distinguished those features in that uniform, waiting for me in the doorway, I thought it was all over. He had discovered us and was here to break my legs. Or maybe Natalia, in a fit of honesty, had finally confessed to him. His silhouette, bisected by the sunlight falling across him, seemed like that of an executioner edging closer and closer to his victim. I almost wanted to pray, or hunt for a weapon; do *something*.

"What's wrong?" he said. "You're pale. Has something happened?"

"Nothing, nothing." My voice cracked. "What brings you here?"

"I need to talk to you for a few minutes, Gustav. It's urgent."

"All right, let's go somewhere safe."

I took him to one of the institute's labs, not far from where Heisenberg and his team worked.

"So?"

"Well, since you weren't at the meeting yesterday, I came to tell you. It's set."

"For when?"

"July 15."

"So soon?"

"Stauffenberg thinks it isn't soon enough," he replied.

"And you?"

"I'll stay with Olbricht to wait for news from Wolf's Lair," he said calmly, as if talking about the most routine, trivial matter. "That's when Operation Valkyrie will be put into action. Stay on the alert."

"Don't worry about me," I stammered. "I'll be ready."

12

Once I knew the date, I felt as though I'd been issued a death sentence, like a prisoner who has just been told the hour of his execution. I sincerely doubted the coup could succeed, and I know many of my fellow conspirators felt the same way, although they never would have admitted it. Even if we did pull it off, it would still mean, in some way or another, the end of my life as I knew it. The end, perhaps, of my affair with Natalia. And that was what frightened me the most: I only had two days left, two more days by her side. . . .

Our rendezvous on the thirteenth and fourteenth were perfectly dreadful. I struggled not to show any signs of panic, but Natalia had a sixth sense when it came to danger or threats lurking nearby. She said nothing—she knew I'd never answer her, anyway—and so we both feigned a tranquillity and peacefulness that neither of us really felt. We hardly said a word to each other; there was a wall now, an inevitable icy remove between us. We kissed each other only in the most perfunctory fashion, as if it were more obligation than pleasure, and we would return to our respective seats, separated and alone, like two strangers sharing a train compartment. A train that was about to derail. And we both knew it.

13

From the minute we woke up the morning of the fifteenth, Marianne also knew something serious was happening. Once again, I tried to keep her out of my various concerns. Every one of her questions and pleas felt like an invasion of privacy, a cruel and unwanted intrusion on my own quiet anguish.

"Don't worry," I said as I left. "I'll see you tonight."

"Are you going to another one of your meetings?"

"Don't wait up for me, Marianne," I said before leaving. "Try to sleep."

According to the plan, I was to stay in my office all morning, until someone made contact with me, and then I was to assume control of the Kaiser Wilhelm Institute, with or without Heisenberg's consent. The assassination was to take place at noon. If everything went according to plan, the coup would extend to the rest of the country by one or two in the afternoon.

By three o'clock, nothing had happened. No message, no signal, no warning. I started to get impatient. Finally, at 3:30 I telephoned General Olbricht's office. Heinrich himself answered the phone.

"Impossible" was all he said, the disappointment echoing in his voice. "We'll have to change it for another day." And he hung up.

I was desperate. There is nothing worse than having the ground move beneath you when you are already trembling with doubt. Without thinking twice, I ran out in search of Natalia.

"Are you crazy?" she said as she opened the door. "What are you doing here? Heini could come home at any moment."

"No," I said. "I just saw him. He'll stay right where he is all afternoon."

Reluctantly, Natalia let me in.

"For once and for all, will you finally tell me what's going on? Has something bad happened?"

"No. Not yet, at least."

"Thank God," she exclaimed, sinking into one of the chairs in the living room.

I walked over to her and began to cover her face with gentle kisses: on her temples, her closed eyelids, her eyebrows, the corners of her mouth. Suddenly, she began to cry. Never before had I seen her this inconsolable, this vulnerable.

"Are you all right?" I asked, kneeling down at her side upon the rug.

"No," she answered. "I'm not. Not at all. Gustav, I'm pregnant."

She said it just like that. Suddenly, without any warning at all—a sad, pain-filled confession. Had the circumstances been otherwise, I would have asked who the father was, but I knew. We had known it for years: I was sterile. In her womb, Natalia was carrying the child of my friend. Her husband. My rival.

"How long have you known?"

"A week, maybe more."

"So why are you telling me now, Natalia?"

"I'm sorry."

"You're sorry?"

"Yes."

"So, are you still—" I stopped myself. There was no need to torture myself anymore. The situation was crystal-clear.

I hated her. I hated her and I loved her. I had respected Heinrich, yet I had deceived him at the slightest provocation. I wanted to spend the rest of my life at Natalia's side and at the same time I wanted to kill myself. I could have done anything right then, I could have made one of a thousand different decisions, but instead, without realizing it, moved by self-pity and bitterness, by my loyalty and the intensity of my feelings, I did the very worst thing possible. Ever so delicately, I gathered Natalia in my arms, as if she were a little girl, a little, wounded child, and carried her into the bedroom. Gently, as always, I removed her clothes, kissing every last bit of bare skin and showering her with my tenderness, determined to prove to her that despite everything, I still loved her.

14

A new date was set for the coup: July 20. This was our last chance, we couldn't postpone it any longer now. General Keitel had harshly reprimanded Olbricht for having suspended Operation Valkyrie for no good reason, and one more wrong move would spell disaster, for it would raise far too much suspicion at this point. It was now or never.

On the night of July 18, I couldn't get out of our last meeting, which was held at Stauffenberg's house on Tristanstraße, though I contributed little to the discussions and strategy planning. The general mood was somber, almost devastated. Every so often someone would say something clever, an uplifting quote or a snappy comment, to alleviate the tension and boost the spirits in the room.

As the colonel and his guests discussed the final details of the plan, Heinrich dragged me into an adjacent room so we could speak privately.

"I have some extraordinary news to tell you," he said. "I'm going to be a father, Gustav."

"Congratulations," I said, automatically extending my hand.

"Aren't you happy for me?"

"Of course, of course . . . it's just so unexpected." I was trying hard to be polite. "Not now, that is. I mean, just look at the situation out there."

"General Olbricht has decided to send me to Paris—I leave tomorrow."

"So you won't be here when—?"

"I'm afraid not." His tone of voice was monotonous and dry, without any inflections whatsoever. "I think I have been chosen to act as General Stülpnagel's contact."

"I'm sorry to hear that."

"Maybe it's better this way."

Once more, Heinrich was off. And once more, Natalia would be alone, which meant that she would need me again. His words gave me a ray of hope.

"I've seen you."

At first, I didn't understand what he was talking about. The comment, however, seemed to come straight from the very core of his soul, like some kind of uncontrollable outburst, a sudden, involuntary reflex that had nothing to do with me at all.

"What?"

"I've seen the two of you, Gustav," Heinrich said. "You and Natalia. The afternoon of the first attempt."

"I don't know what you mean, Heini. You must be mistaken. . . ." I was trembling now.

"I'd suspected it for some time," he said, ignoring what I'd just said. "But then, after Marianne called, I had no other choice but to see if it was true."

"Marianne?" I nearly jumped out of my skin at that.

"She was very worried about you. She told me that you seemed especially tense recently. One day she came to the institute looking for you but you weren't there. That was the only clue I needed. From the instant I began walking home, I knew what I was about to discover, and I wasn't wrong."

"This is all a big misunderstanding, Heinrich," I said, stalling for time.

"It doesn't matter now, Gustav." Heini's words hurt terribly. "Under any other circumstances I would have broken your neck, my friend, but not now. Just promise me that you'll look after her if you make it out alive and I don't, all right? That you'll take care of Natalia and my child. All right?"

"Heini, for God's sake."

"Do you promise?" It wasn't a plea, it was an order.

"Yes, I promise."

He didn't offer his hand for me to shake. He didn't even look at me. The next day he boarded a train for Paris.

15

I don't think I need to repeat the fateful events of July 20. All I can add is that, once again, I took my position at the institute and waited for word. And just like before, the wait was agonizing. After several long hours, once again it seemed that nothing was going to happen. Again. Another delay, another error—what was it this time? I had no way of knowing. I made contact with General Olbricht's office at the Bendlerstraße headquarters. An official, whose voice I didn't recognize, informed me that in fact Hitler had been killed in a bombing. What was I to do now? Heisenberg wasn't even in the building—he had gone straight to his family in Bavaria.

Overcome by panic, I ran for cover at Natalia's house, instead of commandeering the institute in the name of my fellow conspirators. I had to see her, I could only think of her. Nothing else mattered to me—not Hitler, not my country, not the coup, not Marianne, not Heinrich. Only Natalia.

"Do you know what's happened?" Natalia asked me as soon as I arrived. This time the door had opened instantly.

"Of course. But I needed to see you."

"Heini and I talked before he left."

"And so you know?"

Natalia nodded mournfully.

"What are you going to do, then?" I pressed.

"There's only one thing *to* do, Gustav," she replied. "I have to stay here with my family."

"What does that mean?"

"Go home to yours, Gustav. Marianne needs you more than I do."

"Natalia, you can't be serious."

"I've never been more serious in my life, Gustav," she whispered. "I love you, you know that, but for once we should do the right thing. Go . . . please."

"Forever, is that what you mean?"

"Yes, Gustav."

16

I left Heinrich's house furious. Or worse, devastated. My mind couldn't focus on anything. The world—my world—had suddenly come crashing down around me, and there was nothing I could do about it. I can't even remember what I did in the many long hours that followed. When I finally heard the radio broadcast announcing the failed coup attempt and the Führer's survival, I was hardly surprised: That day was destined to go down in history as one giant failure. A stupid illusion. A lost opportunity. A lie.

From that moment on, whether repentant or not, we would all be branded as traitors. I had been one for a while now, anyway.

"My God!" Marianne exclaimed. "What's going to happen to us?"

By the time I learned of the coup's horrifying final chapter—the deaths of Stauffenberg, Olbricht, Beck, and everyone else that same evening, and of Himmler's fast and furious witch-hunt—I had no other choice but to tell her the truth. For once, I actually believed she had a right to know what was going on.

"Why didn't you tell me before, Gustav?" she asked in a maternal tone of voice. "Now I understand why you've been so distant. I would have understood, my dear. You know I'll always be here for you."

"What for?" I retorted cruelly. "I finally tell you and all you can do for us is pray!" She was silent for a few minutes.

"What about Heinrich?"

"I don't know, we're still waiting to hear."

"Can I call Natalia?" I was waiting for her to ask that question.

"Yes," I replied. "Tell her that if she needs anything, she can count on us. And tell her to keep us informed."

After that, I began to pray, too.

17

I've already told the rest of the story. In early August, General Stülpnagel and several members of his unit—including Heinrich—were arrested and subjected to the most excruciating torture, lengthening the already-long list of traitors.

We all suffered terribly in the days that followed, teetering on the edge of madness, fearful as to what might happen to him (and to ourselves), but those days also offered what might have been a brief respite, one last chance to recover all that we had lost. The three of us—Marianne, Natalia, and I— once again found ourselves alone, but we barely even saw one another this time around. For those few agonizing days, Marianne and I wandered about the house like strangers, or ghosts—two bodies that barely acknowledged one another's existence, more absent than present. Natalia, meanwhile, had barricaded herself inside her house. Individually, we each contemplated the awful hopelessness of it all. And to my horror, I discovered that in the final hour there was nobody to free us from this terrible affliction.

18

Only two weeks after the coup attempt, the Reich *Gauleiter* gathered in the city of Posen to conduct the trial of the coup plotters, as ordered by the Reichsführer-SS Heinrich Himmler, who had been authorized by the Führer himself to supervise the proceedings.

Those men, the key operatives of the Nazi party in Germany, had been summoned to provide Himmler with detailed information regarding both the conspiracy and the sentences applicable to those involved. Their declarations would be a testament to the Führer's providential salvation as well as a threat to anyone even thinking of openly defying the authority of Hitler and his ministers. At one point, Himmler turned to them and said:

"This horrible crime is to be judged exactly as it would have been in ancient Germany. It is so repugnant in nature that the accused should be treated as severely as the ancient Teutonic tribes treated their own traitors. It is the only way to purify our nation and ensure a just punishment for these beasts." In his typically cold, calculating voice, he continued: "For this reason, in this case we will ascribe full responsibility not only to each individual but to their entire clan, in keeping with the historical practices of our people. You can read up about it in the Teutonic sagas. When they placed a family under the ban and declared it outlawed, or when there was a blood feud in a family, they were utterly consistent. When the family was outlawed and banned, they said"—Himmler now invoked the voice of a medieval soldier—" 'This man has committed treason; the blood is bad; there is traitor's blood in him; that must be wiped out.' And in the blood feud the entire clan was wiped out down to the last member. The family of Count Stauffenberg will be wiped out down to the last member . . . as well as that of the other traitors and every last member of their families. . . ."

After the execution of Stauffenberg and the trial of his brother Berthold, the Nazi authorities carried out Himmler's decree and arrested the remaining members of his family: a second brother, who was stationed in Athens, and knew nothing of the conspiracy; the wives and children of his two brothers, including a three-year-old boy; and even one of his ancient uncles, an eighty-five-year-old man. After authorities seized the family's possessions, Countess Stauffenberg and her mother were sent to the Ravensbrück camp, while the children were placed in an orphanage and rebaptized with the name of Meister. The families of Tresckow, Oster, Trott, Goerdeler, Schwerin, Kleist, Haeften, Popitz, and many others received similar punishments.

19

The last time I ever saw Natalia was just after Heini's arrest. She had been avoiding my calls, telling me she didn't want to ever see me again, and had given her maid specific instructions not to let me in the house. She ignored all my pleas, something I knew was terribly painful for her, so initially I decided to honor her wishes. I also knew how weak she was, and assumed she would eventually come running back to me and the solace that only I could give her.

But that afternoon I couldn't stand it any longer. I went to see her and, without waiting for her to say no, broke into the house. Natalia, hearing the noise, came downstairs wearing a tan robe. I looked at her impassive, silent figure at the top of the stairs—she looked like an ancient statue about to crumble into a million pieces. Her sweet gaze had all but disappeared, and in her eyes the only thing I could see was a dark void that I knew I couldn't fill. At that moment, I knew I had lost.

"Please leave, Gustav." Her voice was barely more than a whisper.

"I know how you feel," I said.

"Pain," she said, in a listless, stony voice, "is all I have left. And I won't let anyone—especially you—take it away from me, not now. I don't want to see you again, Gustav. Go."

"But I love you, Natalia!" I cried, although I knew that I wasn't really speaking to her anymore, but rather the shadow of who she had been. "Please forgive me."

On the seventeenth of August, a Gestapo unit forcibly entered Heini's house, just as I had done a few days earlier, and arrested Natalia, who defended her husband to the end. A few weeks later, just like her husband, Natalia was executed.

Her world shattered, Marianne was unable to endure any more. In one way or another, we had all abandoned her. By the time the war was over, I learned that she had finally put an end to her pain. I was the only survivor.

DIALOGUE V: ON THE PRIVILEGES OF INSANITY

LEIPZIG
NOVEMBER 9, 1989

This morning Ulrich has stopped by with good news. He tells me that my case is being reviewed (again) and that if everything goes well, they may very well release me, finally set me free. Freedom, after more than four decades of being locked up. Forty-two years surrounded by the howls of the insane, the lunatics and the psychopaths who have been my sole companions for so very long. Freedom at last.

All men of science—and in spite of it all, I still count myself among them—know that no theory is ever completely true, that no law is absolute, no statement is immune to the fickle nature of the passage of centuries. Even Newton couldn't elude criticism, revision, and ridicule; even the theories of Einstein and company were eventually added to history's list of brilliant mistakes, astonishing errors, and marvelous but false metaphors. And if science is nothing more than an amalgam of dubious propositions that require constant revision and correction, then how could I—and the age in which I live—be anything more than a jumble of ambiguities and shadowy, uncertain recollections? I have been called a hero, a criminal, and then a hero and then a criminal again—and a madman, too. Far too many transformations for the anonymous space inhabited by a single lifetime. If this could happen to me, I think it's safe to assume that the same fate could befall any and all the great heroes and villains of the world, as well as all the great ideas and great lies of our time.

Now, as we prepare to sing the anthem that will herald the end of days, the purification of humankind, and the definitive conclusion of the horrors—Hitler committed suicide over forty years ago, and the Soviet Union has only just begun to do the same—I can't help but wonder if this joy is really meant to last. I have a hard time swallowing the idea that suddenly the whole world is in harmony, that we can just blame all our present ills on yesterday's criminals. I hate to burst everyone's bubble, but all I can do now (and all I could do then, as well) is cling to the consolation that nothing is certain, that my role in history will never be fully ascertained. There will always exist the possibility—before, it was referred to as "hope"—that everything, absolutely everything has been one giant calculation error. And if that is true, then history will begin again.

"I've told you the whole truth," I say to Ulrich with a serenity I haven't felt for ages.

"The truth, the truth," he says, smiling. "Sometimes I wonder if you actually believe the things you say."

Like clockwork, the friendly, impressionable Ulrich slowly turns into the dark, insensitive doctor who cares little about my past or my suffering. At first I thought he was different, that he would sympathize with my pain, but I think he's been fooling me all along. His friendly bearing is just a strategy he uses to corner me, to prove me wrong.

"Professor," he says calmly, "something doesn't fit. I understand your suffering, but I get the sense there's something you still haven't told me. I still have nothing that explains why you've been locked up here for so many years."

"Are you sure you're not a mind reader?" I asked sarcastically. "You're right. There is a piece missing from the story. The missing link in all the betrayals. The worst betrayal of all. Would you like to hear about it?"

"Naturally, Professor."

"It was the end of the war, and I had lost everything. Everything I loved and everything I ever gave a damn about. My country. My mathematics. My home. And more than anything, I had lost Heini, Marianne, and Natalia. But then, someone came into my life. Someone who came to trust me. Someone who could be a substitute—if only for a brief while—for all those people I had loved and who were now dead. A new friend, you know? He was a physicist, and also a member of the American forces who liberated Germany from the clutches of the Nazis. And by one of those odd twists of fate, he needed me to help him get to Klingsor. His name was Bacon. Lieutenant Francis P. Bacon."

Klingsor's Revenge

1

Bacon felt like a puppet. How could he have been so stupid? Irene tried to apologize, to forge a kind of a belated bond of trust, but he wasn't that stupid. She had waited until the very last moment to confess her betrayal— only after she had been found out, when she had no other choice but to throw herself at his mercy.

"How could you?" he had said, trying to demonstrate both his outrage and the powerful feelings he still had for her. He didn't accuse her right away, nor did he threaten to turn her in. He merely repeated those ironic, pitiful words over and over again.

To offset the shame she claimed to feel, Irene resorted to tears. Tears always come in handy: transparent, wet, and cold. Easy to manipulate. A good round of sobbing can always subdue an unruly lover. "I'm sorry, I had no other choice." Didn't she? Couldn't she have told him at the beginning? Couldn't she have trusted him, if in fact she had ever really loved him?

"Who's paying you for the information?" Bacon continued, trying to hang on to at least a shred of dignity. "Who are you working for? The Russians?"

It was rather clear that Irene's best option right then was to shut up and nod her head, which she did. Words always have a destructive effect, they always come back to haunt you, whereas people generally forget pauses and silence.

"Why?" Lest we forget, Bacon was still so young, and he wanted to know. To understand her reasons. Well, what he really wanted was some way to justify his lover's actions. Maybe they threatened her, maybe she was in danger, maybe . . . Irene knew exactly how to respond: "Oh, I'm so, so sorry!" The same melodrama as always. But, my God, Frank was actually beginning to believe it. He *wanted* to believe it.

Next she employed a tactic which worked like a charm, despite being one of the oldest tricks in the book: "I was supposed to make you fall in love with me. But then everything changed. Everything started to go wrong, Frank. I

began to care about you but I had no other choice. I had to keep on working for them. They want Klingsor no matter what." A brilliant move on her
part, worthy of a true thespian. "Maybe it started out that way, but I never
dreamed I would end up falling in love with you. I swear! Every day was torture. I wanted to tell you but I was too scared. I should have done it a long
time ago, before you found out for yourself. I love you."

As the lieutenant listened to her, his heart leapt. How could she have used
such a common, mediocre strategy on him? Did she really think he was that
gullible? Was this her way of trying to seduce him? My Lord, if I could have
been there to shake some sense into the lieutenant, to make him see what a
third-rate confession that was. Unfortunately (and I speak from experience), love is a curse that clouds one's perceptions and destroys the soul. All
Bacon wanted to do right then was hold her tight against his body, shower
her with kisses, and make love to her as they never had before, and never
would again. But, of course, he was an intelligence officer and knew that this
was precisely the last thing he should do in these circumstances. But at what
point would his emotions overcome his restraint? At what point would his
passions conquer his intellect?

Frank stormed out, leaving her alone and (supposedly) crestfallen, and
took to the streets of Göttingen in search of an explanation, an answer, a
compromise. He loved her. He loved her more than anything.

2

"Frank, you're back!"

For the first time in a long time, the happiness in Irene's face was real. I
cannot confirm whether this was attributable to her profoundly intense
feelings for Lieutenant Bacon, or if she was moved by the faint hope that he
might absolve her. But one thing I am sure of is that upon seeing him, she
knew this would be her last chance to convince him and save not only their
relationship but her professional career and perhaps her life.

"You're back because you believe me, right?"

"I don't really know why I've come here, Irene," said Bacon, trying to
sound tough, but his presence alone was enough to indicate a certain degree
of weakness.

Irene tried to embrace him, but Bacon prudently stepped back. Any sign
of renewed enthusiasm was still a bit premature; Irene would have to be
patient on that count. She had almost won the game, and at this point she

would be foolish to get exasperated and risk everything just because of a meaningless rebuff on Bacon's part.

"Frank, I love you." Irene had done her homework; every step of the way she recited her lines like a true professional. The Soviets must have quite a manual on the seduction of foreign agents.

"I know," he lied.

If that wasn't a capitulation, it certainly sounded like one.

"What can I do to make you believe me?" Another chess-style move, and a very clever one at that, especially for a lady. Sacrifice a pawn early on in the game to gain a better position in the middle of the board.

"I want the truth, Irene." Well, what else would he want? "The *whole* truth."

The truth. Again. Why are we so obsessed with the truth—begging for it, asking for it, demanding it, when all we really want to do is confirm our own vision of reality?

"I'll tell you everything you want to know." She couldn't have phrased it better: Everything *you want:* I'll tell you what pleases you, what seduces you—not what I know or think. Not the truth.

"I'm listening," Bacon intoned his make-believe threat.

"You know, we're not all that different, Frank," she began. "We've both fought for the same thing—don't forget, the Nazis were our enemy as well. For years they were bent upon destroying everything I loved. When Hitler became chancellor, my father was arrested. He belonged to the German communist party, you know. He died in prison before the war even began. My family lost everything, Frank. I had to fight them, just like you did."

"And so what did you do?" The fact that Bacon was even showing an interest was yet another sign that he had fallen for it.

"When I was fifteen years old I paid a visit to a friend of my father's, a communist who had survived by going into hiding," said Irene, continuing her heroic account. "I told him I wanted to join the party. That man stood there, staring at me, surprised that a tall, skinny kid like me could be so impassioned about something. I'm sure he thought I would be far better off playing with my dolls. 'Are you sure?' he asked me. 'Yes, comrade,' I said, sure of myself. He took a few minutes to think it over and then, finally, he handed me a slip of paper with an address. 'Very well,' he said. 'Go see this man and he'll tell you what to do.'"

"And you went."

"I went!" Irene exclaimed. "It was in one of the worst neighborhoods in Berlin. A toothless, red-haired man answered the door. I gave him the slip of paper and waited. 'What do you want from us, little girl?' he asked, seeming uninterested. 'I want to join the party,' I said. He laughed so hard I could see all his broken, moldy teeth. 'I can see you've made up your mind, young lady. What's your name?' 'Inge,' I told him. That's my real name, Frank, Inge Schwartz. And he said, 'Well, from now on you will be called Irene Hofstadter. You can work for us, but we won't have you join the party. Nobody must find out about it, is that understood? You can be much more useful to us this way.' "

"So am I supposed to call you Inge from now on?" muttered Frank.

"Whatever you want, Frank."

"And of course, you don't have a son named Johann."

"No."

"So you became a spy."

"At first, I just worked for them as a messenger," Irene continued. "He would ask me to deliver packages to certain people, and for a while that was the extent of my work. I was kind of disillusioned, actually, but I was confident that in my own small way I was helping the cause. I was sixteen when they gave me my first real assignment. I no longer looked like such a little girl, and Karl, the redheaded man, told me that I was finally ready to take on more serious operations. 'You have become quite a lovely young woman,' he said. 'Perhaps we can turn that loveliness into a weapon.' "

During his years working for the OSS, Bacon had heard tales of the beautiful women who worked for the Soviets, but he had never imagined that he would actually get involved with one of them.

"So you seduced the men they assigned you to, to get information out of them."

"It was just my way of working for the cause. A mission like any other, Frank. Like yours, for example." Irene (or Inge) added this last bit slightly mockingly.

"It's hardly the same."

"And why not?" she countered. "You've used your scientific knowledge to serve your country. It's the same thing, Frank." Lieutenant Bacon, at this point, had no choice but to keep quiet and hear her out. "I fought for my ideals the best way I knew how—you can't condemn me for that. We had to stop Hitler, no matter what the cost."

"How many times did you do it?"

"What?"

"Sleep with men to fight for your ideals."

"What difference does that make?" By now, Inge (or Irene) had managed to take the upper hand in the conversation. "What do you want to hear, Frank? Dozens, dozens of times."

"The only thing you cared about was the fulfillment of your duties, is that right?"

"Yes. And I became one of the best, though I'm not particularly proud of it."

"So I suppose I should be flattered," said Frank sarcastically.

"The Russians consider you a top priority," she continued, unperturbed. "That's why they sent me, Frank. But I don't want to work for them anymore. For the first time in my life, I am truly in love."

"With me?" Frank laughed derisively. "Why should I be any different from the rest? Why on earth should I believe you?"

"Because I love you, don't you understand?" Inge insisted. "I would give everything up for you. Absolutely everything. The only thing I want is to be with you. We'll go wherever you want, Frank. What do I have to do to prove it?"

"Are you telling me that you're willing to betray the Russians?"

"Yes."

Bacon said nothing for a few minutes. Underneath it all, there was one thing he was terribly, horribly certain of: Even if she was blatantly, outrageously lying to him, he still loved her.

"Would you come with me to the United States? Would you come and work for my government?"

"I'll do whatever you ask," said Inge without missing a beat. She was determined to win.

"All right," mused Bacon.

A broad smile came across Inge's face. She had done it! Bacon finally allowed her to kiss him, passionately, furiously, gratefully.

"I'll say it again and again, Frank: I will do whatever you say."

"I would leave all this, too," Bacon ventured. "I'd go back to being a physicist. I'd go back to my numbers and my theories."

"Wouldn't that be marvelous." Inge was beginning to overdo it a bit.

"I'll take care of all the arrangements," said the lieutenant, batting his eyes at her. "We'll have to leave Germany as soon as possible."

Unfortunately, there was one small piece missing. A minor detail. One final task that she had to complete.

"Frank," she said, gently caressing his cheek. Practically on her knees, she faced her lover—her victim. "I'm afraid it isn't going to be that easy. I can't leave just like that. The Russians won't allow it; I know them. If we want to fool them, we're going to have to keep up the game to the end."

"What do you mean?"

"I have to fulfill the assignment they gave me. Otherwise they'll hound me for the rest of my life. They'd rather kill me first."

"Well, what on earth do they want?" exclaimed Bacon, indignant.

"The same thing you want," she said. Obviously. "Klingsor."

"But you and I don't even know who Klingsor is!"

"Oh, but we do, Frank."

"What are you talking about?"

"Links."

3

For several painful minutes now, Bacon had been debating this possibility in his mind, but even so it was a shock to hear it out loud.

"Gustav? We don't have a shred of evidence . . . Inge. Yes, maybe he botched the investigations, but that doesn't make him a criminal."

"Look, if I'm willing to risk telling you, it's because it's true, Frank," she said dramatically. "You've asked me to tell you the truth, and that's what I'm doing. All our investigations point to him."

"Look, I know you never warmed up to him; that's one thing. But to believe that he—"

"From the beginning he's tried to pin it on Heisenberg," Inge said. She wouldn't let up. "He had you start this endless investigation, which he carefully mapped out so that you would reach this ridiculous conclusion. Both you and I know that Heisenberg may have worked closely with the Nazis, but he was never one of them. He was conceited, proud, and maybe even disloyal, but he was not a monster. Links, however, was."

"Evidence! Evidence! Evidence!" Bacon exploded, exasperated. "Without proof your suspicions are worthless, Inge. I want one piece of evidence."

"I'll tell you everything I know, and you can decide for yourself." Inge was speaking faster now, as if she were nervous (which she wasn't). "What do you know about Links outside of what he himself has told you? The only thing that seems to absolve him is that he did participate in the July 20 coup attempt—and he wears that little fact like his personal coat of arms. Still, you have to consider that fact very carefully. Links says that when the Nazis got wind of the coup and snuffed it out, Heinrich von Lutz, his best friend and one of the brains behind the conspiracy, was responsible for his arrest. And do you know why? Because supposedly Lutz discovered that his wife, a woman named Natalia, had been having an adulterous affair with Links. I think the reverse is far more likely to be true: that Links turned Lutz in to get rid of his rival."

"All right, Inge, maybe you can prove that Links has lied. You can even prove something worse: that he betrayed his best friend not once, but twice—first when he slept with Lutz's wife and second, when he turned Lutz over to the authorities. I can hardly think of anything more despicable, and if it's true, he should pay for it." Bacon was doing his best to sound reasonable. "But his behavior, as depraved as it may be, is really a crime of passion. None of it proves that he's Klingsor."

"All right, then, listen to this," she countered. "After his arrest, Links was to have been tried and sentenced just like Heinrich and the rest of the conspirators. But it didn't work out that way. He claims that a stroke of luck saved his life: Precisely when his verdict was to be delivered, the People's Court was hit by an Allied bombing raid flying over Berlin. Judge Roland Freisler died instantly: A chunk of the ceiling cracked, fell, and split open his head. This fact is undisputed: In effect, yes, Freisler died and the sentencing of the accused was suspended indefinitely. However, according to the transcripts of the proceedings, only four men were to be sentenced that day and Links was not one of them. According to Links, he was shuttled from prison to prison, until an American unit finally freed him. But there isn't any proof of that. At the end of the war he just turned up in Göttingen, and nobody knew exactly where he had come from. Later on he underwent 'de-Nazification' by the British, but the Soviets always remained highly suspicious of him. Don't you get it? The most likely scenario is that he was never asked to participate in the coup—he learned about Lutz's involvement through Natalia, and used that information to do away with his rival."

"There's one thing that doesn't fit," Bacon observed. "Links told me that Natalia, Heinrich's wife, was detained and later executed. If Links is Klingsor, why wouldn't he have saved his lover's life?"

"I suppose that, in spite of it all, Links never dreamed Hitler's revenge would go so far. By turning Heinrich over to the Nazis, he played his best hand and lost. Perhaps that's why Marianne, Links's wife, ended up committing suicide in Berlin."

"All right, I admit your story makes sense, but that doesn't mean it's true." Bacon did try to defend me, almost to the end. "It's just one interpretation of the facts. There could easily be others. Imagine, for a moment, that maybe Links was able to save only his own life by ratting on his friend. That would explain everything, without necessarily making him Klingsor."

But Inge wouldn't let me off the hook. Not when she was so close to victory.

"Despite Hitler's supposed lack of interest in atomic research," she said, changing the topic, "the truth was, he needed to have a man in the project who could feed him constant progress reports. This information became more and more critical as the war ended. Remember, in 1945 the bomb was Hitler's last hope for achieving a victory. Who better for this job than Links? He worked with Heisenberg, he was totally up-to-date on the advances in the research." Inge could barely hide her animosity. "From the moment Heinrich and Natalia are detained, he disappears without a trace and then suddenly reappears, safe and sound, in Göttingen. Only someone like Klingsor, who had the power to pull strings within the Nazi administration—and who was also able to hide behind a facade of respectability—could have pulled it off. It all fits, Frank, admit it. The Russians think Links is Klingsor. If I don't turn him over, I'll be the one who has to pay for it. Won't you just let them decide? It's my only chance to save my *own* life."

A perfect story, clean and transparent, astonishingly cohesive. Too bad it was pure fiction. It was her best move yet.

"I can't." Thanks to his show of indignation, Bacon was able to hang on to one last shred of dignity. "If I give Gustav over to the Russians, not only will I betray him but I will be betraying my own country, too."

"I have to give them someone who could be Klingsor," she insisted. "It's our only hope."

"You're asking too much, Inge. That's a terrible ultimatum: you or him."

"I don't like it either, Frank. But I didn't make the rules of this game."

Of this game. For once she was speaking the truth.

"And what do they want me for?" Bacon was suddenly wild, his face red. "Do they need my approval?"

It took the lieutenant several minutes to regain his composure, but he eventually managed to control himself. He got up, as if waking up from a bad dream.

"This part of the country is under British control," Inge explained, trying to finish things up. "There's only one safe place to trap him."

"The home of an American soldier?" Bacon laughed maliciously. "Are you going to corner him in my own apartment?"

Inge chose to ignore this question.

"I love you, Frank" was all she said, beseechingly. "This is the only way we can be together. Have faith in me . . . have faith in our love."

4

For the first time in his life, Bacon had to make a life-or-death decision. Up until this very moment all he had ever done was run away from his problems—and himself, perhaps. Science had freed him from unhappiness; it had freed him from Von Neumann, from the romantic conundrum of Vivien and Elizabeth; the war had freed him from his difficulties in achieving success as a physicist; Inge had freed him from his loneliness; and I freed him from his responsibility in Germany. Over and over again he had behaved like a subatomic particle, subjecting himself to the imperious forces of bodies far more powerful than he.

But now, all of a sudden, everything was gone. That neat, tidy plan, that universe in which things just had a way of happening by cause and effect, was destroyed. Whom could he trust? Inge? God, no. Von Neumann? Einstein? Heisenberg? Me? He was out of excuses: This time, neither science nor love could save him. The pillars of his existence had come crashing down because he and everyone around him were trying so desperately to escape the truth. Bacon felt an odd combination of rage and sadness well up inside of him. Old Epimenides had gotten it wrong: It wasn't just Cretans. *All* men are liars. If there was really no such thing as an absolute truth (or worse, if Bacon just couldn't find out despite his best efforts), then how could he know if Inge loved him or if she was just using him again? How could he know if I had been a friend or a traitor, betraying him as I had betrayed Heinrich? How could he ascertain the depths of my iniquity? And how would he ever figure out what to do?

Suddenly he realized that the situation was, in fact, simple, painfully simple. For some reason, it was now his turn to decide what was true and what was false, what was virtue and what was vice.

Thanks to some kind of cosmic flight of fancy—call it ambiguity, call it uncertainty—he now faced the agonizing task of making history. He would now have to select from the countless parallel universes Schrödinger had mapped out, and decide which one would be ours. Even if that woman was a liar, Bacon could try to vindicate her. Even if I was innocent—or guilty, though on very shaky grounds—he could determine my punishment. Who cared if Klingsor had tricked us, or if we had never been close to catching him at all? With one simple act of will, Bacon would sit in judgment upon every single one of us. He had to do it—he had to forget the principles of science, justice, reason, and ethics in order to test a no less audacious invention: the love of Inge.

What followed was merely a matter of procedure. Perhaps I should have seen it coming, but for some reason I still believed in Bacon. That afternoon he called for me, but asked me to come to his house rather than to his office. This one detail should have been enough to make me suspicious, but I kept the date nevertheless, arriving at his house at the appointed time. I was hoping he had come to his senses, that he had finally realized how Inge was manipulating him. Fantasies.

I rang the doorbell. I found him alone, sitting on top of a wooden trunk. It was impossible to discern any emotion—rage? disappointment?—from his face. Some kind of veil or spell kept his feelings well hidden. He was trapped, just like me. As I made a quick inspection of the room, I noticed that all of his personal objects were gone. Half a dozen suitcases were scattered about the room.

"Planning a move, Lieutenant?" I said with open sarcasm.

"This place has become too small for me, Gustav," he said in a neutral, empty voice. "I'm tired. Perhaps I was mistaken from the beginning."

"You're going back to the United States." It was a statement, not a question.

"Yes," he lied. "This matter is beyond us, I'm afraid."

At that very moment I knew. He didn't need to say anything else. I knew exactly what was to happen. She had gotten to him. She had gotten to *me*.

I stopped the conversation. All I could do was stall for time, pray for a miracle.

"Would you like to hear about the third act of Wagner's *Parsifal*?" I asked him abruptly. "You wouldn't want to miss out on the ending, Lieutenant."

He paused for a moment and then nodded.

"A long time has passed since the end of the second act," I began quietly. "The curtain rises and we find ourselves in the middle of a breathtaking forest, one of those Teutonic woods the Nazis were always dreaming of. Hidden among the brambles we see a tiny hermitage that belongs to Gurnemanz—do you remember him?" Bacon made a face. "One of the old Grail knights we met in the first act. Very well, then. Gurnemanz emerges from his little hut and suddenly hears a sigh—no, it is more like a wail. He begins to search the surrounding woodlands and there he sees her: Kundry, reclining against a pine tree. She appears to be in a state of trance, or delirium—all she says is 'Serve, serve,' like an incantation or a poetic refrain. In the distance, Gurnemanz makes out the figure of another human being. Who else could it possibly be? Parsifal. Remember, Lieutenant, after Klingsor's castle was destroyed, Kundry placed a curse upon the young man for not succumbing to her powers of seduction."

"I remember," said Bacon.

"That curse has condemned Parsifal to years of aimless wandering, lost, in search of the castle of Monsalvat and the Grail keepers. Finally, after a long pilgrimage filled with adventures and misadventures, he has come close to finding what he has been looking for. Gurnemanz recognizes him and tells him the sad story of all that has happened in his absence: After his duel with Klingsor, the universe has begun a slow, painful decline. Titurel has died, and old Amfortas, robbed of his divine counsel, has forbidden the celebration of the love feast, in order to precipitate his own death." A sinister spark is now detectable in Bacon's eyes. "As fate would have it, Parsifal has arrived to rectify the situation. Now that the Spear of Longinus is in his hands, he is ready to be anointed as the new king of the Grail. He is no longer an innocent youth, but an adult filled with wisdom and a healthy dose of doubt. The first thing he does is to baptize Kundry, freeing her of the curse that Klingsor placed upon her. The woman rises up and then sinks down at Parsifal's feet. And then we witness one of the most magnificent scenes of the entire opera." For one brief moment, my spirits were lifted. "The Good Friday Spell. The music, Lieutenant, is sublime. I can assure you of that. Parsifal goes up to the castle at Monsalvat and there he finds the ailing Amfortas, who begs him not to reveal the Grail but to usher in his death for once and for all. The hero then pulls out the spear, raises it to the old man's festering wound, and frees him from his terrible agony. The Grail keepers gather around once more, this time singing 'A miracle of salvation.' And then they add the following mysterious words: 'Redemption for the redeemer.' Lovely, isn't it? Now, would you like to know how the opera (and the myth) ends, Lieutenant?"

"Go on."

"Kundry approaches the altar, which is the repository of the Grail," I say dramatically. "And instantly falls to her death, finally free of all sin. To be saved, she must die, Lieutenant—you understand that, don't you? It is the only way to rectify her betrayal."

I had barely finished the sentence—an allusion to one last possible solution, one last possible means of redemption—when we heard a thunderous boom. We both turned around and contemplated the scene before us: two tall, burly men, in peasants' clothes, had burst into the room. Behind them in the background, vaguely hidden by the shadows in the hallway, was the fearsome beauty of Inge.

"What is happening, Lieutenant?"

"I'm sorry, Gustav," he apologized. "The game is over."

"Don't try to play innocent, Professor Links!" One of the men with Inge (perhaps her boss) shouted at me in a Slavic accent. "Or perhaps I should say *Klingsor.*"

"Klingsor?" I sputtered. "My God! That's impossible—Lieutenant, you know that better than anyone."

"The game is over," said Bacon.

"And have I lost?"

"In this game we all lose." Those were the last words he ever spoke to me. It was like the kiss of Judas. Repentant or not, Bacon had turned me in.

The Soviets bound and gagged me, and I spent the next few hours in the trunk of an automobile. When I awoke, I found myself in that odious wasteland that is still known as the German Democratic Republic. According to my captors, their unit in Göttingen (to which Inge belonged) had put together a thick dossier on me, filled with incriminating evidence. Yet despite the torture and interrogation they subjected me to in the months that followed, the Russians were never 100 percent certain that I was, in fact, Klingsor. Given the doubts that still remained, they hid their failed investigation (and smartly averted a diplomatic scandal that would have surely ensued) by locking me up in this dark asylum. That was forty years ago: four decades during which time, just like my beloved and long-forgotten Georg Cantor, lover of infinity, I have done nothing but ponder the dark coincidences that saved me from death as well as the other, far more ominous circumstances that condemned me to this long life behind bars. Sometimes I think this is the most appropriate deliverance of all. In the end, dear Natalia, you have allowed me to hold on to your eternal memory and beg your forgiveness, day in and day out, until the day I die.

Bacon betrayed me because of a woman. He deliberately delivered me to a life of torture and exile, to prison and maybe even death, without just cause. After chasing the illusion of that silent, sinister man who hid behind the name of Klingsor, Lieutenant Francis P. Bacon finally fell prey to his curse. This new, misbegotten Kundry had rendered him a liar and criminal as well. In his defense, would it count for anything if I said that I would have done the same? That in some way, I *did* do it? His punishment is perhaps even worse than mine, for he will never be free from the specter of uncertainty that lurks behind his love. And as hard as he may try, he will never be able to forget the torment for which he alone is responsible. And in the end, both our destinies recall that of the cursed, abominable Amfortas: Far from God, our bloody wounds will continue to fester for all of eternity.

—Mexico City,
January 1994–Salamanca, February 1999.

END NOTE

Though Gustav Links would claim otherwise, this book is, in essence, a novel. And though most of the scientific and historical information is factually accurate, the narrator's point of view is always within the bounds of fiction.

Werner Heisenberg's attitude toward the Nazis was ambiguous at best, but there is no evidence proving that his wartime politics constituted anything resembling criminal activities. In any event, the debate is still alive and well, and the interested reader will find ample discussion of the topic in the many Heisenberg biographies.

At the same time, I cannot resist mentioning a curious coincidence, one among the many that have surrounded this novel. In May of 1998, just as I was finishing the final pages of this manuscript, a play by Michael Frayn called *Copenhagen* (Methuen Drama, 1998) opened in London. In *Copenhagen,* the English playwright re-creates an episode which also appears in *In Search of Klingsor*: the tense encounter between Bohr and Heisenberg in the Danish capital in September of 1941. In the final appendix to this play, Frayn presents an ample array of perspectives regarding this fascinating topic, and the interested reader will find it is well worth a look. I would also like to add that the serendipitous similarities between *In Search of Klingsor* and *Copenhagen* were first brought to my attention by Carlos Fuentes, who noted the connection in an extremely generous book review, and for that I offer my sincerest gratitude.

Finally, with respect to the elusive Klingsor, I would only like to add that though there exists no explicit mention of such a historical figure, the *Reichsforschungsrat*—the Reich Research Council—carried out duties very similar to those ascribed to Hitler's so-called scientific adviser in the novel.

As for my own research, I would first like to mention some of the great scientific biographies of the twentieth century. In the case of Einstein and Bohr, the splendid works of Abraham Pais, *Subtle Is the Lord: The Science and Life of Albert Einstein* (Oxford University Press, 1982), *Einstein Lived Here* (Oxford University Press, 1994), and *Niels Bohr's Times: In Physics, Philosophy, and Polity* (Oxford University Press, 1991). Other essential works include *Einstein* (Fontana, 1973) by Jeremy Bernstein; *Einstein: The*

Life and Times (Hodder and Stoughton, 1979) by Ronald Clark; *Einstein: His Life and Times* (Jonathan Cape, 1948) by Philipp Frank; and *The Private Lives of Albert Einstein* (Faber & Faber, 1993) by Roger Highfield and Paul Carter. I also made good use of works by Einstein himself, especially *The World As I See It* (Citadel Press, 1991) and *Ideas and Opinions* (Alvin Redman, 1954), as well as his correspondence with Michele Besso (Tusquets, 1995). And finally, Ed Regis's reportage on the Institute for Advanced Study, *Who Got Einstein's Office?* (Addison Wesley, 1987).

For Heisenberg, Nazi science, the development of the bomb, the Nuremberg trials, and the July 20, 1944, conspiracy plot, I owe much to David Cassidy's *Uncertainty: The Life and Science of Werner Heisenberg* (Freeman, 1992); Thomas Powers's *Heisenberg's War* (Penguin, 1994); Robert Jungk's *Brighter Than a Thousand Suns* (Harcourt Brace, 1958); Heisenberg's autobiographical essay *Physics and Beyond* (Harper & Row, 1971); David Irving's *The Virus House* (Collins, 1967); Richard Rhodes's *The Making of the Atomic Bomb* (Simon & Schuster, 1988); Mark Walker's *Nazi Science: Myth, Truth, and the German Atomic Bomb* (Plenum Press, 1995); Jeremy Bernstein's *Hitler's Uranium Club: The Secret Recordings at Farm Hall* (American Institute of Physics Press, 1996); Joseph E. Persico's *Nuremberg: Infamy on Trial* (Penguin, 1994); and Joachim C. Fest's *Plotting Hitler's Death: The German Resistance to Hitler* (Phoenix, 1997).

The Schrödinger biography by Walter Moore, *A Life of Erwin Schrödinger* (Cambridge University Press, 1994), was useful, as were the scientist's own expository works, specifically *My View of the World* (Cambridge University Press, 1964), *Mind and Matter* (Cambridge University Press, 1958), and *What Is Life?* (Cambridge University Press, 1947). For Von Neumann, William Poundstone's essay *Prisoner's Dilemma* (Doubleday, 1992) was useful.

Other, more general works were extremely useful in the evolution of this novel: *Personaggi e scoperte della fisica contemporanea* (Mondadori, 1976) by Emilio Segrè; *Men of Mathematics* (Simon & Schuster, 1965) by Eric Bell; the translation of *The Autobiography of Science* by Forest Ray Moulton and Justus J. Schifferes (Doubleday, 1945); and George Gamow's *The Great Physicists from Galileo to Einstein* (Dover, 1988).

I must also note my great debt to one more book, one of the most fascinating I have ever read and which inspired the idea for this novel: Douglas R. Hofstadter's *Gödel, Escher, Bach: An Eternal Golden Braid* (Basic Books, 1979, and Tusquets, 1987).

I would like to thank Fernanda Álvarez, Raquel Blázquez, Natalia Castro, Sandro Cohen, Robert Goebel, Luis García Jambrina, Luis Lagos, Gerardo

Laveaga, Jesús Rodríguez, Eloy Urroz, and Sergio Vela for their detailed readings and suggestions. Drs. Shahen Hacyan, Luis de la Peña, Jaime Besprosvany, and Víctor Manuel Romero, of the Physics Institute at the Universidad Nacional Autónoma de México, provided invaluable comments on the scientific aspects of the novel. I thank Antonia Kerrigan, Andrew Wylie, Benita Edzard, Eva Romero, Luisa Herrero, María Pijoan, René Solís, Jesús Anaya, and Patricia Mazón for the great enthusiasm with which they have championed my writing, and to the judges of the Biblioteca Breve prize: Guillermo Cabrera Infante, Luis Goytisolo, Pere Gimferrer, Susana Fortes, and especially my editor Basilio Baltasar, without whom I would still be searching for Klingsor.

J.V.